PRAISE FOR ᴮʸ WINGED CHAIR

"A wildly original and magical twist on the Robin Hood narrative, Kendra Merritt's *By Wingéd Chair* is packed to the spokes with complex characters, wry humor, and flawless world building."

-Darby Karchut, best-selling author of DEL TORO MOON and FINN FINNEGAN

"With a wonderfully crafted blend of swords and sorcery and characters based on Robin Hood, Merritt tops this story off with the lead character readers need nowadays; a strong, independent, powerful female mage who also happens to be in a wheelchair. Readers will be constantly turning pages to see what happens next to this fun group of characters through the twists and turns they won't see coming."

-The Booklife Prize

"Kendra Merritt's prose is fresh, with one-line descriptions that crack like a whip, and she doesn't miss an opportunity to surprise the reader. From the first line to the last, I was enchanted with *By Winged Chair*."

-Todd Fahnestock, best-selling author of FAIRMIST and THE WISHING WORLD

Catching Cinders

Mark of the Least

KENDRA MERRITT

You're worth fighting for!

BLUE FYRE PRESS

This one's for everyone who's ever wanted to see a Cinderella like them.

For all of us wobbly and imperfect princesses. Fight for yourself. You're worth it.

CHAPTER ONE

M ost people would consider talking to flames a bad sign, but for me it was a problem when the fire stopped talking back.

"Ember?" I whispered, kneeling beside the hearth. The foyer loomed behind me, empty, but only for the moment.

The logs sat in the clean grate, silent and cool.

I set aside my dustpan full of ashes and leaned forward. "Ember, can you hear me?"

With a fierce crackle, the wood burst into flame. Heat seared my skin and made tendrils of blonde hair dance around my face. I rocked back on my heels with a sigh of relief.

"Don't do that," I said, glancing around the front hall to make sure we were still alone. "This isn't the place to play." She and I belonged in the kitchen. But the housekeeper needed some extra help and who better to clean fireplaces than Sooty Cindy.

The fire chuckled, a high burbling sound full of joy that never failed to bring an answering smile to my lips, no matter how annoyed I was. I could never really be angry with the fire sprite. We'd grown up together, and she'd been the last gift my mother had given me.

I shook my head, suppressing a chuckle. "You're going to get me into trouble again, aren't you?"

The fire made a noise, as if to say, "Who me?"

I shifted my knees and reached up to grab my rough wooden crutch. Now that we were done, maybe I could get out of the front hall before we were caught somewhere we weren't supposed to be.

The murmur of voices came through the big archway at the end of the hall and made my heart skip.

"Muck," I said under my breath and clambered to my feet, using my crutch for balance. Even before I was steady, I held my hand out to the flames. "Quickly now," I whispered.

This time Ember didn't hesitate or play tricks. A streak of fire shaped like a tiny cat leapt from the flames. She scampered up my arm, leaving a line of warmth along my skin before she settled in her normal hiding spot under my loose braid. Her weight pressed into my neck, a comforting pressure.

I took a crooked step toward the servants' door across the hall.

"Thank you so much for letting our party stay the night," a male voice said. "But we're due back in the capital within the week."

I gasped and shrank against the door of the parlor. Too

late now. I'd never make it across the hall before someone caught me, and I couldn't slip into the parlor behind me. That led to the rest of the house and more forbidden territory. But if I stood still in the shadows, the light from the fire and the high windows wouldn't touch me.

Ember dimmed herself as I tried to blend into the wood.

"Of course. Our door is always open." That voice belonged to the Lady Hargrove, Viscountess of Yarrow, and mistress of the house.

She stepped into view through the archway that led to the rest of the manor. The lady wore her vivid gold hair in intricate braids pinned to the back of her head.

Beside her strode a dark-haired young man in a deep blue suit and cream waistcoat, a top hat in his hand. His hair had been cut short at one time, but it needed a trim, especially on the top where black waves threatened to fall into his eyes. Another man followed in his shadow, with dark hair and an immaculate blue uniform.

The butler stepped into the hall with the first man's riding coat and gloves. "Your Highness," he said.

Highness? I glanced again at the man and saw the indigo ribbon he wore in place of a tie, the Valerian Dark Sun hanging on his chest. Almighty save me, the Crown Prince of Valeria stood less than twenty feet from the fireplace I'd just cleaned?

I tried to shrink even farther into the shadows, as if I could melt into the door against my back.

Lady Hargrove noticed the movement. She pinned me with a confused glance, and I could imagine the questions going through her mind. What was I doing here? Why hadn't I scurried about my chores already? I wondered if she even recognized me or knew that I wasn't exactly a maid.

The Prince himself hadn't looked up from shrugging on his coat and pulling his gloves over his long lean hands.

"Thank you for an enjoyable visit," he said, drawing Lady Hargrove's attention back to him. "I look forward to speaking with you more next time you're at court."

She laughed. "It may be a long time before we're able to attend. My lord is so comfortable here with his books, and I have my patients to look after."

"I commend you for your diligence, madam."

The butler opened the front door, letting in the sounds of several horses and the babbling conversation of a large group of people laughing and preparing for a journey.

My eyes darted between the butler and the lady of the house. I might actually get away after all. Lady Hargrove didn't seem to mind I was here.

But then she hadn't been the one to banish me to the kitchen.

The door behind me opened, sending air whooshing past the ragged edges of my skirt. A hand clasped my shoulder.

I gasped and stumbled back, barely catching myself against the doorframe.

Lord Hargrove, Viscount of Yarrow, glowered down at me, his dark brows drawn together in a heavy frown.

I trembled as I faced my father for the first time in eleven years. I'd only ever seen him from a distance since the day he'd married my stepmother.

Ember pressed herself against my skin, her flickering light casting orange and red sparks across Lord Hargrove's face.

"What are you doing here?" he said, voice hissing between his teeth.

I opened my mouth to answer but nothing came out.

He glanced into the hall and I followed the movement only to see Lady Hargrove give us a baffled look before sweeping out of the entrance hall, her wide skirts brushing the polished wood floor. The Prince must have left while I was distracted.

I was left alone in the big empty hall with the father who'd told me he never wanted to see me again.

My throat clogged, stealing any words that might brave his forbidding expression.

"You can't be here," he grated out, as if speaking to me hurt him. "I don't want you here. Go back to the kitchen. Stay there."

His open palm struck the doorframe above my head, and I found the courage to move. I staggered across the front hall, my crutch clicking unevenly across the polished wood. In the back hall it sank into worn carpet, and finally it clattered against the old flagstones leading into the kitchen.

I leaned my head against the closed kitchen door and breathed as pots clanged and voices raised in jest on the other side.

"Yes, sir. Right away, sir," I said under my breath. "You know you wouldn't see me if you just closed your eyes, sir."

Ember burbled under my ear and a wave of warmth swept me as her flames brushed my skin.

"Of course I'll never say it to his face," I said. "Servants are supposed to grumble, but they're not supposed to actually talk back."

The fire sprite chirped in discontent and batted the strands of hair that tickled her face. The ones she touched curled with the heat. It didn't matter how angry she got, I knew she'd never intentionally burn me. But there was always a chance for accidents. I had faint scars from the few times she'd lost control.

"Fine," I said to her. "We can switch places. You can say anything you want while I set fire to everything in sight."

"You know it's a bad sign when you start talking to yourself," a familiar voice said.

I jerked my head up to see Jason, one of the footmen, leaning against the wall opposite me.

I grinned and straightened. "Ember thinks she knows better than me," I said.

"Ember thinks she knows better than everyone," Jason said, bending his head a little to get a look at the fire sprite under my braid. He was tall enough he had to duck to do it.

Ember usually hid from anyone outside the kitchen, but she stuck her head out from under my hair to make a face at Jason. He reached out to tickle her chin and she swiped at his hand.

"Just remember when she sets fire to the hay rick, she's not the one who comes to rescue you."

"It was only that one time," I said. "And I took your kitchen chores for a week to thank you."

"That doesn't mean I'm ever going to let you forget it," he said and tweaked the end of my braid.

I wrinkled my nose, and he laughed as he pushed the door open for me. The clink of knives and the smell of mutton washed over us. The familiar scent made my shoulders relax even as Jason's smile helped me forget my father's scowl.

Bess sneered at me from the sink where she stood elbow deep in soapy water, her thin face made gaunt by a severe bun. "Sure took you long enough, Sooty Cindy. If you were anyone else, you'd have been fired by now."

Jason frowned at the soapsuds but didn't say anything. I hadn't expected him to.

I didn't bring up the fact that it took me twice as long just to move as everyone else. It would only prove her point. And I'd stopped trying to defend myself years ago when I'd realized I was the only one who cared.

"I'll see you later, Cindy," Jason said. He gave me a wink that made me flush. My nickname didn't sound so bad when he said it like that.

It had started when I sat in the fireplace the first time, and the cook had called me a sooty cinder-mite, like the little mice that burrowed in ash piles for their warmth. It evolved to Sooty Cindy, and now everyone just called me Cindy. Except for Bess who couldn't resist adding the first part anytime she got the chance.

I hobbled toward the fireplace and Bess came with me, hissing over my shoulder, "Don't get any ideas about Jason. I have my eye on him so just keep your hands off my things. You don't see me touching those books of yours."

That's because actual knowledge might scald you and send you back to whatever demonic pit you came from, I thought to myself. But I didn't say it out loud. Bess was spiteful and full of venom, but her mother had died when she was three and her father hadn't taught her anything different.

"Yes, Bess," I said. "Will you tell your grandmother I'll have more spare clothes for her as soon as the housekeeper gives me the cast-offs?"

She snorted as I pulled the little stool out of its corner by the fireplace and sat as close to the flames as I could stand. I knew better than to sit where I might get in the way.

"Still acting like the lord's daughter even down here in the muck with us?" she said.

I sighed as I held out my arm and Ember flowed down my skin and into the fire. My father might have banished me to the kitchen but my mother's lessons on nobility and duty had never faded.

"If I stopped trying to help people I'm sure you'd have something to say about that, too," I said.

Bess watched with narrowed eyes. She was closer to twenty but even at seventeen I stood a couple inches taller than her. "Fine," she said. "You might have found something useful to do, but useful is all you'll ever be. With the way you walk, you'd better get used to living alone. I mean, Jason's known you forever and he hasn't even tried to kiss you ever, has he?"

I stared at the pattern hammered into the iron at the back of the fireplace, a phoenix painted orange and red by the flickering flames. "Thank you for the reminder, Bess," I said.

Ember made a rude noise from the crackling logs and a loud pop sent a cloud of cinders toward us.

Bess shrank back, cursing, and returned to her soap-filled sink.

I just sighed and brushed the cooling ash from my apron, making sure I hadn't caught fire.

"Careful," I said. "I'm combustible."

Ember burbled.

"I know it wouldn't be on purpose," I said. "But that doesn't make it any better if I end up as cooked as the roast."

The morning after the Prince had left, I passed a bundle of old linens to the gardener outside the kitchen door.

"There you are, and you can tell Mrs. Gustafson there will be extra coal in the delivery this week, for her son-in-law."

The gardener touched a gnarled hand to the brim of his floppy cap. "Thank you, Miss Hargrove. She'll appreciate that. And my wife thanks you for the sheets. Though she can't figure out how you knew they were needed."

I winked and pushed him out into the yard. "I always know," I said. Most people just didn't open their ears. If you sat quiet and out of the way, you could learn all sorts of things.

What you did with the knowledge was the important thing.

Ember cavorted around my feet as I limped back to the fireplace. I'd seen her wrap her flames around herself to look like a bird or a butterfly the color of smoldering coals. But mostly she stayed a cat with whiskers she could twitch in exasperation and an expressive face to show her curiosity.

I sank down onto my stool in the fireplace, my sleeves rolled above my elbows to keep the soot off. I made a note in my tiny stained journal to ask the housekeeper for more linens. She didn't mind handing over the ones that were too worn to be used upstairs anymore.

There was always a lull in the kitchen right after breakfast before the rest of the cooking started when I could steal a few precious moments to read. I reached for the shelf set into the wall beside the mantle. It held three darkened books and the roll of bedding I slept on at night. In the secrecy of my own head, I liked to pretend it was a vast library with every book I might ever even want to read waiting at my fingertips.

"Cindy, you're needed upstairs."

I jumped, my fingers just brushing the cover of Hillford's *Analysis of Minosan Mythology*. My bare feet shifted in the ash as I spun to see Jason in the doorway. "What? I'm never called upstairs." My father had made my place very clear.

Ember sat up in the flames, her face wreathed with tongues of fire.

"Well, Lord Hargrove wants you for something."

I stared, the words so unexpected I didn't even register them at first. I hadn't spoken to the man in eleven years and now I was going to see him twice in two days?

I struggled to my feet and grabbed my soot-streaked crutch from behind me. Its handle had been worn smooth over the years, and my hand slipped once before I settled it firmly under my arm.

"What does he want?" I whispered as Jason led me down the hall and up the back stairs.

A disgruntled chirping made me stop on the steps. Ember scampered up the back of my skirt, buoyed by her own heat before she leaped up to her usual perch under my braid.

"I don't know," Jason said and started up the stairs again.

I followed, placing each foot carefully, using the banister and my crutch to haul myself up.

Lord Hargrove had to be angry about the day before. My palms grew sweaty against the handle of my crutch. I'd broken the rules and now I was going to face his scowl and whatever punishment he thought fit my crime.

At the top of the steps Jason pointed down the long hall to another set of stairs at the end. "He's on the roof." Then he looked back at me and frowned in concern. "Do you need some help?"

I gave him a tight smile, hiding the way my heart hammered in my chest. "No. Thank you, Jason." I hardly ever climbed stairs, and I didn't need anyone else witnessing the way I moved like a drunk horse, all awkward limbs and knees that bent the wrong way.

He tried to grin back, but I could tell he was just as confused as I was. Then he tweaked my braid and turned to go.

I opened my mouth, but I had no idea what to say, and he was gone before I could think of anything. Bess flirted with Jason all the time. But I'd never gotten the hang of letting a boy know I liked him by joking and teasing him, then acting affronted when he joked and teased back.

I shook my head and started off down the long hall. Only

a featherhead would think of flirting at a time like this. Besides, I had more practical things to worry about, right now.

Carpets were malicious things that tried to trip me every chance they got, so I kept my head down to watch my feet. Which meant I didn't see Lady Hargrove until the edge of her wide burgundy skirts blocked my way.

I looked up. Ember shivered under my braid, making herself as small as possible.

The lady of the house tilted her head, her lips curved in a tentative smile.

I hunched my shoulders. Nobility never smiled at people like me. Not unless they wanted something. Had she learned where all the cast-off linens and clothes were going?

"My lady," I murmured, moving to go around her.

"You're headed to the roof?" she said, making my feet freeze on the plush carpet.

I nodded.

"Would you mind bringing my lord his breakfast?" she asked and it was only then I noticed she was holding a basket of pastries. "He skipped his this morning."

My mouth parted and I blinked. Why was she asking me to do something instead of telling me? And why was she still smiling at me?

"Yes, ma'am," I said, and bobbed my head in a mockery of a curtsy. My twisted legs would spill me on the floor if I tried a real one.

She handed me the basket and hesitated. "You could have one," she said and nodded to the pile of sugar-covered pastries. "They're my lord's favorite, but he won't notice one missing."

I couldn't imagine anything more inappropriate than a servant eating off her master's plate, but she stood there, waiting, watching me. I just wanted her to leave, so I took the smallest pastry on the plate and bit into it. The sugar clogged my nose and mouth, and I almost gagged. I concentrated on swallowing it without spitting it all over her.

"Thank you, ma'am," I said and finally she moved around me so I could continue down the hall. I juggled the basket and my crutch and staggered to the stairs.

When I looked back, she had disappeared to do whatever it was country ladies did, besides terrorizing innocent kitchen staff.

The stairs led to an open trap door which let the morning fog roll down into the house, raising goosebumps along my bare arms.

At the top of the steps, the roof stretched to either side of me, flat and narrow, and edged by a little wrought iron fence that only came to my knees. Ahead of me, someone had arranged an worn armchair, a table stacked with five books, and a mage globe lamp, its light dimmed in the morning fog.

A tall figure with broad shoulders stood with his back to me at the edge of the roof, close enough to the fence to make me sweat.

Did I clear my throat? Yell out that I was here? I didn't even know what to call him. He'd been Papa when I was little. But that had been years and a lifetime ago. I was older now and he was a stranger.

I shifted and deliberately scraped the tip of my crutch against the tiles of the roof.

He turned, brow furrowed in a puzzled look as if he wanted to tell me something but couldn't quite remember what it had been.

I swallowed and tried to stiffen my spine. "My lord," I said, just to fill the silent air.

He stared. Gray streaked the dark hair at his temples and for the first time in eleven years I realized that while I was growing up, he'd been growing older.

"Did you want me for something?" I said, prompting.

He shook his head violently, but I didn't think that was the answer to my question. Was he old enough to get confused? Jason's grandmother wandered away from her house in the village all the time, forgetting where she was going or for what.

"I brought your breakfast," I said and held out the basket of pastries.

Finally, he stirred and came toward me to accept one of the sugar-coated monstrosities that had tried to kill me earlier. He didn't seem to have a problem with it. He just ate slowly while I stood there, the hazy morning sun glinting from a gold pin in his lapel.

Eventually he finished and looked at the sugar coating his fingers. Then he took a deep breath, blinked, and when he looked at me, the confusion had left his blue eyes.

"I often come up here to think," he said, startling me. Then he pulled out a handkerchief and brushed off his fingers. "I feel like I think better in the fresh air. Do you ever notice how thick the air is in the house? It stops thoughts like flies in honey."

I opened my mouth, but he wasn't actually looking for a response.

He frowned like he realized he wasn't making any sense. "Muck on it, my head feels too thick to get anything out of it."

Actually, maybe I did know what he was talking about. My head was starting to feel thick, too.

I put my hand to my temple and tried to concentrate. What was he saying?

"—realize how long it's been. Or how much you've grown."

I tried to focus my attention—this sounded important. But I couldn't draw a full breath. The air swelled sticky and heavy in my lungs. Why couldn't I breathe?

"I wanted to explain," he started. Then he saw my face. "Are you all right?"

He reached for me but the edges of my vision grew fuzzy, clouds rolling in. Everything seemed so dark.

His voice went sharp and anxious, and I heard him say my name. I hadn't heard it in so long, and I tried to pay attention, but I couldn't see him anymore. Everything was so dark.

A curse and a clatter. Pressure under my head.

Mumbled words, the shape of which would have been familiar if I could have concentrated through the shadows.

I thought I should be frightened of the dark. But it was softer than the blankets I slept on by the fire. Its voice sounded like my father, and it sounded like he loved me after all.

But then light and fire swept through me, taking away the soft-edged dark. It didn't seem fair that the light hurt as it cleared away the cobwebs in my head. It burned everything, examining the pieces of my heart and head, leaving clear, white light behind.

It wasn't just in my head. I blinked and realized the light was the sun trying to burn through the fog above me.

A face blocked the light, and I turned my head, my neck stiff. Instead of my father, a girl watched me, a couple years younger with straight black hair and skin the color of copper.

Isol. Lady Hargrove's younger daughter.

"Can you breathe?" she asked.

I nodded before I thought about it, then took a deep breath just to make sure I still could.

"What happened?" I said, my voice hoarse. I didn't remember much besides the difference between light and dark. Why was my head filled with the image of flames wrapping around the darkness and snuffing it out?

"You don't remember?" Isol said.

"Of course she's going to claim memory loss," another voice said, full of spite and arrogance.

I turned my head enough to see a tall young woman, about my age, with thick dark gold curls and the same copper skin and black eyes as Isol. Anella, Lady Hargrove's eldest daughter.

"That's what criminals do," she said and lifted her chin. She probably didn't realize that from where I lay that just made it easier to see up her nose.

Ember burned in my pocket, giving off enough heat to tell me where she was hiding. Pastries lay scattered around me, but I couldn't see any sign of my father.

"Where's Lord Hargrove?" I said.

"There." Anella pointed.

Down. Over the edge of the roof.

I drew a painful breath and rolled into the wrought iron fence.

Below me, the roof slanted at too steep an angle to stop a fall. And a broken twisted body lay on the gravel of the carriageway.

"There," Anella said again. "Where you pushed him, you murderer."

CHAPTER TWO

All my stepsisters seemed to care about was locking up the murderer, but I couldn't stop seeing my father's body lying on the gravel of the carriageway.

Even as they dragged me to the cellar and shoved me stumbling down the steps, I couldn't focus my whirling thoughts. What had happened while I'd blacked out? What had he wanted to tell me after eleven years of silence?

Had I really knocked him over the edge?

It wasn't until they shut and locked the door at the bottom of the stairs that I came back to myself to realize what was actually happening. Murky black closed around me from either side, as if the walls leaned in. I couldn't get a deep breath, and I sank down against the door as shivers raced through me.

My hands clutched uselessly at the door, trying to anchor myself in the dark. I beat against it, scrabbled at the wood until something sharp tore at the tender skin on the side of my hand. I hunched over the pain.

As I shuddered on the floor, a glow grew in my lap. I fixed my gaze on it until it pulsed and Ember's light steadied. She crouched on my apron, one paw on my bloody fist, her tail lashing back and forth.

I took a deep gulping breath, then scooped her up and held her to my chest as I swallowed down the sobs that wanted to claw up my throat.

"What am I going to do?" I asked her.

She chirped in reply.

"You didn't see what happened?"

She burbled.

"I know he fell," I said. "What was I doing?"

She hesitated a moment before she spread into a bright translucent puddle in my lap. Her flames flickered and resolved into a picture, and I recognized the rooftop, but seen from behind a wisp of hair and the curve of an ear. My ear.

The image moved as if she showed me her own memory. Lord Hargrove spoke, but the picture didn't seem to translate sound. Her whole view wobbled and I realized I must have been swaying on my feet as that fuzzy feeling took over.

Then suddenly I was on the ground and Ember stared up through the curtain of my hair.

Lord Hargrove came into view, face pale and mouth tight. He spoke again, though I couldn't make out the words. Ember glanced down and saw the pastries spread on the tile roof. I must have knocked them off the table as I'd fallen.

She looked back up to see my father peering at her intently. He reached as if to grab her and I recognized her name on his lips.

The image dissolved into blackness and I remembered

that she'd been cowering in my skirt when I'd woken up. Lord Hargrove must have frightened her into hiding.

She hadn't seen what had killed my father on the same morning he decided to talk to me for the first time in years. Was Anella right? Everything I felt about my father was twisted up with confusion and anger. Could I have actually killed him?

I pressed my hand to my head. I...I couldn't remember. Everything after I'd come out onto the roof seemed dark and fuzzy around the edges. Lord Hargrove had tried to speak to me, but what had he said?

I groaned with no one but Ember to hear it. Anger, guilt, and deep gut-wrenching sadness clogged my throat again as tears streamed down my cheeks.

I sat in the cellar alone for what felt like days. I couldn't tell in the dark. Maybe they couldn't decide what to do with me. Murderers were hung in the Refuge of the Saint of Justice. Was there a reason her Disciples hadn't come to drag me away to face execution or imprisonment yet?

I almost climbed to my feet to check the door again. But I knew it was locked. Besides, what would I do if I managed to escape? I couldn't run. Not without help. And I refused to put anyone else in danger for this stupid, mucked up life I was failing to live. Not to mention my stepsisters had left my crutch on the roof when they'd dragged me down here.

I'd stay put. The only one who would be hurt by all this was me and I could at least keep it that way.

I tried to sleep, to bury my panic in gentle oblivion. But I couldn't get comfortable against the cold wall and the packed dirt floor. My legs cramped and every little noise made me jump and jerk awake.

Finally, the door creaked open, and I squeaked.

"Shh," a voice said. "It's me."

"Jason?"

He knelt beside me, his face coming into focus as he leaned into Ember's light. He held out a dinner roll and a chunk of cheese. My crutch was tucked under his arm.

"Thank you," I said in a whisper and tore into the bread.

He set my crutch on the ground and sat back on his heels to watch me eat with a worried crease between his eyebrows. Then he stood and retreated into the dark beyond Ember's circle of light.

In another moment a soft glow suffused the cellar as Jason went around finding and lighting the gas lamps.

I breathed a sigh of relief, and Ember climbed back into my pocket to sleep.

Jason returned to squat on his heels beside me.

"What time is it?" I said.

"Breakfast."

Again. I'd been down here all day and all night. No wonder I was so hungry.

"What's happening?" I asked after I swallowed.

"My lady is meeting with my lord's solicitor. To go over the will and...to discuss what to do with you."

I gulped and suddenly didn't feel ravenous anymore. I placed the bread and cheese in my lap and clenched my hands together. My mouth grew dry and I swallowed convulsively.

"She's going to hang me as a murderer, isn't she?"

"No." His emphatic denial wasn't loud, but it rang in the cellar and my heart all the same. He took my hands in his, and I gasped.

"Not if I can help it," he said. "Come on, I'm getting you out of here."

He tugged on my hands and tried to pull me to my feet, but I didn't budge.

My fingers tightened around his. "Jason, stop."

He froze and looked down at me. Did he really think I hadn't already been over and over this in my head? I'd made my decision. And besides, my legs were asleep.

"I can't run."

Even in the dim light of the lamps I could see him flush with embarrassment. "I-I can help you," he said.

I shook my head. "That's not what I meant. Stop and think a minute." I took a deep breath as he sank back down on the dirt beside me. "I can't run," I repeated. "I wouldn't even get off the property before they caught me. And if you help me, you wouldn't just lose your job, you'd lose your life. Even if we made it away, we'd be fugitives. You'd never get to live free again."

He'd offered to give up everything for me, and that realization filled all the empty corners of my heart. That in itself was enough. I couldn't ruin his life by letting him smuggle me out of the cellar.

He opened his mouth to speak and I covered his lips with my finger.

"I'm not worth the effort, Jason. Don't throw yourself away for me."

He stared at me in the gloom, and I wished Ember would come back and light up his face so I could tell what he was thinking. I shrugged uncomfortably and lowered my gaze to my lap.

"Besides," I said. "I need to know what happened to my father." If I hadn't killed him, what had? The pastries? No, couldn't be, otherwise I'd be dead, too.

I looked back up to meet his eyes and found him inches from my face. He let go of my hand to cup my cheek and leaned forward to touch my lips with his.

I held my breath.

I'd always thought if anyone could ignore my legs and love me anyway, it would be Jason, but I'd never even had a hint he felt anything for me.

I closed my eyes and let my hand grip the edge of his coat. He turned his head to deepen the kiss.

A step on the stairs behind us made him jerk back and swear. His frantic eyes met mine before he leaped to his feet and cleared his throat.

He straightened his coat as he stepped through the door. A voice murmured on the stairs and Jason replied something about bringing me food. Then his footsteps continued up the stairs while another pair descended, accompanied by the swish of long skirts.

Lady Hargrove opened the door and peered down at me, her long blonde hair pulled into braided loops behind her head and a crease of consternation marring her white fore-head. She looked like a true Valerian lady. From her daughters' deeper coloring, I assumed her first husband had come from overseas.

The lady of the house glanced around the cellar at the dim gas lamps, the wine in its dusty racks, and then down at the packed dirt floor. She stepped fully inside before gesturing behind her.

Isol followed her with a stool which she set on the ground where Lady Hargrove indicated.

The lady took her skirts in her hands and sat on the stool arranging yards of fabric and petticoats with a nonchalant grace I couldn't help envying. Isol stood behind her mother and a movement out of the corner of my eye told me Anella lingered in the doorway.

I swallowed as Lady Hargrove stilled and her bright blue eyes focused on me. They were red and raw and the delicate skin under her eyes looked dark as if she hadn't slept.

"Do you have enough to eat?" she said. Even in a cellar, facing one small kitchen drudge, she pitched her voice to be heard and obeyed.

"Yes," I said. I wouldn't dare say otherwise even though my stomach had still been growling a minute ago. It had stopped now. It was too busy being clenched in a painful knot.

"I'm glad," she said and started to reach forward then stopped as if unsure of my reaction. "It was not my intention to starve you."

She folded her hands as I tried to decide what she wanted me to say. Nothing apparently, for she went on.

"Do you remember what happened on the roof?"

I shook my head and my braid whipped behind me. "No, my lady."

"Nothing?"

"I'm sorry, my lady. I remember I-I saw you in the hallway," I said.

"And then?"

"I took my lord his breakfast and then I think he tried to speak to me." For the first time in eleven years, and I'd lost the opportunity to hear what he'd wanted to say. I took a shuddering breath. "But I fell down and blacked out. I don't remember anything after that. I woke up and he was dead. And-and I'm sorry." In horror I heard my voice degenerate into sobs. "I'm sorry."

Her eyes widened, and heedless of her skirts, she fell forward on her knees to throw her arms around me.

It was the last thing I expected and I froze, the tears still streaming down my face.

"Oh, you poor thing. No, no, don't cry. It was an accident. A horrible accident."

Over her shoulder, Isol's mouth dropped open, and she cast a look at her sister, who looked as affronted as a swan out of water.

Lady Hargrove stroked my shoulders and without meaning to I relaxed into her arms. It had been so long since someone had held me, and the past day had been so awful I couldn't help but lean toward her.

Finally she sat back, her hands sliding down my arms to hold my hands.

"Your dress," I whispered. Her skirts would be stained irreparably.

"Muck on my dress," she said, making me gasp at her language. "I'm more concerned about you. I didn't mean to leave you down here thinking you were going to be hung as a murderer. Forgive me?"

I gaped at her as she looked down at my sticky hands. Her breath hissed as she noticed the gash still bleeding sluggishly.

She snapped her fingers and Isol handed her a small satchel she'd been carrying. Lady Hargrove took out a small vial and a roll of pristine white bandages.

"My first husband was from Torraca," she said conversationally as she tended my hand. She cleaned the cut thoroughly, tucking the bloodied bandages back into her satchel and wrapping my hand in a clean one. "They practice different medicine than we do. He taught me everything he knew before he died."

She patted the bandage into place and met my eyes.

"This has all been a misunderstanding...but..." She looked away and bit her lip.

"But what?" I said.

Her hands tightened on mine, making me wince, and she turned back to me. "But others might not see it that way."

"What do you mean?" Now I was clinging to her hands, too, despite the sting.

"Well, you were on the roof with him. Alone. And he hasn't treated you very well, has he?" She bit her lip. "Some people might think you pushed him." She glanced back at Anella who drew herself up and raised her chin.

"But I would never..." I spluttered. "I was happy in the kitchen."

She shook her head, stopping me. "Of course you were. It was safe and familiar. I am only seeing all the possibilities. It's something I'm cursed with, you see." She smiled ruefully at me, like she'd shared a secret. "I have an overactive imagination, and I can't help worrying about what other people might see."

I swallowed. She was right. This all looked so bad. I'd even doubted myself in the night. Had I pushed him and blacked out from the horror?

"What do I do?" I whispered.

She drew my hands to her and held them between her own. "Nothing. That's my job now. I will protect you the way I protect my own children." She reached out to tuck back a lock of my hair that had come loose.

"They call you Cindy, don't they?"

Sooty Cindy. It wasn't my name, but I'd lived with it for so long it felt more natural than anything else.

"Yes, my lady."

She shook her head. "Call me Melissa. Cindy, I'm going to do everything in my power to keep you free. You don't need to worry anymore. I have a plan for you."

CHAPTER THREE

Nik had spent weeks on the road and days in the saddle, all to finally get to the capital. It figured that now he was home, the first thing he was going to do was walk through a portal to take him somewhere else. But his grandfather had requested his presence, and one didn't refuse the former king of Valeria.

He didn't even glance out the windows at the city as he strode through the halls of the Blue Palace, his bodyguard at his side. He didn't need to see the roofs of the townhouses, the dome of the opera house, or the spires of the Chapel of the Almighty in order to feel like he was home. He could breathe it in the air and feel it in the way it sat on his skin.

He nodded politely to a court matron and her daughter touring the Guard's Tower. The two stared at him for a split second before sinking into deep curtsies, then they broke into nervous whispers after he'd passed.

Nik tried not to let their wide eyes and excitement bother him. He tried to tell himself they were only awed by Merrick who walked beside him in the full formal panoply of the ServantGuard, complete with gleaming breastplate, a plumed helm held under his arm. But Nik knew he was lying to himself. He was used to the way their gaze saw only his crisp coat and the Valerian Dark Sun he wore on an indigo ribbon around his neck. The way they completely missed the man underneath the regalia.

He was a prince. The Crown Prince. Nikolas Alyxander Humphrey Rannard, Duke of Arcangele, heir to the throne of Valeria.

Plain old Nik was lost under all that.

Three flights of stairs—the Guard Stairs, the Officer's Stairs, and finally a set no one had bothered naming—brought him to the cupola on the roof above the palace. From here he could just make out the enormous stone angels guarding the Seraph Gate at the east end of the city.

Below him spread the Blue Palace which played host to hundreds of visitors every day, housed courtiers and foreign officials, and provided sanctuary to the royal family.

And tucked in a cupola on top of the roof, it hid one of the marvels of modern magery.

Nik turned from the view. There was no doorway or glowing frame in the air to step through. Merely a pattern of colored tile laid into the floor, polished to a shine from all the monarchs of Valeria who had stepped across.

Once when he was a child, he'd asked the mage in charge why they couldn't move armies with the Byway Portals. The mage had explained in great detail the way so many people and so much mass would tear apart the delicate *vytl* holding the spellwork together, leaving all those people and all that mass, scattered across Valeria in too many pieces to put back together.

Nik had been nervous to step through the portal ever since. He glanced at his bodyguard who stared resolutely at nothing and everything at the same time. Merrick wasn't nervous about anything. Nik strongly suspected Merrick was made of stone.

A mage stood at attention in the corner of the cupola waiting for Nik to acknowledge him. He looked a little young to hold his post, but on his lapel gleamed the sunburst pin of a licensed mage.

"Ready when you are, Your Highness," he said, then gulped. "I mean, the Byway Portal attendant awaits your command and your pleasure."

"I preferred the first one," Nik said with a grin.

The mage relaxed a fraction. "Me too," he said. "But standards must be maintained to ensure our traditions thrive."

It sounded like he was quoting someone. Probably Nik's father.

"I'm familiar with the concept," Nik murmured. Then he cleared his throat. "I am ready to cross the Byways," he said louder this time. "Open the portals."

"Yes, sir." The mage summoned a bit of blue fire to his fingers and knelt to touch the tiles. The fire raced out between the lines of the pattern, making them glow. Starting from the little whorls around the edge, then spiraling toward the center in greater and greater eddies.

"Of course it's not really opening anything," the mage continued. "More like a road that only takes a step to—"

Nik stepped into the fire and the familiar jerk tugged

under his feet. It was a lot like stepping onto a train as it moved away from the platform, but instead of scenery moving past, the world around him smeared, as though he moved too fast to distinguish individual colors.

A moment of vertigo seized him before he stepped out on the other side. He put his hands on his knees and breathed, keeping his breakfast down by an act of will.

A presence loomed beside him, and he looked up to see Merrick, unruffled, waiting for him to recover.

Nik pushed himself to standing, adjusted his coat and the regalia around his neck, and tried not to be jealous for the iron stomach of his bodyguard.

When he felt like himself again, he set off with a nod to the mage who manned this side of the portal. This one, much more venerable and long in the tooth, merely nodded back as he passed.

The long hall of Saint Calahan's Refuge stretched before him, lined with windows. Outside, mountain slopes stretched on either side of the peak where the Refuge had been built.

Nik drew in a deep breath and tried not to gasp. The air always felt a bit thinner up here. Or it could be the nerves that were making a mess of his stomach. He spoke with his grandfather often enough that a summons wasn't unusual. But Nik knew exactly what the old man was going to ask and he wasn't looking forward to the conversation.

The hallway eventually opened onto a library with floor-to-ceiling windows that looked out onto the valleys below. Stacks of books made a labyrinth of the floor as Nik threaded his way between them, careful not to start an avalanche.

The Disciple of Calahan sat in a deep chair beside one of

the windows, his gray head bowed over a book. Two Care-takers dressed in sharp black suits and white gloves stood along the walls, waiting to attend the former king should he lift a finger.

Nik sat.

The Disciple turned his page.

Nik's stomach settled at the familiar ritual. At least he had a few minutes' reprieve before the interrogation started. He sank deeper into the plush armchair, waiting on the Disci-ple's pleasure. The old man was used to getting to things in his own time. Some of it came from having ruled Valeria for thirty-seven years, some of it came from being the only living Disciple of the highest Saint of the Almighty. But most of it came from being stubborn and stuck in his ways.

Nik's many times great-grandfather had started the tradi-tion, abdicating his throne when his son was ready to rule and becoming the very first Disciple of Calahan. He'd served as an adviser to the monarch, using his years of experience to guide Valeria from the background. And when the first Disciple had died, his son had continued the tradition by becoming the next Disciple.

Now the succession of the monarchy depended on the death of the Disciple, not the death of the monarch. When Nik's grandfather died, Nik's father would become the new Disciple and Nik would become—

The Disciple snapped his book closed and laid it aside, spearing Nik with his glance. Green eyes met green eyes.

"Good afternoon, Grandfather," Nik said as if he'd just sat down.

"Back from the Confederacy?" the old man asked and

scratched his beard. When he'd been king, he'd kept it short and professional. He'd let it get a little scraggly in recent years.

"Just this morning," Nik said and sank farther into the chair. He couldn't slouch anywhere else. Even in his private rooms in the palace, he was still on duty. Here, his grandfather took charge so seamlessly, Nik felt he could let his guard down.

"Find anything interesting?" his grandfather asked.

Nik met his eyes as his lips thinned. "No," he said. "I did not find a bride."

His grandfather grunted. "Hmph. Too picky. I remember women from the Clans being quite beautiful in my day."

Nik stood and paced to the window and back. "But I'm not looking for beauty. If I was looking for beauty, I would have married Adelaine years ago and been done with it."

"That the one with the hair like copper you pushed into the mud?"

"I was seven."

"She was beautiful even then." His grandfather paused, thoughtful. "Is she still available?"

"That's not my point," Nik said and flung himself down into the chair again. It squeaked against the hardwood floor.

"What are you looking for? Love?"

Nik waved a hand. "Don't be silly. I don't have the freedom to marry for love."

"Then what?"

Nik wanted badly to run his hands through his hair, but as comfortable as he felt in old King Ambrose's presence, he couldn't look like he'd survived a windstorm when he returned to the palace later.

"I'm looking for honor," he said to his hands clenched between his knees. "Compassion. The ability to listen and command and obey. Marriage is for life, yes, but I have to be doubly careful who I choose simply because of who I am, who I will be. I'm not looking for a bride, I'm looking for a queen."

"Too picky," Ambrose said again.

Nik's jaw clenched.

The Disciple waved his finger in Nik's face. "Queens are made, not born. Kings too, come to think of it. You think you popped out of your mother holding a scepter?"

Nik winced at the image. "No, but—"

"Whoever you choose will grow into her role. She'll be trained and polished. And as long as you choose quickly, she'll have time to be."

Nik glanced at him sharply. "What?" he said. "Why? Has something changed? Do you..." How did you ask someone if they thought they were dying?

"I'm sick."

"Are you sure it's not just a cold?"

His grandfather glared at him. "Every cold and ache could be a death sentence when you get to be my age."

Nik blew out his breath in a sigh. This was just more of his grandfather's usual moaning. The man had been convinced he was about to die at least once a year since Nik's father had assumed the throne and Ambrose had become the Disciple.

"Grandfather—"

"Your grandmother died before I became king."

Nik blinked at the non sequitur. "I knew she died fairly young, but I didn't realize it was that soon."

"We had three young children to raise and a country to rule together and she left me to do all of it alone."

"Grandfather, I don't think she meant to die."

"Of course she didn't. But that doesn't change the fact that I was supposed to have a partner. And I ended up ruling by myself. I decided then and there I didn't want that for any of my children or grandchildren. Once you're King, you'll be too busy to waste all this time 'deciding.' You'll be alone and you'll regret it. I married your father off early, and I told him to marry you off years ago. "

Nik hid his distaste for that. "I'm working on it."

"Not fast enough. I could keel over dead at any minute. Your father would move here to the Refuge, and you, you'll be smack on the throne."

Nik knew his grandfather had a morbid streak and a tendency to exaggerate his own mortality. But he wasn't wrong either. If the Disciple died tomorrow, Nik would be king. Tomorrow.

He swallowed.

"You have a choice," Ambrose said, leaning forward to pin Nik with his gaze. "Choose a bride by the end of the month, or I will choose for you."

Nik jerked. "What?"

Ambrose sat back, a small smile playing with his lips. "That's right. If you want to choose for yourself—find one with honor and compassion and everything else you listed— do it by the Sun Festival at the end of the month. If not…" He shrugged nonchalantly. "I'll marry you to the one I choose. And respect and competence will come from there. Like it did with your mother, like it did with your grandmother."

"A month?" Nik said, mind spinning.

Ambrose picked up his book and opened it. "Don't let me keep you."

CHAPTER FOUR

My stepmother might not believe I killed my father, but that didn't make him any less dead. Three days after my time in the cellar we buried Lord Hargrove, and I moved from one agony of uncertainty to another.

Funerals were supposed to be dreary. We'd had sleet and thunder when we'd interred my mother in the family sepulcher. But the sky had the bad manners to be a clear and painful blue the morning of my father's funeral. The sun beat down, broiling us under black and gray linen and a playful wind whipped my stepsisters' veils around their necks like a playful sprite.

The same wind merely ruffled the edges of my stepmother's skirt. Not even an ill-bred breeze had the audacity to misplace a blonde hair on her head.

The family and staff stood somberly as the Disciple of Woejoy, Saint of Passing, read the Comforts aloud, ignoring the wind which tried to steal his red stole.

I stood alone. I didn't belong with my stepfamily in their

gray taffeta gowns and their sheer black veils, but I wasn't exactly one of the staff, who mourned Lord Hargrove only as the master of the house.

My fingers clutched each other and I stared at my white knuckles. I'd expected to be sad, not filled with this shattering uncertainty. Nothing felt familiar; not my place in the world, or the people I was supposed to trust. Not even the bright sunlight. I'd spent so little time outside in the past eleven years, my eyes watered from the light.

I'd left Ember in the kitchen fireplace. Lady Hargrove had been kind to me so far, but I didn't want to risk her finding out about the fire sprite. It wasn't exactly illegal to carry a creature from the DierRealms around in your pocket, but technically you were supposed to be a licensed mage if you did.

Another Disciple carried a smoking brazier ahead of a group of men dressed in the traditional scarlet cowls of the Dead Keepers. The acrid smoke stung my nose as they carried my father's bier across the crisp grass.

"And even as we grieve, the Almighty lifts Lord Hargrove's spirit, leaving behind his earthly body and giving him a heavenly body to sit beside the Almighty's throne and eat at His table."

What did that even mean? If the words were meant to make the living feel better, then they should talk about what happened to those who were left behind. My father's death shook my solid little world. Why were they called the Comforts if they just left me with more questions?

The Disciple speaking bowed his head as his words came to a close and then he raised his hands to the sky. The sun glared off the marble roof of the family sepulcher, dazzling my eyes. It was a compact building, complete with a peaked roof and smooth columns made to house the dead. It had felt so grand when I was five and my mother had been carried inside, but now I couldn't see the point. Dead was dead. What did my father need a marble house for?

Frowning at the ridiculousness of it, I didn't notice my stepmother step forward until she turned to give me a perturbed glance and gestured with a lace gloved hand. I blushed and stumbled forward with my stepsisters to place a sprig of rosemary on my father's bier. The herb represented our Pledge to use our sorrow as an act of worship for the Almighty for as long as we grieved. Or at least as long as society dictated was appropriate.

Those carrying the bier took this as their signal and moved toward the open door of the sepulcher.

My stepmother placed her hand on a marble door post, bowing her head and whispering silent words of farewell to her husband. My stepsisters held hands as they bowed their own heads in sorrow. I stood awkwardly, waiting for a grief that wasn't coming.

At an unseen signal, the staff moved away, leaving us to mourn alone outside the little marble house.

I tried to weep, but I'd poured out all my grief and fear in the dark cellar with the image of my father lying broken on the gravel below. Now all I could muster was heavy regret. He'd exiled me, ignored me, and treated me as less than his family, less than his daughter. But he'd still been my Papa, and I could wish things had been different, if only in my own head.

I turned and made my way back to the staff. That was where Lord Hargrove had wanted me in life so it was where I felt comfortable after his death.

Ruben, the cook, gestured me closer and reached up to pat me on the shoulder. In the kitchen he used a stool, his short round stature making him look like some kind of dwarf king ruling over his kingdom. I'd told him that once when I was too young to realize it might have been insulting. Ruben had just laughed and said he'd eaten so much of his own cooking his body had given up on growing up and settled for growing out.

He'd been the first one to call me cinder-mite.

"How are you doing, mite?" he asked.

Oh, I'm just lovely, I thought to myself. My father is mysteriously dead, and I have no idea how to prove I didn't kill him. How are you?

"I'm fine," I said instead, knowing Ruben didn't want to hear the rest.

He patted my shoulder as if that's all he expected.

Jason shifted beside me. He hadn't said a word to me since he'd kissed me in the cellar. I could only assume he regretted his rash act of affection since I wasn't going to be hanged tomorrow.

I tilted my chin to meet his eyes, but his gaze remained fixed on the grass. I shook my head. Jason might be able to forget what that kiss had felt like, but I didn't find it so easy.

Lady Hargrove approached, Anella and Isol following her. She didn't need to clear her throat or hold up her hand to get our attention. She just had to raise her chin and the staff fell silent for her.

"Thank you all for your presence and your dedicated service as we send my lord to his place beside the Almighty," she said, her voice steady and confident. "I know his passing will cause some changes. As soon as arrangements can be made, we will be moving the household to the townhouse in Namerre."

The servants around me stirred with a mixture of confusion and curiosity even as my stomach plummeted toward my shoes. Leave the manor? For the capital? Where there were about five million more people to ask about my father and how he died, and wasn't I there with him?

The staff dispersed, making their way back up the dirt road toward the manor at the top of the hill while I stood in the bright sun, stiff and empty. Lady Hargrove stood talking quietly with the head Disciple while Anella and Isol glided toward the carriage.

I sucked down a breath and limped to Lady Hargrove, placing my crutch carefully in the grass so I wouldn't trip.

"My lady," I murmured the moment her conversation with the Disciple seemed over.

She turned with a welcoming nod. "I told you, Cindy. Please, call me Melissa."

"M-melissa," I said. The name sat leaden on my tongue.

She tilted her head, her smile urging me to continue even as years of not questioning my betters tried to keep me quiet.

"I just wanted to know what was going on. What's in Namerre?"

Her expression softened and she moved to wrap her arm around my shoulders as the Disciple excused himself and went to speak with his fellows.

"The Chapel of the Almighty is in Namerre," she replied. "Your mother made a pilgrimage and planted a life Pledge didn't she?"

I nodded. Years ago, right after I had been born, she'd made a Pledge of lady's mantle, dedicating her motherhood as worship to the Almighty. Most people left their little bits of greenery on the altar of their local chapel to signify their devotion, but a life Pledge was planted in order to last.

"Your father's last wish was that his life Pledge, rosemary, be planted beside your mother's to signify his devotion to her even after death."

I looked to see if Lady Hargrove was bothered by her late husband's devotion to a wife other than her, but she seemed as serene as ever.

"But won't being in the city draw more attention to..." Me. But I couldn't finish the thought.

Lady Hargrove withdrew her arm so she could turn me and meet my eyes directly. "I don't want you to worry," she said. "This is for the best. We can't ignore your father's last wishes, and removing you from the area will protect you. Already some of the locals have started asking questions."

She glanced over her shoulder to where the Disciples talked amongst themselves. My shoulders jerked. I knew these men and women, along with almost everyone from the village. I'd sent them extra food for their tables, coal for their stoves, and clothes for their children. Pain shot through me as I imagined my people giving me suspicious looks.

"This will be a good thing," she said and touched my cheek. "I promise."

And that was that. Less than a week later the Hargrove

household packed up and left the only home I'd ever known and the people I'd tried to care for the best I could. I'd left detailed notes with the housekeeper about who was likely to need what and when. They might have been asking questions like Melissa said, but that didn't mean I could abandon them completely.

It took most of three days to travel across the rolling plains of Valeria's lushest farmlands before we crested the last hill and looked out at the city stretched before us. The bright blue ribbon of the River Liren wrapped around it and to the east we could see the masts of ships in the Port of Namerre. Canals split the city into dozens of islands of commerce and entertainment and residence as smoke from chimneys and factories mingled above. And to the west, against the trees of the King's Park and the wide curve of the river stretched the distinctive roof of the Blue Palace.

The sight almost made all the worry and exhaustion worth it. Almost.

Ember took one look at the crowded plain filled with buildings and people and noise and scampered back down my neck to hide under my apron. She'd been restless without a hearth to hide in, and I put my hand over her to try to comfort her. I didn't really want to admit to myself that I missed my seat beside the fireplace just as much.

CHAPTER FIVE

Nik doubted it would solve anything to stand up and declare the Ruling Dukes were stubborn old men who argued in the council chamber because their wives wouldn't let them argue at home. But he really, really wanted to.

Twelve ornate chairs stood in a circle on the lowest floor, occupied by twelve Dukes representing their duchies.

Around them rose tiers of benches designated for the public, circling and circling until Nik felt like he sat at the center of an arena made of blond wood with dark mahogany accents.

It wasn't a bad comparison. He'd always thought that if he gave the Duke of Chatham a short sword, the loudmouth would leap across the chamber to finish his opponent with as much blood and cheering as there'd been in the ancient games of the Vemiir Empire.

"Gentlemen," Nik said, smoothly inserting himself as the Duke of Chatham took a breath. "The Torracan ambassador makes a good point," Nik said. "This compulsion magic his country has struggled against is similar to the blood magic we so abhor. We should at least consider his proposal that we limit it in the same ways."

The Torracan ambassador stood in the petitioner's box just above them, his copper colored skin and black robes standing out among the Valerian Dukes. His dark eyes darted from one face to another as he tried to gauge their reactions. The others obviously missed the significance of the man's full formal attire, with the heavy gold braid and red sash. But Nik knew that in the sweltering desert sun of his home it was considered a concession to the solemnity and importance of the negotiation.

"The compulsion," the ambassador said. "It is insidious. It takes away one's will. It steals a person's most basic choices. And it uses blood. The blood of the victim turned against them." The man hesitated. "I have a friend. An expert who knows more about the details than I do. He could come. He could tell you the dangers, if that would convince you."

The Duke of Chatham drew in an affronted breath. "Are we to allow ourselves to be told what to do in our own country, in our own council chamber even?"

The argument devolved from there. It had taken Nik's great-great-great-grandfather twelve years to get the blood magic laws put into place. It was starting to look like it would take just as long to include compulsion magic.

"It sets a dangerous precedent," the Duke said. "Bowing to outside influence. Just like this demand that the Disciple of Calahan has made. Are we to stomach that as well?"

You're not being asked to stomach anything, Nik thought. *It's my life and my marriage on the line.*

The fading sunlight filtered through the high windows, glinting off the Duke's ridiculous pink glasses. The man had started the trend a few months before, claiming the colored lenses helped him spot a liar from a hundred yards away.

Nik raised a hand. "The Disciple's role has always been one of adviser," he said. "He's not demanding anything. My grandfather merely wishes me to avoid the same mistakes and misfortunes he lived through." Nik would have gladly ignored his grandfather's ultimatum, but he wasn't going to sit here and let a bunch of crotchety dukes malign his right to make it.

"Is the King going to support this decision?"

King Julius was across the palace attending the Monarch's Council session, but Nik knew his father well enough to answer that. "Of course. Unlike some, my father respects the Disciple's advice."

The Duke smiled sourly. "Then you will be looking for a bride."

Nik returned the smile and the sentiment behind it. "Yes."

"I might have someone in mind."

Nik's mouth twisted and he almost abandoned all diplomacy to flat-out say, "I will not marry your sister, you power-grabbing son of a cow." But instead he said, "If we have nothing better to do than gossip, I suggest we adjourn for the day. I'm late for a meeting."

Only the Master of Ceremonies was supposed to adjourn council sessions, but the man took the heir's hint and tapped his staff on the polished bronze disk set into the floor and declared the session complete.

Nik shot from the council chamber fast enough he was surprised he didn't leave a wake in the parquet floor.

Merrick, who had been waiting in the background, stepped after him. Nik often wondered if the man ever sat down while he waited, but so far the Prince had never caught him at it.

Outside the chamber, the broad hallway opened up onto another, newer wing of the palace. Technically it belonged to him, as a home for the heir and his family. It came with all the amenities of a modern house, large bedroom suites, indoor plumbing, its own driveway, the occasional ballroom.

Nik hadn't moved in because he couldn't imagine rattling around in the place by himself.

Double doors at the end of the hall led out onto the open promenade of the King's Gallery, where they could take a sharp left into the gardens.

He didn't have to go far to find his next meeting, just across a narrow bend of the River Liren. The sun was only a hand span above the horizon when cries of outrage and laughter rose from behind a hedge ahead of him. He walked through an archway covered in climbing morning glories and stopped for a moment to take in the sight.

Most of the palace gardens were carefully cultivated and manicured, but this patch of ground had been left flat and bare of anything except grass, a couple of trees, and the lamps that lined the space. His family had long ago appropriated it for game night and by royal decree the gardeners weren't allowed to do anything with it except trim the grass.

Nik's mother and his thirteen-year-old sister, Eriana, currently wielded croquet mallets to whack balls across the lawn, making the rules up as they went. From what little he could see, Nik assumed the object was to hit the other person's ball and make it fly. Colin, as steadfast at seventeen as any ancient councilor, lay on a bench, a book propped on his knees. Nik envied the way he could distance himself from the world with only a page or two of text.

"Take the night off, Merrick," Nik said and stepped across the lawn to his family.

"Yes, sir," he heard behind him. It was an old joke. Nik would pretend he could send his bodyguard away and his bodyguard would pretend he could go. Really, Merrick would join the other ServantGuard around the edges of the lawn.

Queen Terese finally looked up as her son joined them. "Oh good, you made it. We were going to start thinking up penalties." She stretched up to give him a kiss on his cheek. Her hair had started fading toward gray, but in the lamplight you could barely tell.

Eriana pouted. "Foo, I wanted to come up with something really foul, too."

Nik tugged her long red-gold hair. "I knew you'd come up with something evil so I hurried."

"They were talking about toenails, last I heard," Colin said without looking up from his book. "But I didn't catch what they were actually going to do to your toenails."

Nik made a face. "Scary."

Family nights were rare and therefore rigidly enforced. Anyone who missed had to endure a punishment thought up by the remaining members of the Rannard family. And Nik's brother and sister were truly imaginative.

"You can help us come up with something for your father," Queen Terese said.

"No need," the King's baritone said from the archway. "I made it."

The King was short and stocky. Built to wear armor and carry a pike, if only he'd been born a hundred years before, he'd always said. Nik got his height from his mother's side of the family.

Eriana skipped up to their father and threw her arms around his neck. The King grunted and returned her embrace.

"So what are the rules tonight?" Julius asked after his youngest child had released her death grip.

"Whatever you want them to be?" Colin muttered from the bench.

Queen Terese made a face at him.

Eriana pointed to the two trees on the other side of the lawn. "The trees mark the goal line. The object is to hit the other person's ball through the goal. If you knock theirs in, you get fifteen points. If they knock yours in, you lose ten."

"Ah, good," Julius said taking a croquet mallet. "I was just thinking I needed to hit something."

Nik hid a snort behind his hand as the King's mallet cracked against Terese's ball. His father looked tired after battling the Monarch's Council, but then his father always looked a little tired.

"So did the Torracan ambassador make any progress with the Ruling Dukes?" Julius asked. Behind him Eriana shrieked as the Queen whacked her ball between the trees.

Nik gritted his teeth. "No. They were more interested in

Grandfather's ultimatum and whether you were going to enforce it."

His father raised his eyebrows. "I think he has the right idea. Saints know nothing I've said has stirred you to make a choice."

Nik picked up a croquet mallet, finding he now had the urge to whack something, too.

"I want to make the right choice," he said.

"You're thoughtful and responsible and you're old enough to know yourself," the King said with a look at his son. "You're unlikely to make the wrong choice. As long as the girl is willing to learn, she will become the woman you need beside you."

"I don't think I want to leave something that important to chance." Nik stripped out of his carefully tailored jacket and loosened his collar so he could swing his mallet without ripping anything.

"It's not chance," his father said. If he'd been anything less than a king, he'd have rolled his eyes. "It's life. People change. Spouses learn and grow. Usually together. If you're trying to find the perfect woman right now, you're wasting your time." He paused as he watched his wife and daughter argue about whether a ball had gone over the line or not. "You're wasting the kingdom's time."

"So I'm not perfect?" Terese said, abandoning her argument to put her arm around her husband.

Julius turned his head to plant a smacking kiss on her lips.

"Ewww," Eriana said and whacked another ball.

"And look, you can make your sister squirm, too," Julius

said with a pointed look at Nik. "You just have to choose a partner."

Nik stepped up to the line and swung the mallet in a perfect arc so it cracked against his father's ball and sent it sailing over the hedge.

A faint cry of alarm reached them through the dark.

Terese sent a rueful look after the ball. "Perhaps we've exhausted the topic."

Nik flexed his hands on the handle of the mallet and forced his shoulders to relax.

"I think that's cheating," Eriana said.

"How can you tell?" Nik said. "You're playing by made-up rules."

"And I'm making one up right now that says that's cheating." She skipped to him across the lawn and gave him a kiss on his cheek to soften the blow. "You're being far too pragmatic anyway," she said into his ear. "You should find someone you love, no matter what any of them say."

His arm tightened around her, but he didn't respond, unable to shatter her idealism. He'd had to let go of the fantasy of love a long time ago.

"That only makes the job harder," he said quietly. "That's two impossible criteria to meet."

She laughed and returned to the game. But Nik hadn't really been joking. He already had to find a good queen. How was he supposed to find someone who also saw him as more than a prince?

He strode to Colin's bench, moved his brother's feet, and plopped down beside him. Colin raised an eyebrow and closed his book.

"Who's right?" Nik asked quietly.

Colin had made it his duty to learn everything the world could teach him. Neither of them had said anything about it, but considering how little time Nik had for learning, he knew his brother would be his chief counselor and the wisdom behind the throne whenever he became King.

He was already the wisdom behind the heir.

"Everyone's right," Colin said, sitting up. "Taking your time to choose carefully isn't a bad thing."

"That's what I was trying to say—"

"But they're right in that trust and respect grow over time. Anyone you choose will grow. So will you."

Nik slumped on the bench.

"Even Eriana's right. A partnership based on love will be even stronger than one based only on respect and skill."

"So I have to meet everyone's requirements. In less than a month."

Colin gave him a sympathetic look. "I'm glad I'm not the heir."

Nik grimaced. At seventeen Colin was only two years younger but no one had even mentioned marrying him off yet.

"Colin, it's your turn," Eriana called. "And Nik, we're still missing a ball."

Nik sighed and Colin chuckled as they stood up.

"Good luck," Colin said as Nik started for the archway.

He got the impression Colin didn't just mean the ball.

"I hope it didn't roll into the river," Nik said under his breath.

CHAPTER SIX

The city was bigger than I expected. I'd had a vague concept of lots of people and buildings crammed into one space, but it was one thing to imagine it and another to get your toes run over by a cart while pedestrians pushed you off the sidewalk.

"Is it always going to be like this?" I asked Ruben as I hobbled after him. Ember leaned out from under my braid and chattered angrily at the people in my way. I shushed her but needn't have bothered. Everyone else seemed too busy to notice the fire sprite on my shoulder.

Ruben chuckled. His short stature meant he was overlooked and trod on far more than me, but he'd grown up in the city and the crowd didn't seem to bother him at all.

"You didn't have to come with me," he said. "You could have stayed cozy by the fire." He'd left his apron, smeared with meat and vegetable juices, by the fire as well.

"I wanted to see the city." I missed my people in the village and the busywork I'd made for myself, helping them.

So with the Hargrove ladies busy getting fitted for new gowns and Ruben taking a trip to a local chapel, this had seemed like the perfect opportunity to get out of the townhouse.

We wove down the street and crossed the Grand Canal to the large market that stood just off a big green park. Several stalls sold the little bundles of greenery that served as Pledges for those heading to a chapel, and Ruben took his time choosing a little bunch of cut daisies, each petal pristine.

I hesitated before I chose one daisy and one sprig of rosemary and laid down half of my savings for the Pledges. I'd always followed Saint Needsmeet, since that was what all the servants did. But I felt guilty not pledging rosemary in remembrance of my father.

I tucked my offerings into the pocket of my apron and wedged my crutch under my arm to follow Ruben. The number of people thinned and tapered off as we reached a modest chapel on the edge of a narrow canal.

I glanced at the chapel in consternation. It wasn't any bigger than the one dedicated to Saint Woejoy back at the manor and it was significantly less ornate.

Ruben turned to head inside, but I hesitated.

A young woman stood beside the steps, her shoulders hunched under her threadbare shawl and her hand out for alms. Her head ducked as if all she expected was a kick or a slap.

Two or three other people entered the chapel and they didn't even look at the young woman.

"What's the matter?" Ruben said as he came back down the steps to take my arm. "You've seen beggars before."

I had, of course, but none of them had struck me the same

way as this one. She looked no older than me. And from the state of her clothes I'd say she hadn't been on the street for long. I could imagine her story and something in me wanted to write a better ending for it.

"Go on," I told Ruben. I fumbled my Pledges out of my pocket. "Put my offering on the altar for me. I think the Almighty will understand."

Ruben frowned, but I didn't budge, and finally he sighed and left me on the step.

By the time Ruben had returned, the woman had a crust of bread and a cup of fruit juice I'd bought with my last two coins.

"Well then, mite," Ruben said. "You ready to head back?"

I turned from the young woman who sat on the steps with her bread and her juice cradled close to her chest as if they were the most precious thing.

"This is Renny," I told Ruben. "She's been a lady's maid for two years, but her mistress passed away and Renny's been out of a job since. She has a little sister who stays with a seam-stress nearby."

I hadn't been in the city for long but it didn't take a hard-ened resident to see where Renny's story was headed. The longer she was on the street, the harder it would be for her to find a decent position. One opportunity, one chance was all she needed. And it seemed like one missed chance was all it took to ruin her completely.

"What is it you want, then?" Ruben asked reaching for his wallet.

"I want to take her back to the townhouse," I said. "There's no reason she can't have a job with us."

Ruben spluttered, his hand frozen. "No reason— You're so high and mighty now you're hiring?"

I flushed. "No, of course not. I just mean there's plenty to do. Renny can scrub floors or dishes. She can sweep and mop and fold laundry. She's far more useful than me. It doesn't have to be forever, just until she finds something better. Lady Hargrove can afford one more maid. She won't even know Renny's on the payroll." I spoke all my arguments in a rush before he could head me off.

Finally, I took Renny's hand and pulled her up beside me. Then I raised my chin and waited for Ruben's response.

He was going to argue. He opened his mouth several times to do so. Then his gaze settled on my expression and he blew out his breath.

"You look just like your mother when you do that," he said. "No one could ever talk her out of something once she got it into her head either."

Ruben turned and set off in the direction of the townhouse.

"I think that means, 'yes,'" I said to Renny and hurried after him.

"Why are you doing this, miss?" Renny said as we crossed the Grand Canal.

"They call me Cindy," I said.

"Cindy," she said. "But why? You spent your money on me and everything."

I shrugged uncomfortably. "You needed the help."

"Yes, but...I've had loads of people pass me by, some even stop to give a coin. But no one has ever actually done anything."

I frowned at the cobblestones, trying to put my thoughts into words. "I guess a coin or two would have helped. But it wouldn't have changed anything. Not really. Do you know the Saint of Service's name?"

"Needsmeet," she said quietly.

"Yes, meeting needs. That's how we serve. I'm not...I'm not a very useful servant," I said looking down at my awkward gait. "But I can do this one thing. I can help you when you need help. Surely that counts for something."

Renny looked at me then took my hand as we turned up the street toward the townhouse. "I think you were the Almighty's servant today."

Like every other house on the row, the Hargrove house had a pristine facade with tall narrow windows and a flight of stairs leading down to the service entrance below the front door.

I was thinking of how to get Renny settled when Jason met us just inside the service entrance. He hadn't paid me much attention since the move. We'd always been friends but ever since he'd kissed me in the cellar, he'd been avoiding me.

I stared at him steadily, waiting for some sort of reaction.

He met my eyes for the first time in a week, but his words weren't what I was hoping for.

"Lady Hargrove has been looking for you all morning," Jason said.

My heart thumped, and I tried to convince it there was nothing to worry about. "Why?"

"I don't know, but you'd better go quick. She's been waiting."

I cast a quick look at Renny. "Jason, can you find her an

apron and tell Ruben I'll be back to take care of her later? I'd better go see what Lady Hargrove wants."

I climbed the stairs as quickly as I could, using the banister to pull myself up each step. Up to the second floor where Lady Hargrove and her daughters slept.

The three of them stood in Isol's room while two seamstresses bustled about with tape measures, pins, and other mysterious tools I didn't know the use for. As a kitchen drudge, my education in all things lady had been seriously lacking, including needlework.

"There you are," Lady Hargrove said, making me jump. I could feel Ember settle closer to my neck as my stepmother closed in on me from the other side of the room.

"Where have you been all morning?" Lady Hargrove said, consternation written in the crease of her forehead. The lady didn't frown if she could help it, but her eyebrows had no trouble expressing displeasure.

"I was with Ruben, my lady," I said.

"It's Melissa," she said firmly. "I did say that we were all getting measured for new clothes today. The seamstress has been waiting."

My jaw dropped, and I could only stammer. "I-I didn't think you meant to include me."

Lady Hargrove cupped my face and gave me a sympathetic smile. "Of course I meant to include you, dear child. You're family, aren't you?" She turned to the women with the implements of measuring. "We'll need the last court dress ready by tomorrow for my stepdaughter. Based on the approximate sizes I sent to you last week."

"Why would I need new clothes?" A sick feeling settled

in the pit of my stomach as my mind raced through all the possibilities and came up with one that filled me with dread. Isol watched me, her face smooth as a mirror reflecting no feelings. Anella's lips twisted and she raised her chin.

"You don't expect me to come with you to court," I said, voice rising with disbelief.

Lady Hargrove glanced at the seamstresses, where they worked with their heads down, and pulled me aside.

"Yes, I do," she said, quietly so only I could hear. "I have a plan to protect you but you must play your part too, do you understand?"

I was busy trying to arrange my arguments when her hands gripped my shoulders.

"We must establish your innocence. In every sense of the word. The weak, the helpless, the sick. They are never blamed for things like murder because people inherently believe they're incapable of such things. Do you understand now?"

"Yes." She wanted me to play dumb. She assumed that if I looked sick and helpless, then no one would be able to blame me for my father's death. And she would be free of the taint of association.

"I will need your help," she said. Her hands slid down my arms to grasp my hands. "Can you help me?"

"I've never been very good at lying." She'd said she'd sent ahead. How long had she been planning this, and she hadn't thought to warn me?

"You don't have to lie. You don't have to open your mouth. You just have to be silent and people will make their own assumptions. I'll do my part, too."

She wasn't wrong. Strangers always looked at the way I walked and assumed my brain was broken along with my body. Unless I spoke up to defend myself, her plan could work.

"But why does it have to be at the royal court?" I said. "Couldn't I just be meek and helpless here?" I gestured around Isol's bedroom with its flowered wallpaper and canopied bed. It wasn't exactly familiar territory but it was better than court.

"No one will know you're meek and helpless if they don't know who you are," she said. "You need to be seen. You have to trust me. Do you trust me?"

I opened my mouth without an answer, but she didn't need one.

"Of course you do," she said. "You're so good that way."

Heat flooded my cheeks as I tried to decide if that was a compliment or an insult.

She turned to check the seamstresses, and Ember whistled alarm in my ear.

I batted at her. I had my own mixed feelings about this; I didn't need to deal with hers.

Melissa turned, an eyebrow arched in question. "Did you say something?"

I pulled my hair over my shoulder to hide the fire sprite. "No."

I didn't want to alienate the only person who'd tried to help me since Jason had lost interest. And this wasn't a terrible plan; it only required my silence and my cooperation. Even if it meant I would have to go to court and endure all those people staring.

Would I have to stay quiet the rest of my life? Surely she didn't mean to parade me around forever. In time, the court would forget about my father's untimely death and I could go back to the life I was used to. Maybe I could even go back to the manor and my people.

A clink of a tray behind us announced the arrival of tea.

Melissa looked up and stepped back, distracted.

"Who is this?" Melissa said.

I glanced back to see Renny carrying the tray carefully in two hands, a clean white apron covering her threadbare dress. Her eyes widened when the lady of the house noticed her.

I limped to her as quickly as I could. So much for slipping her into the house unnoticed.

"This is Renny," I said firmly. "She, uh, she was hired right after the move." I raised my chin as an idea clicked into place. "She can be my maid. If I'm going to be going to court with you, I will need someone to help me dress and...and do my hair."

I'd been dressing myself for eleven years and couldn't imagine needing Renny to do my buttons, but ladies had maids. Maybe well-bred women were allergic to button-holes.

"I don't know," Lady Hargrove said. "We're going to be very busy with the presentation at court. We won't have time to train anyone new."

I squared my shoulders. "She's experienced, and this way I won't have to take one of the upstairs maids from you or Anella and Isol."

I realized then that I was going to go along with her plan to make me look helpless. The thought sank around my shoulders like a weight, but it wasn't like I had any better ideas.

Renny stood frozen, the tray still in her hands. I was impressed it didn't even wobble. Lady Hargrove's gaze examined Renny from head to toe, then swept to me. I don't know what she was looking for, but she found it in my eyes. The lines at the corners of her mouth stretched thin but she gestured outward with her hand.

"Very well," she said. "I can see you are determined, and I don't see any harm in letting you have your way this once."

I grinned at Renny, relieved. Her dark eyes were huge as she moved to set the tray on the low table in the middle of the room.

"Now then," Melissa said and took my shoulder to turn me back to the seamstresses, who waited with their tape measures. "If we are finally pulling in the same harness, let's get you ready for court."

CHAPTER SEVEN

It turned out I did need Renny's help dressing. The simple dresses I'd worn in the kitchen hadn't prepared me for the number of buttons, stays, and petticoats a court gown possessed. And all the fastenings were in the back, where even a first-rate contortionist couldn't reach.

I stood in front of the mirror and felt like I stared at my mother. Her rust-colored eyes gazed back at me from a heart-shaped face and her lips twisted self-consciously. Her hair had even been the same shade of honeyed blonde.

Then Renny reached over to tug my hem straight, breaking the fantasy.

I smoothed the fabric down my front. A gray silk skirt hung around me like a bell. I'd refused to wear the petticoats that would have made it stand out two feet to either side of me because I'd never be able to walk in the ridiculous things, especially not with the flimsy court canes Melissa had given me. The seamstress had grumbled about shortening my hems to compensate, but I couldn't see the difference when yards of fabric still swung around my legs.

A low-cut bodice hugged my torso and pushed my chest up. Who knew I had a chest to push? I'd have to be careful not to lean over or the blasted things might fall out onto the floor.

Instead of my usual braid, Renny had spent an hour with a hot iron gathering my straight hair into a cascade of curls that fell down my neck and shoulders.

Melissa had declared my rough wood crutch too crude for a lady and had ordered a pair of dark mahogany canes capped with silver instead. They didn't provide nearly as much support as my crutch, and I hoped I wouldn't wobble all the way to court. Maybe that was part of Melissa's plan. If I looked wobbly and weak, no one would think I was strong enough to push my father off a roof.

Renny bit her lip and looked down as she handed the canes over.

I checked my reflection again. "Have I dislodged something important already?"

"No, Miss Hargrove," she said, clasping and unclasping her hands. "I just...I just wanted to thank you. I had no idea you were a part of the family when I followed you home the other day."

"You know, neither did I," I said, giving the top of her bowed head a bemused look. "We were both in for a shock."

Renny finally met my eyes, startled.

My smile turned rueful. "Until the morning I met you, I was a servant. Mostly I peeled potatoes by the fireplace."

She laughed. "Is that why you still sit so close to the flames?"

I glanced at the fireplace in my new bedroom. Melissa had insisted I move up here, instead of staying on my pallet in the kitchen. It was only one of the spare rooms on the third floor, but it had an actual bed and a window that looked out over the palace wall so I could see a slice of the gardens and the royal chapel.

"The ashes remind me of the kitchen hearth," I said.

"Cindy?" my stepmother called from the stairwell. "Are you ready?"

I drew in a sharp breath. "Coming."

From the fireplace, Ember chirped and then streaked across the carpet and up my dress.

"It's going to be boring," I said. "Are you sure you want to come?"

She hummed and wrapped herself around my wrist. As her fire dimmed her shape changed until she looked like a bracelet made of orange and black stones. A surprisingly pretty complement to the gray of my dress.

Renny watched her with wide eyes. "Does it burn you?"

"Not unless she gets really angry. Mostly she feels like sunlight on your bare skin." I lifted my wrist and spoke to the fire sprite. "You have to stay hidden. And you can't make me laugh at odd moments."

Ember made a shushing noise that I assumed meant consent, and I headed for the stairs. Melissa hadn't noticed my constant glowing shadow, and I was reluctant to reveal her presence. The fire sprite didn't think much of my stepfamily and she'd likely get me in trouble by being rude at the wrong moment.

Anella watched me jolt down the stairs, her lip curled in disgust. You'd think her twisted expression would ruin her beauty, but her dark gold hair and coppery skin still gave her a unique allure despite her haughty look. Her sister remained stony and unreadable. They both wore the same dark gray as I did. Normally, young women were presented to the court and the King in white, but since we were in mourning, gray was more appropriate.

Melissa wore full black and managed to make it look elegant and a little alluring. We each wore a sprig of rosemary pinned to the shoulder of our gown to remind us of our Pledge to the Saint of Passing.

Melissa clapped her hands at the sight of us standing together. "Are we ready, ladies?"

She led the way outside where our carriage waited on the street. Jason jumped down from the driver's bench and opened the door for us. I tilted my head to meet his eyes. He glanced up, blanched, then turned a deep red before locking his gaze on the cobbles.

He was very careful not to look at me as he handed my stepfamily into the carriage, and I bit my lip in amusement.

I tried to be as graceful as the others climbing up the step but the heads of my canes were new and unfamiliar. I fumbled them and fell onto the seat.

Melissa helped me get settled while the carriage lurched into motion, and my ears burned furiously. Isol just watched, but Anella made a disgusted noise and rolled her eyes.

"Everyone remembers their protocol?" Melissa said.

She'd gone over the etiquette of a court presentation in thorough detail the day before. The whole idea seemed very elaborate to me, but according to my stepmother it had been even worse before King Julius had cut the pomp to a minimum.

"Yes, Mama," her daughters responded.

"Cindy?" she said and looked at me.

"Yes, Melissa," I said.

Anella snorted. "As long as she doesn't trip and fall on the way to the throne," she said, then turned to her mother. "I still don't understand why we're bringing her along. She'll make us look ridiculous."

"Because she's family," Melissa said.

"She never was before." Anella's voice took on the hint of a whine. "Why now when we're actually getting to go to court?"

I bit my lip, wondering the same thing. Even my father hadn't thought of me as family.

Melissa's eyes narrowed and she pinned her daughter to the cushion with her glance. "Because I said so. Is that good enough for you?"

Anella's face contorted as if she was going to keep arguing, then her expression went blank, and she subsided with a murmured, "Yes, Mama."

I was impressed. I remembered my mama well enough to know the words "because I said so" had never worked for her. She'd always been careful to explain things so I understood why I was asked to do something.

Anella said nothing else the rest of the trip, just stared sullenly out the window. Isol held her peace, watching.

Melissa squeezed my shoulder and I gave her a tentative

smile back. For the first time I could remember, someone actually wanted me here.

Outside the window, rows and rows of townhouses and shops passed. We rolled over a canal and turned to follow it all the way to the great wrought iron gates of the palace. I craned my neck, trying to get a glimpse of the blue tile roof the palace had been named for and the dome capped with the golden statue of an archangel.

"Close your mouth," Anella hissed. "You look like a tourist."

I sat back, flushing.

The carriage pulled up to a set of wide, curving steps, and Jason jumped down to open the door for Anella and Isol to step through. I hesitated on the bench, intimidated by the staircase.

Melissa reached a hand out to touch my trembling fingers. "I know it's frightening," she said. "But this is the best way to keep people from asking too many questions."

Frightening was the wrong word, but I couldn't come up with the right one to describe the swirling mix of nausea and cold sweat that made my palms slippery on the shafts of my canes. Why couldn't hiding in my fireplace be the best way to defend myself?

She sat back with a bemused look. "I have something for you," she said. "I thought to give it to you on the way home, as a treat for getting through the ordeal of court. But maybe now is better."

She reached into her reticule and pulled out a pendant, the long silver chain sliding through her pale fingers. She turned it deftly so the oval of glass backed with silver caught the light and glimmered.

A sprig of lady's mantle lay perfectly preserved under the glass, its tiny yellow flowers set against some crisp greenery. The beautiful piece of artistry caught my gaze and held it.

"It's wonderful," I murmured. "But why lady's mantle?" It was Saint Nurture's Pledge. Pregnant women and mothers followed her Path by dedicating their motherhood to the Almighty.

"Your mother followed Saint Nurture," Melissa said, looking down at the pendant with a soft gaze. "I thought it would be a nice way to keep her with you always. And I wanted you to know that I will protect you like a mother, but I will never try to replace your memories of her."

My throat closed and I had to blink to clear my eyes. After years in the kitchen where everything I owned including my clothes had been given grudgingly, I didn't even know how to handle such an unexpected and thoughtful gift.

"Thank you," I said with quiet sincerity.

She leaned forward to clasp the chain around my neck. The pendant settled cool and heavy against my collarbone, and I touched it self-consciously.

Then Melissa climbed from the carriage, and I took a deep breath and followed. If she said this was the only way to keep me free, I believed her.

Jason took my hand to help me down. He squeezed my fingers and winked when I looked up in surprise. I'd been waiting for him to do something—anything—since that moment in the cellar and he chose now when I didn't have time to do more than blush?

My stepfamily was already climbing the stairs, so I hurried to catch up.

Inside, the Grand Foyer rose until the ceiling disappeared in a curtain of shadows at least three stories up. A palace footman dressed in deep blue livery met us at the door and told Melissa court was being held in the gardens today. He led us through a long hallway where we passed several galleries full of art and armor and out into the summer sunshine.

Several gazebos shielded an array of brightly dressed courtiers all grouped in little pockets of conversation and laughter. The footman escorted us to the largest of these and bowed us over to the master of ceremonies who stood at the edge, waiting for our names and titles.

In the center of the gazebo stood a man dressed in a sharp black suit, an unassuming circlet on his brow. The morning sun brought out the stark white strands in his black hair. He was shorter than I'd expected but he turned to greet us with a courteous nod as we stepped close.

"Lady Hargrove, Viscountess of Yarrow," the master of ceremonies said, voice pitched to carry without shouting. "Her daughters, Miss Anella Hargrove, Miss Isol Hargrove, and Miss Cindy Hargrove."

I hiccuped in surprise. For some reason I'd thought he'd use my real name, but it was too late to correct him now.

My stepfamily sank into deep curtsies, and I felt eyes on the back of my neck as I bent over my canes and bowed from the waist. An actual court curtsy was out of the question the way my legs shuddered, but the canes kept me upright, thank the Almighty.

The King murmured a bland greeting and a few words of conversation to my stepmother. For a terrifying moment I found his eyes on me, and I held my breath.

Then he turned back to his companion and that was it. That brief interaction allowed us to attend court functions, mingle with the gentry, and it would allow Melissa to find husbands for Anella and Isol.

My stepfamily backed away. I lurched with them, the tips of my canes clicking with every step.

Now that we were free of protocol, Anella and Isol drifted toward a group of young women who looked about our age and Melissa was beckoned by a matron old enough to be my grandmother. Before she went, she gave me a significant glance, and I ducked my head.

My stepsisters were to spend the morning making friends and connections they'd use for whatever nefarious purpose young women needed such things for while Melissa was hoping to find new patients to replace the ones she'd left in the country. She treated mostly older women who didn't want to bother with doctors for so-called "women's ailments."

My job was different, though simple enough. I was supposed to stay out of the way, keep my mouth shut, and look as feeble and incompetent as I could manage.

I moved to the edge of the gazebo and wondered if I dared wander off in search of a bench. Even as I shifted out of the center of attention, it was clear I didn't fit with these graceful beautiful people. Eyes followed me, then darted away in pity or revulsion. I was used to both but not here where I couldn't tuck myself into the fireplace and disappear.

I propped myself against one of the highly polished

pillars which supported the roof of the gazebo and breathed deep, controlling the pounding of my anxious heart. I kept my gaze down, discouraging any interaction and struggled to remember that this ordeal was for my own good.

Ember pulsed on my wrist, sending a steady heat through my skin which did more to steady me than all my stepmother's remembered words.

My gaze drifted to the other courtiers. Now that I wasn't trying to wade through them, they weren't quite so terrifying. It seemed like the chief occupation of a noble was to stand around the King and talk. I may not have been a part of the conversations but body language alone spoke volumes.

For instance, the man with the peacock blue suit was obviously trying to impress the older woman beside him. Another clearly wished he was anywhere else as a girl barely out of the schoolroom chattered in his ear.

One young woman with fiery red hair caught my eye. She was possibly the most beautiful person I'd ever seen, and she flirted outrageously with anything male within twenty yards. She threw back her head to laugh and the men all laughed with her. She frowned and they scurried to make her happy again.

All, that is, except one young man with mousy brown hair, a staid tan suit, and the pin of a licensed mage displayed on his lapel. He watched the red-haired beauty with hurt eyes, and from the way she glanced at him to be sure her flirting was noticed, it wasn't hard to guess something had happened between them.

I looked away, wondering how anyone could miss the story of pain and misunderstanding in their postures.

When I turned, my gaze caught on Melissa in her stark black. She stood talking with the King again. This time his dark head was tilted toward her in intense concentration, as if her words held the weight of the world.

I swallowed, my throat suddenly dry. What could Melissa possibly have to say to the King? I'd assumed when she'd told me to stay quiet and out of the way, she would be following that rule, too.

My breath stuttered. Unless she wanted me to stay out of the way while she betrayed me to the King?

My fingers crept to the necklace she'd given me less than an hour before. The glass felt warm under my fingertips and I forced myself to think. She wouldn't betray me. Not after she'd been so nice. Not after she'd defended me to her own daughters. And if she'd really wanted me to hang as a murderer, she'd already had plenty of opportunity back at the manor.

I was overreacting. There, now she was gesturing to Anella and Isol in turn.

Oh. A shiver of unpleasant realization crept across my skin. She did have an ulterior motive for dragging me to court. It just wasn't one I'd been expecting.

Compared to me, Anella and Isol looked beautiful and competent. Perfect marriage material despite their mixed heritage. A couple of the older matrons were looking askance at their darker skin, but the younger set hadn't seemed to notice. Was I here to serve as the ugly counterpoint to her own daughters?

Ember tightened against my wrist with an inquisitive chirp.

"It's nothing," I whispered. "I think I've just been standing for too long. You'd think they'd have some chairs or benches out here." My legs already trembled from the abnormal exertion.

One of the black and orange beads of my fake bracelet raised itself like a head and Ember trilled. Then before I could stop her, she slipped off my wrist, morphing into her sleek cat form, and darted away through the sea of wide skirts and trouser legs.

"Ember," I hissed. "Ember get back here."

Muck on me, I hadn't expected her to actually go looking for a seat. I hurried after her, stumbling around courtiers before I stepped into the sunlight and onto a flagstone path.

A streak of firelight drew me away from the gazebos and farther into the gardens. I ducked around a row of manicured hedges, the noise of the crowd fading. With each step my wide skirts wrapped the canes, threatening to trip me.

Now my legs really were going to give out.

The path opened onto a wider walkway beside the river. This lazy meander of the Liren glinted in the sunlight, picturesque and pristine, like a river next to a palace should be.

I finally caught sight of Ember, a tiny flaming cat sauntering down the path toward a bench that backed up to the riverbank.

My breath caught. Two men stood talking beside the bench, one in the polished breastplate of a ServantGuard.

"Oh no," I said under my breath as Ember propped her front paws on the leg of the bench and looked back at me, twitching her whiskers in triumph. I hobbled forward, hoping to get there before the men noticed the flaming cat.

As I lurched off the path, my skirts caught my left cane. I stumbled, tried to right myself, and overcompensated. Too late to stop my forward motion, I pitched down the steep bank, palms skidding in the grass.

I yelped and tucked my shoulders so I rolled. The sky, the riverbank, and the bench whirled above me like streamers in a carnival dance.

There was a splash and suddenly the world was still again. A creeping wetness around my feet and calves told me I'd landed in the river.

I buried my head in my hands with a noise that caught halfway between a groan and a laugh. A quick mental survey told me I wasn't hurt, but I could just imagine what I'd looked like doing a cartwheel down the riverbank in full court attire. And now I sat half in-half out of the water doing my best impression of a frog. Laughing was the only response that seemed to fit the ridiculousness of the occasion.

Ember streaked across the grass to my lap, careful to keep her paws out of the water as she chirped and whistled in concern.

A shadow fell across us and she squeaked in surprise before burying herself in my voluminous skirts.

"Muck in a saint's handbasket," a voice said as hands caught my elbows and hauled me upright. "Are you all right?"

I looked up and froze, my heart thudding in my chest.

Green eyes stared at me out from under a sweep of stark black hair. The same hair I'd noticed needed a trim in the manor only weeks ago. And if I'd had any doubt about whose hand was wrapped around my elbow, the Valerian Dark Sun worn only by the King and the heir hung around his neck.

The man in the ServantGuard uniform held my other arm and the two of them lifted me back onto the path, my legs swinging like a pendulum between them. Tick-tock like a broken clock.

"Were you going after the cat?" the Prince said. "I thought I saw one just before we got to you."

His lips quirked in a grin, inviting me to respond.

I unlocked my jaw but couldn't for the life of me think of anything to say besides "tick-tock." I snapped it shut again before I could humiliate myself further.

And it was a good thing, too. If I tried to come up with something witty to impress him, I would completely ruin Melissa's plan.

I realized I was staring and dropped my gaze to the Dark Sun he wore on an indigo ribbon. It looked like a compass star —sixteen symmetrical points arrayed around a circle of brilliant silver eclipsed by a black disc. It signified the Darkness which occurred every thousand years, the Darkness Valeria had been built to endure.

"Did the fall knock the words out of you?" he said. "I've never fallen into a river, but I've tumbled off plenty of horses. I know it can take the wind right out of you."

I couldn't help huffing a laugh, and I nodded, snatching the excuse he'd given for my silence.

"Well, just give it a moment," he said. He glanced down at my dress and he cleared his throat.

My face burned as I realized with his height all he'd see

was cleavage. But like a gentleman, he ignored the obvious and bent to brush bits of grass from my skirt.

Mortified, I batted at his hands. A day ago, I'd barely needed a lady's maid and now I had a prince checking me for grass stains.

"Let me find you some help," he said. "Merrick—Oh, thank you." The ServantGuard handed the Prince my canes, which had gone flying, and he held them out to me.

"Merrick, can you stay with her while I find someone?"

"You know I will not leave your side," the man rumbled in the deepest voice I'd ever heard.

The Prince sighed. "You are impossible." He tilted his head to meet my eyes. "Will you be all right if I leave for a moment? You won't try jumping into the river again?"

I shook my head emphatically. Anything to get him to leave so I could let the ground swallow me without interruption.

He backed up a step and held his hand up palm out. "Stay there. I won't be long."

He trotted off in the opposite direction, toward the palace proper with his bodyguard following a precise two steps behind.

Almighty save me, that was Prince Nikolas. Crown Prince Nikolas Alyxander Humphrey Rannard. He had half a dozen other titles I couldn't think of right at the moment but just the one was enough to make me smack the silly out of myself.

How close had I come to completely blowing Melissa's plan? If the Prince himself started asking questions about me, there was no way I'd remain free and innocent for long. He'd learn the truth, and I'd be hung as a murderer.

Which meant there was no way in hell I was sticking around until he came back.

I turned on my heel and hurried back toward the gazebos as fast as I could. Ember finally emerged from my waistband with a whistle and slid back toward my wrist.

I gave her a look out of the corner of her eye. "I'm still mad at you, you know."

She immediately cooled against my skin and gave a low apologetic murmur.

I stopped beside the hedge separating me from the court and glanced down. I made a distressed noise in the back of my throat. I'd hoped to slip back in unnoticed, but my gray gown was soaked to the knees, not to mention my shoes.

"Now what?" I whispered.

Ember chirped, then with a sharp whistle and click the wet silk began to steam. In seconds the bottom half of my dress was dry enough you'd never know I'd just got dunked in the river. That is, if you ignored the fact that it was discolored and a little shrunken.

"Good enough," I said. "And thank you."

Her noise this time was clearly contrite.

I shook my head with a snort and moved to disappear within the court.

CHAPTER EIGHT

No matter how urgent Nik's quest to find a wife was, he still had all the normal obligations of the heir. Like attending the opening of the Royal Academy's new observatory. Since the Rannard family had generously sponsored it, they'd had to sit through an hour of speeches.

"Maybe I should marry a scientist," Nik said, watching the lead researcher gesturing wildly with her hands as she explained the giant telescope to Colin. Nik's eyes would have glazed over by now, but Colin nodded as if he understood her words perfectly. He probably did. Colin understood everything.

"I didn't know you were so interested in science," the woman beside him said. Lainey tucked a curl of bright red hair behind her ear.

"I'm not," he said. "But she'd have the problem-solving skills she'd need as a queen, not to mention drive and dedication."

"She'd be bored running a country," Lainey said. "A

woman who is used to mapping the stars is not going to settle for being a pawn in someone else's politics."

The bitterness in her words rang across his nerves and he gave her a sidelong look. "I take it your brother's been talking at you again."

Lady Adelaine had been cursed with an ambitious older brother, the Duke of Chatham, who was determined to see her crowned queen. Luckily she'd also been blessed with a steady common sense and self-awareness. She and Nik had decided when they were thirteen that they would never be married. Lainey knew she would be a terrible queen. And Nik knew that deep down Lainey wanted to marry for love. She'd never be happy settling for friendship.

But that same friendship made her the perfect woman to escort to this sort of thing. He had someone intelligent he could talk to, and she never read anything more into his attention.

"There were several new girls introduced in court today," Lainey said. "I saw a couple that had potential."

"Yes, I pulled one out of the river this morning." He chuckled at the memory.

Lainey started to snort, then instantly her posture changed, leaning toward him like he was the center of her world. "Oh, Your Highness, you're just too funny."

He looked at her askance. "Why are you talking like that?"

"Like what?" She put her hand on his arm and tipped her head back to laugh. "Almighty, sometimes I don't understand what goes on in men's heads."

Nik frowned, then caught on. He glanced around and

sure enough he caught sight of Christoph, the King's Mage, lurking in the background. His gaze fastened on Lainey's face, then he spun away.

Nik sighed. "Stop using me as a way to make him jealous."

"It's not just you," she said with a fake tinkling giggle. "There are plenty of men willing to play the game."

He removed her hand from his arm. "I'm serious, Lainey. Stop it. You should just talk to him."

The bright smile fell from her face and her lips thinned. "He was the one who stopped talking to me. He made it very clear he wasn't interested anymore."

From the way Christoph watched Lainey every chance he got, the mage was clearly still interested, but Nik wasn't about to make assumptions for other people. It was bad enough being friends with two sides of a quarrel.

Across the room, Nik's father broke away from his conversation with other patrons of the observatory and made deliberate eye contact with Nik. He jerked his head and stepped across the tile floor to the wide windows.

Nik took the opportunity and excused himself from Lainey.

The Queen had spent the day hashing out a referendum with the Bicouncil, leaving Julius free to assume the social obligations of the crown for once. But that didn't mean his father was off-duty.

The Valerian summer night let in a cooling breeze, ruffling the edges of the curtains as Nik joined his father beside the window.

"Find anyone you like?" Julius said before Nik could ask what he wanted. "Or are you reconsidering Adelaine?"

Nik kept himself from clenching his jaw and covered his annoyance with polite attention. Always it was the bride hunt. His parents never seemed to want to talk about anything else nowadays.

"How do you know I was looking?" he said.

"You get this intense expression anytime you look at a girl. Like you're tallying up all the pros and cons in your head. You do know you're looking for a bride, not the perfect riding horse, right?"

Nik moved past his father to grip the windowsill. How else was he supposed to look at his marriage with a deadline looming over him? He was already a week into his allotted month and all he had was lists in his head.

"I hate to take you away from something so important. Especially when you're finally concentrating on it," Julius said, and Nik could read the hesitance in his father's voice.

He turned to lean against the windowsill. "What's wrong?"

Julius opened his mouth, thought better of whatever he was about to say, then started over with no preamble. "Someone has been destabilizing the Blood Bond."

Nik straightened in shock. "What?" The Blood Bond linked every noble to the Rannard monarch. Erestan the Gentle had established the bond hundreds of years ago in order to strengthen the Valerian people with Rannard blood. In times of trouble, the monarch could send his own strength straight to his nobles, who could then feed it into their people.

If someone broke that link, it could undermine Valeria's strength as a country.

"Have you felt anything?" Julius asked. "As the heir you're the closest to the Bond besides me. Your mother and siblings might be affected, but not as much as you."

Nik closed his mouth and thought. "I have felt...off-balance once or twice, but I thought it was everything going on in my head. Do we know who it is?"

Julius straightened. "I have a guess. The Lady Hargrove brought it to my attention. How well do you know her family?"

"I stayed with the Viscount and Viscountess on my way home," Nik said, brow furrowing. "I believe Lord Hargrove passed away recently, leaving behind a couple daughters."

"Three," Julius said. "It is the eldest I'm concerned about. I asked Lady Hargrove to bring her to court so I could see her for myself. She's blonde, quiet, walks with canes."

Nik nodded in recognition. "Yes, I helped her out of the river this morning." He remembered her face quite well, but he hadn't bothered cataloging Miss Hargrove as a potential bride. Not because of the way she walked, but because of the way she'd avoided his gaze and run from his help. His queen couldn't be meek. She had to have a backbone.

Julius raised an eyebrow. "She's ill. But as her father's only daughter, she holds the Rannard Blood Bond in her veins. Therefore she is linked to every other noble in Valeria and the Rannard family. When she comes of age, she will receive the spell key to the Bond which requires a certain amount of mental control. But if she's incapable of that control, it's entirely possible she is the one destabilizing the Bond."

Nik frowned. "Can one person do that? I thought the point of the Bond was to spread strength, not weakness."

"I don't know. We've never had someone with her limitations in the Bond before. And I've never felt this sort of destabilization before. It stands to reason they might be linked."

"And you want me to investigate," Nik said.

"I want you to figure out the truth of the issue. If she is unfit..." Julius shrugged. "Well, we can't remove anyone from the Blood Bond, it doesn't work that way. But if we know where the weakness is coming from we can protect against it. I know she's not a candidate for marriage, so this will take time away from your bride hunt. But it's important. I've invited the Hargroves to the memorial tomorrow so you can talk with her and begin your initial assessment."

A piece of Nik—a not very princely piece—sighed in annoyance. As if he didn't have enough to worry about. But a larger part of him actually relaxed a little in relief. Constantly evaluating every conversation partner for her potential as queen was exhausting. It would be nice to just talk to a girl without wondering whether she would destroy the country if he married her.

Of course it would leave less time to make his decision, and the end of the month was only getting closer. Could he do both? Could he investigate this girl and find himself a bride by his grandfather's deadline?

Nik squared his shoulders. It wasn't a matter of could or could not. He simply would have to do it. He was the heir.

He was already training for a nearly impossible job. What was one more thing on top of it?

The Royal Memorial was supposed to be an austere and elegant building, but I couldn't help thinking that it squatted between two hills like an old dog with a bad case of indigestion.

"Over five hundred years ago, Master Arcturus Pellon, King's Mage to Gallan the Second, insisted on building the Royal Memorial with magic," the court's herald said, his voice carrying easily to the mass of courtiers waiting beside the crooked building.

"He lost control of his spell and sank the memorial deep into the palace grounds, where it has remained ever since, a testimony to Saint Calahan's proclamation that Valeria be built by hands only and never magic."

I tilted my head to look at the memorial. The front half stood above the ground, enough that we could walk through the door. But the back half of the building sloped down until the entire thing was immersed in the gardens.

Someone had tried very hard with the facade where enormous alcoves housed statues of previous monarchs, but since the whole thing tilted at an angle, the past kings and queens of Valeria looked like they'd had too much to drink and were sleeping off the effects of their debauchery.

I grinned and then bit my lip, trying to match the solemnity of the courtiers around us. The Memorial for Ancient

Kings was supposed to be a day dedicated to ritual and ceremony.

Still, it was hard to concentrate on the history of the ceremony when old Queen Ullele the Devout leaned on the wall beside her with her eyes closed and her mouth open.

Around my wrist, Ember caught the direction of my gaze, and she made a faint snoring noise.

I choked down a laugh, covering it up with a cough.

A pale blur caught my eye, a face staring directly at me and not at the herald. Prince Nikolas stood with his family beside the doors, watching me with a curious expression.

Saints protect me, why was he looking my way? Was he imagining me knee-deep in water again? Muck on me and my clumsiness for being so memorable. I dropped my gaze to the grass-blades beneath my canes and shifted so Melissa's bright curls and wide sleeves hid me from view. I didn't look up again until it was time to move into the memorial itself. Then I was too busy watching my feet to worry about princes or why they'd notice me.

Inside, the crush of courtiers made it hard to breathe. Too many of us crowded the open foyer and all of them glanced at me sidelong as if wondering what I was doing here.

I had no answer for them. I went where my stepmother led and she'd insisted I would find the memorial interesting.

After the ceremony, most of the court clustered in the foyer around the buffet tables. The hall extended down into the earth, but it was well lit with mage globes, and the solitary space beckoned me away from the press of people.

Melissa had only reminded me to be meek and quiet. She

hadn't said I couldn't wander off by myself. And she hadn't seemed upset after I'd disappeared the day before.

I moved down the slope, away from the foyer, placing my canes carefully on the smooth flagstones in front of me and bracing for each step. The noise of the crowd faded as I walked farther and farther into the memorial. Ember raised her head from my wrist and chirped.

"You promised not to get me in trouble today," I reminded her.

She gave me a woeful hum and ducked her head back against my skin.

I headed for a branch off the main hallway. The halls were laid out in a grid so I wouldn't get lost, but I liked how I could turn a corner and feel completely alone.

Apparently, I wasn't the only one who'd tried to get away from the crowd, though. I stumbled across two women tucked away in one of the many alcoves.

I recognized the redhead as the young woman who had flirted outrageously the day before. She leaned on her dark-haired friend's shoulder, weeping.

"I hate myself for it, but how else do I get him to look at me?" the redhead was saying. "I miss him, Bianca."

Not wanting to be seen, I hurried deeper into the memorial. I wanted to go up to her and hold her hand, try to rewrite her story like I'd tried with Renny. But I was a stranger and she was a lady. And could I really know what was best for her and her estranged love just by seeing them interact once or twice?

Farther down the slope the hallway grew darker as the

skylights disappeared and the mage globes were spaced farther apart.

"All right, Ember," I said to my wrist. "You can come out now."

I raised my arm and Ember climbed up to sit on my shoulder. She flared into her cat shape, small enough to fit in my palm, and cast flickering orange light on the murals carved into the walls and the deep alcoves housing dead kings and queens.

I found the silent stony company of the statues restful. These companions demanded nothing from me. Not even my presence. Even after I left, they'd go on watching over the kingdom from their marble pedestals.

I wandered among them, reading the plaques that described their great deeds, or serious piety, or magical brilliance. A few lines of text on their plinths hinted at each one's story.

Where could I find the rest? Even great kings and queens had to come from somewhere. They all had childhoods that had shaped them into men and women who could do great things.

I leaned forward so Ember's light fell on the plinth and I could squint at the words under Erestan the Gentle's feet. His stone hands held a tiny child, but his sad eyes seemed to say there had been a lot of pain before he earned the title of gentleness.

"I've always liked Erestan," a voice said. "He was actually convicted as a blood mage before he became king."

I whirled and caught myself on the plinth.

The Prince stood in the hall, watching me in Ember's

flickering light. The bodyguard stood in the shadows behind him.

I propped a cane against the plinth and closed my fist around Ember. She dimmed to a dull ochre, pretending to be a stone. No one had ever tried to send her back to her Dier-Realm, but that could be because she'd never let anyone see her long enough to think they should. Perhaps he would just think she was a fire-stone. Lots of people kept those around.

Today the Prince wore a deep indigo suit. The color was reserved for use by the royal family on special occasions. It meant that he was being especially formal today.

And yet he wasn't off, seeing to his many duties. He was here, his head cocked as he studied me.

I shifted my feet. What did he want?

"Are you a mage, then?" he said, nodding to my clenched hand.

I shook my head and brought my fist to my chest. Muck on this court dress. It didn't have pockets. What dolt designed a gown without something so practical as a pocket?

He frowned and stepped forward. "Are you...can you speak?" His words lengthened and his tone grew gentle, like he was talking to a wounded animal.

I lifted my chin and opened my mouth to defend myself, but then thought better of it. Melissa had said the best way to keep people from asking questions was to remain silent.

But I could already tell, refusing to answer this man's questions would only make him more curious. There was something in the way he looked at me that said he was already forming answers in his head. The best way to get him to leave me alone would be to talk to him.

Besides I was supposed to be meek and sick, not mute.

"Yes," I finally said.

He raised his eyebrows in surprised delight. Maybe I'd taken so long to answer he'd given up on me.

"There, see. Was that so hard?"

"Yes," I said. The playful answer startled me, since my sense of humor stayed tucked behind my teeth most of the time.

His green eyes widened, and his mouth quirked up in a grin as he realized I was teasing. "Do I intimidate you that much?"

"Yes," I said and grabbed my other cane again.

Ember slithered back up my wrist to be a bracelet, but the Prince wasn't watching now. He leaned against the wall, his polite smile hiding something sad and resigned, making him look a lot like Erestan the Gentle.

"Don't let the title fool you," he said. "Prince is just a job description. Like cook or carpenter or juggler. It doesn't mean I'm not a person, too."

I wanted to ask him if he knew how to juggle but that last bit caught me. I knew what it was like when people only saw the outside of you, the obvious bits, and never bothered to look any deeper. Was being a prince that much different from walking with canes if people assumed that was the only important thing about you?

"So I know you're one of the Miss Hargroves," he said. "But which one?"

My brow furrowed, and I looked pointedly at my canes.

He flushed. "That's not what I—I meant, what's your name?"

I smirked and shook my head.

"You're not going to tell me? Or are you only answering yes or no questions?"

"Yes."

He rolled his eyes heavenward. "Oh that's cruel."

I snorted at his melodrama.

"Will I have to guess?"

"Yes." I turned to continue walking down the line of statues.

"Is it Esther?"

I turned to see him squinting at the nearest plinth.

"Esther the...I think that says reluctant. Are you Esther the Reluctant?"

I giggled. "No."

"You could get out your light again and help me."

I hid a chuckle and turned to keep walking.

"Jessamine the Cruel?"

"No."

"Octavia the Decadent?"

"No."

"Maxwell the Barbarian?"

I turned to mock glare at him. "No."

He grinned at me.

I could spend the rest of my life making him smile like that.

"Cindy!" My stepmother's voice rang around the stone walls of the memorial.

I drew a sharp breath and lowered my gaze to the floor. Meek, mild, sick. Not a threat. These were the things I was supposed to be. Flirt was not on the list. Saints save me, what had I been thinking?

The Prince folded his arms over his puffed up chest. "Ha," he said. "Now I know your name. Cindy the Reticent."

Melissa hurried beside me and took my arm in her gentle fingers.

"There you are, my dear. I worried you'd gotten lost. Are you feeling all right?"

I nodded, gaze still stuck to the floor as I fumed at myself.

"I'm sorry, Your Highness. I hope she wasn't a bother. She's very ill, you know. Sometimes she wanders off and can't get back on her own." My stepmother babbled like a runaway brook, clearly trying to fix what I'd already ruined.

"Not at all," the Prince said. "She was perfectly polite, just very quiet."

I could hear the confusion in his voice, but I didn't dare raise my head. I'd already proved I couldn't trust myself in his presence. I knew the consequences, I knew what was at stake, and yet I'd acted like the silliest flirt in the world. Something in me had wanted to respond, to make him laugh, to think myself worth a prince's attention.

"Come along, Cindy," Melissa said, towing me inexorably back up the sloped floor. "We're planting your father's Pledge today and we must get to the Chapel. The carriage is waiting outside so you don't have to walk so far."

"Thank you," I whispered. I didn't dare turn to see the Prince's expression as we walked away. He would forget about me in a day or two. So many women flirted with him, he surely wouldn't remember one with a limp.

And I would do better next time. I'd stay away from him in the future.

Nik watched the Hargroves make their way up the memorial, his polite smile devolving into a frown.

There was no doubt in his mind that Cindy Hargrove was not the source of weakness in the Blood Bond. She couldn't be and still respond to him with cleverness and interest. But there still had been something decidedly odd about her.

First he'd practically had to chase Miss Hargrove into the depths of the building. He'd never had to chase a woman in his life. He'd been surprised to find it an uncomfortable feeling. Then—another new experience—the girl had refused to talk to him.

All right, if he was being honest with himself, that part had been fun.

And finally, when Lady Hargrove found them, the girl had acted like she'd been caught doing something horrible. Or at least indiscreet.

Lady Hargrove had described her stepdaughter as sick. Like she needed the guiding hand Lady Hargrove had rushed to give her. But Miss Hargrove had seemed perfectly capable until her stepmother showed up. Sure she was a little wobbly and quiet, but she'd certainly responded to him with wit and intelligence, even if she'd masked it under coquetry.

Nik's frown deepened as he and his bodyguard climbed the slope back to the abandoned foyer, the courtiers having left for more interesting venues. Why would Lady Hargrove want him to believe her stepdaughter was sick?

His thoughts flicked to the rest of the family. Lady Hargrove had two daughters of her own. Both of whom were the perfect age to snag a prince. He almost groaned out loud. He was no stranger to conniving mothers and throne-seeking daughters. It was a wonder he hadn't noticed it right away.

It was entirely possible Lady Hargrove was maligning her stepdaughter to redirect his attention to her own daughters.

CHAPTER NINE

That afternoon, I regretted all the walking I'd done at the memorial. I stood in the Pledge gardens of the Chapel of the Almighty, shifting from foot to foot as my calves threatened to seize and cramp.

An acolyte knelt in front of us, dressed head to toe in white, clearing a space among the carefully cultivated ground cover. He moved a small rosemary plant from its pot to the hole in the ground, and he pressed the soil down around it as he murmured prayers.

Melissa and my stepsisters bowed their heads with him.

I tried to pay attention as well but my gaze caught on the tall healthy specimen of lady's mantle planted beside the rosemary, its little yellow flowers already blooming. A bright bronze plaque in front of it bore the inscription:

AMELIA MARIE HARGROVE

4E 880

I was supposed to be thinking about my father as we honored his last wishes, but I couldn't help remembering my mother and wondering what kind of woman would love a man who ignored their offspring.

I touched the necklace Melissa had given me, burying the conflict deep inside me.

The Chapel acolyte finished his prayer and stood, the knees of his white trousers stained brown and green. He brushed them off with an unhurried flick of his fingers.

Chapel acolytes didn't grow Pledges for worshippers to pick and lay on the altar like common farmers. They nurtured the living Pledges left by thousands upon thousands of faithful pilgrims. Some only required a sheltered home and plenty of water, but others had to be planted and replanted year after year. The acolytes cataloged every Pledge ever made, where it had been planted, when and by who.

"You may stay as long as you wish, my lady," the acolyte said before retrieving his tools and returning to the Chapel whose marble domes towered behind us.

Melissa put an arm around my shoulder as we stood looking at my father and mother's Pledges.

I was shifting my aching feet when Melissa straightened.

"What did the Prince have to say to you this morning, Cindy?"

I jerked. I'd been expecting her to ask ever since we'd left the palace, but she'd waited to ambush me here.

I swallowed. "Nothing much," I said. "I was just looking at the statues."

"Princes like him don't talk to people like you," Anella said, looking down her nose at me. "What did you do to get him to come over to you?"

"I didn't do anything," I said.

"Liar."

I rocked back on my heels, drawing an angry breath.

Anella didn't pause long enough to let me defend myself. She turned to her mother with a sneer. "She has to be lying. She did something to get the Prince to notice her when he's supposed to be looking at me. You promised me the crown."

Melissa sent her a quelling look. "I also promised you would have to work for it."

Anella crossed her arms with a pout.

My gaze darted between the two. Of course Anella wanted to be queen. Any fool could have guessed that. But what did I have to do with any of it?

Melissa sighed. "Anella is right about one thing, Cindy. You had to have done something to attract his attention. There's no other reason for him to have sought you out. Did you speak first?" Melissa said, her voice gentle but firm.

I shook my head, the curls pinned to the back of my head swishing with the movement. "I was trying to get away from the crowd."

I didn't mention that I'd been holding a burning fire sprite when the Prince sought me out. Maybe he really liked magic. I'd be more careful to keep Ember hidden from now on.

Melissa wasn't done. "What did you say to him when he did speak to you?"

"Just yes and no. I thought it would be rude to ignore him."

She sighed. "We brought you here to be noticed," she said. "But in a general way. If the Prince himself learns what happened with your father, I don't know if I can protect you from the consequences."

I scowled at the dirt scattered on the footpath. "Yes, I know." Did she really think she had to remind me?

Melissa touched my hand. "It will be all right. Just avoid him when you can, and when you can't, come find me and I will redirect his attention."

Her gaze flicked to Anella, who swung between annoyance and glee.

It was for the best, I knew, but I couldn't help the pit that formed in my stomach. The thought of the Prince paying any kind of attention to nasty, simpering Anella gave me a case of indigestion.

"I know you can do it," Melissa said. "You just need to try harder."

On my wrist, Ember vibrated, and for a split second, flames licked up my arm.

I clapped my other hand on top of her.

Melissa's eyes narrowed but her response was cut off by the return of the acolyte.

"My lady. I'm sorry to interrupt but there's someone asking for you."

Melissa's brow creased. "Who on Térne would bother us here?"

"She says she's the Dowager Lady Hargrove, madam."

Melissa blinked, her mouth parting in surprise.

"Don't stir yourself on my account," another voice said, and a woman appeared beside the acolyte, shifting him out of the way with the sheer force of her presence.

Short and stout, the woman known as the Hargrove Harridan didn't look like much. Contrary to popular style, she'd pulled her iron gray hair back into a loose bun instead of curls and her skirt was very narrow compared to the wide frothy layers we wore.

I frowned. What was my father's mother doing here? My only living grandparent had been abroad since my father had remarried.

Melissa shook herself and stepped forward. "Lady Hargrove," she said. "We weren't expecting you."

"Of course you weren't," the Dowager said, pulling off a pair of black gloves. "I didn't send word. But then, neither did you. I expected to find you in the country."

"We came to honor my lord's last wishes," Melissa said. "He wished for his Pledge to be planted in the Chapel gardens."

"I know what he wanted," the Dowager said. "That's why I'm here. My own solicitor sent for me when he saw my son's will."

"I-I would have invited you, of course, if I'd known you were interested. I assumed you were too busy in-in Minosa to attend."

"I was in Ballaslav," the Dowager said with a gleaming glance at Melissa. "When I learned of my son's death, I immediately booked passage on the first steamer heading south. I figured it was high time to return to my family and protect my interests."

She glanced at me where I stood frozen on the path, so quick I easily convinced myself I'd imagined it.

Melissa flushed, the first time I'd seen her discomfited by anyone or anything. I never would have imagined anyone ruffling Melissa's feathers but the Dowager had been the Lady Hargrove long before my stepmother had assumed the title.

"You've been out of the country for so long—"

"That doesn't make me an idiot," the Dowager said, walking toward Anella, who scrambled out of her way less than gracefully. "Anella," she said, tipping her head toward the girl. "You are as beautiful as your mother. May you learn to use that as well as she ever did."

Isol stood still, face unreadable when the Dowager turned to her. "Isol, still hiding everything behind your eyes. Hang onto that, girl. It makes you useful."

I kept my gaze on my feet, expecting the Dowager to ignore me the way my father always had. She'd been out of my life for so long I couldn't imagine her paying any attention to me now. But she circled my stepsisters and stopped on the path in front of me.

"Granddaughter," she said.

I glanced up into sharp blue eyes. "My lady."

"You're going to stand on ceremony when I've come all this way just for you?"

My chin jerked. "Me?" I said. "Why?"

"You are my granddaughter, aren't you?"

"I didn't think you cared," I said and nearly bit my tongue. I hadn't meant to say that out loud.

The Dowager winced, pain racing across her face.

Melissa came forward and put her arm around my shoulders. "Cindy is very tired today. Perhaps you can spend more time with her after she's rested."

My grandmother's eyebrows shot up. "Who is Cindy?" she said.

"It's her nickname," Melissa said. "You would know if you'd ever been around."

Melissa steered me toward the Chapel and the road beyond, and I let her. She was protecting me from the disturbing emotions in my grandmother's eyes. I didn't know how to read them, or read her.

"Well, now I'll be around enough to learn these little things," the Dowager said behind us.

Melissa paused and looked over her shoulder. "You'll-you'll be staying with us?"

"Of course. The townhouse is my home. Saints, Melissa you can be slow sometimes."

It seemed court was now a daily routine, and the Dowager would be joining us as well. The next morning I sat wedged beside the Dowager in the carriage while Melissa, Anella, and Isol occupied the bench opposite us. I leaned so my arm brushed the wall instead of my unfamiliar grandmother.

Today court was being held in the Grand Receiving Parlor at the end of a long hallway. My grandmother had been presented decades ago, so she didn't have to go through the whole rigmarole we had. Instead she drifted off to greet some old friends, ignoring the King.

Across the room I caught a glimpse of the Prince's big bodyguard in his immaculate uniform. Close beside him stood Prince Nikolas in a dark green frock coat and tan trousers.

He turned my way and I ducked behind my stepmother.

I had no idea what I'd done to attract his attention the first time, but it couldn't happen again. The Prince could so easily destroy Melissa's plan to keep me free of murder charges.

I retreated to the far side of the room and tried to keep the rest of the court between myself and the Prince.

"What's going on?" someone asked at my elbow and I jumped.

My grandmother had snuck up on me.

"Nothing," I said automatically.

She raised a disbelieving eyebrow and didn't seem to be in any hurry to move on. She just waited, light blue eyes steady on my face.

I sighed and decided to tell her at least some of the truth. "I don't really belong here," I said. "Court makes me feel like a pigeon in a peacock pen. I was trying to hide."

"Hmm," she said, lips pursed. "I can understand that. Court certainly has its uses, but most featherheads use it as an excuse to check their intelligence at the door. Come, there are more enjoyable pursuits."

She turned and headed for the open archway that led to the rest of the palace. I wavered, caught between following her and staying put. But then I noticed the Prince scanning the room as if looking for someone. Possibly me.

I hurried after my grandmother, choosing her as the lesser of two evils.

The Dowager headed unerringly for a small foyer off the main hallway and a pair of glass-paned doors leading out into a garden. A footman saw her coming and threw one open so my grandmother could step outside.

I paused on the threshold. "Are we allowed to leave?" I asked.

My grandmother raised an eyebrow. "Do you think the King keeps us caged like pretty birds, displayed for his own amusement?" She snorted. "That may be what people like Melissa think. But court is for business, and this is my business today. Are you coming?"

She held the door for me.

Squaring my shoulders, I followed the Dowager into the bright sunlight. It was pleasantly warm in the shade but a bit too hot for a walk in the direct sun. My grandmother stepped down into the garden as if she didn't even notice the heat, and I had no choice but to follow her. Greenhouses lined the paths, full of every kind of flower, some I could name, most I could not, and a fountain burbled in the center of the garden.

"Why do they call you Cindy?" the Dowager asked abruptly.

I watched my feet where the tips of my canes sunk into the gravel. "It's just a nickname," I said. "It makes me feel like I'm back home."

"So it's your choice?"

It felt odd to have someone asking me questions who actually seemed interested in the answers. "It wasn't at first," I said. "If I could have chosen, I would have wanted to be named for fire. But Ruben told me fire doesn't last. It's the ashes and soot that are left over when the fire is gone."

She cast a glance at me from the corner of her eye. "I was wondering if you still had the fire sprite."

Ember raised her head from my wrist and chirped.

My grandmother stopped and acknowledged her. "There you are."

"I'm surprised you remember her," I said with a frown. "You left when I was so young."

My grandmother held out her hand and Ember flowed from my arm into her palm without hesitation.

"She's hard to forget. Especially after your mother used her to burn out your illness. I thought the idea was insane, but she'd read about Dierlings somewhere and that was all she needed to save your life. I'd never been a great reader, but that day convinced me books could save the world."

I blinked. I'd never thought of that story from someone else's perspective. I didn't remember much of it, but it was one of the last clear images I had of my mother, leaning over me, wreathed in light.

Ember chattered and the Dowager let her jump down to the gravel path, where she darted ahead of us as a cat. "Do you like to read?" she said.

I hesitated, trying to catch my breath. Sitting by the fireplace all day hadn't prepared me to walk and talk at the same time. And I had a hard time believing she really cared what books I'd read.

"Do you interrogate everyone like this or just me?" The little stones shifted under my feet and canes, making everything twice as hard.

I stopped in the middle of the path to breathe, and the Dowager gave me a quick glance up and down. "I think you need to walk more. Work on your wind."

I scowled. "Or maybe my legs don't work and there's nothing wrong with my wind."

She tilted her head to regard me. "Maybe. That doesn't mean you can't try. How hard do you push yourself?"

I went quiet. The truth was no one had pushed me to do anything more than sit by the fire since Mama had died. And I hadn't pushed myself because it had never occurred to me. No one cared enough to see me do better, not even me.

I shook my head. She didn't understand. She hadn't been around during the hard years. It didn't matter how hard I worked. I was broken. Melissa understood. She was the only one who had accepted that and moved past it.

"Why do you care so much?" I said instead of all the things that swam through my mind. "Does it really matter how well I walk and what books I read?"

She fixed me with her stare again.

"If it matters to you, it matters to me," she said. "And believe it or not, you're a Hargrove. Your education as a noble is important to this country."

I laughed without meaning to. "You are the only person since Mama who's ever even mentioned education."

"Surely your father..." she trailed off when she saw the look on my face.

"My lady," I said, deliberately reminding myself of my past. "Until Lord Hargrove died and Melissa took over, I worked in the kitchen. I peeled potatoes, cleaned fireplaces. My education? I was self-taught based out of the books I could find downstairs. But mostly I learned to stay hidden because other people had things to get done and I was in the way. Father was the first one to teach me that."

I turned away to avoid the dawning horror and realization on her face. This was the part where the interest she'd shown would turn into pity. I'd learned to accept it from everyone else, but for some reason the idea of it from her made me want to hit something. And I just wasn't the kind of person who punched anything.

My canes struck the gravel path, emphasizing the discontent churning in my gut. I couldn't decide if it was anger or regret or just frustration that this was how the world worked. Whatever it was it left a sour taste in the back of my mouth.

Ember raced past me and circled around. Halfway through her circle, she hit a metal waste bin beside a greenhouse and something clanged.

I frowned and leaned over the bin to see what would make that noise out here in a garden. At the bottom of the mostly empty bin a couple pieces of burlap sack fell to the side.

Underneath lay a knife, its blade blackened by fire and the hilt cracked.

Other than its condition it looked like a normal pen knife, something a footman or a steward would carry for any number of mundane tasks. But something about its placement in the garden, hidden here in an incongruous trash bin, made me frown.

I reached in and used one of the pieces of burlap to grasp the hilt and draw the blade from the bin.

Ember jumped to the rim of the bin to see what I'd found.

Her nose twitched, then she screeched and leaped away. The burlap in the bottom of the bin caught fire and fell away as ash.

"What's got her so upset?" the Dowager asked stepping up behind me.

"I'm not sure." I turned to hold out the knife to her. "I just thought it was odd, a burned knife."

My grandmother fell still, her gaze locked to the knife in my hand.

"What is it?" I said, voice hushed. Whatever it was had spooked her.

"I could be wrong. But it looks like the knife of a blood mage."

I drew in a sharp breath and held the thing at arm's length. "How can you tell?"

"I've spent the last three years traveling Ballaslav. Even now they still have problems with blood mages running rampant. There's not enough *vytl* up there and mages fall to temptation every day, using blood to power their spells. And they all know to cleanse a blade with fire to remove the traces of themselves."

"Ember?" I said. "Can you tell if it was used for blood magic?"

Ember had retreated around the corner of the greenhouse. Only her head poked out and she chittered at the top of her voice.

"What did she say?" the Dowager asked.

"I think you understood as well as I. She doesn't like it, whatever it is. She senses impurities in stone and metal.

Maybe blood magic leaves an impurity so deep even fire can't hide it from her."

"Then there's a blood mage in the palace," the Dowager said, voice flat.

"We have to tell the King," I said. I wasn't supposed to talk to anyone at court, but this was too important to keep to ourselves.

The Dowager shook her head. "The King's Mage," she said. "He will be the one to handle accusations of blood magic. I'll find him. Stay here. I don't want that to move too far from where we found it, in case that's important."

A bit of relief swept through me when I realized she would be the one to do the talking. "Yes, my lady."

"Grandmama," she said firmly. "No one else gets to call me that. It's your privilege and yours alone."

I bit my lip. She still wanted to be my grandmother, even knowing where I'd spent the last eleven years.

"You said you came back for me," I said, as she turned for the palace. "Why?"

The lines around her mouth deepened in hurt and disapproval. "You weren't the only one exiled by your father. When he met Melissa, he 'encouraged' me to travel. I always assumed Melissa didn't want me around. When I learned he'd died, I knew you would be here alone with her. I thought I was coming to rescue you."

She hurried off.

My mouth opened and closed a couple times, but I wasn't sure what I would have said if she'd stayed. Did she expect me to fall into her arms for a hug? Or break down crying? I was old enough to know how the world worked and benevolent relatives only showed up in stories, not real life.

Still, I wanted to believe her. Something inside of me soaked up her words, and for a moment the world felt open to me.

But if the Dowager knew what had happened at the manor, she wouldn't be so accepting. Like Melissa said, she'd think I killed my father, and the first real family I'd had since Mama died would abandon me.

She didn't have to find out. If I never told her about Father's death, she wouldn't have to choose between love and justice.

Male voices from across the garden made me jump, and I quickly wrapped the knife in the loose burlap.

"—told you to stay away from my sister."

I clutched the evil little bundle against one of my canes and peered past the greenhouses to see two men, one heavyset with florid features and a pair of ridiculous pink glasses, the other tall but slender in a rumbled brown suit.

I was far from familiar with everyone at court but I'd seen the tall man before, and the pin of a licensed mage gleamed from his lapel. This was Master Thane, the King's Mage.

I spun to call Grandmama back, but she'd already disappeared into the palace.

"I've done everything you demanded, Your Grace. I haven't spoken to her in weeks." Master Thane's voice was tight and unhappy.

"Then why is she moping around the house like a sick cat? Explain that, Master Thane."

"I can't." It sounded like the mage spoke through his

teeth. "I've cut all ties with her. I will not make the woman I love choose between me and her family."

"The woman you love," the Duke mocked. "As if you truly cared about her and not her title."

"You have forced me to lie to her," Master Thane said. "But I will not lie to you or myself."

I glanced between the two. The mage stood rigid and silent. He didn't fight back, but his back remained straight under the Duke's abuse.

Without thinking, I started forward. I was no knight in shining armor to come to his rescue. But if I was distracting enough, maybe the Duke would stop haranguing him.

"Master Thane," I said, hoping to interrupt.

The Duke spun to glare at me. "Leave your betters alone while they're talking, girl."

I stopped short, drawing an affronted breath. Ember caught up with me and raced up my skirt, hissing.

Clearly, I wasn't important enough for the Duke. I set my jaw. But that didn't mean I couldn't distract him.

I took another two steps, trod deliberately on the edge of my gown, and let myself stumble into Master Thane's chest.

Like a gentleman, he caught me.

"Oh, sorry," I said, keeping it simple. Melissa still didn't want me talking to anyone, and the Duke didn't seem like someone who'd appreciate a chatty stranger.

"It's no problem. Are you all right?" Master Thane looked back up at the Duke. "Please excuse me, Your Grace. This young woman..."

"Miss Hargrove," I said.

"Miss Hargrove requires some assistance." Master Thane

turned us so our backs faced the Duke, giving him a very clear message.

The Duke spluttered, but Master Thane didn't look back, and finally the man harrumphed and stomped away through the gravel.

"Thanks for the rescue," the King's Mage said, giving me a sad little smile.

I straightened away from his support and resettled my canes on the gravel. Then I remembered I still had the knife pressed against one of the hafts.

I transferred both canes to one hand and unwrapped it. Then I held it out, balanced carefully on my palm.

He frowned and reached out to take it, using the burlap to pick up the blade.

"Where did you find this?" he said.

I pointed back the way I'd come. "Waste bin."

"Do you know what this is?"

I opened my mouth, hesitated, then nodded.

"How?" he said.

"Grandmother."

He tilted his head to eye me. "You're quite terse, you know that?"

I gave him a crooked smile and a shrug.

"Well, thank you for this." He held the knife up with both hands and bowed his head. "I'll take care of it."

CHAPTER TEN

Christoph found Nik in the stables stealing a moment of peace with the horses. Nik looked up as the King's Mage stepped toward him, a serious expression on his face.

"What's wrong?" he said.

"We have a problem." Christoph ran a hand through his dark hair, which stood out at odd angles. The King's Mage had never taken much care with his appearance, even less so when he was around the heir. He might have been appointed as the magical advisor to King Julius, but his youth and personality had made him a friend of Nik's.

"We have a blood mage in the palace," Christoph said.

Nik stiffened in shock. "You're sure?"

Christoph blew out his breath and leaned against the wall of a stall. "There's no doubt. A knife was recovered. The blade was cleansed with fire, which removes enough evidence that I can't trace its owner, but it doesn't remove the residue of *vytl* taken from blood. I can tell what it is even without spells. It feels...greasy."

"I'll take your word for it," Nik said. "I'm not doubting your competence. But a blood mage loose in the city is bad enough. One here..." A thought occurred to him and his brow furrowed. "Could this have anything to do with the instability in the Blood Bond?"

Christoph's eyebrows went up and he straightened. "It... yes, yes it could. We hunt down blood mages because they power their spells by hurting victims. That's common knowledge. But less well known, is that a blood mage would be able to wreak havoc on the Blood Bond."

"Muck on me," Nik said, pacing from one side of the aisle to the other. "Is that why Valeria is so hard on blood mages?"

"One of many reasons," Christoph said. "We should enact the protocols. Lock down the palace."

Nik's hand slashed through the air, cutting him off. "No. That will only start a witch hunt. Maybe even another Time of Blood and Hope. And it will spook our quarry. Namerre hasn't seen a blood mage in...decades. The last one was hunted down by my grandfather."

"And beaten to death in the square before the Guard had a chance to arrest him. I remember that story," Christoph said quietly.

"We'd better handle this quietly. Especially since it involves the Blood Bond. And thanks to you, we have a head start on the man." Nik clapped a hand to Christoph's shoulder.

Christoph gave him a rueful grin. "Actually, I didn't find it."

Nik raised an inquisitive eyebrow.

"Her name is Miss Hargrove." Christoph rubbed the back

of his neck. "I was right there in the same garden. But somehow she saw something I missed."

Nik grunted in surprise. "That's...interesting."

"What would you like me to do?"

Nik chewed his lip. "Start your spells. Discreetly. If he's working in the palace we at least know where to start. I'll do the non-magical legwork. Questioning, investigation." He winced. "As if I have time for this."

Christoph gave him a sympathetic look. "Don't forget you're scheduled for the Chapel unveiling tomorrow and the hunt in King's Park is the next day."

Nik would have preferred to toss a few of those obligations aside in favor of investigating a blood mage, but he still had his duty. And if he didn't want to start any rumors he had better show up for it.

Not to mention he still had to find a bride.

"Everyone loves a hunt," the saying went. And the courtiers who rode their horses in the bright sun of King's Park certainly looked happy about it. But whoever had come up with that piece of wisdom obviously hadn't been one of the ones stuck on the ground.

I shaded my eyes with one hand and leaned on one of my canes with the other. Could they leave already? All this ceremony was even worse than the memorial had been. That at least had been interesting. I just wanted to find some shade and sit out this hunt without mucking up Melissa's plan even more. And every time the Prince looked up from his horse, it felt like he was searching for me.

Over thirty horses milled around the meadow while their riders laughed and flirted above them. I caught a glimpse of my stepsisters, Anella looking vibrant and athletic in the sunlight and Isol looking as quiet and competent atop a horse as she did in every other part of her life. Prince Nikolas waited patiently at the head of the pack, the dark flanks of his horse matching his hair.

I shook my head as the horns blew and the riders set out with a great deal of laughter and encouraging cries. The horses streamed by, and I shielded my face from the sun again, telling myself I was looking for my stepsisters, not the Prince. But it was impossible to ignore the confident man on his dark horse, leading the charge into the forest.

I turned away as the last of the hunters thundered by and started to make my way to the tent where those of us too dignified or sick to sit a horse waited for the rest of the court to return.

The long grass clung to my skirts and the tips of my canes, making me stumble.

Someone took my elbow, and I glanced up at Melissa. She gave me an indulgent little smirk. "Here, Cindy," she said. "Let me help you."

Ahead of us, the Dowager cast me a look over her shoulder, her brows lowered and forehead creased with disapproval. I remembered what she'd said in the gardens the day before, about pushing myself, and tried to pull my arm from Melissa's grasp.

"I can do it," I said.

Melissa's mouth flattened, etching deep lines around the corners. "Nonsense," she said and gripped my arm tighter. "Why shouldn't you have help when you need it? Let me find you a seat."

I glanced at the older women gathered at the other end of the tent, all whispering and casting me those looks with smiles that weren't really smiles. Luckily Melissa led me to a different corner.

"What about over here? I know how you don't like to be in the way."

She made a great show of helping me into a chair.

"Thank you," I said. Surely she was done now and would leave me alone.

She gave my arm a pat before leaving me to join the other matrons. They laughed as she joined their ranks and I flushed, trying to ignore the niggling thought that they were laughing at me.

Ember uncurled from her hiding spot on my wrist and raced up my shoulder to hiss in Melissa's direction. I gasped and snatched the fire cat. "Stop that," I said under my breath.

She grumbled before she flowed back down my arm.

"I don't like it either, but what am I supposed to do about it?"

"You're allowed to tell her no," Grandmama said, making me jump. She moved to stand beside me, her arms crossed.

"I did. Melissa doesn't take no for an answer."

Grandmama's mouth thinned.

"It's all right," I said before she could turn into the Hargrove Harridan and go after my stepmother. "It was just this once. I'll be more forceful next time."

"Sure you will," Grandmama said with a sigh. She dropped the subject, gazing out at King's Park with her sharp eyes.

The land here beyond the palace had been left uncultivated for occasions just like this. Our meadow was the only break in the trees for miles except for the wide curve of the River Liren, a thoroughfare for any water traffic that wanted to circumvent the city entirely.

A few footmen passed with trays, carrying drinks to the courtiers left behind. Even here in the near wilderness standards had to be maintained, and it seemed like half the palace staff had accompanied us to provide refreshments.

The matrons of the court were still talking and laughing. Melissa spoke with a couple of them, passing out homemade remedies from a satchel she carried with her. They were far enough away that I could ignore them, and I felt sure that they were ignoring me.

I chuckled to myself, and Grandmama turned her sharp glance back on me. "What is it?"

"I'm glad you showed Renny that trick for pockets," I said. "Otherwise I'd have to sit here with nothing to do except keep Ember from giving herself away."

Slits in my skirts and underskirts gave me access to a large pouch tied under my clothing. Now I could stow anything short of a draft horse.

I pulled a book from my pocket, and Grandmama barked a short laugh.

"*Andre's Verses*," she said. "Very nice. That will keep you occupied for ages." She hesitated. "Will you be all right here? I wanted to speak with the Baroness of Whitecliff."

I opened my book pointedly and glanced at her over the pages. "As long as you stop talking to me so I can read," I said.

It felt dangerous to joke, but she snorted and grinned in appreciation before moving away.

Grandmama might laugh, but I didn't think it was considered polite to read at court. So I checked to make sure no one was watching and kept the book low where my voluminous skirts would hide it from view.

My mother had read from a version of *Andre's Verses* when I was a child. The rhythm gave me a little trouble until I stopped thinking about it as poetry and just read it like a story. The author had clearly spent time in court because I recognized the caricatures he portrayed in the courtiers around me.

Ember burbled a question in my ear.

"No, I won't read it aloud," I whispered to her. "I don't want to look like a crazy person."

She whined in disappointment and flattened herself again.

"But you can read along with me."

I didn't think she could actually make sense of the words, but she always liked pretending. I tilted the page so she could see, and she leaned over with a studious expression.

I chortled to myself and settled in for a long morning.

No one bothered me, and from the crick in my neck, I could tell it had been hours since I'd shifted when a shadow spread across the page like the ink had run out of the words.

"Must be a good book," a voice said. One that was becoming familiar.

My head jerked up and my breath hitched.

Prince Nikolas stood before me, a smirk on his lips. Anella clung to his arm, pouting.

Saints take me, I'd completely missed the return of the hunters. Now that I wasn't engrossed, the clamor of voices and the calls of horses and grooms nearly deafened me.

The Prince craned his neck to see my book, and I snapped it shut as heat rushed up my neck to my cheeks. Ember flattened herself against my wrist.

"Well, she has to keep herself occupied somehow, Your Highness," Anella said, giving me a sour smile. "She's not good for much else except sitting. Were there pretty pictures, Cindy?" she said with a condescending coo. She made my nickname sound like a disease. "Yes, I'll bet there were."

I clenched my teeth and ducked my head. It was a low blow, since she knew I couldn't defend myself.

"Anella," my grandmother's voice cut like a razor's edge, and I saw my stepsister jump. "Don't you have anything better to do?"

Grandmama stepped up beside me.

Anella gaped for a moment before her mouth snapped shut, and she twitched her chin up. I could almost see her digging in her heels. "I'm just trying to include my poor step-sister in the conversation," she said. "Little Cindy was hiding over here all by her lonesome. It's not good for her to spend so much time by herself."

My face burned as the Prince's eyes examined me, head to foot.

Grandmama crossed her arms, but Anella was speaking again before she could do more than glare.

"Did you hear the news, Cindy? The Prince caught a

murderer last spring." Anella stroked his arm, long tan fingers caressing his sleeve.

I recoiled, knowing perfectly well why Anella would think I'd want to hear about something like that.

The Prince frowned and looked like he wanted to say something but wasn't sure where to start.

"Yes," Anella said, obviously responding to the look on my face. "The man was tried and convicted of murder but appealed for King's Justice." She simpered up at the Prince. "Luckily our own Prince Nikolas pronounced him guilty and had him executed. Isn't it wonderful how he protects us from those sorts of dangerous people?"

My fingers wrapped around my book, the edges cutting into my skin.

"The story is more complicated than rumor would have you believe, Miss Anella," the Prince said. "Miss Cindy, I wanted to ask you some things."

I refused to raise my gaze. What could he think I had to say to him? Had Anella already hinted that I might have more in common with that murderer than he thought?

"Your Highness," Melissa's voice oozed between us and for a moment I struggled between relief and annoyance. I didn't want to talk to the Prince, but I also didn't want to hear what she had to say about me.

I slipped the book back into my pocket before she could see it.

"Is there something I can help you with?" Melissa asked, perfectly reasonable.

The Prince drew himself up. "I was hoping to speak with Miss Hargrove for a moment," he said.

I made the mistake of glancing up and he caught my gaze. "Would that be all right?"

He was asking me, but Melissa answered, "I'm sorry, it's not."

At the same moment that my grandmother said, "Of course it is."

Melissa gave my grandmother an arch look. Grandmama glared at her.

Prince Nikolas stared directly at me.

"I'm afraid my stepdaughter is overtired from the day," Melissa said. "I'll be taking her home early."

She reached for my arm and hauled me to my feet. Something in the Prince's expression pulled at me, something too much like the pity I saw from everyone else in the world.

"Come Cindy, I know you're exhausted."

The only thing I was tired of was the way she spoke to me.

"I'm not," I said.

Her eyes flashed wide, but only for a second.

Her strong fingers closed on the back of my arm and pinched hard.

I gasped and jerked away from the pain. Shock rolled through me. Yes, my response wasn't exactly on the list of Melissa-approved words, but that had hurt.

Ember flared, sending a wave of heat up my arm. I covered her with my other hand to keep her from leaping at Melissa.

"Don't be silly. Of course you are," Melissa said, putting her arm around me and drawing me away from the group of people. "Your Highness," she said over her shoulder. "Anella can answer any questions you have, but I'm taking Cindy home."

"Melissa," the Dowager said, tramping through the grass after us. But Melissa didn't stop to let her catch up, practically dragging me toward the dirt track where a dozen carriages waited to take the hunters home.

I cast one last glance over my shoulder to see Anella towing the Prince away, triumph lighting her eyes.

Melissa's arm tightened around my shoulders and I dropped my gaze to the grass again.

Safely away from the Prince's attention, I had better worry about my stepmother who wouldn't be pleased with any of what had just happened.

Nik allowed Miss Anella to pull him away from Miss Hargrove, but only as a strategic retreat while he pondered his options. He'd wanted to speak with Miss Hargrove alone, to ask her about the knife she'd found. But her family had conspired against him.

First Anella had brought up that macabre rumor about the murderer he'd executed. He could hardly tell anyone that the man had turned King's Witness, and his execution had been staged for his own protection. Now the man was hidden away in Royal Custody.

Then Lady Hargrove had stepped in and made it clear he was not welcome to talk to her stepdaughter. She clearly wanted the world to see Miss Hargrove as some kind of invalid.

But Nik now had proof she was more than she was letting on. That hadn't been some picture book in her lap like Anella had intimated. It hadn't even been one of those tragic romance novels his sister wouldn't admit to reading. He'd seen enough of the text to recognize *Andre's Verses*, a scathing social commentary written in iambic pentameter. Nik remembered throwing the same book across the room when it made his head hurt.

But if Miss Hargrove wasn't some invalid who couldn't string two words together, why was she pretending to be? She'd stayed silent while Anella humiliated her. And she didn't speak up when her stepmother treated her like a fragile child.

Anella dragged him back toward the rest of the hunters, chattering about the hunt and how much she loved riding. Nik barely paid attention. Clearly Lady Hargrove wanted to keep Anella front and center as the favored candidate for his bride. He was used to such antics and manipulations, but this time he had little patience for it since it hindered his search for a real threat.

If Miss Hargrove was clever enough to enjoy *Andre's Verses* and perceptive enough to find evidence even Christoph had missed, she could be the perfect person to help him find the blood mage that hid in the palace.

That is if he could ever get her to talk to him. He could force the issue, pull rank on Lady Hargrove and tell her he needed Miss Hargrove for his investigation. But he wanted the girl's willing cooperation. It seemed like she had enough coercion in her life already.

The royal huntsmen returned to the meadow, carrying

the stag slung over the back of one of their horses. Nik hadn't struck the killing blow—he'd never been able to stomach killing for sport—but he'd helped chase the animal until they'd cornered it against a steep bank of the river.

A slow grin spread across his face as Anella prattled on, oblivious to his thoughts.

That was exactly how he had to handle Miss Hargrove. This was a hunt.

He just had to keep after her until he'd caught her.

And now he knew her weakness and just where to corner her so she couldn't run.

"I told you to keep your head down and stay out of the Prince's way," Melissa said as the carriage lurched over the cobblestones and into the city proper. Melissa had left instructions with a royal footman to be sure Anella and Isol made it safely home in another carriage.

I rubbed the back of my arm where she'd pinched me, sure there'd be a bruise. "It's not my fault he spoke to me," I said.

"What's going on, Melissa?" the Dowager said from the bench next to me. "What was that—" My grandmother stabbed her finger at the window where we could see the trees of King's Park disappearing behind the buildings. "All about?"

I lowered my eyes to my lap and twisted my fingers in my skirt.

Melissa drew a breath and shook her head slowly. "We

are treading a delicate balance," she said to me, ignoring my grandmother's question. "I know it's difficult, but we need people to think you're helpless. Not wonder why a prince thinks you're so interesting."

I ground my teeth. "I know. I'll try harder." I didn't want her to say any more while Grandmama sat beside me, her eyes flicking between me and Melissa. She still didn't know the truth, and I wanted to keep it that way.

But my grandmother was sharp and used to getting her own way. She crossed her arms and fixed Melissa with her stare. "Care to explain?"

"I'm protecting her," Melissa said.

Grandmama snorted. "Protecting her?" she said in disbelief. "More like you want to keep the way clear for your own daughters."

It would actually be a sort of backhanded compliment if it was true. But I didn't think Melissa saw me as competition for my stepsisters. Only as a foil to make them look good.

Melissa's eyes narrowed. "Nothing of the sort. Cindy needs my protection or didn't she tell you how much danger she's in?"

Panic crawled up my throat. "Please don't," I said, crossing my arms so my fingers clutched my elbows.

Melissa cast me a pitying glance but my pleas had no other effect. "I think your grandmother deserves the truth, don't you?"

"Spit it out, Melissa," the Dowager said.

Melissa turned to her with thin lips. "I'm protecting her from a murder accusation."

Grandmama stiffened on the bench beside me. I flinched away.

"Murder?" Grandmama said.

Melissa sighed and looked back out the window as if the situation was sad rather than life altering. "I'm afraid when your son fell from the roof, the only one with him was Cindy. If the Prince ever found out..." She shivered dramatically. "I don't think anything would save her from a formal investigation. And without proof either way, she'd live with that doubt for the rest of her life."

The carriage jerked and swayed as it stopped outside the townhouse.

Melissa smiled kindly at me. "This is the best hope for her future. Make people believe she'd never be capable of that kind of violence, so if the question does ever arise, no one will accuse her. That's why we must keep the Prince away. It's still too early. He wouldn't believe her innocence now."

Melissa stepped out of the carriage and up the steps to the front door.

I sat still, not meeting Grandmama's eyes.

"Is it true?" she finally asked.

I took a deep breath that shook a little. "Yes, I was with him," I said. "But I-I passed out. I don't remember what happened. I didn't push him, Grandmama, I swear. I didn't kill him. I just don't know what happened."

"Relax, child," she said putting her hand on mine to calm me. "I know you didn't murder your father."

The tension drained out of me and I sagged against the plush seat. "You do?"

Her sharp glance was full of regret and exasperation. "Of course I do. I just wish you'd told me in the first place."

I bit my lip and looked away.

She sighed, interpreting my silence. "No. You're right, you have no reason to trust me, yet. I understand what Melissa is trying to do, but I don't think this is the best plan. You need to tell someone who can help you. Someone like the Prince. He seems fair enough. And interested in you already."

"No," I said quickly, fingers gripping the edge of the seat. "Not him. You heard what he did to that man who sought King's Justice. He'd have me executed without a thought."

"I'm sure the circumstances are different," she said firmly.

I shook my head. "Melissa's right. I have no proof I didn't do it."

"There's no proof that you did, either," she said.

"Then she's wrong?" I said, looking up at her, eyes wide. "People won't believe I murdered him."

She opened her mouth, then hesitated. Too long. "No," she said. But she didn't sound very convincing. "At least probably not. If everyone stays quiet about the circumstances..."

"And if they don't?" I asked. "If the Prince learns I was there with him when he died?"

She drummed her fingers against the windowsill. "We need another plan," she said, almost to herself. "Something that doesn't rely on Melissa."

I rubbed the back of my arm where she'd pinched me. I couldn't believe my stepmother had been so vicious about keeping me quiet. But then she had been trying to protect me. I'd been about to ruin everything with my thoughtless reaction.

My grandmother saw my expression and reached to pat my hand. "We'll think of something," she said. "Don't worry. I will not allow you to be executed as a murderer."

She stood, making the carriage sway, and shifted around me to step down into the street.

I hesitated before following her. So much of me hated Melissa's plan, but I was mired in the court now. The only way to keep from attracting the wrong kind of attention would be to hold my silence. Grandmama could look for all the solutions she wanted, but I would stay in the background, quiet, unassuming, and hope that would be enough to protect me when everything inevitably fell apart.

CHAPTER ELEVEN

Another courtier bumped my shoulder, turned to apologize, and then gave me a pitying look as they realized who I was. Ember chittered in irritation. I slapped my hand over my wrist where she clung, looking like a bracelet.

"I'm not going to bring you anymore if you keep making a nuisance of yourself," I whispered to her.

Throngs of noblemen and women crowded the Grand Receiving Parlor today, so Grandmama and I stood close to the wall.

I sighed. Looked like Melissa's plan was working. Everyone around us either stared openly or glanced at me only to look away quickly and whisper behind their hands. "Do you think Melissa would let me stay home tomorrow?" I said.

Grandmama snorted beside me. "Muck on me if I know what's going through that woman's head."

My breath huffed in a shocked laugh. "Grandmama,

language. What will all these people think?"

My grandmother waved airily. "It's amazing how the older you get, the less energy you have to worry about what other people think of you. I'd rather save it for more important things."

"Like cursing?" I said with a straight face.

"It's more satisfying than anything else."

I turned away from another courtier who was eying my canes, his mouth pulled tight in a frown. "Do you think we could escape to the garden again?"

Grandmama looked pointedly at the windows. Gray clouds swirled outside and summer rain streaked the glass. "I think you're stuck here."

A cough behind me made me turn to survey the older man who'd cleared his throat.

"Excuse me, miss. Madam," he said. "I've been instructed to make the library available. If you would like to follow me..." He tilted his head in invitation.

I perked up at the word "library."

Grandmama examined the man up and down, like she was appraising a horse. He didn't flush or fidget. I assumed from his iron gray hair he was old enough to have learned Grandmama's lesson about not caring what other people thought, and from the orange stole he wore over his black suit, he was a Disciple of Saint Wonderment and probably had more spiritual concerns.

I checked with Grandmama, who just shrugged.

"Go ahead," she said. "The library is as good a place as any to wait out the storm. I'll join you after I've spoken with the Countess of Ainsborough."

I smiled at the holy man and turned to follow him when he led the way out of the parlor.

"I'm Father Philip, Abbot of Saint Wonderment," the man said as he led me down a long corridor lined with doors.

"Cindy Hargrove," I said after a moment's hesitation. I still wasn't supposed to talk to anyone outside the house, but how could I distrust a man whose life purpose was to read? His quiet self-assuredness soothed me almost as much as the feel of ash under my feet when I sat in the fireplace.

All I knew about the various Saints in Valeria was what I'd read in books, but I did know that Disciples of Wonderment had dedicated their lives to scholarship and lifelong discovery.

"I normally live at Wonderment's Refuge," he said. "Outside the city. But the Disciples are responsible for the royal library, so I come once a year to make sure everything is in order."

He led me through a pair of doors at the end of the hall into a huge marble-lined foyer. He kept his pace slow without being obvious about it.

I took a moment to orient myself and realized we must be near the King's Council chambers at the end of the palace. From the silence I assumed this half of the Bicouncil must not be in session today.

"The library is just through here," Father Philip said. He pushed through a pair of doors on the north side of the council chamber, and I stepped through.

The sight hit me like a physical force, and I stopped to catch my breath and cling to my canes, as if I'd fall over from the mere idea of so many books in one place.

Almighty, I'd known there were libraries like this, I'd imagined them often enough. But to actually see one...

The wing itself was well over three stories, completely open except for the balcony where we'd entered. Shelves lined the walls below where we stood and extended out into the center of the room, leaving only a decent corridor between them. More shelves filled the spaces between the tall windows here on the balcony, and I could see another walkway above us where I presumed there were even more shelves.

I wished I could see it when there wasn't a storm, when light would pour through the windows and fill the spaces between thousands of books with glorious warmth and brilliance.

It was a far cry from having to sneak one or two books into the kitchen at a time.

"I've never seen so many stories at once," I said, my voice hushed.

Father Philip's expression went soft and understanding, like he knew exactly what I felt. "I'm partial to my library at home, but this one is something special."

"It's beautiful," I said. "I would love to spend even a fraction of my life here."

"Would you like to become a Disciple?" he asked with a chuckle. "We could always use that kind of enthusiasm for study."

I laughed along with him. If I was free to choose my own path, I would definitely consider a life devoted to Saint Wonderment. "Maybe," I said. "Thank you for bringing me here. Is the history section nearby?" I started to move down the aisle. "Do you know if you have any books about Erestan the Gentle before he became King?"

He raised his eyebrows. "I'll see if I can find you something, but why him?"

"Someone told me he was a blood mage before he became 'the Gentle.' I want to know what could change a person so much. It sounds like a fascinating sto—"

"Ha!" A tall figure in a dark gray suit with the Valerian Dark Sun around his neck stepped out from behind the shelf in front of me. "I knew you could say more than yes or no," Prince Nikolas said. "You can't avoid me now."

I clapped a hand over my mouth. Saints take me, what had I done? The wonder of the place had made me completely forget what I was supposed to be doing at court.

I backed up and hit the shelf behind me with a thud. A slim paperbound volume fell to the floor, and I winced.

The Prince frowned at my reaction. "Come now, I'm not nearly so scary as all that. Won't you talk to me?"

I shook my head hard enough to dislodge a curl from its pins.

Father Philip glanced between the Prince and I, forehead creased with concern. "Your Highness, are you...did you use me to trap this young lady?"

The Prince avoided the man's eyes. "Trap is such a strong word. I merely wanted to speak with Miss Hargrove discreetly. Away from anyone else."

"I do not like that you've involved me in separating her from her chaperone."

"I assumed you were chaperone enough, Father," the Prince said, with a sour little twist of his lips.

He looked like a little boy who'd gotten his hand rapped for stealing pies. His expression was almost enough to make me laugh. But no matter how devious the Prince's plan had been, I knew he hadn't trapped me here for anything inappropriate like Father Philip imagined.

The Prince craned his neck around Father Philip, and he got a good look at my face. The sheepish expression left, replaced by concern.

"You really are frightened, aren't you?"

He took a step toward me and Ember let out a shriek. She morphed into her cat form and leaped from my wrist toward the Prince.

I gasped and lunged for her, catching her around the middle as she hissed and spat at the Prince.

"Stop that," I whispered vehemently. "You can't attack a prince."

She grumbled as I stroked her arched back but finally settled into the crook of my arm with a glare at the men.

The Prince cleared his throat and tugged the hem of his jacket straight. "I apologize," he said. "I didn't mean to frighten you." He tipped his head at Ember. "Either of you."

He faced the Disciple of Wonderment. "Father, will you trust my intentions are honorable long enough to let me speak to Miss Hargrove privately? I think the lady is well defended, don't you?"

The abbot frowned and glanced back at me, as if in question.

I had no answer to give. I didn't want to speak to the Prince at all, but I'd somehow missed the lesson on how to refuse royalty.

"I'll be within earshot," Father Philip said. "Looking up some things about fire sprites." He gave the Prince a scathing glare before retreating past the next shelf.

The Prince sent a rueful grin my way and a fierce little spike of joy made me gasp. I forcefully reminded myself that Prince Nikolas had had someone like me executed, someone who'd sought King's Justice. Any Valerian convicted of a crime could appeal to the King for a final judgment, as long as they believed they were innocent. But this prince had ignored that murderer's plea and had him executed.

Prince Nikolas knelt and retrieved the book I'd knocked to the floor. "Can we start over? Good morning, Miss Hargrove. Are you well today?"

I chewed my lip and gave him a wary look before answering. "Yes," I said.

His mouth twisted. "Back to yes or no answers again, are we?"

"Yes," I said. I couldn't help the small smile that tried to crowd out the frown on my face.

He sighed. "Very well. If that's what I can get, I'll take it. Are you enjoying your time at court?"

I didn't have to think about that one. "No."

He huffed a laugh and scratched his head. "Is that because of me?"

I tilted my head and shrugged.

"What does that mean? Maybe? Maybe not?"

"Yes," I said.

He clutched his chest, his face twisted in mock pain. "Ouch. Your honesty is as cutting as it is admirable."

I snorted. Ember wrinkled her nose and climbed to my shoulder.

"Look, I know I'm not very good at talking to you. But I needed to speak with you alone. I want to ask you some questions."

My eyes narrowed. "Why?"

He blinked and his lip twitched. "Did we just add a third word to our repertoire?"

I rolled my eyes. "Yes. Why?" I repeated.

"Because you found the knife of a blood mage on palace grounds."

My fingers clenched on the heads of my canes. I'd passed that off to Master Thane. He was supposed to deal with it, not involve me.

"This isn't about you not talking to me," the Prince said. "This isn't about your stepmother throwing Anella at me. This is much bigger than that." He paced to the opposite bookshelf and back. "Something is destabilizing the Rannard Blood Bond."

"Yes?" I said. What did that have to do with me?

"You don't have to worry. We don't think it's you anymore. I've ruled out your stepmother's concern. Now I'm certain it's related to the blood—"

"Wait. Me?" I held out my hand to stop him, his words jumbling in my mind.

He paused, studying me with an intense focus. "Lady Hargrove told my father you were sick. That your illness would destabilize the Blood Bond. My father asked her to bring you here so we could evaluate the possibility." He hesitated. "You didn't know?"

I drew a quick, sharp breath, barely noticing as Ember sank her claws into my shoulder to balance.

He was chasing me for a reason. But I'd been so worried about being accused of murder I hadn't even thought about the Blood Bond that connected all the nobles of Valeria with the monarch. With my father gone, I was the next descendant in the Hargrove bloodline.

I shook my head, a dozen emotions racing through me, too fast to register.

Ember chattered in my ear, making her opinion known. I shushed her. I couldn't think when she did that.

"Lady Hargrove lied to you," the Prince said, his voice dark and sharp.

I shook my head again. Not in denial but because it was so much more than that. She'd set into motion the investigation that made the Prince so interested in me. She'd put me directly in his path. After everything she'd said about keeping me safe.

I opened my mouth, all my thoughts ready to spill out in a torrent of confusion and betrayal and fear. Then an image crossed my mind, my father lying crumpled on the gravel below me and Anella whispering "murderer."

Nothing had changed. I was still the prime suspect for my father's accidental death. And the man who could convict me stood there looking perplexed.

I snapped my mouth shut and swallowed down every outraged protest.

"Let me help you," the Prince said, low and earnest.

I shook my head. "No."

He was a part of Melissa's plan. She wanted the royal

family to investigate me. She wanted them suspicious. Even if I didn't know exactly what she planned, I should stay away from the pieces of her plot.

Except I hadn't so far. I couldn't seem to keep away from the Prince and his flirting and his questions.

I pushed off the shelf and hobbled away as fast as I could.

"Wait," Prince Nikolas said, and I could feel him following.

He'd catch me again. Make me talk. He'd learn the truth and Melissa would use him to destroy me.

"Father Philip!" I called and the Disciple didn't hesitate. I glanced back to see the holy man place himself between me and the Prince, allowing my escape.

I pushed through the double doors and ran smack into Grandmama.

"Almighty, what has you in such a hurry?"

"We have to go," I whispered fiercely. "I have to stay away from the Prince."

She craned her neck to scout behind me where Prince Nikolas argued with Father Philip. "He does seem persistent."

I shook my head. She didn't understand. "Melissa lied. She asked the King to investigate me. She's the reason he won't stop asking questions."

Her brows came down in a dark frown. "She what?"

"She's planning something. I don't know what, but it won't be good for me. And he's part of it."

Her eyes flicked to the Prince again before she took my arm. "Come on. We'll outrun him while he's arguing."

CHAPTER TWELVE

In the morning, Melissa called from downstairs that it was time to leave. I exchanged a look with Renny who finished buttoning my day dress, a practical green linen affair perfectly acceptable for around the house but not for a day at court. I took a deep breath and hobbled my way down to the front hall where Melissa waited with Anella, Isol, and my grandmother. Melissa's brow furrowed when she saw how I was dressed.

"Cindy, what are you doing?" she said. "Are you trying to make us late?"

I steeled myself, prepared to tell her very firmly that if she wanted me at court she'd have to drag me to the carriage. The night before, Grandmama and I had come up with a whole speech to confront her about her lies. I'd even planned to ask her flat out why she had set the Prince on me.

But her scowl completely derailed me and my thoughts frantically backtracked. Whatever lies she'd told me, she still held all the power. She could have me arrested at any moment. And without knowing her plan, I couldn't know for sure that I was in the right.

Without courage or belief, the words died in my throat, unsaid and unheard.

Grandmama frowned at my silence, but I just dropped my gaze to my feet. She wasn't the one facing Melissa's displeasure.

My stepmother's eyebrows drew down, and she stepped toward me. My pulse sped up.

She traced a finger down my cheek, and I swallowed.

"Are you feeling all right?" she said.

"Actually, no." I seized hold of the lie.

"You do look pale," she said finally. "Maybe we've overdone it a bit. Would you like to stay home?"

"Yes."

"I suppose that would be all right. But I worry about you without anyone to take care of you."

I bit my lip. She sounded like she meant it. But I knew she couldn't. Was I really so easy to manipulate?

"You can stay. As long as you promise not to leave the house. I can't protect you if you go wandering around the city."

I agreed easily. Where would I go? I had no friends to visit or appointments to keep.

Finally, she stepped away and gestured for Anella and Isol to follow her out the door. Grandmama waited till they were out of earshot before turning her gaze on me. "What happened to that argument we worked on?"

I rubbed my forehead. "Sorry, but you're not the one she would have arrested if she gets mad."

She pursed her lips. "True," she said, grudgingly. "But we can't even be sure that's true."

"Then I'll take the opportunity to find out if it is," I said, a new plan forming in the back of my mind.

She tilted her head. "What are you going to do?"

"I'll look for any sort of proof she might have kept. Anything that points to my guilt or innocence."

"Good," Grandmama said. She glanced out the door where we knew Melissa was waiting. "I would stay and help, but I want to keep an eye on her. Make sure she doesn't spout any more nonsense to the King. Will you be all right by yourself?"

I made a face. "You're starting to sound like her."

She rolled her eyes heavenward. "Saints defend me. I suppose that's your way of telling me to leave already. Don't worry, I can take a hint." She waggled her fingers and stepped out the door.

I turned back toward the house. They planned to attend a play the royal family had commissioned and a luncheon afterward. Which meant I now had most of the day to search for any more secrets Melissa might have kept from me.

Nik paced from one column to another, waiting in the shadows of the Grand Foyer as courtiers trickled into the palace, chatting amicably. Nik hid when he saw the Duke of Chatham escort Lady Adelaine through the big double doors. Lainey looked bored, but Nik did not risk catching the eye of his childhood friend or her brother. He had other prey today.

Except his quarry hadn't shown up yet. Every courtier in regular attendance at the Blue Palace would be here for the play, and Nik had made sure the Hargroves were included on the invitation. But as he'd already proved several times, he could trap Miss Hargrove well enough, but he was muck at making her talk.

She was presenting him with all sorts of new experiences. He wasn't used to being bad at anything.

Merrick stood against the wall, back straight, eyes vigilant even though they were in the palace proper, the safest place in Valeria.

There, finally, the Hargroves stepped into the bright sunlight streaming through the windows of the Grand Foyer, Melissa in the lead. Nik's eyes counted the figures: Lady Hargrove, Miss Anella, Miss Isol, and the Dowager. But no one else followed them. No limping figure with honey-colored hair and hunted brown eyes.

He frowned then surged forward as the Hargroves gathered themselves on the threshold. He stopped just short of Melissa and gave her a correct nod. Merrick followed and stopped behind him at a precise distance only he could calculate.

"Lady Hargrove," Nik said, shortly. "You're missing someone today."

She took a quick defensive step back, and he cursed himself for letting his discomfort rattle him.

She rallied quickly enough and touched a hand to her fading golden hair. "Yes, my stepdaughter wasn't feeling well today. She is resting."

"Nothing serious I hope," he said through clenched teeth.

Had the woman done something to her? She was already lying to Miss Hargrove. What if she'd taken it a step further and made sure her stepdaughter missed court today?

"Just the usual," she said, giving him a sad smile. "I don't know if all this excitement is good for her, to be honest."

"With all due respect," Nik said before he could think better of it. "You were the one who brought her to court."

Lady Hargrove's eyes flashed and her lips thinned, but she managed a credible nod. "Yes, under the direction of your father. Now I'm thinking that was a mistake."

Nik glanced at the other women in the family, wondering how much they all knew. Miss Anella and Miss Isol looked bored and wary respectively, while the Dowager regarded him with sharp eyes.

"What else were you expecting when you asked him for his judgment?" he said.

"I assumed he would assign someone who recognized my stepdaughter's delicacy and act accordingly. I did not think I would have to protect her from someone blundering about making her uncomfortable."

Nik flushed. Her words skirted the edges of treason but didn't cross the line. And he could hardly imprison someone for pointing out the truth. At least not in this enlightened day and age. He found himself in the strange position of wishing they lived in a time of royal tyrants before indoor plumbing.

Lady Hargrove's hands twitched, then fell still. "Surely you have all you need to make a decision," she said. "Please stay away from Cindy, Your Highness. I'm not sure what influence your attention will have on her health."

She swept her wide skirts around her and sailed off across the marble hall with her daughters trailing behind.

Nik stared after her, his face going hot then cold and back again. That had sounded like...

"Did that sound like a threat to you?" the Dowager said.

Nik just kept himself from yelping. He'd almost forgotten the Dowager was there. "What is going on in your household?" he asked with quiet vehemence.

She threw up her hands. "Muck on me if I know."

That surprised a laugh out of him. His tutors, usually older women, had always rapped his knuckles when he'd used language like that. Now to hear it coming from someone with the same iron gray hair and upright posture gave him a case of vertigo.

She waited until he'd stuffed his chortle back under a prince's calm before she gave him a sharp look. "Well, are you going to find out?" she said. "Cindy needs someone on her side."

He gave her a mocking bow. "I would love to, my lady, but your granddaughter has made it nearly impossible to talk to her."

"Maybe if you didn't go after her like a bulldog with a bone."

Nik choked on the image.

The Dowager just raised an eyebrow.

"Yes, my lady," he managed to reply.

She stared at him for a long uncomfortable moment before nodding sharply. "Good enough," she said. "Here's the address." She drew a card from her reticule. "I believe I can tell you Cindy is home, alone for the moment. And we will be otherwise engaged until early this afternoon. Tell her I sent you and she might let you through the door."

"Thank you," Nik said, taking the card.

She didn't release it immediately and they were left holding two ends of the stiff paper, standing uncomfortably close.

"Tread carefully, Your Highness."

"Yes, ma'am," he said.

She gave him a disbelieving "Hmm," and finally released the card before following her daughter-in-law.

Nik ran his fingers over the edge of the calling card, a simple rectangle with the Dowager's title printed on one side and her address on the other. He resented the implication that he had no grace or finesse, but when it came to Miss Hargrove, it was no less than reality.

He wanted the truth, yes, but charging after it might hurt Miss Hargrove more than it could help her.

If he wanted to do this right, he needed to do it one step at a time.

CHAPTER THIRTEEN

I'm not sure why I'd thought Melissa would keep incriminating evidence lying around the house. My step-mother was a lot of things, but stupid wasn't one of them.

I limped into the kitchen late in the morning, my legs as sore from climbing the stairs as they'd been my first day at court.

Ruben stood on his stool kneading the dough for dinner. He glanced at me while I leaned my elbows on the table beside him. "Haven't seen you much lately, cinder-mite," he said.

I opened my mouth to respond then closed it because I didn't have an excuse for not visiting him. It seemed so pretentious to tell him I'd been too busy at court. But maybe it was a good thing I'd come in here. Ruben ruled the down-stairs the way the King ruled Valeria. He knew things no noble would ever give him credit for.

My fingers twisted together. "Ruben, do you know if

Melissa brought anything from the manor? Anything that had to do with my father's death?"

His hands stilled for a moment on the dough before he went back to pounding it into submission. "Why are you looking, mite?"

I shrugged, trying to appear nonchalant. "No reason. Just something someone said."

"Anything of importance, like my lord's will, would be in his study," Ruben said. "Unless she left it with the solicitor."

I sighed. I'd already checked the study. No servant in Melissa's house would leave anything so obvious as a layer of dust, but the room had that fusty smell that told me no one had used it in years and the desk had been empty.

Ruben must be right. Melissa probably left anything important with the solicitor before leaving the manor.

My knees complained, so I pushed off from the table and hobbled to my old stool which still sat in the corner of the hearth. I lowered myself to the seat, and Ember wasted no time sliding off my wrist to settle among the flames. She burbled, making the logs crack and pop.

I reached to unlace my shoes. Jason had cobbled them together years ago when my ankles had started protesting the twisted way I walked. The wood rods kept my ankles straight but the leather pinched something awful, and I preferred to go barefoot when I could.

I kicked the shoes and my stockings to the side and scrunched my toes in the ashes with a small sigh.

"Look at you," Jason said when he pushed into the kitchen a few minutes later. "It's like you never left." He leaned against the opposite side of the hearth and gave me a wink.

I gave him a broad grin, relieved he was talking to me again. In the last couple weeks, Jason hadn't said anything about the one kiss we'd shared in the cellar. I'd assumed he'd been ashamed. That he'd just felt sorry for me or thought better of it. But maybe he'd been as disconcerted by my elevation to one of the family as I'd been. And maybe seeing me back in my old place by the hearth made him remember everything that had led him to kiss me in the dark.

"Yes, look at her, vacationing in the slums," Bess said, passing Jason and casting a spiteful glare at me. "I guess the high and mighty like to get their feet dirty every now and then before they go back to their silk and fur."

I ground my teeth.

Jason opened his mouth as if about to say something, and I leaned forward. But then he shook his head and just frowned.

"Miss Cindy." Renny raced through the kitchen door, making my heart jump. "Miss Cindy, you have a visitor."

"What?" I straightened fast enough make my stool rock.

"A man asked to see you," she said hurrying over to the hearth where I sat in the ashes. "The butler put him in the parlor to wait for you."

"Who is it?"

"He didn't say his name."

I hesitated, my mouth gaping, before I clambered to my feet and reached for my crutch. I'd left the polished canes upstairs since there'd been no one to impress.

Ember cooed in surprise and leaped from the flames to scurry up the back of my gown and wrap around my wrist.

Renny's brow furrowed as she peered at the ashes on my dress. "Do you think you have time to change?"

"Not unless this man wants to wait another hour while I climb up and down the stairs."

My crutch clacked against the kitchen flagstones. Who would come visit me? I didn't know anyone in the city. Father Philip was the only one from the palace that I knew personally. Maybe he'd found a book on Erestan the Gentle. He'd said he would look for one.

Renny trailed after me, brushing at the soot that stained my hem.

"Cindy, your shoes," Jason said hurrying after me, my shoes clutched in his hands.

I almost stopped, but it would take another five minutes to struggle with the damn things. Surely a holy man wouldn't judge me for my bare feet.

Jason rushed forward to throw open the parlor door for me. I stepped through and faltered, clutching my crutch for balance.

Prince Nikolas stood before the fireplace, his polished boot propped on the grate. The big bodyguard stood in the corner, making the room seem smaller with his bulk.

Prince Nikolas turned at the sound of the door, and I found myself off-balance with bare feet and soot to my knees while the Crown Prince of Valeria stood calm and immaculate in our front parlor.

"Your Highness," I said, my mouth dry.

Jason hid my shoes behind him, and Renny glanced at the

soot on her hands before folding them demurely to hide her black palms.

"Miss Hargrove." Prince Nikolas gave me an elegant nod.

I knew I should curtsy or something, but with my clumsy crutch and no shoes I'd likely end up on the floor.

We stood silent, staring at each other. The last time I'd seen him, I'd run from him. I should run now, but how much farther could I go? The man had followed me home.

The Prince raised his chin and pinned Jason and then Renny with his gaze. "I was never here," he said. His tenor voice was built for palace halls and sounded strange and uncomfortable in a townhouse parlor. "If your mistress asks, no one came to the door today."

"Miss Cindy is my mistress," Renny said, her voice quiet but firm.

Jason nodded and threw his shoulders back before meeting my eyes. "Mine as well," he said. "If Miss Cindy says you weren't here, that's good enough for me."

I blinked. Jason had never called me "Miss" Cindy in his entire life.

Prince Nikolas stood there, glancing between me and the servants.

I raised my chin. If he was waiting for me to dismiss them, he would wait till the next Darkness. I had absolutely no desire to be alone with the Prince.

"I wanted to speak with you," he finally said.

I heaved a gusty sigh. That was nothing new.

"I thought you might feel that way," he said, face full of chagrin. "Look, I know your stepmother would rather I spent time with Anella."

We both grimaced.

"But you can't spend your life doing everything she tells you to. Your grandmother said to tell you she sent me. She said you needed someone on your side."

I opened my mouth. Then closed it. "Oh," I said.

"Is that all you can say?"

I frowned. "Of course not. But you knew that already."

He broke into a wide grin. "Yes, I did. But it's nice to see you finally admit it."

"Because you like winning?" I said with an exasperated eye roll.

His levity disappeared. "Nothing about this feels like winning. I want to help you. Why do you let your stepmother treat you like an invalid? Why are you hiding?"

Because I might be a murderer and you execute murderers.

I shook my head to clear it of the thought.

"I'll talk to you, Your Highness," I said grudgingly. "Since my grandmother says so. But not about that. Those are my terms. You can either agree or you can leave."

Over my shoulder, Renny choked on a laugh. I was glad this was amusing to someone. The bodyguard didn't react. He could have been carved out of granite for all I knew. At least he'd left the gleaming breastplate back at the palace. In my parlor he wore a simple dark uniform with an indigo stripe down the side.

Prince Nikolas spread his hands in defeat. "All right. If that's all I can get, I'll take it. But why agree to talk to me if you won't let me help?"

I gave him a look out of the corner of my eye. "You

followed me home. Like a stray dog. What else am I supposed to do?"

The Prince's mouth twisted. "That's the second time today I've been compared to a dog. Am I really that bad?"

A mixture of affront and shame suffused his royal features, and I bit my lip to keep from laughing.

"Persistent," I said. "Which is more annoying than anything. I think you have beautiful women throwing themselves at you all the time, and you had no idea what to do with someone who genuinely didn't want to talk to you."

He rubbed the back of his neck and shifted his feet, proving I wasn't wrong.

"I'll admit, it's maddening," he said, meeting my eyes with a rueful grin. "But I tracked you down for other reasons, too. I have questions about the knife you found."

I spread my hands. "Master Thane knows more than I do. I only found the thing. Ember helped."

I moved around the end of the sofa to the fireplace and held out my arm. Ember trickled down my wrist and leapt into the flames that crackled in the grate.

"So am I allowed to ask about the living fire that doesn't burn you?" he said.

My lips quirked. "She can burn if she wants to. But she likes me."

"Is that why you're covered in soot?"

"I'm not covered," I said with a glare. "Covered is what happens when I clean the fireplaces. Not sit beside them."

"You clean your fireplaces?" Prince Nikolas said with a frown. He glanced at Renny and Jason. And I could hear the question he didn't ask. Isn't that what servants are for?

CATCHING CINDERS | 153

"I—" I could have explained that I'd lived as a servant for most of my life. That would certainly clear him out in a hurry, but a strange sort of shame filled me when I thought about telling him how my father hadn't wanted me around.

"I follow Saint Needsmeet," I said instead. Plenty of eccentricities could be explained away with religion.

He drew back, his brow furrowed. "Needsmeet? But he's the Saint of Service. Servants follow him."

"The purest form of worship is selfless service," I said, quoting the Writings of Needsmeet. "Maybe you should consider Pledging to the Path of service as well."

"Why?" he said with a chuckle.

"Because a monarch's greatest duty is to serve his people faithfully."

He stopped laughing. "I thought my greatest duty was to lead my people wisely."

I put my hands on my hips. "And how do you think you do that?"

He looked genuinely flustered. "By...leading them, of course."

"Of course," I said, more than a hint of sarcasm leeching into my voice. "So you walk out in front of them and hope they'll follow along behind. Like sheep." My ankles started to ache from standing on them for so long, so I turned to gesture at the sofa.

He sat and I plopped. No chance of grace here. The bodyguard didn't move. He scowled at the paintings on the wall like they'd personally offended him.

"I take it you follow Saint Calahan," I said.

"It's how I was brought up," Nik said. "The Rannards have always Pledged their leadership to Calahan."

"You know, you scoff at the Saint of Service, but it was Needsmeet that helped put Calahan on his throne."

His lips twisted.

"It's true," I said with a shrug. One of the soot-stained, dog-eared books beside the fireplace at the manor was a history of the Saints. I'd read it so many times I'd lost count.

"After unifying the duchies, Calahan went to Needsmeet weary and lonely. All he wanted was to serve the Almighty as a Disciple. But Needsmeet told Calahan that was exactly the reason he should be Valeria's first king. Because his greatest wish was to serve. It's why they didn't give him a special name after his canonization. He considered himself the least of the saints. Their follower."

"Why have I never heard this before?"

"Were you always diligent in your lessons?"

He winced and I smirked.

"I didn't think so. You never wondered why the royal guard are called the ServantGuard?"

"I...I always assumed it was because..." he trailed off, his face as red as the coals in the fire.

"Because they serve you?" I laughed. "No. It's because they guard the servants. Supposedly." I sat back self-consciously, realizing I was lecturing him.

Prince Nikolas looked at his bodyguard. "Merrick?"

The bodyguard's eyes flicked to the Prince. "Miss Hargrove is correct," he said, though his gravelly tone made it sound like he wasn't happy to admit it.

I must have made a face because the Prince laughed.

"Don't mind Merrick. He's in a bad mood because I dragged him into the city. He's not used to it."

"I take it you don't call on many women in their homes," I said.

He laughed. "No. I don't usually have to chase them down either. They tend to stay where I can see them."

It was clearly supposed to be a self-deprecating joke, but the truth in the statement made me remember I was talking to a prince. A prince who was rumored to be bride shopping.

I studied my hands, suddenly awkward. What was I doing talking to this man like I was his equal?

"Presumably so I won't forget about them," he said. "I do have a lot of things on my mind, after all."

The arrogance in his voice popped the bubble of self-consciousness, and I rolled my eyes. "The exercise will be good for you. You wouldn't want to start taking all those beautiful women throwing themselves at you for granted."

His eyes widened and then he barked a laugh. "I don't know why your candor surprises me. Even when you weren't speaking to me you were honest."

He stared at me, a small smile playing with his lips.

"What?" I said.

"You have a way of talking to me that makes me forget I'm a prince."

"Maybe because no matter who you are, you should be a man first. Your Highness." I added the last part as a deliberate afterthought.

He shook his head with a laugh. "Don't go and ruin it with that. I'm Nik. Or Nikolas if you can't bring yourself to shorten it. 'Your Highness' makes me feel invisible."

"You're the most public figure in Valeria besides the King," I said. "How can you be invisible?"

"People look at me and all they see is a prince. They don't see Nik."

I blinked. "I can understand that," I said, quietly. Now I felt bad for laughing at him. "People judge you based on the one thing they can see and assume it's all they need to know about you."

"Exactly."

"I have the same problem. People prefer to pretend I'm not there."

His gaze remained fixed on my face when he asked. "Why?"

I raised my eyebrows and nodded to the crutch resting on the sofa.

He shook his head, either oblivious in truth or deliberately ignoring the obvious.

"Really, Your Hi—Nikolas, pretending there isn't a problem doesn't fix it. It only makes you look dense."

His cheeks reddened. "I'm not pretending. Why should they act that way? Just because you don't walk well?"

"I remind them of things they'd rather not think about. Like the fact that life isn't always easy or pretty."

"Then that's their problem," Nikolas said. "Not yours."

I stared at him in consternation. He looked like he believed what he was saying. "You keep saying you're not just a prince. That you're like everyone else underneath the title, but you're really not."

"Why? Because I see you and not the crutch?"

"Because of how you talk to me even after you see the crutch."

He shifted uncomfortably. "I've learned to see every woman as a potential wife and queen. To evaluate them for specific qualities. I guess the way you walk has no bearing on whether you'd be a good queen or not."

I could only laugh. There was no other response. "Well then I guess it's a good thing I'm not in the running. You can talk to me like a normal person."

"It will be a new experience for both of us."

I bit my lip and looked down at my hands in my lap. Why did I have this funny feeling in my chest? Like happiness but more complicated.

I had to admit to myself I wouldn't have been nearly this fearless about talking to him if I actually had a chance with him. I'd have been tongue-tied and worried and not nearly so candid. But knowing he would never consider me an option freed me to speak my mind.

I swallowed down all the complications. "You didn't come here to talk about the Saints, or Ember, or...or anything else."

"No, I came to ask for your help. I need to track down this blood mage, and I think you can help me."

I gaped at him. "Why? What could I possibly do?"

"You notice things. Things other people miss. You're clever and quiet. I've seen you watching. You don't mess about trying to be noticed, so you see things. I need that."

Almighty, he'd thought this through. It wasn't some whim or misplaced interest in someone who refused to talk to him.

"Miss Cindy, the time," Renny said quietly from the corner.

Nikolas glanced at the clock on the mantle. "I should go," he said, standing. "Your family will return soon."

I struggled to my feet, and Nikolas put a hand under my elbow to help. Over the Prince's shoulder I caught Jason glaring. I hoped the Prince couldn't feel the heat of the footman's gaze. The bodyguard certainly noticed and had no qualms about glaring back, his hand resting on his sword hilt.

"May I call on you again?" Nikolas asked.

"Why?" I said. "Do you need the exercise?"

I grinned up at him as he held my arm, and we walked to the front hall, our entourage following us.

"Well, I haven't gotten the answer to my question yet," he said. "So, I'll have to return." He paused. "Miss Hargrove, if this blood mage is destabilizing the Rannard Blood Bond, it could potentially destroy the entire country."

I drew in a quick breath and he glanced at me.

"Yes," he said. "It's that serious. If he's doing it deliberately, then he's planning to use the weakened Bond for something. Maybe an attack on Valeria or an attack on the royal family."

I thought about the knife in the bottom of the rubbish bin. The wrongness of it. Then I met his earnest gaze, and I couldn't help the little surge of pride that made my chest puff out. The Prince needed me.

"I will help you, Your Highness," I said with quiet intensity. "In whatever ways I can."

The grin he flashed my way made me catch my breath.

"I'd hoped that would be your answer. And that makes my gift all the more appropriate."

I stopped in the front hall near the door and gave him a puzzled look.

He pulled a book from his pocket, a slim leather-bound volume, tooled with gold leaf.

"Father Philip found a biography of King Erestan the Gentle."

I touched the binding with cautious fingers. A first edition. "I can't take this. It's too valuable."

Nikolas shrugged. "It wouldn't be a worthy gift if it didn't have value. Please, take it."

I bit my lip and accepted the book. "Thank you."

"Erestan the Gentle was once a blood mage. And he was the one to establish the Blood Bond. Maybe there's something in there to help us."

I wrapped my arms around the gift and nodded.

He shifted from foot to foot, glancing at the front door like he wasn't sure what to do next. I realized if he'd never called on a woman in her own home, he'd probably never said goodbye to one there either.

"Thank you for an enjoyable visit," he said.

I winced. Even I knew that was stilted, and I'd grown up in the kitchen. I could see Renny roll her eyes from where she'd positioned herself beside the stairs.

"You're welcome?" I said.

He started to turn, thought better of it, and grasped my hand. He pressed his lips to my knuckles, cocked an expressive eyebrow at me, and spun to leave, his bodyguard following.

CHAPTER FOURTEEN

Two evenings later I sat on a gondola with my stepfamily, kicking myself for agreeing to help Nikolas's investigation. Otherwise I could have been at home with my feet in the ashes, reading the biography he'd given me.

But Melissa had insisted the invitation included me, and this would be the perfect opportunity to listen for rumors of blood mages testing the Blood Bond.

Now I was trussed up in an evening gown—which was only slightly better than court attire—and on my way to a party I didn't want to go to with a stepfamily I didn't trust.

The waterways had been built mainly for shipping goods in and out of the city, but a couple of decades ago the elite adopted the idea, creating the Grand Canal which wound its way through the townhouse district.

Jason perched in the back of the gondola poling us along the waterway. Many of the wealthier families hired their own polemen and barges, but a lesser viscount's widow had to make do with reassigning a footman.

Water lapped the sides of the gondola with a wet slapping noise.

Grandmama was away at her own social engagement, but
Melissa and Anella chattered about some Duke or Earl I'd
never heard of while Isol sat quiet in the bow of the boat. She
turned as if she could sense me looking and caught my gaze
before I could look away. Her dark eyes and deep golden skin
gave her a very calm and exotic appearance, but the watchful-
ness behind her gaze echoed the wariness that wavered in my
own mind.

Under the bridge and past the market where I'd met
Renny, one of the big residential squares had been razed and
turned into a large park. Rows of identical townhouses lined
the massive green and the Grand Canal cut straight through
the west side of the square. To our left, a smaller canal
ducked between the townhouses leading to a private boule-
vard lined with elegant mansions.

The gondola jerked as Jason brought it up to the private
dock outside the Duke of Chatham's immense residence.
Little mage globes hung on strands across the canal, their
lights winking and flitting in the water below us.

Other partygoers laughed and shouted greetings from the
open courtyard as Melissa climbed gracefully from the
gondola to the dock. Jason extended his hand to Anella, then
Isol, and then finally to me. But my legs had gone numb from
being folded for so long.

I fell, sprawling halfway between the dock and the
gondola while the latter bobbed alarmingly.

Several people cried out and Jason lunged forward. Then
Melissa was there to take one of my arms while Jason hauled

on the other. The footman gave me an apologetic wince as they set me on my feet, and Melissa cooed in distress.

Once I regained my balance, I dragged in a shuddering breath and wrenched my arm from her grip.

"I'm fine," I said, voice shaking.

"You're not," she said. "You're trembling."

I always shook after a fall, while the shock of it coursed through my veins. But having her lying hands try to steady me was worse.

"I'm fine," I repeated. "I just need a minute. Away from everyone."

She eyed me skeptically, and I dropped my gaze. Could she read the defiance in my eyes? What would she do if she did?

"Very well," she said. "Why don't you find a nice quiet corner? You're very good at that."

I scowled at her back as she moved away.

Melissa's friends greeted her with a chorus of sympathetic noises.

"The poor thing," one of them said. "It must be so difficult."

"She tries so hard," Melissa said in response. "She's such an inspiration to me and my girls. Just for getting out of bed in the morning."

I clenched my fists on the heads of my canes.

"And you are such a dear," someone else said. "Giving up so much of your time and effort to care for her."

"It's what any mother would do. It's one of the reasons I became a healer as well—"

I turned away before her false sacrifice made me gag.

Was that why she'd dragged me around court? So she could brag to her friends about how selfless she was?

I was glad I'd made Ember stay home. She'd been very vocal about her dislike for Melissa recently, and I didn't want her getting me into trouble again. She was back at the townhouse now, probably burning sullenly in the coals of my fireplace.

The well-dressed guests began parading into the house through the big glass-paned doors, most of them casting me pitying looks. I'd seen those looks my whole life. I understood them. I'd accepted that this was the way I would live my life.

So why did something dark and tight burn in my chest?

I glanced back to the gondola, but Jason had already disappeared into the house through a service entrance.

I clutched my canes and limped across the courtyard to the glass doors. Inside stretched a ballroom lined with mirrors on one side and murals of the saints on the other. A string quartet played somewhere out of sight, a mage funneling the sound into the room so it could be heard in every corner.

Courtiers danced through the room, the colors of their gowns and coats blurring until they looked like loose blossoms tumbling down a waterfall. The laughter and music stopped me at the door like a physical wall.

I could easily imagine what it would be like to step inside and have the laughter hush as a wave of discomfort spread from person to person, each one catching sight of me.

Nikolas wanted me to help him search for a blood mage among the nobles, but my clumsiness didn't belong in that world of merriment and movement.

If he was right, and I really was the kind of person he needed to help him, then I was going to do it my way.

I made for the service entrance and the narrow hallways clearly built for the servants who made this vast edifice run. This was a better plan if I wanted to hear anything useful. Nobles thought they knew everything, but really it was their servants who traded information like coin and called it gossip.

A very different sort of laughter drew me forward. I passed the kitchen where cooks and scullery maids bustled about preparing finger foods and little sandwiches to ferry to the guests. I kept going until I reached the Servants' Hall, the large room where the downstairs staff relaxed and slept after the family retreated to bed. Here, the servants that had come with the guests gathered until they were needed.

I stood on the threshold, shifting from foot to foot, too afraid to step forward, too ashamed to go back. But if I didn't belong out at the party and I didn't belong here, where did I belong?

Then Jason caught sight of me lurking in the doorway and called out. I passed two other tables full of maids and footmen to join him near the fire.

My gown clearly set me apart from the soberly dressed staff, but when Jason said "Miss Cindy" and moved over to make room for me on the bench, the rest assumed I belonged and turned back to their conversations. If a footman accepted me, I could easily be a governess or secretary dragged along to the party by my mistress.

The typical conversation resumed around me. Whose

mistress was mad at whose master. Whose master had walked out on their family. These were upstairs maids and valets and the occasional footman or poleman, the servants trusted implicitly by their employers and yet strangely invisible. They saw everything.

The ebb and flow of it was familiar, and I settled into the rhythm like a dance that didn't need my feet. With my mouth closed and my ears open, I'd hear anything worth hearing.

"Can you believe it? He just walked out. Not a word or nothing to anyone," one conversation went.

"Well, my lady says she's no better than a Torracan mind mage with the way she makes the men around here hop to," another one said.

"And Lady Lainey was so heartbroken. She really thought the King's Mage was serious with his courting."

The last one came from a maid sitting just a few spaces down and made me sit up and listen. It wasn't anything about blood magic, but it was about people I knew.

"Lady Adelaine?" someone else asked. "The Duke's sister?"

"Of course," the maid said with a sniff. "My lady Lainey. His grace is the only one who calls her Adelaine."

"What happened with the King's Mage?" I asked.

"He flat-out stopped calling on her," the maid said. "She cried on my shoulder for weeks. There she was thinking there were wedding bells and now he won't say more than two words to her."

"That's men for you," another said.

"She must have scared him away," another one said.

"Men don't like when a woman starts talking weddings before he's proposed."

"She never did," the maid said. "Besides, I saw them often enough. He was as smitten as she."

"So now she flirts with everything that moves trying to make him jealous," I said, biting my lip.

"Exactly." The maid eyed me up and down. "Do you know my lady?"

I blushed. I was supposed to be listening. "Only in passing," I said.

The maid raised her eyebrows. "Well, the mage better hurry and make up his mind. My lady's brother is dead set on marrying her to the Prince."

My stomach dropped for no good reason.

"But if Lainey is still in love with Master Christoph, she wouldn't agree to marry the Prince, would she?" I asked, fingers clenched on the table.

The maid gave me a philosophical shrug. "Well, the mage isn't doing much to change her mind now, is he?"

And he wouldn't since Lainey's brother had threatened him away from her.

I chewed my lip. "What would Lainey do if she knew it wasn't the mage's fault?"

She narrowed her eyes. "What?"

I leaned forward. I hadn't intended to do anything with the information I carried, but now I had the chance to help two people who were hurting. "What would Lainey do if she knew her brother threatened Master Christoph and told him never to call on her again?"

The maid's mouth fell open. "Are you—Are you serious?"

CATCHING CINDERS | 167

Beside me Jason frowned, but he said, "Miss Cindy's been to court. I would trust her."

"I don't know what she would do," the maid said quietly.

"But she deserves to know the truth," I said. "Don't you think?"

The maid bit her lip, then in a decisive movement pushed back on her bench and stood. "Thanks," she said and disappeared through the door of the Servant's Hall.

Jason leaned back and crossed his arms, a scowl settling onto his features. "You just did that because you don't want the Prince marrying someone else," he said.

My mouth fell open. "What?"

"He's been sniffing around you and now you want to keep him to yourself."

I snapped my jaw shut and clenched my teeth. "The Prince can marry whoever he wants," I said, voice tight. "It has nothing to do with me."

"Don't pretend you told her all that out of the goodness of your heart. Jealousy doesn't look good on you."

"I told her because I knew the truth and I want them to be happy."

He scoffed. "Right." His bench scraped against the flagstones with a screech as he stood.

I stared after him as he left.

Why would I be jealous? To be jealous, you had to actually have a chance with someone. I'd been taught my whole life that no one would ever want me that way. Jason himself had taught me that by kissing me and then never doing anything about it.

Maybe I was letting the Prince's attention go to my head.

I couldn't pretend I was completely indifferent. I loved talking with Nikolas. It was the reason I was in so much trouble in the first place. But that didn't mean he felt the same way.

My best chance of a life without loneliness was with a footman who hadn't done a single thing in over a month. And now I might have ruined my chances with him over a prince who was as out of reach as the sky.

I scrambled over the bench. I couldn't worry about Jason and his moods, not when Nikolas had trusted me with something as important as the Blood Bond. I was supposed to be investigating. Not getting flustered over a brooding footman and a prince with an infectious grin.

So what was I looking for? More tools like the knife? Probably not in some nobleman's house when we knew the mage was somewhere in the palace.

But there were other things that I could search for. I hadn't gotten far in Erestan's biography yet, but I already knew that blood mages left a trail of suffering behind them like ripples in a pond. They drew energy from their victims, draining them gradually until they died. That kind of violence left traces.

I drifted from one table to another listening for rumors of exhausted servants, missing siblings or friends, wounds that wouldn't heal. Anything that would show the trace of a blood mage's passing.

Finally, a cluster of scullery maids whispering near the fireplace caught my attention.

"Did you see her? Pale as a Ballaslavian milkmaid."

"And her eyes all sunken. Exhausted, unless I miss my guess."

The maids cast glances at another girl already on her way out of the hall. She was dressed in a simple gown and could have been a downstairs maid or even a kitchen drudge.

I limped after her.

Expensive mage globes lit the hallway outside, even here in the servants' section, and I caught a glimpse of her pale face and limp blonde hair.

"Miss," I said, hurrying after her. "Miss."

She turned, eyes down, and she clasped trembling hands in front of her. "May I help you?" she said in dull tones.

I bit my lip. I'd come hurrying out here without much of a plan.

"Could...could you point me to the water closet?" I said. "I'm afraid I'm a bit turned around."

She blinked at me for a moment, then pointed down the hall the way she'd been heading. "It's down there, second hall on the left."

"Thank you," I said brightly. A fierce heat beat in my breast for a moment. If she knew where the water closet was, it was likely she worked here.

She started to turn as if to go, and her clasped hands fell to her sides. For one brief second her sleeve was illuminated in the light of the mage globes. A bright red stain soaked the fabric.

I didn't hesitate. I stepped forward, and took her arm like a doddering old woman.

"Thank you," I said again. "These long hallways are the death of my legs."

As she stood steady, I slid my hand up her arm, lifting the hem of her sleeve.

Bright blood seeped through white bandages, clear enough that I could imagine the perfect rows of slash marks underneath.

Her breath caught, and I gripped her hands before she could pull away.

"Who did this to you?" I said.

"No one," she whispered.

My lips thinned. "Try again."

My tone must have been too harsh. She ducked her head and fell silent.

"Please, let me help," I said. "You don't have to be his victim anymore."

"I'm not his victim," she whispered. "I chose this. It's not like it was in the old days. He's not some kind of monster."

"If he's hurting you—"

She yanked her hands from my grip, throwing me off balance. I caught the wall as she dashed away from me, moving fast enough that there was no hope I could follow.

Muck on it, as Grandmama would say. I'd picked the wrong tactic. If the girl was in the blood mage's thrall and had convinced herself he was doing good, it would have been better to come at her sideways. To insinuate her mage was in some kind of trouble.

Double muck. I wouldn't get another chance at her now. Not tonight, and maybe not ever. The best I could hope for was to send her description to Nikolas and hope he could find her master from his end.

✷

Nik escorted Lainey across the wide tiles of the royal hospital's foyer and fought off a yawn. He'd brought her hoping she'd be able to alleviate his boredom, but the plan had backfired.

As much as he appreciated Lainey's company, he wished he'd had the freedom to bring someone else. He was starting to find her hair too red. He liked a nice dark blonde now. And her gait was too steady, too normal.

Funny how his thoughts kept turning to Miss Hargrove when he had so many different things he could be worrying about. She'd sent him a message just that morning about a possible blood mage victim. He'd passed it on to Christoph to include in their evidence.

Here on this side of the courtyard a statue of Aegis, Saint of Healing, gazed down with what was supposed to be benevolent concern but looked more like pinched disapproval.

"She looks lonely out here by herself," Lainey said.

Nik tilted his head. "They could give her a friend. Maybe I'll suggest they add a statue of Saint Needsmeet to keep her company."

Lainey gave him a startled look. "Why Needsmeet?"

"He's the Saint of Service. Healing could be considered a pretty important service."

Lainey looked at him like he'd suggested they drop bugs down Aegis's toga. "I didn't realize you were so interested in sacrilege nowadays," she said with a playful nudge.

"It's not sacrilege," he said. "You hear about Needsmeet

all the time, but I've never seen him anywhere. His chapels are always small and plain."

She raised her eyebrows. "I believe that's the point. People who follow Needsmeet believe it's disrespectful to put up his image. He was a servant. His aim was to be remembered for his service, not for his looks. You won't see any statues or paintings of him. When he's depicted with the other saints he's always robed and cowled. Even Woejoy, Saint of Grief and Passing, has a face, while Needsmeet doesn't."

Nik gave her an incredulous look. "I didn't know you knew so much about them."

"Religious studies," she said with a snort. "An appropriate pasttime for well-bred ladies."

It was a familiar refrain from their friendship, but this time there was no bitterness in the words. Lainey often complained about her overbearing brother and his plans for her future, but now that he thought about it Nik hadn't heard a word about the Duke since they'd gotten there.

And she hadn't tried flirting with him once today either. That was new.

Nik watched Lainey out of the corner of his eye as he towed her to the buffet. She nodded and murmured to the doctors and statesmen they passed, same as normal, but her movements lacked the mocking edge he'd come to expect from her the last few months. Ever since she and Christoph had stopped seeing each other.

"Are you feeling all right?" he asked.

"I'm fine," she said with a distracted shrug. "Why?"

"No reason," he said. "You just look happy."

"Is there something wrong with that?"

"No..." He couldn't tell her he'd gotten used to her self-destructive pain. So he changed the subject. "I'm sorry I missed your party last night."

She still didn't look at him. She stared off into the distance with a small, secretive smile. "It's all right. The entire world doesn't revolve around you."

His brow furrowed in consternation and he turned to follow her gaze. What had her so distracted?

Under the colonnade beside the wall, Christoph stood, a glass of champagne held awkwardly in his hand. The King's Mage was mired in investigations and duties, but somehow he'd been roped into this social event. He looked their way and flushed.

Beside Nik, Adelaine bit her lip and stifled a giggle.

Understanding dawned, and Nik suppressed his mirth. When had this happened? He'd been trying to get Lainey and Christoph to kiss and make up for months.

"You know, if it's supposed to be a secret," Nik whispered in her direction, "you should stop staring at him."

Lainey flushed a deep red that clashed terribly with her hair.

Nik grinned and then waggled his eyebrows at Christoph. The mage gave Nik a tiny shrug and twiddled his fingers toward Lainey.

Lainey pressed her fingers to her lips and blew him a kiss.

"You two are disgusting," Nik said.

Lainey laughed.

"What happened?" he asked. "Last I knew you were cursing him to hell and back."

Lainey shook her head. "It was really just a little thing all along. I understand him so much better now. He didn't get to grow up with a family, so he didn't want me to lose mine. It's sweet, actually. Misguided, but sweet."

"Your brother isn't going to be happy."

"My brother can take a nosedive off a cliff," Lainey said with a vicious jerk of her chin. "It's his fault we wasted all that time without each other."

Nik frowned. He was happy his friends were happy, but her words poured salt on his own problem. "Family isn't something to just throw away without thought."

"Believe me, I've thought about it as much as you have," she said, knowing full well his dilemma between pleasing his family and finding the right woman. "Besides, you're one to talk. Would your family approve of the woman you're courting now?"

His head snapped up. "What? I'm not courting anyone."

She smirked. "Sure. And you're just suddenly interested in Saint Needsmeet for no particular reason at all. And you're not disappearing at court functions."

Nik opened and shut his mouth, thinking of and discarding a hundred things to say to that. Finally he tried, "I'm just getting to know her."

Lainey nodded sagely. "And you find yourself thinking about her at odd moments. Wondering what she would say or think about this, that, or another thing. Going over her words again and again to look for hidden meanings."

"She says what she thinks, there are no hidden meanings."

Lainey gave him a sympathetic pat. "There are always

hidden meanings. Even if she doesn't think there are, even if she's as candid as the Saint of Honesty. She's a woman, so there are several thousand things going on in her head. Fair warning."

Nik frowned. "Thanks. I think."

CHAPTER FIFTEEN

Two days after the party, Nikolas showed up at my door again.

"Did you get my message? About the girl with the cuts?" I asked when Jason had led me to the front door. "Did you find out who she's working with?" I hadn't seen the girl since, and I'd squandered my opportunity to discover her master for myself.

"We're still looking," Nikolas said. He wore a nondescript dark coat today, maybe to keep himself anonymous. Although how he thought he could pass as a mere citizen when the Rannard eyes stared out from under his dark eyebrows and the Valerian Dark Sun hung around his neck, I didn't know.

I planted my fists on my hips. "Then what are you doing here?"

"I asked if I could call on you again," he said. "And I have a different lead to follow. I thought you would like to be included in this one."

My brow furrowed. "Any particular reason?"

He gave me a crooked grin. "This one has to do with Erestan the Gentle and how he created the Blood Bond."

All right, that had me suitably hooked. "What do you mean? How can Erestan be a new lead? He died hundreds of years ago."

He shrugged. "I guess you'll have to come with me to find out. And if that's not enough of a reason, I brought lunch."

I glanced behind him where his stoic bodyguard stood holding a large wicker hamper. The sight was so incongruous I had to fight not to laugh. Then his words sunk in.

"You mean we have to leave the house."

"Yes, generally picnics require the outdoors."

I bit my lip. "Nik—Nikolas, I'm sorry. I can't go. I'd be breaking all sorts of rules."

He stepped close and took my hand in his long fingers. "You're already breaking the rules by speaking to me. What's one more?"

I looked up into his green eyes and wondered if there was truth in the rumors about the Rannard eyes having some sort of magic. They made me want to do things I shouldn't.

"I like rules," I said barely above a whisper.

"I do, too," he said, his face inches from mine. "But I think this once I'll make an exception. What about you?"

This thumping, fluttering in my heart was stupid. He was here because he needed help investigating a blood mage, nothing more. When that was done he would leave me alone, and I'd go back to whatever passed as normal in my upturned life. But he was making it harder and harder to protect my heart.

"My stepfamily will be home this afternoon," I said.

"I'll have you back before then. I promise."

Ember streaked out of the parlor and clambered up my dress to perch on my shoulder, claws sinking into the fabric.

I shook myself, then nodded. "Let me get my maid," I said. "As a chaperone." And it would put someone else between me and the green eyes I couldn't ignore.

"Do you doubt my intentions?" he said with a wry quirk of his lips, releasing my hand.

I gave him a look over my shoulder. "We could always ask Father Philip to join us."

He raised his hands with a laugh. "Saints defend me."

As I moved back down the hall, Jason fell into step beside me.

"I'm coming with you, too," he said in a furious whisper.

"What? Why?"

"I don't trust him."

"Jason, don't be ridiculous."

"I'm not being ridiculous," he said. "You're being reckless."

I glanced over my shoulder to see the Prince staring at us while I had a heated discussion with a footman. Did other nobles have to seek approval from their servants?

"I'm helping my prince with an investigation. He asked me specifically."

Ember chittered at him, shaking her head in irritation.

Jason blew out his breath. "If you leave without me, I'll... I'll stowaway on the back of the carriage."

I froze, my hand on the kitchen door.

"He doesn't care about your safety," he said, quietly. "I do."

"Fine," I said, giving up. "If you're going to be dramatic about it, I guess I don't have a choice."

In the end, five of us left the townhouse. Jason and Renny followed me down the steps while the bodyguard glowered over Nikolas's shoulder.

I stopped short when I saw the carriage the Prince had brought. Clearly he'd hired it from some anonymous stable, and the horse looked big enough to pull freight for a living.

"Where on earth are we going?" I asked.

"You'll see." Nikolas rubbed the back of his neck. "I kind of want it to be a surprise."

Jason jumped up to the box. The bodyguard gave me a sharp look before climbing up beside him, and Nikolas handed Renny and I into the carriage.

"I don't think your bodyguard likes me very much," I said as the Prince closed the door behind him and we lurched into motion.

"Merrick?" Nikolas looked startled. "Why would you think that?"

"He's always scowling at me."

"Ah," Nikolas said, his confusion clearing. "No, you're mistaken."

I crossed my arms. "I'm pretty sure I'd remember if he ever cracked a smile."

Nikolas grinned. "No, I mean, he scowls at everyone. Not just you."

"Is that supposed to make me feel better?"

He chuckled. "Merrick is very intense, yes. But it's part of his charm."

I made a face. "If you say so."

"Do you know how the ServantGuard are chosen?"

"They're Disciples of Saint Discipline, patron of combat," I said. The city sped along outside the windows as we left the townhouse district behind.

Nikolas nodded. "They're taught self-sacrifice, honor, fortitude, and of course, discipline. The best of the best are sent to the Blue Palace to become the ServantGuard."

"And Merrick was one of the best?"

"More than that, he doesn't care about normal things," he said with a slight frown. "Friendship, wealth, none of the things most people want make him happy. He doesn't want time off, he doesn't need to take breaks. All he does is eat, sleep, and watch. He can't be bribed, even by me." Nikolas gave Renny and me a self-deprecating grin. "I've tried to lose him before, just to see if I could, but he always finds me and gives me a look like I've murdered someone. Then he says, 'Your life is my honor. If anything happens to you, it will be broken.'"

"What does that mean?" I said.

Nikolas gave a self-conscious shrug.

"I don't know. I think he finds the thing he's going to care about, and that's it. That's the rest of his life. Nothing can shake him from his duty."

The buildings receded as we passed through a gate in a crumbling ancient section of the city wall. We turned off the main road and rumbled onto a much narrower track through a rare piece of wilderness.

"This lead seems to be a long way out from the city," I said, casually.

Nikolas refused to rise to my question.

The carriage jolted to a stop, and I lost my balance. I had to grab one of the straps attached to the ceiling to keep myself from falling off the bench. Ember screeched and buried her front claws in my hair, her tail twining my neck. Outside, the horse made an affronted noise.

"Saints take me," Nik muttered as he pushed out the door. "What's happened?"

"Road's washed out," Jason called. "Horses have been through here, but nothing with wheels since the last storm."

Nik swore and disappeared to investigate.

"Looks like we'll have to turn back," Jason said. He sounded gleeful.

I sighed. "What's wrong with Jason? He's been in such a bad mood recently."

"Don't mind him," Renny said. "He's just jealous."

I blinked. "Jealous?" I said. "Of the Prince?"

"Of course. Jason's been sweet on you forever. But then the Prince started calling on you, and it's thrown him good."

I shook my head. "I used to think...but he's had years," I said. "Why hasn't he ever said anything?"

Renny shrugged. "He probably thought you wouldn't have anyone better show up. Serves him right."

I rubbed my eyes. "The Prince isn't competition," I said. "He's just investigating this blood mage. When he's done, he'll move on."

"Of course he will," Renny said with a smirk. Her tone said she didn't actually believe that.

I pursed my lips and thrust the door open. Then I climbed carefully down into the muddy road. I wasn't going to sit inside while Jason made a fool of himself for nothing.

I squelched and slipped to where he and Nik argued at the head of the horse.

"What's going on?" I said.

Nik ran a hand through his hair. "We're not going any farther this way," he said. "Not in this mud."

"How far is it to where we are going?"

"Another half a mile, I'd say."

"Can we walk?"

"No, Cindy," Jason said coming around the horse. "You're not walking half a mile in the mud."

Nik drew himself up. "Does he always talk to you this way?"

I sighed and met Jason's eyes. "Yes. I've always liked that he's honest with me."

The footman swallowed but held his own.

"You could take her on the horse, Your Highness," Renny said, stepping from the carriage. "If we unhitch it."

"Then you could catch up on foot," Nik said.

"Your Highness," Merrick said, a scowl deepening the lines around his eyes. "I do not like this plan."

"I know, I know," Nik said. "You can't guard my body if my body is somewhere else."

I stifled a chuckle at Nik's tone. He'd obviously heard the argument before.

"I don't know any other way to get to there, do you? You'll catch up, you always do."

Merrick's lips thinned.

By the time Jason and Merrick had unhitched the horse, I'd had time to work up some nerves. My heart pounded looking up at the smooth sides of the enormous horse.

Grudgingly, Jason cupped his hands to give the Prince a leg up. I had to admit, Nik looked magnificently calm and confident with no saddle and the overlong carriage reins. But that didn't keep me from gulping with fear.

Nik grinned and held out a hand. As if he would just pull me up beside him like an inanimate saddlebag.

"I don't know how to ride," I said, wishing I'd been brave enough to speak up before.

"Merrick will help you up. And I'll be here the whole time."

Merrick stepped up. The top of my head barely reached the man's shoulder. Before I could protest he grasped my waist and lifted me to sit in front of Nik. Ember clung to my shoulder with her claws while I swung my leg over the horse's neck, trying not to think too hard about the fact that ladies did not ride astride. But there was no way I was riding side saddle without a saddle.

"You'll need these," Renny said and handed me the picnic basket and my canes.

Nik's arms tightened around my waist, and he clicked to the horse.

Jason and Merrick's twin expressions of disapproval blurred and disappeared behind us. I tried not to shriek and clutch the basket. I'd probably break the wicker. Instead I leaned back into Nik's solid warmth. He seemed steady enough on the back of the horse, even if I felt like I was about to fall from the roof of a building.

Trees whipped past, and Nik chuckled in my ear. He really liked this whole pelting through the forest thing.

"Do we have to go so fast?" I said.

"What do you mean fast?" he said. "This is just a trot."

I gulped. If this was trotting, I never wanted to see what running was like. Galloping? I wasn't even sure what to call it.

My fingers clung to the arm he'd snugged around my waist, and I closed my eyes.

It couldn't have been long but it felt like a lifetime later when Nik did something to make the horse stop.

"Well?" He twisted as if to look at my face. "Did you have your eyes closed the whole time?"

"No," I lied, even though I knew he could see me. I snapped my eyes open.

Nik gave me a strange look, sympathy marred by regret. He shook it off and gestured expansively to our surroundings. "Well?" he said again.

It was a hill. Admittedly it was a big one, with odd jagged clumps at the crest and a hole in the base directly in front of us. A couple of people in canvas aprons moved about purposefully.

"I'm not sure what I'm looking at," I admitted finally.

"Come on. I'll show you." Excitement infused his voice.

He slid off the back of the horse to land on the ground. I wobbled, squeaked, and dropped the basket so I could clutch the horse's mane. Nik lunged to catch the basket, then dropped it again so he could lunge to catch me when I slipped down the horse's side.

I hit his chest with an "oof" and grabbed a double handful of his jacket. He staggered, and my face stung with embarrassment.

"You should have told me you didn't like horses," he said with a wheeze.

"I didn't know I didn't like horses. I've never been on one. I could have liked horses plenty and just never realized it."

He chuckled breathlessly and moved to set me on the ground, but my right leg was tangled in the reins. The horse stood placid as any pony as Nik shifted to help me.

"What's this?" he said, and to my horror he knelt in the mud before me.

"What's what?" I said, brushing horse hair from my dress.

He took my foot and raised it so we could both see my boot, a sturdy leather affair with worn laces and two wooden bars glued upright against the ankles.

I tried to twitch my skirt back over my feet. "It's a shoe," I said.

"I know it's a shoe. Why does it have these bars?"

"My ankles are weak and sometimes they twist. Those keep them straight and supported. Can we talk about something else? You're making me uncomfortable." I didn't want him wondering why my shoe was so worn with ragged laces.

He shot to his feet, a bright red flush creeping up his cheeks. "I apologize. I let my curiosity get the better of me."

He handed over my canes, which had fallen with the picnic basket, and lent me his arm. I used one cane and leaned on him with the other. It seemed so natural and homey, and I let myself imagine for a moment what it would be like to live my life with someone who knew exactly when to lend an arm and when to let me do it myself.

He snatched the picnic basket with his other hand before escorting me to the hill.

The hole in the base turned out to be an entrance shored up with timbers like a mine. A young woman in a practical brown gown and a dirty apron checked things off on a sheaf of papers as we approached.

She looked up and the expression on her face went from annoyed to welcoming. "Your Highness," she said. "I knew you'd show up as soon as we uncovered the tomb."

"How could I stay away? This could help us immensely."

"Tomb?" I said, realization dawning. "It's a dig site, isn't it."

Nik bowed his head. "It is. Miss Hargrove, this is Miss Beatrice Lawford. Miss Lawford, Miss Cindy Hargrove."

"Pleased to meet you, Miss Hargrove," the young woman said. "I'm the Assistant Historian for the site. If you'll follow me, I'll give you the nickel tour." She turned and started underground.

The air became cool and clammy as we moved out of the sunlight.

The tunnel only lasted a few feet and then we stepped out into a vast cavern. Square-cut blocks tumbled over the ground, and tiny ruined houses filled the vast empty space under the hill. Most of the buildings had collapsed, but some still stood tall enough for a man to enter.

"We're certain now, this was a necropolis for the original settlers of Namerre," Miss Lawford said. "Refugees from the collapse of the Vemiir Empire started burying their dead here nearly two thousand years ago."

It should have been creepy. But it was too fascinating to be creepy. Above us, a good amount of the roof had caved in, leaving a wide ragged hole which filled the cavern with filtered light. Moss grew on the stones, and between some of the houses trees and bushes had taken root, giving the whole place a glowing green allure.

"It's beautiful," I said. Much more welcoming than the cold white family crypt back on the Hargrove estate.

"We found it because the ceiling collapsed there." She pointed, then started moving around the perimeter, and we followed. "We bury our dead in crypts above ground, but even just a few hundred years ago it was still common to build entire graveyards underground. This whole place was hollowed out to provide a city for the dead. And we could have missed it entirely if not for the cave-in."

Nik cleared his throat, clearly waiting for something. Miss Lawford gaze flicked to him and back. "Then we realized, given the antiquity of the place, several of the old monarchs of Valeria could be buried here."

"Including Erestan the Gentle?" I said, giving Nik a side-long look.

"I told you old Erestan might help us out still," Nik said. His arm under my hand jiggled with excitement.

"I wouldn't get your hopes up, Your Highness," Miss Lawford said. "There's really not much left of the tomb itself. It's one of the oldest in here."

Despite her words, Nik beamed as Miss Lawford showed us to a crumbling sepulcher. It looked much like the others in the area, but inside Miss Lawford pointed out the faded peeling frescoes and a worn effigy.

"It's hard to tell, but I don't think he's wearing a crown," she said.

I stepped closer to the almost faceless carving. "Erestan

refused to wear a crown after all the pain he caused as a blood mage." That must be how they knew whose tomb it was.

"That was one of the reasons he created the Blood Bond." Nik bent to squint at one of the frescoes. "To strengthen Valeria with his blood. He wanted to make up for his past mistakes."

Miss Lawford tilted her head. "What were you hoping to find that might help you?"

Nik straightened and shrugged. "Tools? Artifacts? I'm not really sure. I guess deep down I was hoping for an instruction manual on how to catch a blood mage. Something that isn't in our history books."

Miss Lawford's lips twisted in a rueful grimace. "Sorry. That's not how archeology works."

A voice called the young woman back to the front of the dig site.

"Feel free to look around," Miss Lawford said before leaving us. "Be careful around the edges of the site, though. The main cavern is as safe as we can make it, but stay out of the farther reaches, there're a couple of phoenixes nesting that we're trying not to disturb."

"Phoenixes?" I said as she left. "I thought they were from the DierRealms."

Nik shrugged. "They are. But there are places where Dierlings can come through sometimes. Or sometimes mages summon one and they escape. Is that where yours is from?" He nodded to Ember on my shoulder.

I touched her warm back. "Yes. But she didn't escape. My mother hired a mage to summon her. But when Mama died shortly after, no one thought to return Ember to her home. By the time it became an issue, she didn't want to leave anymore."

Ember rubbed her head against my cheek, leaving a line of warmth in the cool tomb. Then she flowed down my shoulder and sauntered over to light up the fresco in front of us.

Nik sighed. "I was really hoping for something more than an empty crypt and a legend."

He frowned at the wall, and I felt the pull of his disappointment.

I followed Ember. "It might not help us right now," I said quietly. "But it's still fascinating."

He leaned in beside me. When he glanced my way I realized how close he was.

I cleared my throat and pointed. "Look, I think this part shows the creation of the Blood Bond." I leaned over to examine the cracked and faded figures. "See, crownless Erestan is joining his blood to his people."

"That's still how it's done today," Nik said. "It's pretty rare though, since the Bond is passed down through the blood. The only time we need to add new people is if a bloodline completely dies out, or a new title is bestowed."

I tapped my teeth in thought. "Could someone do it themselves? Insert themselves into the Bond without you knowing? All they would need is a bit of the Rannard blood and their own."

"And knowledge of the binding ceremony," Nik added, but a shadow of doubt crossed his face. "Are you saying that's what someone is doing to destabilize the Blood Bond?"

I shook myself and laughed. "I have no idea," I said. "I'm not a mage. It was just a horrible thought that crossed my mind."

Nik started to say something, but Ember burbled at the wall, interrupting him. She looked up at me.

"I don't know," I said. "I wouldn't try it though."

"What's she saying?"

"Fire sprites can burn out impurities in things like metal and rocks. She wanted to know if she could burn away the dirt to help us see more of the fresco."

"I doubt if that would be good for it," Nik said. "But thank you for offering."

He held out his hand as if to shake her paw, and she looked at it blankly. She sniffed it like a real cat would, sneezed, and then turned to saunter out into the main cavern.

"I think that means 'you're welcome,'" I said with a laugh. I followed her, placing my canes carefully in the treacherous terrain.

"Can you always understand her?" Nik said behind me.

Ember's bright flames lit the surrounding ruins with flickers of orange and yellow and red. She chuckled with pleasure.

"Most of the time," I said. "But it's not really like understanding language. It's more like I've lived with her long enough to catch the nuance in her inflection. She thinks this place is amazing."

"What about you?" he said.

I glanced at him over my shoulder. "I do, too. How did you know I would like it?"

"You seemed to like the statues in the Royal Memorial.

And you asked Father Philip about some really old books. I assumed you must like history."

"I like stories. And history always seems to have the best ones."

We passed a couple more little houses and suddenly the area in front of us opened into a large flat circle, almost like a meadow if we hadn't been underground and surrounded by tombs. Above, the ceiling gave way to the sky, and the sparkle of magic where spells kept the roof from fully caving in glimmered against the clouds. Grass had taken root here, but every few feet the green gave way to blackened spots, the blades curled from heat.

Ember darted in front of me, leaving steaming footprints in her wake. She leapt up onto a moss-covered stone and gave a piercing whistle of excitement.

A shriek answered her, ringing around the wide cavern. Across the field, beyond more ruins, a flutter of wings made all three of us freeze. Light bounced back and forth across the rocks, like a flame in the breeze, and two birds as large as eagles leaped into the air above us.

They had feathers of flame and tails of sparks, one burning gold and orange and red, the other a deep bright blue like the heart of a candle flame with feathers that faded to gold at their tips.

Ember streaked across the meadow to me and raced up my skirt to my shoulder.

The pair of flaming birds shot to the top of the cavern and spun together, sending waves of sparks to fall around us. A hand took mine and I jumped, startled from my reverie by Nik's touch. He smiled at my reaction.

"It reminds me of the fireworks at the ball last year," he said. "Only far better than anything a mage could come up with."

"I haven't been to many balls," I said. I might have to change that if this was what I could expect.

Nik eyed me sideways. "Why not?"

I blushed. I couldn't explain that as a kitchen drudge my world had been limited to the hearth. "I don't dance," I said instead.

His grin grew mischievous, and he drew me out onto the grass under the sparking phoenixes. "It's not hard," he said. "I can teach you."

"Nik," I said. "I can barely walk. What makes you think I can dance?"

"I think you can do anything."

He stopped, and I lumbered into him. He didn't comment on my clumsiness, just put his arm around my waist and stepped gently to the left.

I tried to follow gracefully, but my movements were just as jerky as ever.

Nik's gaze remained on my face and he stepped again. I stumbled after him.

I put my hand on his shoulder and let him take my other hand in his. The next time he stepped, I leaned on him and moved in time.

"See, you just need the right partner," he said.

As long as I trusted him to hold my weight as I moved and he knew the way I swayed when I shifted my weight, it actually worked. I looked up to see his green eyes only inches from mine.

I swallowed and tried to distract myself. When his investigation was over, life would go back to normal. I didn't want to miss him more than I had to.

"You must do this with all the women in your life," I said. "Lure them underground with phoenixes and food."

He laughed and we both glanced at the abandoned picnic basket lying beside a crumbling wall.

"I actually haven't been on a picnic since I was a child," Nik said. "I think I smeared custard in Lainey's hair."

"Lady Adelaine?" I said, trying to imagine Nik as anything other than this competent young man.

"She was one of my best friends growing up."

I bit my lip. "There were rumors you were going to marry her," I said carefully.

Nik snorted. "You shouldn't believe everything you hear," he said. "Lainey would make a terrible queen. And she wouldn't have me even if I did want her. She's quite taken."

I breathed a sigh of relief and told myself it was just because I was happy for Lainey and Christoph, not for any other reason. "I'm glad for her."

Nik's eyebrows drew down as if he had to think about that. "I guess I am, too. Her family won't be happy, though."

"Her brother wanted to use her for his own gain," I said. "You approve of that?"

"No of course not," he said, but he wouldn't meet my eyes. "But it's exactly what I expect for myself. I have to marry to please my family as well."

Above us the two phoenixes trilled and flashed as they disappeared through the hole in the ceiling.

Ember trilled a long, wistful note.

Nik watched the sky and a twinge of regret made me turn away. If I hadn't said anything, we'd still be dancing in the green light.

"What's it like?" I said. "Having a family that's so close?"

He finally turned back to me, then sighed and retrieved the picnic basket. "Crowded," he said and pulled a blanket out with a flourish.

I tipped my head in question.

"Mostly in a good way," he said as he tucked the blanket around a rock sized perfectly for a seat. "I'm never lonely. Not with Colin or Eriana around." He held out his hand and helped me sit.

I tried to imagine talking about Isol or Anella the way Nik talked about Colin and Eriana. It didn't work. "What are they like?"

"You know how the Arcangele duchy is named for the archangels sent by the Almighty to tell Térne the world was forgiven? I imagine Colin and Eriana as two angels. Related but very very different. Colin represents the practical side and Eriana the passion."

"It sounds like they must argue a lot."

"Hardly ever," Nik said. "They manage to balance each other out."

He peeked into the basket and made a face. Then he angled it toward me so I could see the mangled contents.

I laughed and pulled out some squashed bread. It would still taste all right, despite its hazardous journey. Ember peered over the edge of the basket, burbling to herself as she tilted her head this way and that.

"Your family wasn't ever close?" Nik said.

I bit my lip. "Maybe once," I said. "But my mother died when I was six. Things fell apart after that."

"I'm sorry," Nik said. "You must miss her. Is that why you carry lady's mantle with you?"

I touched the necklace Melissa had given me. "It was her Pledge when she alive. Even after I got sick she still Pledged to the Saint of Motherhood, not the Saint of Healing. I guess she saw me as her daughter first. Not some invalid." I frowned to myself. I'd never thought of it that way, until now.

"How did you get sick?" Nik said quietly. "Do you mind if I ask?"

My fingers tore off pieces of bread, crumbling it into a distracting mess. I could talk about it as long as I didn't meet his eyes.

"I hardly remember it. At first it was just a fever but then I started getting weaker and weaker. My muscles didn't work anymore, and none of the doctors or healers could help. Then it got hard to breathe, and Mama decided to do something...drastic."

"Like what?" Nik asked.

I stroked Ember, curled up in my lap. "I said Ember's kind can burn out impurities, right? Mama brought her to me, and she burned out the sickness. Some damage was permanent, which is why I still walk funny."

Nik reached out to scratch the top of Ember's head. "Wow. Why doesn't every healer in Valeria have a fire sprite?"

The flame cat rolled so he could rub her belly. "There's a price. A fire sprite burns out all impurities, even from your mind. If you're not completely sure of who you are and what makes you who you are, you can end up with your entire self burned away."

He snatched his hand back, then laughed at his own response.

"Don't worry," I said. "She's only ever done it twice. The first time she took the shape of who I was from Mama's mind, not mine, so I survived."

He caught the meaning behind my words and stilled. "What happened the second time?"

"My mother died." The bread now sat in a pile of crumbs, so I knotted my fingers together and laid them in my lap. "She caught the same illness I had. She said she was strong enough to hold onto herself, but I think she was sicker than she let anyone know. Ember tried her best but she burned away too much. By the end there was nothing left."

"I'm sorry," he said. "I'm surprised you still carry Ember around with you."

I shrugged. "She was only trying to save her. It wasn't her fault. I don't blame her for what happened, I just don't ever want her to have to do it again."

"Understandable. So what happened after your mother passed away?"

With a sharp gesture I swept the pile of crumbs into the grass. "Nothing," I said.

"That was years ago," Nik said. "Surely something has happened to you in the meantime. Your father must have taken care of you after that."

"My father," I said with a bitter laugh. "My father was so ashamed of me, he pretended I didn't exist after he married Melissa."

His mouth opened and closed. "I'm sorry. I didn't realize. I just wanted to know more about you."

"Why?" And why couldn't he read the discomfort in my words and leave me alone? Like everyone else.

"You're interesting."

I snorted. "No, I'm not."

"Why do you think that?" he said, his brows drawing together in a frown.

"Why shouldn't I?" I snapped, fed up with his willful obliviousness. "I'm worth less than everyone else. It's how I've been treated my whole life. Why are you the only one who can't see that's how the world works?"

"Maybe that's how you've been treated but it doesn't have to be."

I gave him an exasperated harrumph. "One person can't change the world."

"One person could change your world," he said. "Wouldn't that be enough to start?"

I laughed but it didn't feel mirthful. It felt like the edge of a sob. "I don't want to believe the world can be better. I want to believe this is just the way things are. That way it hurts less when nothing changes." Why was he making me question everything I'd ever believed about myself? I'd been happy. If I was content with the way things were, I didn't have to hurt when no one else wanted to make it better.

He leaned forward and grasped my hands. "It's all right to be angry. What they did to you was wrong. The lies they made you believe—"

I yanked my hands away. "Lies? They taught me the truth. Papa didn't think I could be a daughter so he sent me to the kitchen. Said he never wanted to see me again. You want to know why my servants talk to me like I'm one of them? Because I was. I grew up with them. I couldn't be a daughter so I was made a servant. But I couldn't even be a servant. They're not allowed to be useless either. I was a burden. A waste of space. I lived there on charity and everyone knew it."

I buried my head in my hands and sobbed. Years of suppressed unhappiness and fury warring in me until I couldn't do anything but cry. God Almighty, what had I said? If I'd gone on even a second longer, I might even have confessed I was a murderer.

Nik's solid weight settled beside me on the rock and his arms wrapped my shoulders until my head rested on his chest.

What was this man doing to me? Making me question everything. Changing me from the inside out until dissatisfaction clogged my throat and made me want more.

Something cold and wet hit the back of my hand, and I looked up, blinking. Dark clouds rolled across the small scrap of sky above. We'd been so intent on our conversation we hadn't noticed the light change. Ember made a dissatisfied noise and flowed back up my arm to hide under my hair.

Nik looked up and swore with vehemence.

I raised my eyebrows. I wouldn't have thought a prince would know any of those words.

"We're going to have to make a run for it," he said.

I glanced at the broad expanse of grass. "Um."

"Saints, I'm sorry. I didn't mean—"

"No, you run," I said without rancor. All my bitterness had been expended in tears. "I'll walk."

The drizzle turned to an outright downpour.

"Like hell," he said and helped me to my feet. Then he shook out the blanket and draped it over our heads. "Now."

We shuffled as fast as we could across the grass while rain pelted the light linen blanket with steady insistence. A flash and sizzle made us glance up halfway to see the phoenixes ducking back through the collapsed ceiling. Calls from the other end of the site told us the archaeologists were covering parts of the work threatened by the rain.

By the time we reached Erestan's tomb we were soaked through and giggling. Nik ducked into the sepulcher, dragging me with him.

He stopped so abruptly I lost my balance and swayed. He put his hand on my waist to steady me, and I reached my arm around his neck without thinking. One last laugh escaped my lips as I met his eyes, dark in the gloom of the necropolis. Only the faintest hint of green shone through, like the moss on the stones behind us.

He leaned down and pressed his lips to mine. Rainwater mingled with his kiss as his ragged breath matched mine. Warmth seeped into me and my fingers closed on the back of his neck, his short hair soft under my fingertips.

My heart stuttered in my chest. Could he make my heart stop with just a kiss? Did I care?

Finally, he pulled back.

"What was that for?" I asked, breathless.

"I wanted to," he said. "Forgive me?"

I huffed a laugh. "Definitely not. I think I liked it."

"Hmm, you're not sure? I must need more practice."

"Practice? Shouldn't a prince be good at everything?"

I was only teasing but he drew back a little and looked... was that embarrassed?

"I've never actually kissed anyone before."

My jaw would have dropped if I hadn't thought that would completely mortify him. "What? Never?"

"Your Highness?" we heard Miss Lawford call. "There are people here looking for you."

I ignored her and stared at Nik. He shifted his feet, and I couldn't help thinking how adorable he looked when he was less than confident.

"My grandfather taught me never to kiss a girl unless I was willing to make her my queen."

Now my jaw did drop. My stomach joined it. "What?" I said.

"Hadn't you guessed? I'm courting you."

I should have told him to stop being ridiculous. I should have said a prince couldn't marry someone like me. But he'd broken something loose in me, and I couldn't go back to the way I'd thought before. Just because everyone else looked at my twisted legs and thought I was less didn't mean they were right. And this man looked at me and saw past all the things I couldn't do.

"I think I'm getting the idea," I said.

"If it's only an idea, then I'm doing it wrong." His expression was soft and full of promise as he studied me. A strand of his hair straggled across his forehead, and I brushed it back with trembling fingers. A strange possessive feeling swelled in me. I could touch him like this and no one else in the world could do the same. It was as if by returning his kiss I had branded him as mine.

CHAPTER SIXTEEN

The trip back wasn't nearly so pleasant with Renny and I huddled in the carriage, but I kept replaying Nik's kiss in my mind, and I couldn't help grinning foolishly out the window at the rain.

Outside, Nik and Merrick walked with the horse, urging it on through the soggy road while Jason guided it from the driver's box. It felt like every few feet they had to stop and push when the wheels got mired. By the time we reached the edge of town they were so covered in mud it was impossible to tell the Prince from the footman and the bodyguard.

Ember crouched on the sill, spitting with anger. Water couldn't actually hurt her, but it slowed her down and she spent hours recovering her flames after a good dousing.

Rain continued to pour while we clattered over the cobbles and pulled onto our street. But instead of stopping in front of the townhouse, the carriage jerked and kept going around the corner.

I glanced out the window and caught my breath as I saw

Melissa, Anella, and Isol step into the house under heavy black umbrellas. My stepfamily had beaten us home.

Renny and I looked up as an argument broke out above us.

The moment the carriage stopped, I pushed the door open and stumbled down the step. The tips of my canes slid against the slick cobbles.

Nik and Jason stood in the middle of the street glaring at each other.

"What are you doing?" Nik glared at him. "She can't walk from here."

"Do you know how much trouble we're in?" Jason yelled back.

"If you don't calm down," I said, coming to a halt beside them. "The entire street will hear you."

"If this moron hadn't dragged you out of the house," Jason said. "You'd still be safe at home." Jason stepped forward to do who knew what, but Merrick was suddenly between him and the Prince.

Jason fell back, swearing.

"My stepmother is home, Nik," I said. "Jason was right; I can't go in the front door."

Nik's shoulders sagged. "I promised to get you back on time. I'm sorry."

I shook my head. "You didn't know it would rain and mire the carriage," I said. But my heart was pounding. What was I going to do? I held Ember close under my arm, protecting her from the rain as much as I could. She still chattered and hissed, her flames dimmed so she looked like a sputtering coal.

"I'll help you get inside," Nik said as Renny descended from the carriage to join the conversation. "I'll sneak you in somehow."

I shook my head. "It's sweet of you, but it would be worse for me if Melissa catches you here. You have to go."

"I can't leave you here with no way to get inside."

"We'll go in the back," Renny said. "There's a gate into the alley where Ruben puts the trash bins."

Jason crossed his arms. "Only if it's not locked."

Nik looked at me, his eyes full of things unsaid. "I don't want to leave you like this," he said.

"I'll be all right," I told him. "Melissa won't...won't hurt me." My voice lost its strength as I remembered the way she'd pinched me to keep me quiet.

He took hold of my hands. "Are you sure?" he asked in a voice that was only for me.

"I am," I said, as much to convince myself as him. "Go."

"Only because you say so."

I could tell he wanted to kiss me again from the way he held my gaze, but he just raised my hand and brushed his lips against my knuckles. I shivered and tried to think of something to say, but he'd already pulled away.

He climbed the carriage to the driver's box and clicked the horse into motion. Merrick leaped up behind and they were away, Nik casting one last look at me where we stood on the curb.

I shook my head to clear it and said, "Come on. The sooner we get inside, the sooner we can get dry."

"Do you have any idea what you're doing?" Jason said through his teeth as we moved past the houses to the alley behind, the two of them matching their pace to mine. "You're risking everything for a man who wouldn't have looked at you twice when you worked in the kitchen. Do you really think he means what he says?"

I wanted to. I wanted to badly. But I wasn't going to tell Jason that. I was going to keep this possessive hopefulness tucked deep inside where I could guard it with every thought I had.

"That man is going to break your heart."

"Probably," I said, fed up with him in that moment. "But what are you going to do about it?"

I stopped in the narrow alley, forcing him to face me or push past.

He dropped his gaze and refused to answer.

"Just help me get inside," I said. "You can do that much, right?"

He jerked, and I felt a twinge of guilt for pushing him so hard before I twisted around on my reluctant feet and continued along the alley.

We counted the gates until we came to ours and Renny tried the latch.

"You were right," she told Jason.

"Could you go over the wall and unlock it from the inside?" I asked Jason.

Renny was the one to answer. "Not without the key."

"We don't have time," Jason said. "Here. I'll give you a boost." He knelt as if to help me mount a horse.

I looked up at the wall surrounding the tiny yard behind the house. It was barely taller than me and a scraggly little tree peaked its branches over the top, but it might have been three stories for all I could climb it.

"I'll get you to the top, then you can let yourself down the other side," Jason said. "As long as you take it slow, you'll be fine."

I huffed in consternation, but I didn't see another option. I tucked Ember under my braid, where she grumbled.

Jason managed to get me high enough to drape my arms over the rough stones, then pushed at my legs until I lay flat across the top of the wall.

I glanced back and saw him avert his gaze, a bright red flush creeping up his face.

Who knew I had enough appeal to make a footman blush, as well as a prince?

I clung to the stones, their jagged edges catching the cloth of my gown as I let my legs swing over the other side. I hung there, gasping with effort until I felt my feet touch the ground. It took a couple tries to lock my knees so they would take my weight.

"I'm over," I said raggedly.

Jason helped Renny over the same way and then followed without much difficulty. Apparently the life of a footman kept him fit enough for some acrobatics.

I pressed a hand to my chest, trying to catch my breath. "Now, let's get inside before—"

"What's this?"

I froze, Melissa's voice making the hair on my neck stand on end. She stood in the doorway to the kitchen, her austere gray gown making her look like an avenging angel guarding the Saint of Passing.

I glanced behind her for Grandmama, but the only one standing behind her was Bess. My grandmother must have stayed at court.

"I came home to check on you," Melissa said. "Make sure you were feeling well. Imagine my worry when I couldn't find you in your room, or the kitchen, or indeed anywhere in the house."

Her voice sounded soft and sweet as it always did but now there were sharp edges to her words.

I looked around for an excuse for being outside, but the little yard at the back of the house was bare and paved, with only the scrawny tree standing in its planter.

"I've...been here," I said.

She tilted her head. "In the rain?"

Renny and Jason stood quietly beside me, eyes wide. I raised my chin. "I like the rain."

Melissa stared at me, her blue eyes steady on my face. "You've been outside this house," she said.

"No."

She stepped into the yard, the rain soaking her hair and dress. "Really?" she said. "Bess told me you had a visitor."

I glared at the scullery maid who skulked in the doorway, a smirk on her thin face. "She was mistaken," I said.

Melissa sighed. "I have been trying my best to protect you. To put you in a position of safety, but you are undermining me at every turn. All I want is what's best for you."

"Then why did you tell the King to investigate me?"

For a moment the mask of kind concern dropped, and Melissa looked truly shocked. Then she took a deep breath and her expression closed off. "Everything I've done, I've done to keep you from being branded as a murderer. It's not my fault if you can't see that."

"How does bringing me to the attention of the King keep me safe?" I said.

"Enough." Her hand slashed through the air as if to cut me off.

I kept myself from jumping.

"I will not stand for this disobedience."

"I've done nothing," I said, holding my ground. I didn't know what else I could do. I could hardly admit what I'd really been doing that day.

Melissa's lips tightened, and she moved back toward the kitchen. "I forbade you from leaving the house while I was gone. You were not supposed to interact with anyone outside the family without my supervision, and now you've done both."

"I haven't."

She spun back to face me. "You are lying." Her voice rose and her eyes turned to slits.

I swallowed.

She took a deep breath, her nostrils flaring, then she straightened and stepped into the doorway. "Jason, Renny. Please come with me. I believe it's time my stepdaughter learned that there are consequences for her actions."

My eyes widened. "No." I hobbled to the door. "You can't. They didn't do anything." I reached out to grab her sleeve.

She looked at my hand and her lips tightened. Without flinching, she wrenched her arm from my grip and slapped me hard across the face.

My ears rang. I staggered and fell across the stone step.

Something snapped and pain exploded up my arm. I curled into a ball, white lights flashing before my eyes.

Ember streaked out from under my braid, shrieking. The rain pelted her, making her sputter, but she reached flaming claws for Melissa, who stepped easily out of the way. The wet fire sprite fell to the doorstep, guttering on the stone.

Melissa sneered and nudged her off the step with her toe. My heart clenched.

"You bring this on yourself, Cindy," Melissa said through the haze of pain. "I have only tried to help you."

Melissa called for a surgeon to set my arm, saying, "We'll tell him you fell. It's the truth and no one will believe anything else."

The surgeon said only one of the bones in my left forearm was actually broken. He set it, splinted it, and strapped it to a sling, effectively halving my mobility.

He gave me a sedative before he left, leaving me to sleep through the worst of the pain.

I woke with my head full of fog and the blackness of full night outside my window. Grandmama snored in a chair beside my bed.

Ember lay curled along my bad arm, her flames dimmed, still recovering from the rain. Melissa had left her huddled below the kitchen step but as soon as my stepmother's back was turned, Renny had scooped the fire sprite up and hidden her in her apron. Now Ember managed to draw away the heat and ease the swelling in my arm.

She raised her head as I shifted. I raised my good hand to pat her head. "Are you all right?" I said.

Grandmama snorted and sat up, rubbing a hand down her face.

Her bleary gaze met mine, then cleared. She stood and strode forward.

"Show me," she said, her eyes worried, her face gaunt and pale.

I pulled my bandaged arm out from under Ember, who grumbled and settled herself on my chest. Her voice sounded normal, and I knew she wouldn't have the strength to complain if she'd been truly hurt.

Grandmama turned my arm over carefully, though there wasn't much to see: just a splint and some bandages. Her mouth twisted in a tight unhappy line, and her chest heaved once, like she held her breath, waiting for her anger to pass.

"Renny told me you had an altercation."

"How is she?" I asked. "Melissa threatened them, too."

"She and Jason are fine. Your stepmother didn't touch them. Apparently she felt like she got the point across."

I grimaced.

Grandmama placed my arm back on the covers and sat back to regard me steadily. "I sent the Prince here so you could work with him on his case. Prove your character to him. Not so you could run off across the countryside."

"I know. I'm sorry."

She grimaced. "One good thing has come from all this.

Melissa has shown her hand now. I'm not letting you stay here another—"

The door opened, interrupting her. Isol appeared around the edge, her dark eyes calm and collected.

"What do you want?" Grandmama said without preamble or warmth.

Isol didn't seem bothered and took that as invitation to step inside and close the door behind her. She wore a long white nightgown. "I heard voices," she said. "I wanted to see how Cindy was doing."

"Fine," I said. What else was I supposed to say? Your mother broke my arm but don't worry, I'm all right with it?

"I thought you might want something for the pain." She held out a vial of liquid. It looked a lot like the ones Melissa carried around.

I drew back warily. I didn't have any reason to distrust Isol, but she also hadn't given me a reason to trust her either. "I didn't know you were an herbalist, too."

"My mother taught me," she said.

"Be sure that's the only thing you learn from her," Grandmama said with a sniff.

"It might already be too late for me," she murmured.

I frowned, but she looked up to meet my eyes before I could reply.

"It's not too late for you, though. You know she doesn't mean you any good, right?"

"I got the idea, yes," I said with a snort.

She opened her mouth to respond, then hesitated, her gaze going to my good arm. Her fingers reached out, and she grasped it gently. A long shallow scratch marred the skin along my wrist. It was deep enough to have bled but it had scabbed over quickly enough that my sheets were still clean.

"When did you get this?" Isol said.

I chewed my lip, realizing I didn't remember. I hadn't had it before when the surgeon checked me. And it looked familiar. I'd seen wounds a little like this before. When I'd talked to the servant at the Duke's ball. She'd had cuts all up and down her arms, half healed and seeping. I only had the one.

But maybe one was how it started.

My mouth went dry and I struggled to swallow down the panic creeping up my throat. Was Melissa the blood mage Nik was looking for?

I cleared my throat. "I must have gotten it climbing over the wall," I told Isol.

Her eyes narrowed in clear disbelief. But she didn't press the issue.

Did she know what her mother was?

I kept my lips tight on the question. She wouldn't have answered me if I asked anyway. She was used to keeping secrets behind a cool expression.

She pressed the vial into my hand. "This will help your arm without leaving your head fuzzy. You'll need it if you want to protect yourself."

Grandmama laughed, short and sharp. "You do have some sense, then," she said. She turned back to me. "You can't stay here anymore. This," she tapped my arm, "changes things."

I used my good arm to throw the covers back. "Are we leaving the city?" I swung my legs over the side and tried to stand with only one arm to support me. I wobbled, then steadied. "Do you have somewhere we can go?" She was used to traveling. Maybe she'd take me with her to see the best libraries in the world.

"I don't think running will solve everything," Isol said. "You have to fight her."

"Like some kind of warrior?" I snorted. "Right. Besides, you saw how well that worked."

"Now you know what she's capable of, you'll be better prepared."

"Isol, I couldn't even defend myself," I said. My hand shook where it clutched the mattress.

My door opened for the second time, making me jerk upright. Ember squeaked and streaked across the carpet to dive into my fireplace.

Melissa strode into the room, dressing gown flowing behind her like a court dress.

"I thought I heard voices." She stepped toward the fireplace and smirked at the flames. "A fire sprite certainly explains a few things. She doesn't have to worry, I'm not here for her."

She cast a glance over her shoulder at the Dowager and then Isol. "You're not bothering Cindy, are you? She needs her rest."

Isol dropped her gaze to the carpet and sank back into the shadows of the room.

My grandmother drew herself up and ran a hand over her rumpled dress. "This ends now, Melissa. I'm taking my granddaughter away from your schemes and your abuse. Did you really think I would let her stay here after you broke her arm?"

Grandmama moved to support my elbow.

Melissa crossed her arms. "I don't think that would be a good idea. Cindy really isn't feeling well."

My good hand clenched on the bedspread. It was the same thing over and over again. She pointed out my weaknesses, then exploited them. But it didn't have to be that way anymore.

I straightened.

Heat then cold washed over me, erasing the thought I'd been trying to express. I trembled as a shower of bright sparks exploded in my head, and the room disappeared behind a smear of color.

When I blinked, I found myself on the floor looking up at Grandmama's worried face and Isol's frightened one.

Behind them, Melissa's small satisfied smile disappeared quickly enough I doubted I'd seen it.

"There," she said, tone gentle and conciliatory. "Now you see what I've been trying to tell you."

"What happened?" I said, my tongue thick and clumsy in my mouth. My arm ached worse than before.

"You—" Grandmama looked at Isol. "You had some sort of fit."

"It was like you were trying to hit something," Isol said.

"Has this ever happened before?" Grandmama said.

I started to shake my head, then froze. It *had* happened once. I'd blacked out on a roof. And when I'd woken up my father was dead.

"Yes, it has," Melissa said simply.

Isol sank back on her heels, avoiding my gaze.

Grandmama put a hand under my shoulders to help me sit up.

"Clearly your granddaughter is ill," Melissa said. "She needs to be cared for in a safe place. A place where she can't hurt anyone. And if you try to take her from my custody, I will do more than break her arm to keep her safe. I will tell the King about these fits. I will tell him that the last one killed her father."

"That's not true," Grandmama said, but there was a hesitance in her voice that made me wince.

Melissa spread her hands. "With this new evidence? It's very damning. And if you try to defend her, he will remember the last person you tried to defend. How well did that go?"

The blood drained from Grandmama's face, leaving her pale. Her hands shook on my shoulders.

"How do you know about that?" Grandmama whispered. "Those records are sealed."

"You told your son," Melissa said. "And I was his wife."

Grandmama's breath came in short, sharp gasps beside my ear. I put my hand to her fingers and squeezed, trying to reassure her. Whatever she was remembering, whatever this new threat was, it had struck deep inside my grandmother.

"It's really very simple," Melissa said with a tiny shrug. "How badly do you want to hurt your granddaughter's chances? Come, Isol."

She left without a backward glance, as if she knew my grandmother's decision.

And she did.

In the morning, we were still there.

CHAPTER SEVENTEEN

Nik rubbed his temples. Why was this so hard? He was a prince, he should be able to get a few old men to agree on one small thing. And the longer they sat here, the more he worried about Cindy and the position he'd left her in. Was she all right? What would her stepmother do if she found out Cindy had been out with him?

The Duke of Chatham refused to compromise on another piece of the legislation, and Nik fought the urge to beat his head against the table.

There was really only one thing he felt free to do at the moment. He turned in his chair and inclined his head toward Merrick. The bodyguard came forward and leaned down so Nik could whisper to him.

"I want you to go check on Miss Hargrove."

"Sir?" Merrick said, giving him a narrow-eyed look.

"I know, I know," Nik said with an exasperated sigh. "You're not supposed to leave my body. Look, we're in the palace. The safest place in Valeria. If you don't think your fellow guards can handle it..." Nik gestured to the other ServantGuard posted in the corners. "Then you should probably have a word with your commander."

Merrick's expression tightened.

"I don't trust anyone else," Nik said before he could argue. "Please, Merrick. Just make sure she's all right. Discreetly."

Finally, the bodyguard gave him a curt nod and turned on his heel. Nik turned back to the deliberations with a sigh.

An hour later Merrick still hadn't returned, and Nik had a bad case of antsy. He couldn't sit still. He couldn't listen to any of these men drone on without his gut squirming.

The Torracan ambassador stared at Nik from across the broad table, his eyes wide and beseeching. It made Nik feel especially useless.

He stood abruptly, interrupting the Duke of Chatham with the screech of his chair.

"Gentlemen, that's enough," he said, raising his voice probably more than necessary. "I would like you to come to an agreement on this issue. But in the end that isn't necessary. By my power as heir, I'm presenting this legislation to the Bicouncil at the end of the week, and I will make it clear to them where they should stand on it."

Nik waited for the men in the room to duck their heads, to back down before his superior authority. This argument was ridiculous. Surely they'd recognize that now and agree.

No one seemed cowed.

The Duke of Chatham pushed back his chair in a deliberately slow movement and stood to face him. "You can, of course, do whatever you wish, Your Highness. But you should know if you force this in the council the result will be disastrous." The Duke smiled coldly.

Nik drew himself taller.

The Duke continued before he could say anything. "You have the authority to present the bill as is, Your Highness," he said. "But the councils still have to vote on it and if you tip your hand like this, you will lose what little support you have. Perhaps you need time to think about the consequences of that."

The Duke gathered his things and left, followed by the other men, each casting disgusted or disappointed grimaces back at Nik as they did so.

Nik stood, blinking, his hands pressed against the wood of the table. Humiliation rushed through him.

What had just happened? He was the heir. He was supposed to lead. Why hadn't that worked?

A phrase floated through his mind spoken in Cindy's voice. "So you walk out front and hope they'll follow along behind." Only now could he hear the sarcasm in her comment.

Nik collapsed back into his chair and glanced at the Torracan ambassador, the only one still at the table. The man stared at his hands, which were clasped in front of him.

"I'm sorry," Nik said without bitterness. "I mucked up your negotiation."

The ambassador finally looked up and met his eyes. "At home we say 'you handled that like a cat in a well.'"

Nik winced, but the description was accurate.

The man began packing the items before him into a bag.

Nik noticed the small rod of metal he'd set up before the meeting.

"What is that?"

The ambassador turned it over in his hands before holding it out to the Prince. "It is...like a tuning fork." He demonstrated by tapping it gently on the table and fitting it into a notched stand. "My friend at the Torracan College of Magery developed the technique. The vibrations protect those around it from compulsion magic."

Nik glanced up in alarm. "Do you think compulsion mages have infiltrated the palace?"

The ambassador hesitated a split second before answering. "I am in the habit of taking precautions, regardless of what I think."

That didn't actually answer his question. Nik folded his arms. "Can you tell when you're under compulsion?"

"It depends on the skill of the mage and the awareness of the victim," the ambassador said, continuing to pack up. "Anyone can use the magic to force their will on you, and you end up a helpless observer as your body obeys another person's commands. But the more skillful the mage, the more the compulsions seem like your own thoughts, directing you further and further out of character. However the more self-aware you are, the more likely you will notice the strange turn of your own thoughts and be on guard against manipulation."

The ambassador tucked away his apparatus, then took a pair of spectacles off and folded them carefully. Nik noticed one of the earpieces hung loose, like it was missing a screw or two.

Cindy's voice kept drifting through his head. "A monarch's greatest duty is to serve his people faithfully."

He'd screwed that up. And now this man worried that Nik's country was in danger.

So what would Cindy do, if she was here?

"Why are you the one presenting this?" Nik said abruptly.

The ambassador looked up from the document he'd been carefully sliding into his bag.

"I mean, why is this law against mind control magic so important to you? Personally."

The man laid the document and the glasses to one side. Then he he rubbed his eyes as if tired.

Nik shifted uncomfortably, aware now that he could have been more tactful.

"Until about fifteen years ago Torraca was ruled by a corrupt Zultaan," he said. "This ruler and his family used magic to manipulate, persuade, and confuse the mind. Even a man's thoughts were not his own. I remember this time. I remember what it was like to not trust your friends, your family, even yourself because your very mind was the battleground."

Nik waited while the ambassador paused.

"The Zultaan and his family ruled for years. Until Valeria secretly sent help to the resistance and our revolution finally succeeded. We won our freedom with your help."

Nik remembered his grandfather telling him about the Torracan revolution. It had been one of his last actions as king. His grandfather had wanted him to know the difference between actions that were public and actions that were not.

"The revolution succeeded," the ambassador said. "But we were scarred from the fight. My daughter, she was beautiful, with skin like the finest copper silk and eyes as sharp as a falcon's. And she was deadly as an asp. She was influenced by the Prince's magic, compelled to fight for him while he fled. She died because she was not allowed to make her final choice in that fight."

"I'm sorry," Nik said. What other response was there?

The ambassador shook his head as though rejecting Nik's empathy. "The Prince fled to Valeria. We know he came here and disappeared. That murderer found a new life here because Valeria has no laws against the kind of magic he wields."

"You're trying to find him?" Nik said. "For revenge?"

A second time the ambassador shook his head. "What use is blood shed to my daughter? It would serve her none and my country even less. My vengeance is this." He placed a steady hand on the document in front of him. "By keeping other criminals from practicing mind control. By preventing other victims, my daughter's death will not have been in vain, and she will rest in peace."

Nik took the document from him to read it once more with new eyes. He'd thought it would fit into Valeria's blood mage policy seamlessly and so he'd supported it. But now he could see it from a personal angle.

"I have been recalled," the ambassador said. "I leave for home before the month is over. And I worry I will not have accomplished my goal before I must leave."

Because Nik had mucked it up. He chewed his lip. What could he do now to salvage the situation?

He couldn't help thinking of Cindy and her quiet, vehement defense of the Saint of Service. And how that man had put Calahan on the throne. So how did you truly serve people?

Nik reached over to snag the ambassador's broken glasses. The craftsmen in the workshops beneath the palace could fix them in moments. It wasn't much. Hardly worth the worry he'd caused the man. But it was something that would make the ambassador's life a little better. And the bigger thing was that Nik was listening now.

Late in the afternoon, Grandmama helped me dress. I couldn't lay in bed all day just because I couldn't use my arm. I'd have to figure out how to get around sooner or later, so I decided on sooner.

The lady's mantle necklace swung from the neckline of my chemise and I caught it with my good hand. The thing made my stomach clench. I loved that it reminded me of my mother, but with that reminder came the memory of Melissa's warm smile when she'd given it to me. Could one object represent such different feelings?

I made as if to pull the thing over my head, but I balked. Even if it had been Melissa's gift, it still made me think of my mother. Was that such a bad thing? Perhaps the memories of Mama could redeem the sour note left by Melissa's lies and manipulations.

With a frown, I tucked the necklace back under my neckline.

Grandmama lifted the sleeve of a simple day dress in a sky blue and guided my arm into it, her mouth tight and unhappy. She'd been quiet the whole day. Ever since Melissa had issued her midnight threats.

"What was Melissa talking about last night?" I asked, partly to distract myself from the pain and partly because I would never know the answer if I didn't. "What happened 'the last time'?"

A muscle in her jaw jumped. She pulled the material up my shoulder and began fastening my buttons.

"I didn't want you to know," she said from behind me. Like it was easier to talk if she didn't have to meet my eyes.

"The same way I didn't want you to know about Father?"

She grunted what could have been a laugh in better circumstances. "Point taken," she said. "I've...made some poor choices in my life."

"This one must have been quite spectacular."

She sighed. "You could say that. It involved a man who eventually became a blood mage. The last one hunted down by the old king."

I kept myself from reacting. Any sort of horror on my part would have kept her from finishing.

"What happened?" I said.

"I defended him," she said. "Before I knew what he was. I couldn't believe the truth and I was very vocal about his innocence. When they proved his guilt, he was beaten to death by the mob before he could face justice."

"Did they want to arrest you, too?"

She patted the last of my buttons, and I turned. She met my gaze finally.

"No. There was no proof that I had known the truth. But King Ambrose asked me to leave court. Said it would be better for me if I gave everyone time to forget my involvement. It's one of the reasons I was abroad for so long. It's one of the reasons your father asked me to stay away."

I winced.

"And it's the only reason I can't help you the way I want to."

"I don't care about any of that," I said.

"You might not," she said, voice sharp like normal. "But others will remember. They'll remember that the last person I spoke up for was actually guilty. And they'll look at you and wonder if I'm wrong again."

I settled my crutch under my arm and staggered to the bed where I could sit. "Then there's nothing we can do."

"I didn't say that," Grandmama said, jerking her chin up. "We just need to have plenty of our own proof before anything comes to light."

A quiet knock on the door made us both jump.

"I'm sorry to interrupt you, Miss Cindy," Renny said. "But you have a visitor."

My heart leaped and then plummeted again. What could Nik be thinking, coming back again so soon, with my stepmother just downstairs in the parlor?

Grandmama took a good look at my face and snorted. "Come, then. I'll distract Melissa."

Renny helped me down the stairs and then slid into the kitchen to distract Bess, the little snitch, while Jason snuck me out the back door into our tiny yard. I shivered when I passed the doorway where Melissa had broken my arm. It still ached, but Isol's medicine had taken away the jagged edges of my pain.

My mouth went dry and my pulse pounded as I hurried past the doorstep. I wasn't sure I'd ever be able to stand in this yard again without thinking of that moment.

The paved space was empty, but I hobbled over to the gate with Jason's help. The footman left me where I could prop myself against the wall and stood back a few paces so he wasn't immediately obvious.

"I'm here," I said quietly.

"Miss Hargrove," a voice said from the alley.

I almost didn't recognize it, since I'd only ever heard the man speak one or two words at a time, and he remained hidden behind the wall. "Merrick?" I said.

"Yes, miss."

Relief warred with consternation as I realized that Nik hadn't risked everything to come see me.

Clothing rustled as he shifted.

"Stay out of sight, please," I said. "I don't want anyone from the house to see you."

The shifting stopped. "His highness wanted to know if you were all right."

"So he sent you."

"He wanted to come himself, but his obligations forbade it."

I could almost feel Merrick's frown of disapproval, and I bit my lip as a piece of guilt stabbed at me. Nik might not have come to see me himself, but I was still taking his mind off his duties. I was a distraction.

"Are you all right?" Merrick asked.

I shifted my feet. "I'm surprised you came," I said. "I didn't think you liked me very much."

A part of me hoped he'd deny it and talk about how wonderful I was, but his next words undermined that hope immediately.

"I go where my prince commands," he said.

"Of course," I said, pinching the bridge of my nose.

There was a hesitation beyond the wall before he spoke again. "I do not mean to offend," he said slowly, as if the words were unfamiliar. "Did I offend?"

I rubbed a rueful smile from my lips. "I take it you don't talk to many girls while you're guarding the Prince?"

"I don't talk to many people," Merrick said. "I only meant it is my honor to guard the Prince and carry out his orders. It is my life and my purpose. I have no other. As long as I am protecting him, I know my honor is intact."

"That must make things...very straightforward," I said. It explained some of why Merrick was so intense.

"If there is peace, I walk beside him to assure it remains peaceful. If there is a threat, I kill it. And if he asks me to leave his side, I go," he said. "Grudgingly."

That made me laugh. "I can see that. It doesn't allow for much nuance."

"Nuance is confusing. Duty is clear. And you aren't allowing me to do my duty, Miss Hargrove."

"What?" I made a face at the blank wall.

"You still haven't told me if you're all right."

I hesitated. It would take months for my arm to heal so keeping the injury secret was impossible, but also there was no reason to worry him right now. "You may tell the Prince I'm fine."

"That doesn't actually answer the question, Miss Hargrove."

I sighed. "It's good enough, Merrick," I said.

He paused. "Miss Hargrove, I may not be very good at talking to people, but I've been trained to read intent in voice and body language. And your voice tells me you're lying."

I ground my teeth in frustration. "All right," I said. "Your job is to protect the Prince, correct?"

"Correct."

"That means protecting him physically, but what about emotionally? What good would it do Nik to know that I was hurt? It would only harm him. It would distract him. So you're going to protect him from himself. You're going to go up to the palace, and you're going to tell him I'm fine because that is what he needs to hear."

A long silence reigned on the other side of the wall.

"So you were hurt," he said.

I blew out my breath. "Yes," I said simply.

A boot scrape against the cobbles of the alley, and before I could say anything, he stood behind the gate, making it look small and insufficient. He peered through the bars.

"Your arm is bandaged."

"It's broken," I said through my teeth.

"How?"

"Did the Prince tell you to find out how?"

His jaw clenched. "No."

"Then you don't need to know, do you?" Until Grand-mama and I figured out a way to get me out of this house and away from Melissa for good, there wasn't anything Nik could do to help anyway.

"How bad is it?"

"It will heal," I said. "I'm well enough to come out here to argue with you, aren't I?"

His lip twitched. Was that a smile or a grimace? I got the impression he still wasn't going to like me after this.

Finally after weighing his options, he said, "Then that is what I will tell him and all our honors will be satisfied."

I blinked. That was...surprisingly reasonable of him.

He turned as if to leave, and I let myself sag in relief.

"I broke a lot of bones in training," he said to the cobbles. "There's a doctor at Saint Aegis's clinic by the docks that does plaster casts. It will still take months to heal, but you can at least use the arm while it does. And you can use it to hit back." He ducked his head in what looked like an awkward bow. "Good day, Miss Hargrove."

CHAPTER EIGHTEEN

M errick must have done a good job downplaying my injury to Nik because a couple days had gone by and I hadn't heard anything from the palace besides the fact that Nik was mired in complications from the Torracan ambassador's legislation. Apparently he was visiting each Duke, each councilor, serving them in small ways, leading them toward the big things.

I relaxed in satisfaction as I sat in my fireplace, bare toes scrunched in the ashes under my feet. It might have been summer, but I still liked the heat coming from the flames. The warmth wrapped me like a blanket and made me feel like I was back in the kitchen even as I sat upstairs in my room.

Ember frolicked in the sparks, making cinders fly out into the air, and I laughed at her.

"Careful," I said and waved the little bits of flame and ash away from my book. "Nik gave this to me."

She might have enjoyed visiting the necropolis, but she

showed no interest whatsoever in the biography of King Erestan.

My door opened, and I stiffened before realizing it was Grandmama.

The Dowager strode across the room to stand before the fire. She liked the heat too, after so many years in snowbound Ballaslav.

"I'm leaving the house," she said abruptly. Grandmama didn't believe in pleasantries.

I blinked. Since Melissa had broken my arm Grandmama had stayed close, remaining at home when the family went to court and spending as much time in my room as she could without driving me crazy. The only time she'd ventured out was to bring the surgeon from Saint Aegis's Refuge that Merrick had mentioned, and now my arm was encased in plaster.

"Where will you go?" I said. Melissa was out running errands with Anella and Isol so I felt relatively safe being here alone. Although my stepmother had taken Renny to carry packages, so I had less help than normal.

"I'm going to look for an explanation for these fits," she said.

By all rights I should be the one talking to healers and doctors, trying to figure out what the strange fit had meant. But Melissa had made it doubly clear that if I left the house without her supervision, she'd do more than break my arm.

"Do you think you can stay out of trouble while I'm gone?" she asked.

I nodded. "I won't be defying Melissa again anytime soon, you can bet on that."

"If she gets home before me, stay out of her way. Don't provoke her. Don't talk back."

"I've had a lot of practice at silent obedience by now, Grandmama," I said with quiet bitterness.

Her gaze flicked to the fire where Ember crouched, watching. "Keep her safe," she said. "Don't let her do anything stupid."

I choked on a laugh as Ember drew herself up solemnly and puffed out her chest.

Grandmama put her hand on my shoulder and squeezed. I touched her fingers once before she left in a flare of skirts.

I didn't really mind being home alone. It gave me a chance to read, and I was deep in my book when I heard the front door open again.

Renny soon poked her head in my room, and I gave her a smile. "Is Melissa home, too?" I said.

Then I registered the tight lines around her eyes and mouth and set my book down. "What is it?" I said.

"Miss Isol asked me to deliver this note while we were out. But I...I read it, and Miss Cindy, I think Miss Isol is in trouble."

She stepped into the room holding out a folded piece of paper. I frowned and took it. "You read it?" I said. It was one thing for servants to gossip about their masters, it was quite another to read their correspondence.

"I thought it might have something to do with you. She asked if you were at all acquainted with the King's Mage before she gave it to me."

What could Isol want with the unassuming King's Mage? And what did I have to do with it?

The message wasn't sealed or addressed. "Who were you supposed to deliver it to?"

"I was supposed to place it directly in the Duke of Chatham's hands," she said. "No one else."

That only made it more suspicious. The Duke had no love for Master Christoph. I unfolded the paper and read the words written in an elegant round hand.

I gave you twenty percent as we agreed. You will get the rest when the mage is either dead or arrested. Isol Hargrove will handle the details.

I froze. Dead?

I wasn't familiar with Melissa's handwriting, but this seemed much more in line with my stepmother than with my quiet stepsister.

Still, murder? Melissa was full of nefarious secrets and plans, but this was a far cry from my unproven guesses.

What had Christoph done to earn her ire? He seemed as quiet as me, most of the time.

I shook my head to dislodge all the questions. The why didn't matter so much as the what. Melissa planned something truly evil for Christoph.

And Isol was right in the middle of it.

"It might be too late for me," she'd said the night Melissa broke my arm. I couldn't help remembering the way she'd ducked her head and melted aside when her mother made her threats. It looked...familiar.

I knew firsthand how practiced Melissa was in manipulation. Could her daughter be as much a prisoner as I was?

I struggled to my feet. Whether Isol was trapped like me, or if she thought she was doing the right thing following her mother, I knew I couldn't sell her out. Even if it would save Christoph.

I'd just have to think of a way to save Christoph without getting Isol arrested.

"Renny, get Jason. I'll need his help getting out of the house without Bess finding out."

"Yes, Miss Cindy," she said without hesitation. "Where are you going?"

"To the palace." Someone had to warn the King's Mage someone was trying to kill him.

Nik stared at the windowsill between his hands, his head reeling. He still couldn't believe it. One of his best friends accused of blood magic. His fingers clenched on the wood. He couldn't even turn to face the young woman who bore the damning evidence up and down her arms.

"Your Highness, your response is clear," the Duke of Chatham said behind Nik.

Nik ground his teeth. The man's voice grated on his ears normally, but today it made Nik want to throw things at him.

"Your Highness—"

"You're sure you know the man that did this?" Nik said, spinning to confront the maid.

She flinched and clutched her apron. Her sleeves had been rolled up to reveal the cuts laid in precise rows on the pale skin of her forearms. Some of them still seeped. Nik remembered something Cindy had mentioned from Erestan's biography, about blood mage victims not being able to heal as quickly after they'd been bled over and over.

He wished she was here for this interview. She could tell him if this was the same young woman she'd seen before. Nik was sure it was; she worked in the Duke's household where Cindy had found her, and she matched the description. But he couldn't be absolutely certain without Cindy's testimony.

The girl's gaze flicked to the Duke, who nodded encouragingly.

"Yes, sir," she said. "I mean, Your Highness. It was the King's Mage. He's forever visiting the Lady Adelaine, and he...he cut me."

Every inch of Nik balked. He'd known Christoph for years, and he couldn't believe the quiet, gentle mage was capable of this kind of horror and deceit.

But he also couldn't ignore a direct accusation from a victim.

He glanced at Merrick in the corner, but the bodyguard gave away nothing, no hint of what he should think or do.

Nik strode to a table, anxious for movement, something to keep him from falling to pieces. "Thank you for coming forward," he said. "You may return home. But please remain available for questioning."

The Duke frowned. "I thought I would come with—"

"No," Nik said. "I'll handle this myself. Thank you."

Every little thing about the Duke rubbed him the wrong way, from his smug smirk to the ridiculous pink glasses perched on his nose.

The Duke drew himself up as if to argue, then met Nik's eye. Something in the Prince's level gaze made the man blanch and reconsider. He hurried the maid out the door. He might have been a pompous ass with too much authority, but he knew when he'd hit a wall he couldn't break down.

Nik returned to the window and braced his forehead against the cool glass. *What do I do now?*

Images of Christoph ran through his head, memories of wisdom shared and deep conversations. Jokes and laughter with a man he'd thought of as a friend. A blood mage couldn't fake that much normalcy, could they? Maybe they *were* normal, until that first decision, that first cut, warped them.

Christoph himself was the one who'd told Nik there was a blood mage in the palace, and he was the one leading the investigation. But what better place for the guilty party than at the head of the search where he could direct attention away from himself?

"The law is clear," Merrick's rumbling voice said. "All accusations of blood magic must be investigated to the fullest. The mage in question must be detained until all evidence is explained. And any mage caught fleeing after a blood magic accusation is killed on sight."

Nik glanced away. "Yes, I know."

"Sir, whatever your personal feelings on the matter, the Duke is right."

"Damn the man."

"You only have one option."

"Thank you, Merrick," Nik said, more forcefully this time. "I know."

He should go to the Captain of the Guard or his father and report the accusation. But he couldn't do that to Christoph. The law might have been clear, but he could at least handle it himself.

"Come on," Nik said and strode out the door.

Christoph had rooms in the palace, not on a main floor where the ambassadors and King's and Queen's households lived, but above the Queen's Tower in a spacious, airy, attic room.

Nik intended to knock, giving Christoph the courtesy of not breaking his door down, but as they approached, raised voices reached them from down the hall.

Nik and Merrick exchanged a look and raced forward. Then they stopped short.

Christoph's door stood open and a dead ServantGuard sprawled across the floor, blood seeping across the polished wood. Christoph knelt beside the body, the knees of his trousers soaking up the scarlet stain. Lainey stood just behind him, hands covering her mouth, trembling uncontrollably.

"Christoph," Nik said, and he couldn't keep the horror out of his voice.

"This man—" Christoph said, face pale. "I found him— I don't know what..."

Nik took a step forward but Merrick reached out to slam a hand into his chest. "Sir," he ground out.

"You don't believe..." Nik said but trailed off.

Merrick had a hand clenched on his ceremonial sword,

but Nik knew if Merrick wanted to kill someone he didn't need three feet of steel to do it. The ServantGuard carried swords, not because they looked pretty, but because if they were up against a mage, the fastest way to take out a spell caster was to cut off their hands.

"Nik," a voice he hadn't expected called him anxiously from down the hall.

"Cindy?" he said, turning to see her limping as fast as she could toward them. "What are you doing here?" A distant part of his mind noticed she only used one crutch.

Ember raced ahead of her to twine around his boots.

Cindy didn't answer as she drew even with him, but she sucked in a breath when she saw what was inside the room.

"Master Christoph Thane," Merrick said. "You're under arrest for murder and suspicion of blood magic."

Christoph's eyes went wide. "What?" He glanced down. "I didn't kill this man."

"Stand up, sir."

Christoph lurched to his feet. "I'm not a murderer. I won't let you arrest me for something I didn't do."

"Hands down, mage," Merrick said and drew his sword.

"I'm just asking you to wait." He held his hands up, palms out. For anyone else, it would look like he was telling them to stop.

But mages used any number of gestures for their spells.

The next few things happened in a blur.

Merrick lunged forward, blade sweeping down to counter the mage. Lainey screamed. Nik reached for the bodyguard's arm, but he was too far.

Ember raced between Merrick's feet and leaped up,

flaring into a bright, blinding bird, making the bodyguard wince and shield his eyes.

Nik's heart stopped as Cindy dropped her crutch and lurched forward to stand between Christoph and Merrick's raised sword.

"No, Merrick," she said. "Look, look at his eyes."

It was enough to make Merrick pause, a moment of calm when they all stared at Christoph's clear blue eyes.

"What about them?" the bodyguard rumbled.

"There's no blood ring. When a mage draws *vytl* from blood, a red ring forms around his irises."

Nik wanted nothing more than to reach out and draw Cindy away from Merrick's blade, but he forced himself to wait. "I didn't know that."

Her own eyes flashed. "You asked me to read Erestan's biography so we would know what to look for. The ring is always present in a blood mage's eyes but can be dark and overlooked, unless you know what you're seeing. However, in sunlight..." She pushed Christoph gently so he stepped back, one step, two. Into the bright sun streaming through his window. "It turns bright red. The color of fresh blood."

Christoph blinked in the light. No blood ring marred his irises.

He hadn't drawn *vytl* from blood. Which meant he was no blood mage.

Merrick lowered his sword, and Nik's breath left his lungs in a whoosh. The bodyguard's eyes were as wide as Christoph's now.

"I nearly killed you," Merrick said to the mage, voice hoarse.

"You were meant to," Nik said. His mind raced over the last hour, turning the facts round and round. "Someone framed Christoph. The real blood mage sent that girl to lie and make sure we caught him."

"And with the laws so stringent," Cindy said. "He was more likely to end up dead before he could explain himself."

Nik's eyes narrowed as he glanced at her. "But how did you know what was going on? Why are you here?"

Cindy lifted her chin, face pale. "I came to warn Christoph someone was trying to kill him."

Nik's brow drew down. "You knew someone was setting him up?"

"Yes," she said.

"How?"

"I can't tell you."

Nik jerked back. "What?"

Her gaze remained steady on him. "I'm sorry," she said. "I can't tell you."

"Why not?" Didn't she trust him? After everything they'd said the other day in the necropolis?

"It could hurt someone...someone who doesn't deserve it."

Nik made a low noise in his throat. Who else could she mean but her stepmother?

"Why are you protecting her?" he asked. "After everything she's done." He went to grip her arm, but she winced. For the first time he noticed her left arm was bulky beneath the sleeve of her gown, and she held it close to herself.

She turned away from him as if to hide.

He stepped so he was directly in front of her and forced

her to face him. Then he gently felt along her arm. A plaster cast.

"She broke your arm," he said, barely keeping the surge of rage in check. Years in the royal court had taught him how to keep his face bland when anger roared beneath the surface, but this nearly broke his control.

"Actually, I fell," she said, and he couldn't interpret the mix of amusement and anger in her voice.

"Muck on that," Nik said.

Lainey gasped at his language, but Cindy just rolled her eyes.

"Merrick said you were fine." Nik glared at the body-guard who drew himself up and fixed his gaze on the paneled wall behind Nik.

"He told you the truth," Cindy said, raising her chin.

"Like hell," Nik said. "How did you even get up all the stairs?"

"Slowly," she snapped back.

"Why are you protecting her?" Nik said again. Maybe this time she would actually answer him.

"I'm not," she snapped. "I'm protecting someone else." She met his eyes evenly, her lips thin and determined. "I told you once before you couldn't ask questions about what went on in my house," she said. "You promised to hold to that."

And he'd already broken one promise to her. He paced to the door and back again, running a rough hand through his hair.

He knew he had to look at this objectively, to see the facts and not the emotions. But when he looked at this room, all he saw was Christoph smiling at Lainey across a hospital courtyard and Cindy dancing with him in green glowing light.

Who did he trust? In the end that was the only question he could answer with absolute certainty.

"All right," he said, and stopped his frenetic pacing. "All right."

"It's not all right," Lainey said, without relinquishing Christoph's hand. "Someone is trying to frame Christoph as a blood mage. This woman has information and you're just going to let her stay silent?"

"I trust her," Nik said shortly.

Faint surprise and gratitude suffused Cindy's face before her expression smoothed again.

"I can tell you the note was confirmation of a plan to get Master Thane killed," she said. "And I also know it was supposed to be delivered to His Grace, the Duke of Chatham."

Lainey went white.

Christoph blinked. "That...makes more sense than it doesn't," he said with an apologetic look at Lainey.

Nik had to agree. The Duke wanted Christoph out of the way more than ever now that he and Lainey were attached. And the Duke was the one who'd brought the maid.

Nik's eyes narrowed in thought. Could he be the blood mage? He'd started that trend with the colored glasses a few years ago. He couldn't wait to knock the stupid things from his face and stare into his unfiltered gaze.

And whether he was the blood mage or not, Nik could come at the other half of the problem through him. The Duke had to know who had hired him to frame Christoph.

"We'll send a complement of ServantGuard to invite him the palace," Nik said. "He'll have some questions to answer." Nik resumed pacing, the worn floorboards creaking. "But whoever sent the note is serious," Nik said. "They wanted you dead or arrested. There is nothing less for charges of blood magic."

Cindy nodded to the dead guard. "And they murdered someone else to make sure it happened."

"Then this murderer is likely to try again. Harder next time."

"We need to protect him," Lainey said. "We need to get Christoph to somewhere safe and hide him."

Nik rubbed his mouth in thought as the late afternoon light crept across the floor toward the bloodstains. "There's something called royal custody," he said. "When the crown knows someone is important but in danger, they'll hide them. The only people who know their whereabouts are the Rannard who arranged it and whoever is sent with them. I did it with a convicted murderer just a few months ago."

Cindy looked stricken. "You...you didn't have him executed."

He shook his head. "No. I started that rumor to keep him safe."

Christoph nodded. He'd been privy to parts of that plan. Enough to believe Nik knew what he was doing.

Cindy's brow pinched, like she was thinking. "We might have to do something similar with Christoph. He can't just disappear," she said. "Sh—They'll know we know something. Then the next time they try, they'll be more secretive."

Nik sighed. "All right, what do you suggest?"

Cindy stared at the low sloped ceiling. "Make it look like they succeeded. But only half way. Christoph can disappear but put out wanted posters, tell the newspapers he's suspected of blood magic. In a few days, leak information on where he might be. Not the real location, of course, but a fake one. If they still want to kill him, they'll try again, but this time you control where they strike. And that way you can catch them in the act."

Nik thought. The logic made sense. But Valeria's laws about blood magic and hunting blood mages were harsh. It was why they'd had so many years of peace while other countries struggled with plagues of blood mages.

If the news went public that a blood mage escaped, someone would have to take the fall.

Nik glanced at Merrick. The bodyguard had stood, sword sheathed and face green through the entire conversation. He met Nik's eyes. Then he swallowed and nodded shortly.

Nik nodded back, acknowledging the sacrifice without drawing attention to it.

Christoph drew himself up. "Very well. I'll be a blood mage. But only until we find out whoever wants to kill me. You just have to promise to get me out of this once we find the real culprit."

CHAPTER NINETEEN

This time, Nik refused to leave until he'd walked me safely to our back gate. For once Merrick didn't accompany him. The bodyguard had stayed behind to arrange Christoph's escape while the Prince ensured I made it home.

I hoped that the plan worked. I hoped that they could catch the Duke and get at Melissa without implicating Isol. Especially after I'd worked so hard to keep her name out of it.

Night closed in around us as we trudged back through the alley. Ember sauntered ahead of us, her flames casting flickering light across the walls and cobblestones. My arm ached, but I did my best to keep the pain out of my expression. The look on Nik's face when he'd first seen the injury still made me shiver. I'd never have thought of my prince as violent if I hadn't seen the way his lips had gone white and his eyes blank. It had only lasted a moment. But it was enough.

We reached the wrought iron gate set into the stone wall,

and I checked the handle. We'd thought ahead this time, and Jason was supposed to be waiting to unlock the gate and smuggle me inside.

There was a click and the handle moved under my hand. I moved to open it, but Nik's hand on my arm stopped me.

"Cindy..." he whispered.

I turned to answer his questions and instead found his lips on mine. I drew in a surprised breath and then let myself kiss him back.

He pulled away far enough to rest his forehead against mine. I'd expected questions. Demands for answers instead of evasions. But all he said was, "Be careful."

I raised my eyes to meet his in the dark, but I couldn't tell what he was thinking with the shadows hiding his face.

"No more sneaking around, no more secret meetings. Not if it puts you in more danger."

I shook my head. I'd said the same thing myself this morning, but the moment someone else was in danger I'd rushed to save them. Clearly I wasn't very good at following my own advice.

"Why do you stay?" he said. "Why don't you defend yourself when she's done nothing but hurt you?"

None of the reasons seemed enough anymore. I couldn't deny what he was saying anymore.

But that didn't change the fact that I'd been silent this whole time. I'd ducked my head and taken her words, the good and the bad, without argument.

I studied his face in the shadows and thought about all the reasons I'd had to stay quiet.

"The man who sought King's Justice," I said. "Did you

really protect him?"

His brows scrunched in surprise. "Of course. When he came to me it was clear he was innocent. Why?"

I bit my lip, holding my breath as I hung poised on the edge of a decision that could change everything.

I opened my mouth to say, "Because I might need King's Justice one day."

But my throat closed, and the confession died unsaid.

"No reason," I said instead and somehow it felt like my voice wasn't my own. Where had those words come from? I wanted to tell him; I wanted to be done with this secret that stole my freedom.

But I waited silently, watching his face move from puzzlement to acceptance.

"You thought I was the sort of man to execute someone who came to me for mercy?" he said. "I suppose I started the rumor so I shouldn't be upset when it comes back to bite me."

He chuckled as if my gut wasn't burning with the need to tell him and the physical impossibility. I couldn't even open my mouth. Maybe I'd lived with fear for so long I couldn't take my freedom when it was offered to me. Like a bird that returned to the cage after flying free.

"Do you know better now?" he asked.

I nodded. I could at least do that.

"Go, and be careful," he said, and kissed my forehead before letting me go.

Bemused, I pushed through the gate expecting Jason to still be there. A figure stepped away from the wall, and my heart stuttered in my chest when I realized it wore a gown and not trousers.

Then my grandmother lifted a glass lantern, and I let out my breath in a whoosh.

"You scared me," I said. My voice seemed to be my own again.

"Good," Grandmama said and lowered a shield over the dancing mage light behind the glass. It let out just enough glow to get us to the back door. "Maybe then you'll think harder next time."

She strode to the door. "I told Melissa you weren't feeling well. They've all gone to bed by now."

"Thank you," I said as we slipped through the kitchen.

Even with the house quiet for the night, I held my breath while I limped past Melissa's room.

I was ready to collapse into bed, but Grandmama followed me through my door and stood with her arms crossed.

"I promise it was necessary," I said as I sagged into the seat at the dressing table.

"We seem to have different definitions of 'necessary,'" she said, her expression darkening. "You need to take a closer look at yourself and decide how much you're willing to risk for a boy."

"He's not just 'a boy,'" I said even though I knew she wouldn't care.

She snorted. "Just because he's got 'Prince' in front of his name doesn't mean anything. He isn't any different from all the other young men at court."

"I don't think any of those other men work so hard without reward, for something as abstract as a country," I said. I'd seen the dark shadows under Nik's eyes and knew he wasn't getting much sleep during all the talks with Torraca. "And none of those men know what it's like to be invisible. They don't see me. They don't demand respect for me. They don't show me how to respect myself."

I met her gaze, certainty making me bold. "I've already decided how much I will risk. And it's everything."

"He must be a fantastic kisser," she said, her expression unchanging.

I flushed and turned away, but her censure didn't shake my certainty. "I'd risk everything even if I could never kiss him again. I'd risk everything for one more moment." I pressed my hands against the dressing table, but they still trembled. "What does that mean?" I said. "What's happened to me?"

Grandmama let out her breath and finally her arms dropped to her sides. "Sounds a lot like love to me," she said.

"Or self-destruction," I said with a self-deprecating laugh.

"That's why it's one of the most wonderful things in the world. And the most dangerous. It can either be the key that frees who you truly are. Or the weapon that destroys you."

Was that why I couldn't tell him the truth tonight? I trusted him too much to worry that he would use it to destroy me. But maybe I worried this new feeling could be destroyed by the truth.

But I didn't have to let my fear rule me anymore. The first chance I got I would tell him the truth about my father. I would fight the fear I'd lived with for so long, and I would beat it.

In the morning Nik only took four ServantGuard with him to arrest the Duke of Chatham. He hoped it would be enough to subdue a dangerous blood mage but not enough to start a riot in the street. The Valerian crown had good reason to keep this arrest secret.

Filmy gray clouds scudded across the sky as two of the ServantGuard dragged the Duke into the walled courtyard outside his grand townhouse.

The Duke tried to wrench his arms free but the Servant-Guards Nik had chosen were massive, even bigger than Merrick.

"What right do you have to come here and drag me from my home and family?" the Duke said, a sneer marring his florid face.

Nik didn't respond. He set his teeth and stepped up to stand toe to toe with the man, using his superior height deliberately.

Nik lashed out and knocked the Duke's colored spectacles from his face. The Duke's head snapped back from the blow, and the lenses shattered against the cobbles.

"You dare to strike one of your nobles?" The Duke spat then glowered at Nik.

His brown eyes flashed and Nik faltered. They looked...normal.

God Almighty, if he was wrong...

A breeze ruffled Nik's hair, the clouds cleared for one moment, and a shaft of sunlight illuminated the courtyard.

Nik's lips thinned in a tight, satisfied smile.

A bloodred ring gleamed around the Duke's dark brown irises.

"You're under arrest for practicing blood magic in the Kingdom of Valeria, for flouting its laws, and for breaking fealty to your king and country." Nik spoke quietly so the Duke's household staring out the windows wouldn't hear, but his voice lacked nothing in conviction.

"And unless you can tell me who hired you to frame Christoph, I'll add conspiracy to commit murder to that list."

The Duke's lip curled. He leaned forward until his face was close enough that Nik could smell the wine on his breath. Nik refused to flinch.

"Add anything you like. It doesn't matter what else you accuse me of. It's a death sentence if I'm convicted of blood magic. A firing squad against the wall, I believe." He straightened with a sneer. "Do your worst."

His utter lack of remorse or fear made Nik's fists clench, his nails cutting deep into his palms. The man was caught, he could at least have the decency to shake in his boots.

Nik examined his fingernails. "Maybe I'll just leave you in King's Way Square with a sign around your neck. 'Blood mage here.' I believe that's where the last one was beaten to death by an angry mob."

The blood drained from the Duke's face, and his fat cheeks went flaccid.

"Take him to the cells below the palace," Nik said, standing aside for the ServantGuard escort.

A sour sort of satisfaction burned in his belly as he watched them march the Duke to the waiting carriage.

The cells below the palace weren't anything special. They'd been there since the Time of Blood and Hope more than eight hundred years ago, when the Blue Palace had been built on top of them.

It was noon by the time Nik made his way down the stairs. Apparently arresting one of the Ruling Dukes involved enough paperwork to sink a battleship.

Ancient flagstones passed under his feet, but the cut stone walls had been plastered over sometime in the last fifty years and freshly charged mage globes lined the hallway, shedding bright light on his repulsive task.

He was not looking forward to getting the Duke to talk. He almost wished the man had tried to run so the Servant-Guard could have killed him for fleeing, but then they wouldn't have had the chance to learn who had hired him to frame Christoph. It was hard to imagine there was someone even worse out there pulling the Duke's strings.

At the end of the hall a couple of guards slouched outside a thick metal door with a narrow window. These weren't ServantGuard. Once the Duke passed into this space he became the responsibility of the prison guards. And the prison guards hadn't had a lot of practice with blood mages.

Nik stopped before the two men. "I'm here to interrogate the prisoner," he said.

"Right," the guard on the left said. He bobbed his head like a pigeon. "Of course, Your Highness. We'll just get the door."

The man turned to fumble a key from his belt.

"There's a girl in with him now, but she won't give you any trouble, I'm sure."

Nik froze. "A girl? What girl?"

"Serving girl," the man said. "Said she wanted to say

goodbye to her master."

Nik gaped at the man who whistled through his broken teeth.

"Why would you let anyone in here? The man is a blood mage." He just kept himself from yelling.

The guard fell back against the wall. "She didn't have any knives or anything with her; I checked real good. She was crying about the arrest. She's just a little slip of a thing, Your Highness. She couldn't be a harm to anyone."

Nik shouldered him aside and thrust the door open.

The Duke lay on the bench, hands crossed over his chest, eyes closed, as if already entombed. His chest was still.

At his side sat the maid servant with the slashed arms who had stood in Nik's office and lied to his face. She lay draped across her master's chest.

She lifted her head and blinked blearily when he burst through the door.

"Now you can't hurt him," she said, voice thin.

Nik strode to her side and grabbed her shoulders. "Why did you do this? Did the Duke order you to kill him? Or someone else?"

She just closed her eyes and her head fell back as she stopped breathing.

Behind him the guards swore.

Nik clenched his teeth, but he laid the young woman down gently. He knelt for a long moment trying to control the waves of regret and anger swelling inside him.

Yes, the problem of the blood mage was solved. But whoever wanted to frame Christoph had made sure there was nothing to connect them.

CHAPTER TWENTY

"My lady, there's a man at the door," Jason said during dinner two nights after I'd snuck out of the house to save Christoph's life.

Melissa looked up from the steak and kidney pie with a frown. "And we just sat down to eat," she said. "So send him away."

"I tried, my lady. He insisted on seeing the mistress of the house. Says it's urgent."

Melissa sighed, wiped her mouth with her napkin, and pushed back her chair.

The moment she left the room Renny rushed over to me and whispered in my ear, "Miss Cindy, that bodyguard is here again. He's waiting out back."

I glanced at Grandmama and my stepsisters before excusing myself and standing up awkwardly.

Grandmama raised an eyebrow while Anella glared suspiciously. Isol just watched, face blank and unreadable.

When Anella opened her mouth to say something

Grandmama speared her with a glance. "So Anella, has your mother found a man willing to offer for you yet? That is why she dragged you all to court, right? For more marriage prospects."

Anella sputtered and I hid a smile while I slipped out of the room. Down the hallway I could hear Melissa arguing with whoever was at the door.

"I will say it again. This is the Hargrove household. Not the Hornminsters."

"Well, I've got this letter for Delilah Hornminster. What am I supposed to do with it if Miss Hornminster doesn't live here?"

"That's hardly my problem, is it?"

In the kitchen Jason stood by the sideboard talking with Bess so that she couldn't see my path to the back door.

Was the whole house in on this ruse?

I limped down the back step and tried to rush across the paved yard. Who knew how long my co-conspirators could keep everyone distracted?

"Merrick?" I said as I drew even with the gate.

"Miss Hargrove." He stood out of sight again.

I leaned against the wall and let my breath out in a sigh that was half amusement and half annoyance. "This is getting to be a habit, Merrick. You know you can just send me a note, right?"

"This was too important for a note. I assumed you would not wish your family to know I was here. Was I incorrect?"

"No, no." I should have remembered the stoic bodyguard had no sense of humor. "That's true. Is the man at the door one of yours?"

"He is a temporary employee," Merrick said. "An out of work actor hired for the occasion."

I laughed. "Really? Nik went all out with the clandestine this time."

There was a pause. "I am not here on his highness's behest, Miss Hargrove."

"What?" I said. "Then why are you here?"

Another pause. "I came for my own reasons. The Prince no longer commands me."

My amusement shattered and I shifted to peer through the gate so I could see him fully.

He didn't wear his uniform. It had seemed so much a part of who he was that to see him without it was like seeing him naked.

"Merrick, what's happened?"

"I've been dishonorably discharged. I am no longer in service to the Rannards or to Prince Nikolas."

I drew in a breath. "But...I thought that was your purpose, Merrick." I couldn't even put into words the way Merrick had felt about guarding the Prince. And the thought of Nik without his silent shadow was wrong somehow.

"It was necessary," Merrick said. "There needed to be a witness to testify that Master Thane and Lady Adelaine escaped together. So whoever framed the King's Mage would believe their plan almost worked. I was the witness. And there are harsh penalties for a guard who lets a blood mage escape."

"But they caught the Duke. The Prince knows the truth."

"The Duke died before he could name the person who hired him. So the plan must go forward."

I stood in silence, guilt and regret washing over me in waves. Christoph's fake escape had been my idea. And Merrick had been the one to take the fall for it.

"Merrick, I'm so sorry," I said but I knew the quiet words did nothing to make up for what I'd cost him.

He shook his head. "You mistake my purpose in being here, Miss Hargrove. I came to thank you."

I snorted. "I'll admit I don't understand you on a good day, but that makes no sense, even for you. *Especially* for you."

"You stopped me from killing an innocent man," he said.

"You thought he was a threat to the Prince," I said quietly.

"What I thought makes no difference," he said and the vehemence behind his words made me jump. "An innocent man still would have been dead at my hand. The Prince was not in danger and therefore the mage did not need to die."

"I'm sorry, I still don't understand. I thought you would do anything to protect the Prince."

"Yes. I would have. Even killing a man who did not deserve it. Miss Hargrove, I don't want to be the kind of person who kills an innocent man in error. Which means I am no longer the right person to guard the Prince. I volunteered to take the fall, to be dishonorably discharged, so I wouldn't have to be."

"I understand the sentiment," I said. "I just...hadn't expected it from you."

"Which tells me I made the right choice. Thank you again, Miss Hargrove."

I shook my head. "But everyone will believe you let a

blood mage escape. They will believe the dishonorable part of your discharge."

"I would rather people think that my honor has been stained rather than know for myself that it was broken entirely."

I fell silent, the humility and the simple truth in his statement making me flush with shame. I was letting people believe all sorts of things about me just because I'd made the mistake of trusting Melissa.

"I just wanted you to know what you did for me, Miss Hargrove," he said from across the wall. "And that I am now in service to you more than I ever was to the Prince."

I stood and gaped while Merrick bowed, turned, and left down the alley.

Nik stared out the window at the mountains, his mind going over and over the Duke's death while Colin and Eriana chattered away to their grandfather. He rubbed his temples. What would Cindy think when he told her how badly it had all gone?

A loud cough caught his attention and he turned to see Ambrose hacking into his hand. Finally the old Disciple glared up at him.

"You don't have much time, see?" he said and gave one last cough to prove his point. "I'll be dead before the end of the month and you won't have a bride."

Nik fought not to sigh. His grandfather had been threatening death for years. He didn't look any closer today than he had the last time Nik had visited.

"I've been trying," he said. "But Father had me on an investigation. It sidetracked me for a while."

"I heard about that," Ambrose said. "The little crippled girl."

It was so much bigger than that, but Nik's fists clenched at his grandfather's willful misunderstanding. "I'll thank you not to talk about her like that," he said between his teeth.

His grandfather didn't notice. He turned to accept a glass of water from one of the caretakers, and he sucked it down noisily. He coughed once more, then fixed Nik with a stare.

"Stop wasting your time with a girl who will never be your wife. Valeria needs a queen. So get off your ass and pick one."

A cold calm washed over Nik and he settled into his armchair, returning his grandfather's stare. "Cindy would be a better queen than anyone else you could come up with, Grandfather."

Ambrose jerked like he hadn't expected Nik to talk back. He opened his mouth, but Nik continued before he could say anything.

"She's reserved," he said ticking things off on his fingers. "She is slow to anger, and doesn't show it when she is. She is humble and kind. She doesn't see enemies or allies. She just sees people and how to help them. And she doesn't believe she's worthy of the crown."

Ambrose snorted. "That doesn't sound like a strength."

"Then you've never seen how badly someone could muck

things up when they thought they knew what they were doing."
Nik thought of the Torracan ambassador and heat rushed
through him. But he kept going. "She calls people to be better.
Valeria needs a queen like that. I need a queen like that."

Eriana stared at him with her mouth hanging open. Colin
just studied him with hooded eyes. Ambrose drew breath for
another tirade.

"Are you saying you're going to marry this girl?"

"I am."

"And I'm supposed to be happy about it?"

"You're supposed to accept it, whether you're happy or
not." Nik stood abruptly, and the armchair screeched on the
flagstones.

He left his grandfather gaping like a fish and strode
toward the long covered bridge. He took a deep breath and
tried to think. Why was he so angry? Seeing other people
disregard Cindy wasn't new. Just about everyone at court
did so.

But there was something different about hearing his
grandfather belittle the woman he'd chosen.

As annoying as Ambrose could be, Nik loved and
respected the Disciple. His father had taught him about
being a man, but his grandfather had taught him how to be a
king. He'd expected to defend his choice. So why did a blow
to Cindy feel like a blow to Nik?

The room that housed the portal had been built on one
craggy peak and the main Refuge perched on another. Nik
didn't bother getting close enough to the windows to look
down. There was nothing that said a crown prince couldn't
be afraid of heights, but he and heights had an understand-

ing. As long as they stayed away from him, he wouldn't be afraid of them.

He was halfway across the bridge when he realized Colin and Eriana had followed him. The thick rug had masked their footsteps.

Colin drew even with him and stared out the window at the jagged peaks. Eriana grinned and linked her arm in Nik's.

"Why didn't you tell us you'd fallen in love?" she said.

Nik stumbled, then righted himself. "I'm not in love," he said, denying her words as well as the churning in his gut. "I'm just choosing a queen. There's a difference."

Colin smirked at Eriana. "I don't think he's realized it yet."

"How do you not know when you're in love?" Eriana said, brow furrowing.

Nik pulled away from his sister and ran his hands over his face. "Stop it both of you. I want Cindy to be my queen. But that doesn't mean..."

He stopped trying to deny it for one moment and instead tried to think like Colin. Why was he upset when he had to defend Cindy to a man he respected? Why was he constantly thinking about her? Why was he thinking even now how he would relate this conversation to her later?

"Muck in a saint's handbasket," he said. "I'm in love."

He hadn't just listed the reasons Cindy would be a good queen. He'd listed the reasons he loved her.

Eriana laughed and took his arm again. "Poor Nik."

"Why do you look like you've been run over by a cart?" Colin said. "Isn't this good news?"

"I didn't want to find a woman I loved," Nik said. "I just wanted to find a queen."

"What's the problem with having both?"

"This wasn't supposed to be complicated. There's much more to lose now. What if she won't have me?" Nik said. Before, that wouldn't have been that bad. He'd have just moved on to the next prospect. But now...now it meant living the rest of his life without her.

"We could find out for you," Colin said, his expression thoughtful.

Eriana clapped her hands. "Oh yes. Let's waylay her and ask her intentions."

"No," Nik said with force. The calculating look on Colin's face frightened him. "No. I don't want you scaring her off."

"Then what?" Colin said.

"Then nothing," Nik said and drew himself up. "You two are just going to have to stay out of it. I don't need you bungling everything up before anything's decided." He glared at his siblings.

Colin dropped his gaze but Eriana pouted.

"But what if I want to meet her?"

"You'll just have to wait until it's official."

Her eyes lit up. "At the Sun Festival ball?"

Nik hadn't thought much about the ball at the end of the month, only as the means to an end. He was supposed to announce his choice of bride during the masquerade.

"Yes, at the ball," he said, his heart leaping in his chest. "But I have a question to ask someone before that."

CHAPTER TWENTY-ONE

The next morning Melissa made sure I was dressed on time. I made sure Ember stayed in the fireplace. She'd become too vocal when she was angry and Melissa made her angry most of the time now. There was no way I could hide her feelings now that my stepmother knew about her.

She spat sparks onto the hearth when I told her she wasn't coming to court.

"That's why," I said.

By the time I got downstairs, Anella and Isol waited in the carriage and Melissa stood by the door.

"I don't trust you to stay home alone anymore," she said, pulling on her gloves. "So you will be coming to court with us."

Grandmama was out speaking with every doctor and apothecary she could find about my strange fit, so I faced Melissa alone.

"No, I won't," I said. It seemed a small thing to argue about. She'd dragged me to court plenty of times now. But even though I'd promised Nik I wouldn't put myself in danger, I also wouldn't take her orders anymore.

"I don't recall asking your opinion."

My hand clenched around the head of my cane and held my ground.

The skin around her lips whitened as she noted my defiance. "Get in the carriage. I will not ask again."

I drew a swift breath to refuse again, no matter the cost. But was this one little victory worth risking Melissa's wrath?

Yes, I thought, pushing the doubt aside.

But then, without conscious effort, my feet carried me out the door to the carriage. The hair on the back of my neck stood on end as I realized I couldn't stop myself.

I tried to brace my good hand against the wall of the carriage to keep myself firmly on the cobbled street, but instead it gripped the edge as I clambered inside.

Melissa settled on the bench next to me, a tiny smirk on her lips.

Anella and Isol watched from the opposite bench. Anella sniffed in contempt while Isol bit her lip and glanced away from me.

A pit formed in my stomach. Saints protect me, what had just happened? I'd been so sure, so determined to defy her over this one thing. And the moment she'd held her ground, my feet had obeyed her.

There was something wrong. More wrong even than all the things I knew about. With the fingers of my broken arm I pushed up the hem of my other sleeve and stared at the cut on my wrist.

There was nothing in Erestan's biography that said a

blood mage could control thoughts, but maybe he hadn't known everything there was to know about blood magic.

Or maybe Melissa wasn't a blood mage. Maybe she was something else. Something worse.

I looked back up at Isol, but she stared resolutely out the window, back straight, until we pulled up in front of the palace.

Melissa followed her daughters out onto the cobbles and turned to look at me. "Come along, Cindy. We don't have all day to wait."

I searched myself for the desire to obey her. Was there some unseen force inside me, urging me toward the door? Or were my actions and decisions my own? How could I tell the difference?

I followed my stepfamily through the palace, deeply disturbed, and retreated to a bench as soon as I could. More pitying looks followed me today than there'd been the last time I'd been to court, and I found them harder to ignore. Each one sent shards of glass to churn in my veins.

Melissa stood over me as if concerned for my fragility, and I ground my teeth, struggling to control my ragged breath.

Another matron passed me with a pitying glance and a tsk tsk noise on her lips. She exchanged a brief sympathetic look with Melissa.

I tried to take the pity. I tried to swallow it and my pride all in one and I choked on the effort.

I pushed up from the bench with my good hand and my stepmother immediately jumped to my side, her forehead creased with concern and her hand under my shoulder.

"What is it?" she said in a voice sticky with sweetness. "What do you need?"

"The water closet," I said shortly. Any excuse would have done at that moment.

"Do you need help? Here, lean on me."

"No," I said and all but wrenched my arm from her grasp. "I'll be back in a minute."

A muscle in her jaw fluttered. "All right. I just want to be able to see you. In case you need anything." Her tone was consoling but her words made me bristle.

"Fine." If she really did control me somehow, this would be a good way to test my boundaries.

"And don't talk with anyone from the royal family," she said, cutting me with her glance. "You've had a hard time with that one, but we can try to salvage some of the situation."

"Yes," I said through my teeth and escaped through a side door into the hallway.

Nothing kept me from turning the corner to find the water closet. No intrusive thoughts convinced me to stay in Melissa's sight. But then she'd really only suggested that I stay nearby.

This section of the palace had been remodeled recently enough to include running water and spacious tiled rooms, and I took as long as I possibly could in the state of the art washrooms.

Finally when I couldn't justify spending any more time in there, I pushed through the door.

A young man stood propped against the opposite wall. He glanced at me and straightened up, like he'd been waiting.

I eyed him, and tried to edge down the hall, away from creepy men who lurked outside women's washrooms.

"Hello," he said, as if he hadn't noticed. He had a pleasant face and thick sandy-colored hair, but there wasn't much about him that was remarkable, except for his eyes. He had the Rannard eyes.

"You're Miss Hargrove, correct?" he said.

I opened my mouth to respond, forgetting Melissa's instructions for one important moment.

My throat closed, and I gagged on the words. No thoughts told me to stay silent, but my body sent a clear enough message. No talking to the royal family, Melissa had said.

"Are you all right?" His brow drew down in concern.

I shook my head and realized that answer would hardly get him to leave me alone, so I tried to smooth my expression and nodded.

He gave me a wary glance. "I'm Colin."

Prince Colin, Nik's younger brother. This was the one who was so clever. Nik had said he'd be Nik's chief counselor when he assumed the throne.

"I was hoping to catch you alone," he said. "My brother is quite taken with you, and I just wanted to make sure you felt the same."

Make sure? Was he threatening me? His face seemed open, studying me like a particularly interesting book.

"Do you love him? Or is it just fun to have the Crown Prince dangling after you? You don't strike me as that sort of flirt, but then I hardly know you. Nik's queen must be strong and dedicated, not flighty. Do you think you'd make a good ruler?"

I laughed in helpless confusion. How could I answer any of those questions? Yes I loved him, but that wouldn't make me a good queen. Strong and dedicated? I couldn't even fight my stepmother to control my own life.

Without thinking I opened my mouth to say something, I didn't even know what, but my throat tightened, cutting off the words. Cutting off my air.

I choked in desperation as I realized I couldn't breathe.

"What is it?" Colin asked.

The edges of my vision sparkled and heat made my skin prickle. Oh no—

Brilliant flashes of color and a wave of cold swallowed the thought that I couldn't have another fit. Not here in the palace. In front of Nik's brother.

My legs collapsed and the walls blurred into bright purple and gold.

When I opened my eyes Colin's white face floated above me. The stranglehold on my throat had released its grip and I could breathe again.

"God Almighty, Nik is going to kill me," Colin whispered. "Miss Hargrove? Miss Hargrove, please be all right."

Gone was the confident young man who had asked intelligent questions. He was replaced by this frightened boy.

"Your Highness, step back," another voice said. "Give her some room."

Colin's head snapped up, and he shuffled back far enough to allow Isol into my field of vision. She settled beside me, skirts ballooning around her. Her dark brows drew together with concern.

"What happened?" Colin asked, voice high with anxiety.

"She fell," Isol said simply. "It happens."

I closed my eyes. It was so much worse than that. I couldn't disobey Melissa. It was physically impossible. Almighty, I didn't even know how far the effect went. Last night, I'd tried to tell Nik about my father's death and my throat had closed. I'd thought it was my own fear, but if I'd tried harder, would the magic have killed me?

"What can I do?" Colin said.

"You can help her stand. Gently. It's easy to get light-headed."

With Isol under my injured arm and Colin under the other they levered me to my feet and set me upright once more. The walls still fuzzed around the edges, but I concentrated on breathing and they finally evened out.

"Thank you, Your Highness," Isol said. "I'll help her from here."

Colin looked like he was going to protest, but Isol sent him a haughty glare and he relinquished his hold on me.

Isol walked me down the hall, keeping her pace slow to match mine, but the moment we were around the corner, I pulled myself free from her support.

"Cindy," she started.

"No." Apparently I could still talk to members of my own family.

She looked taken aback.

"I don't— Unless you want to tell me what she's doing to me, I don't want to talk to you, all right?" The second fit had left me trembling with either nerves or whatever lasting effect it had, and I felt on the brink of tears. I couldn't deal with my mysterious stepsister right now.

She stayed silent, her lips pressed into a thin line, and I took that as her answer.

"Is she doing the same thing to you?" I asked. "Is she forcing you to help her?"

Her gaze flicked away from me. "It's complicated."

I shook my head, but I couldn't refute that. How much worse would Melissa's manipulations be if she was my real mother?

"You know she doesn't mean you any good," I said echoing her own words to me.

"And you don't know how far I've fallen," she said. "You can't save me."

I deliberately caught her eyes. "I know you helped set up the King's Mage."

She looked stricken. "Then...then why haven't I been arrested?"

"I defended you."

"Why?"

I shook my head, lips pressed together. She had her secrets and I had mine. Truth was, I'd felt sorry for her. I'd seen her trapped under her mother's power exactly as I was. But now I couldn't even be sure if I'd made the right choice. If I'd gotten Isol arrested, her mother likely would have followed, and I would have been free by now.

I hobbled off down the hall without looking over my shoulder to see if she followed.

I stared at the passing floor not really caring where I went as long as it felt like "away," but eventually my feet took me to the one place I'd felt joy in the palace.

By the time I looked up, the library stretched on either side of me, books upon books making me feel more welcome than any courtier ever had.

"Miss Hargrove?"

I turned to see Father Philip poking his head out from around a nearby shelf.

"Hello, Father," I said with relief.

"Let me find you a chair," he said. "I can pull one up wherever you like and you can read undisturbed."

"Oh, that sounds wonderful," I said. "But I don't know how long I can stay." Melissa might have sent Isol looking for me, but I imagined she'd be coming herself soon enough.

However, since I was here, I could do a little research.

"Do you know if there are any books on..." I wasn't even sure how to phrase it. "Control of thoughts."

He tilted his head. "Not here." He gestured at the millions of books around us. "Strangely enough, I have some in my personal collection, but they've always seemed so esoteric."

"So they're probably not very helpful anyway," I said, shoulders slumping.

"I wouldn't say that," Father Philip said. "But why do you ask? Are you feeling out of control?"

I opened my mouth and shut it again. Melissa's stricture

kept me from speaking to royalty. Would it strangle me again if I tried to tell Father Philip what was going on?

"No reason," I said. "I was just curious."

His steady gaze made me think he didn't buy my excuse.

"I will see what I can dig up," he said. "But you should know, no matter what happens, we are always in the Almighty's hands."

I winced. I'd forgotten I was talking to a holy man.

"Father, look at me," I said, gesturing awkwardly down at my twisted legs and cane. "Do I look like someone who has the Almighty's favor? I thought following Needsmeet made sense. I'd serve my god and He might find the time to look in on me every now and then. But I've been forgotten by my creator as surely as I've been disregarded by the world."

"Forgetting is a human fallacy," Father Philip said. "So is trying to earn something you've been given. You're not supposed to serve to gain the Almighty's grace and mercy. You serve because you already have the Almighty's grace and mercy. I dedicate my study for the same reason. I celebrate His goodness by studying the world He created."

"Why do you think I have His grace and mercy?" I said wearily.

"The Writings of Saint Aegis say, 'He knows us in the dark of the womb; before the world was formed he made us to be fearsome and beautiful in His sight.'" Father Philip tilted his head. "If He loved you so much before he made the world, do you think he would just forget about you while you walk through it?"

"It certainly seems like it," I said without rancor. "If he could have made me perfect, why didn't he?"

"You're assuming he didn't. What if what you see as flaws are the things that make you perfect for Him? What if those are the things that make you fearsome and beautiful?"

Fearsome. The word ricocheted through me, shining light in all the frightened anxious spaces of my heart. It made me think of some sort of battle angel, all wreathed in glorious wings and armor.

It wasn't an image I was used to associating with myself.

But neither was the cowering invalid that Melissa wanted me to be. And I already knew I was done with that.

If I could pick one or the other, wouldn't I rather be fearsome?

CHAPTER TWENTY-TWO

Nik barely paused on the palace steps to brush the dust from his riding boots before he strode into the Grand Foyer. The new bodyguard that trailed him was having a hard time keeping up. Just a couple minutes ago, the boy had gotten tangled in his stirrups and landed in a heap in the stable yard, making Nik miss Merrick all over again.

Nik sighed and slowed his pace to let the bodyguard regain his place behind his prince. But the moment the boy had caught up, Nik was off again, slapping a nondescript envelope against his trouser leg. He could have left the letter at the Hargrove house when he'd learned the family wasn't home, but he wanted to hand it to Cindy himself.

Actually, he wanted to say the words with all the inflection and feeling he had pent up, but he knew finding a minute alone with her would be next to impossible. So he'd written the letter. And agonized over every word.

He paused just outside the Receiving Parlor, wondering if he would have to search the palace wing by wing and room by room. Just as he thought maybe he should send his guard off in another direction so they could cover more ground, he heard a familiar voice coming from the hallway behind him.

"Honestly, Cindy," Melissa Hargrove was saying. "You only had to remember one thing. Stay in sight. It shouldn't have been that hard, even for you."

Nik turned to find Lady Hargrove striding down the hall, her daughters in tow. Behind her trailed a slight figure, hobbling to keep up with only one cane.

Even the sight of Melissa Hargrove couldn't douse the relief he felt when he saw Cindy. She didn't look well. Her limp seemed more pronounced, and she was paler than usual. But all he could focus on was her presence as he strode toward the Hargrove family.

Melissa saw him first and came to an abrupt halt.

"My lady," he said, giving her a winning smile. He was prepared to do whatever he had to do to get around the woman. "Leaving already?"

"Yes, I'm sorry. My stepdaughter is not well today." She gestured absently to Cindy, who glanced up at him once and then kept her gaze fixed to the floor in front of her.

Nik thought fast, hiding the envelope. "I'm sorry to hear that," he said, deftly folding it behind his back several times. "Especially as I've only just arrived. I didn't get a chance to greet you today."

He reached for Melissa's hand and brought it to his lips even though the gesture made him want to grimace. "My lady," he said simply. If he embellished at all, he was afraid she'd see right through him.

He straightened and turned to her closest daughter.

"Miss Anella," he said and repeated the process with her hand. "You look lovely today."

"Oh, Your Highness," she said and giggled.

He fought not to roll his eyes and turned to the next in line. "Miss Isol," he said and kissed her knuckles. "Are you well?"

"Tolerably, Your Highness," she said, then glanced at Cindy.

Nik finally faced his goal.

Her brown gaze didn't meet his at all, and he caught his breath in worry and disappointment.

"Miss Hargrove," he said, and he couldn't help it when his voice went rough. He took her fingers and raised them to his lips.

Her eyes flicked toward his in surprise as he pressed the folds of the envelope against her palm.

His grip tightened in triumph. "I hope you have a pleasant day," he said.

"Come along, girls," Melissa said, cutting him off. "Good day, Your Highness."

"My lady," he said, but they were already moving off toward the portico where a valet would run for their carriage. Cindy didn't even glance back at him, but Nik could imagine from the way she held her spine that she wanted to desperately.

Nik blew out his breath. It was done. He'd know soon enough.

When he turned, he found Colin leaning against the wall watching the Hargroves disappear around the far corner.

"What are you doing here?" Nik asked. "I thought you were supposed to be spending the day with Mother."

"I traded with Eriana," Colin said. "I wanted to be here."

Nik's eyes narrowed. "Why?" he said, suspicions floating through his head.

Colin avoided his gaze. "I wanted to meet your lady."

Nik made a frustrated noise in the back of his throat. "Colin, I told you not yet."

He crossed his arms, but he couldn't pretend he wasn't interested in the outcome. "What happened?"

Colin loved questions. Almost as much as he loved answers. But he met this one with hunched shoulders and a furtive look.

Alarm raced along Nik's nerves. He hadn't seen that look since they were little and Colin had broken a second era pink vase and blamed it on Eriana.

"What did you do?" He dropped his hands to his sides as they curled into fists and took a step toward Colin.

His brother flinched. "Nothing. I only wanted to protect you."

"How?"

"I just wanted to make sure she wasn't like all the others. Seducing you because she wanted a crown."

"Colin..." Nik resisted the urge to pull out his hair. His brother meant well but..."I had to hound her into even talking to me."

"I got that," Colin said. He looked at his hands, his brows drawn in consternation. "She laughed when I asked if I thought she'd make a good queen. Laughed until she fell over."

"You hurt her?" Nik wondered if he could black his brother's eye. He never had when they were kids but now he wished he'd been a little rougher.

"It was just a little fall. She didn't seem hurt. Just shaken."

"You're sure?"

Colin shifted his weight. "Her stepsister said she was fine. She seemed more subdued as they left, but I couldn't get close to check on her."

Nik paced to the other side of the hallway and back. "Colin, Cindy's spent her life believing she's powerless. She wouldn't even know how to go about seducing someone." Nik flushed when he realized what he was saying. "At least not intentionally. She's definitely seduced me by accident."

Colin looked thoughtful now. "I can see that," he said. "And I can see why you think that would make her a good queen. So has she said yes, yet?"

Nik glared at him.

Colin laughed. "That's a no."

"Do me a favor. Go stick your head in the river."

Colin laughed harder.

Melissa spent the ride home glaring at me, and Anella chattered on and on about how the Prince had singled her out for her beauty. When we pulled up in front of the townhouse, my stepfamily clambered out of the carriage. Melissa barked a short command for me to follow and keep myself to my room for the afternoon.

I climbed down after her, trembling with anger I could not vent.

I had no intention of ever following one of her orders again, but it looked like I'd lost the ability to refuse. My hands clenched and the crackle of paper disrupted the spiral of my thoughts.

The rest of the morning might have been a complete disaster, but I could hold tight to the memory that Prince Nikolas had gone down the line, greeting each woman in my family just so he could slip me a note.

I hurried upstairs as fast as I could and slipped into my room before anyone could interrupt. Heedless of my elegant hem, I plopped on the padded foot stool on my hearth. Ember flared up and burbled a greeting.

I replied absentmindedly as I unfolded the envelope and slipped out the letter inside.

Cindy,

I wanted to say these words to you in person, but it will be days before I have that chance, and I can't wait any longer. I won't wait any longer. I used to be a patient man, but somewhere along the way I've misplaced my tolerance for waiting. I need you to know these things now. Not later.

I love the way you make me laugh. I love your smile. I love looking at the curves of your face. I love the way you defend the people who can't speak up for themselves. I love that you belittle my arrogance and in the same breath make me feel a thousand feet tall. I love that I want to be a better prince, a better king, a better man because of you. Dare I say it?

I love you.

There. It's been said and I can't take it back. I won't.

I've been looking all this time for a woman to be my queen. Someone with the strength and skills to complement me on the throne. I assumed there was at least one woman in the world who would be perfect. I would consider myself lucky if she was someone I could tolerate. But I would not look for love. The likelihood of finding both was too low to contemplate.

But I have.

You see people, Cindy. You see them and you care about them. They talk to you and you listen. With kindness and patience and true compassion you help them. Valeria needs you. I need you.

Cindy Hargrove, will you be my wife? I am not asking as a prince. Only as a man. Will you be my partner?

Yours in waiting,

Nik

I stared at the words as they swam before my eyes. For a moment, I wondered if I was about to have another fit. Ember chittered at my agitation and tried to climb up my leg. I obligingly tilted the paper so she could see, and she stared at it, making coos of satisfaction. It was ridiculous since she couldn't read, but it gave me something to think about besides the impossibility before me.

He wanted me to be his wife.

He'd said as much in the meadow under the dancing phoenixes, but it had been easy to brush off his words as a joke when we'd both been a little tipsy with the moment.

This was something different. Something much more frightening.

This was a thought process laid out in writing. Not something said in one moment and regretted the next.

God Almighty, what was I supposed to do with this?

I stood with difficulty and rushed for the door. Grandmama's room was only two down and the door stood open. She was inside removing her shawl as if she'd just returned from her errands.

I'd forgotten for a moment that she'd even been out.

She saw me in the doorway and shook her head. "Nothing yet," she said. "I have yet to find the solution to our problems."

"Could this help?" I said and thrust the letter at her.

She took it, and I fidgeted impatiently while she read it and read it again. I bit my lip.

Finally she looked up at me, eyes serious and lips set in a small but genuine smile. "Congratulations."

She was happy for me, but I could tell from her expression there was much more than that and none of it was without complication. "But this doesn't solve all your problems. You are still having fits. There's still someone willing to accuse you of murder."

"It would solve one problem," I said. "It would get me out of this house and out from under Melissa's control."

She nodded cautiously. "It would be harder for her to hurt you, yes,"

"No, I mean she's actually controlling me, Grandmama. Even when I plan to disobey, and I've worked myself up to it, I can't. I either talk myself out of it, or..."

"Or?" she said, face white.

"Or I find myself a prisoner in my own body. Like my thoughts and actions are disconnected. Inside, I'm still myself but outside...outside I'm Melissa's good little stepdaughter." I couldn't connect the fits, yet. Maybe they were some sort of side effect when I tried to fight back.

"How long has this been going on?"

"I don't even know. I just noticed it for sure today. But I've been talking myself out of confronting her for —for weeks."

Grandmama's eyes widened then narrowed as if a thought had just occurred to her.

"What is it?" I said. "What have you thought of?"

"Political trouble, oddly enough. Nearly twenty years ago, Torraca was ruled by a corrupt Zultaan."

"The compulsion magic," I said, pieces falling into place. I'd been so distracted thinking Melissa was a blood mage, I'd overlooked the obvious. "Melissa told me her first husband was some sort of Torracan healer."

Grandmama snorted. "Sure he was. But if this is true, then I've been looking for a 'cure' in all the wrong places." She paced away and back again. "It doesn't change what you hold in your hand, though."

I bit my lip. She was right. Nik's offer still held a cupful of promise and a world of complications.

"What do I do?" I said.

"First you stop reacting like a wet firework, sending out confused sparks." She nodded at the letter. "He's done you a favor putting it on paper. You have time to think. You know your feelings best. It's your decision. No one can make it for you."

She swung her shawl back over her shoulders.

"Where are you going?" I asked. I'd hoped she would give me a straight course of action. I should have known better.

"To look in all the *right* places," she said. "Whatever you choose, you're going to need a cure. Badly."

I watched her go, resignation settling in my chest. There was nothing left to do but decide.

I walked back to my room, where Renny was waiting for me. She tsked at my distraction and turned me around to undo my buttons while Ember streaked across the carpet shaped like a glowing fiery cat. She climbed my skirt and up onto my shoulder where she curled around my neck in a comforting warm weight.

"What has you two so worked up?" Renny said, helping pull the court gown over my head, leaving me in my chemise and petticoats.

I brandished Nik's letter. "Nik's proposed."

She drew an awed breath. "Oh," she said. "Miss Cindy. That's wonderful."

"Yes, but now what?" I said.

"You answer him of course. Let me get Jason. He can run your reply over to the palace without Lady Hargrove knowing anything about it." She raced for the door in a bustle of skirts.

"Wait, Renny! I don't even—"

She was gone before I could say I didn't even know what my reply was going to be. She would only tell me I was being silly.

Prince Colin had asked me just earlier today if I thought I would make a good queen. I'd laughed, but now I had to actually answer his question for myself. Nik seemed to think so. And his reasons weren't...incorrect. But was caring about people really the foundation for ruling a country?

Nik had said to answer him as a man, but he evaluated everyone, including me, for their potential to rule beside him. He couldn't even ask someone to marry him as a man. There was always the Prince lurking underneath.

I reached for the dressing gown laid on the end of my bed and shoved my arms into its sleeves.

Grandmama had said I was the only one who knew my feelings, so maybe I should stop and examine them.

Did I love him? Yes. Was I willing to risk everything for him? Yes. Or at least I'd thought so until "everything" included a throne and a potential to ruin an entire country.

Nik had a habit of looking past the way I walked, but I couldn't decide anything without seeing my differences from every angle. Could someone like me be strong and respected?

A shaft of guilt cut through me. Was I being selfish by even considering his proposal? As Nik's queen we'd both have to overcome pity and revulsion every time someone looked my way.

My knees gave out, and I sank onto the dressing table chair. God Almighty, was I really going to say no?

I squeezed my eyes tight, ignoring the way they burned and started to water.

Someone tapped on my door and it opened.

"Miss Cindy?" Jason said quietly.

I blinked rapidly and cleared my throat. "Yes, Jason," I said.

"Renny said you had something you wanted taken to the palace."

My lips thinned and I looked away. "She was a little premature," I said. "I— I haven't..."

When I didn't finish, he stepped closer and closed the door behind him. "She told me what the Prince wrote," he said to the floor.

I glanced back at him and heat rose in my cheeks. He'd seen it from the very beginning, this choice I'd eventually have to make. "Then you know what I have to tell him," I said.

He shook his head. "I don't."

I tossed Nik's letter onto the dressing table but it missed and floated to the floor where it rested on the carpet. "I don't belong on the arm of a prince," I said. "That's what everyone will say."

He knelt to retrieve Nik's letter.

"They'll be dead wrong." He stood and turned the creased page over and over in his hand. "There's something I've wanted to tell you for days now, but I'm a coward of the lowest sort. Now's my only chance so I'll have to just say it, with no elegance and nothing to save me if it goes wrong."

His fingers clamped down on the letter as if to steady himself. "I've loved you forever, Miss Cindy."

I couldn't help sucking in a breath. Half of my mind was saying "two in one day when I'd expected none in my entire life?" The other half was saying "Jason. Jason? Jason!"

"I always thought..." I started to say but couldn't finish. "Why did you never say anything?"

He ran one hand through his hair in consternation. "I was...lazy. I thought I could take my time. I figured you would be there waiting for me. When the Prince started coming around for you, I realized you had a world full of choices and I was at the bottom of the list."

He finally looked up and met my eyes. "I looked at you and thought I was the only one who could love you. He looked at you and saw someone to grab and hold onto before someone else got her. I'm sorry for that. Because now, I think I've lost you."

I blinked. I didn't know what to say.

His mouth twisted. "I just wanted you to know that you deserve better than me. Sure, they'll say you don't belong on the arm of a prince. But that's not true. You're the daughter of Lord Hargrove, Viscount of Yarrow, and a noblewoman of Valeria. And you'll show it to them every day you walk beside him. You'll prove what nobility really means, and you'll prove you belong there." His voice was low and vehement, and he took another step so he could drop Nik's letter on the table in front of me.

I swallowed, trying to get rid of the lump in my throat, and a small part of me raged at him for all the wasted time and opportunity. If he had just said something, maybe...

No. While I cared for Jason as my childhood friend and playmate, my heart didn't flutter at his smile, and he wasn't the one who had ensnared my thoughts more surely than any book or story ever had.

I stood up and went to put my arms around him. He had been brave enough to tell me he loved me knowing he would be giving me up to another man. His words gave me the courage to write my own.

Father Philip had called me fearsome. And Jason had seen it, too.

"Thank you," I told him.

Later, Jason snuck out of the house with my answer. It was one word.

Yes.

CHAPTER TWENTY-THREE

Gilded letters arrived less than a week later inviting my stepfamily to the Sun Festival masquerade. The festival itself normally celebrated the return of the sun after every Darkness, but the royal family had combined it with a ball to honor Prince Nikolas's choice of bride. Anella made a point of mentioning every chance she got that the invitation had included hers and Melissa's and Isol's names but not mine.

I made a point of not mentioning that my invitation had been penned by the Prince himself and sent privately by way of the back gate.

"For how can I announce my bride-to-be if she's not there?" he'd said.

For five days I kept my head down in my room, hiding from Melissa. I just had to make it to the night of the ball without her issuing an order that would keep me home on the most important night of my life.

Grandmama made all my arrangements, and Renny went

to the fittings, since we were of a similar height and build. Jason smuggled the dress into the house late one night after everyone else was in bed.

The night of the masquerade, Melissa stopped by my room, hair immaculate and mask in hand. She was dressed as a black dragon, all shining satin and filmy gauze. Her mask sported glistening scales.

"I trust I don't have to repeat my instructions," she said.

My fingers clenched in the folds of my skirt as I prayed she wouldn't say anything more. "No," I said. "I know them all by now. Don't leave the house, don't speak to anyone, don't ruin your plans." Maybe if I spoke them, she wouldn't bother and the magic wouldn't take hold of me.

She eyed me. "That cheekiness will come back to bite you, Cindy."

I hated the sound of my nickname when it came from her lips. But I wasn't going to let her be the first one to use my real name. It was the last piece of myself that I could keep from her and I would guard it until the right moment.

I kept my lips tight on another cheeky response and prayed she would leave without any more orders.

She huffed and rolled her eyes, suddenly switching tactics. "You know I only want what's best for you, Cindy," she said, and reached out to tuck a wisp of hair behind my ear. I flinched away.

Her fingers pinched my chin even as she smiled.

I bit my tongue to keep from saying anything that would make her suspicious. I just needed her to leave.

When the door finally closed, Renny flew to help me get ready. That night, she pinned my hair up, allowing a few curls to cascade around my face. Over the last month it had gained luster, my face no longer had the pinched, starved look to it, and the rest of me had filled out with all the healthy meals and exercise my grandmother had insisted on.

Grandmama stood by to critique, but she could find no fault. She helped Renny throw the ball gown over my head without mussing my hair, and they laced me up.

Finally, Renny helped me to the mirror.

I straightened up, my chin rising with pride. My gown tumbled around me in shimmery pieces of iridescent blue and orange with a cape attached to my shoulders that draped in a skillfully crafted train. I did not ask how much it had cost, but whatever it was, Grandmama's seamstress had successfully recreated the female phoenix Nik and I had seen on our picnic. Ember raced up my skirt to my shoulders where she spread along my shoulder blades. She lifted the edges of the cape until it looked like I flew on wings of fire. I tied the blue feathered mask behind my head and stared back at the stranger in the mirror.

Renny stepped back. "You look beautiful, Miss Cindy," she said, voice hushed.

"You do," Grandmama said.

I shifted and felt my shoelace give way with an audible snap.

We laughed as Renny knelt to retie it. I couldn't wear the slippers that came with the dress since they didn't have the support I'd need at the palace. My worn boots with their wooden supports would have to do.

"These laces need replacing," Renny said. "They're

completely worn through. Think you'll be able to afford new ones when you're a princess?"

"Just don't put any extra strain on them tonight," Grandmama said.

"You're not getting ready?" I asked. She still wore a sturdy gray dress, the same one she'd worn to travel to the city.

She gave me a look full of regret. "I'm not coming."

"What?" I spun to face her in surprise.

She took my good hand. The other stayed tucked at my side, the wide sleeves of my dress hiding the plaster cast. "You may be betrothed to a prince, but you are still not free. Now that you will be safe under his protection, I'm going to find the counter to Melissa's magic."

"What part of that means you can't come tonight?"

"The answers lie in Torraca. No one here can help now that the ambassador has returned home. But I heard him speak of a friend, an expert in compulsion magic. If I can find him, bring him back...I leave tonight, in fact. If I miss my boat in two hours, I won't be able to go for another two weeks."

"I assumed you'd be with us for the announcement at midnight." I couldn't hide how disappointed I was.

My grandmother cupped my cheek. "You don't need me weighing you down," she said and flicked my flaming wings. "I'm so proud of you, Granddaughter."

Her voice got thick and she cleared her throat. "Now go," she said and pushed me gently toward the door. "I'm paying for that carriage by the hour."

I laughed so I wouldn't cry and hurried as fast I could downstairs where Jason sat on the box of a rented carriage.

I held my breath as I crossed the threshold, onto the street. Would Melissa's magic keep me from leaving? I'd said the words forbidding me to leave, not her, but would that really make a difference?

I walked to the carriage. Nothing took hold of my limbs. No doubts or unexplained thoughts crossed my mind to convince me to turn around.

I was free.

Jason hopped from the box and bowed formally before helping me in.

As he shut the door, I turned to glance at my home one last time. After tonight I wouldn't have to come back here anymore. I wouldn't have to hide every time I spoke to Nik or tiptoe around Melissa. I wouldn't have to worry anymore.

Renny stood on the doorstep with Grandmama and waved. I promised myself that when I had a minute after our betrothal, I would send for Renny. I would still need a maid and a friend I could trust, and I couldn't imagine leaving her behind.

I relaxed against the seat. All I had to do was make it to the palace. The moment Nik made his announcement I'd be under his protection. I wouldn't even have to talk to Melissa again if I didn't want to, and I'd be safe from her insidious instructions.

The short ride felt nerve-wrackingly long, and I spent it watching the scenery to keep myself from thinking of what I was about to do. The palace loomed large at the end of the street. Mage globes lit every window and garlands were strung across the facade. No one else lined the steps since I had arrived late. The carriage pulled up in front of the wide stairs, and Jason was there to help me up the steps. He paused at the doors to raise my hand to his lips.

"You're the most beautiful thing I've ever seen, my lady. I hope the Prince knows how lucky he is."

I took a moment to squeeze his hand. Then I turned to face the doors.

Two of the ServantGuard stood at attention, polished breastplates gleaming in the mage lights hanging above us. A majordomo waited with them to accept invitations. I took a deep breath and hobbled toward him.

He looked me up and down, noting the cane and my costume. His eyes widened when he saw Ember and my flaming wings.

Then he bowed. "Miss Hargrove," he said and opened the doors.

I hadn't expected to remain anonymous for long. My cane and the way I walked would give me away before anything else, but as long as I stayed away from Melissa I would be safe.

I took another deep breath, this one going all the way to my toes, and I straightened my shoulders.

Through the grand foyer I could see the throne room and the three open archways that led to the ballroom. That was the proper entrance, but I knew the palace well enough by now to know I could slip into the ballroom unnoticed if I used the door beside the kitchens.

A floating chandelier lit the ballroom, illuminating the dance floor while leaving the enormous windows in enough shadow to see the stars outside.

No one took note when I made my entrance. No fanfare played. There was no sudden silence heralding my presence.

Only one person noticed as I slipped quietly along the wall, my fingers gripping the head of my cane.

A hand took my arm as I passed in front of a window. "I've been waiting for you."

I glanced up at green eyes behind a blazing red and orange mask. For a split second it felt like I stared at a stranger, and then his mouth curved into a familiar grin and I recognized my prince.

He wore a burgundy waistcoat and jacket with bright slashes of orange and scarlet embroidery down the front and along his sleeves. A half cape was tied across his chest and draped over one shoulder, adorned with streaks of gauzy orange feathers with the occasional flash of blue.

He brought my hand to his lips, his gaze steady on my mask, and he kissed my palm. I swallowed, my throat bobbing convulsively.

He straightened, and I found my mouth dry. Too dry to speak. What was I supposed to say to this man I'd professed to love? All the words, everything of significance had been said with pen and ink, and now I could not put a voice to any of them.

"I find myself faltering when it comes to speaking face to face," he said as if reading my mind.

My breath hitched, and my heart skipped in my chest. What if the feelings weren't real if they couldn't be expressed in person?

He leaned closer and put his lips next to my ear. "I love you."

My knees weakened with relief, and I leaned heavily on his arm.

He chuckled. "That felt fantastic. I think I'll do it again. I love you. See, it's much easier now. It's your turn."

"I don't know, you're doing a pretty good job all by yourself."

"You mean you won't say it?" Real hurt passed through his eyes

I put my hand on the back of his neck and pulled him close. "I love you," I said against his lips.

I felt his grin against my mouth.

"Will you marry me?" he said.

"Yes."

He kissed me while we still stood in the shadows of the window, unnoticed and unremarked upon. It was a luxury I knew we wouldn't have for long, and I took advantage of it wholeheartedly.

At last he let me go, far enough that I could admire him again.

"I like your costume," I said.

He turned as if to show off his plumage. "Thank you. Your grandmother suggested it, oddly enough."

"Hmm, imagine that."

He craned his neck around me. "Hello, Ember."

She trilled a high happy sound and fluttered the edges of my cape.

Nik's gaze caught on something across the room and he sighed. "I made a promise I have to keep," he said.

"And what's that?"

He turned, took my cane in his right hand and tucked my arm in his left elbow. "Come with me."

I hesitated and he felt the tug on his arm.

"I just have to stay out of Melissa's way," I said.

His expression went tight and fierce. "We'll steer clear of her, of course. But she can't hurt you anymore."

He led me along the edge of the ballroom to a buffet table where a young woman seemed to be hiding behind a large ham. She was dressed as an ancient knight, complete with chainmail and surcoat over her gown, and a sword hung at her side. She wore her red-gold hair in a braided crown and carried a helm under her arm.

"Can I meet her now?" she asked as Nik and I approached.

"Only if you promise to stop skulking behind the appetizers. You look like a demented gopher."

She scowled at Nik and tried to beam at me at the same time, making Nik's description seem rather apt.

"Cindy, this is my sister, Princess Eriana. Eriana, Miss Cindy Hargrove."

I started to do my awkward curtsy thing.

"Oh, thank goodness," Princess Eriana said and plopped her helm on a tray of jelly tarts. "Colin would not stop bragging that he got to meet you and I still hadn't."

She didn't seem at all concerned with protocol so I straightened up using Nik's arm as leverage. "I had no idea there was a competition," I said.

"Oh don't worry, it wasn't that cutthroat," she said. "I just wanted to meet you so badly, you see. I'm so looking forward to having a sister."

"Why is that?" I said. My experience with my stepsisters had left me less than enthusiastic, but if Eriana was something to look forward to, I didn't mind expanding my definition of family.

"There are just so many things you can't do with brothers. Like talking about boys, or swords, or anything really."

Nik's face scrunched in affront. "You can't talk to me about swords?"

She patted his arm consolingly. "I can try. But you're kind of hopeless at them."

Nik raised his chin. "A gentleman these days learns to box."

"And I'm sure you're very good at it. But it doesn't really lend itself to a group costume, does it?" She turned back to me. "I wanted to dress us all as knights, but..." She cast a sly glance at my gown. "Clearly Nik had other plans. But it means I've been wandering around dressed as my favorite person and no one here has guessed it."

"You were the one who chose something so obscure," Nik said.

"Nonsense," I said. "Clearly she's Althaea the Wolf." I nodded at Eriana as her mouth dropped open. "The first female knight in Valeria. I recognize the surcoat from Erestan's biography." I mock-glared at Nik. "Shame on you for not knowing your history."

Eriana threw out her arms. "Yes, exactly." She gave her brother a smug look. "See? At least your fiancé has taste."

"My fiancé will probably have read more than Father Philip by the time we've been married a year." He grinned at me. "I'm not even going to try to keep up."

That was something I hadn't thought of as a perk to marrying Nik. Unlimited access to his library. Oh, what would I read first?

"Are you all right?" Nik said. "You look dazed."

"Miss Hargrove, you have to promise to come to my presentation," Eriana said as she grabbed a jelly tart out from under her helm.

I blinked at the abrupt change in subject. "Your presentation?"

"You have to be there. It's traditional for the newest member of the royal family to present the next. I only got to come tonight because of the announcement." She examined the tart from all sides and then stuffed it into her mouth.

"Well, if it's tradition..." I said, glancing at Nik. But he was staring at his sister with a pained look on his face.

Eriana made a noise around a mouthful of jelly tart. "Mother is beckoning," she said. "You make yourself scarce, I'll head her off."

She grabbed her helm, heedless of the stickiness, and strode away.

Nik gave me a dubious shrug. "Should I be apologizing?" he said.

"Why?" I said. "Because your sister has a personality? I shouldn't think so. I like her quite well."

He heaved an exaggerated sigh. "Oh good. Because you're pretty well stuck with her now."

A thrill of pleasure spiraled down my spine when I thought about the future. I threw back my head and breathed deep as I looked out the window at the stars.

"Are you enjoying yourself?" he said and twined his arms around my waist. "Because this party is for you."

I snorted. "And you."

We were starting to attract stares in our matching costumes. It wasn't immediately apparent he was the Prince, but the Valerian Dark Sun glinted out from under his half cloak. And I was recognizable enough as the sickly daughter of the Hargroves.

As I scanned the room my gaze snagged on an austere black figure in the midst of the bright gowns and colorful costumes. Melissa stood across the dance floor, facing me. I couldn't see her eyes behind her mask, but I knew from her posture she'd seen and recognized me.

My grip tightened on Nik's arm. As long as he didn't leave me and she kept her distance, I'd be safe.

"Are you all right?" he said.

"Fine." One little not-quite lie. After tonight I'd be free to tell him everything. He'd know the entire truth. And he'd know my name. He would be the first to use it since my mother died.

Nik glanced at the big gilded clock over the thrones and put his glass down to hold out his hand. "It's almost time for the announcement, but we have time for one dance."

I hesitated. It was one thing to dance with him under a pair of flaming phoenixes in the privacy of the necropolis. It was another to dance in front of all these staring people. But I had agreed to become his queen. My public life started now, and I might as well get used to it. Besides, I felt like I could do anything when Nik grinned at me like that.

I slid my hand into his and left my cane by the buffet

table. We stepped to the middle of the dance floor just as the musicians in the gallery above us began another number. Couples whirled around us, but Nik didn't seem to mind that I couldn't move that fast. He took my good hand in his and put his other on my waist and just like in the necropolis we moved together. He anticipated the way I swayed, and I stepped with him at half the time of the music.

He pulled me closer, and my breath caught. I wasn't used to standing this close to another person, but I leaned against him and trusted him to take my weight and make up for my weakness.

Over his arm, I saw Melissa standing at the edge of the dance floor.

I drew a surprised breath and turned my face away.

A breath against my cheek made me jump. "You feel ill, don't you, Cindy?"

Melissa's voice in my ear. I whipped my head around, but she still stood across the ballroom.

How could she talk to me? Some sort of spell? Or was it part of the magic that already had hold of me?

Nik's face fuzzed around the edges, and I blinked.

"No," I said, but couldn't even be sure the words made it to my mouth.

"Yes, you do. You feel ill."

I tried to draw breath but couldn't seem to get enough air. Colors swirled around us, gowns and capes and masks all reflected in the polished marble of the floor. My head felt thick and fuzzy. I turned my chin, but the world spun in the other direction.

Almighty, I was going to throw up.

Sparks crowded the edges of my vision. It was happening again. I was going to have a fit right in the middle of the dance floor.

We'd stopped and Nik was saying something, his voice heavy with concern, but I couldn't answer. I couldn't even concentrate on his words.

Ember shrieked in alarm. The light weight of her left my back and she snarled as she streaked across the dance floor toward Melissa. A blazing line in my blurry vision.

But she didn't get there. Anella stepped forward and dumped a goblet of liquid across her as she burned past her feet.

Ember squeaked and sputtered, and her flames died.

"Cindy!"

I flinched. I didn't want to hear that voice saying my name.

"Cindy." A cool hand cupped my cheek as I leaned over and tried to keep from barfing all over the marble. "You've overtaxed her, Your Highness. I knew this would happen. I tried to warn you."

I tried to push her hands away, but my limbs didn't want to obey me.

"Back away, Lady Hargrove. Your concern is not welcome." I'd never heard Nik's voice so cold.

"No. I tried to warn you. She'll become violent."

"Why should I believe you? All you've done is lie to us."

Melissa's cool hands braced my shoulders as she helped me straighten and she drew me toward her. "Who's lied to you, Your Highness? Have you asked Cindy why she's so secretive? Did she tell you what happened to her father?"

No. No, no, she wasn't supposed to be able to ruin this.

Her lips brushed my ear. "You're angry with me, aren't you? Fight back, Cindy."

A wave of unfamiliar rage swept through me, leaving burning heat in its wake. I had to stop her. My good hand clenched into a fist as the wave of heat rose again. Anger and fear churned until I didn't know what was real and what was searing emotion.

As if from a distance I heard an incoherent cry and realized even as I moved that it had come from me.

And I was no longer in control of myself.

CHAPTER TWENTY-FOUR

Sparks dashed across my vision, making a kaleidoscope of
lights and color.

I don't know how long I stayed in that blurry place before
I took a deep breath and found that I could at least control
that. Then I tried another. And another.

Gradually the sparks faded, and I realized I was
surrounded by screams. I blinked and squeezed my eyes shut,
willing them to work. Then I opened them on disaster.

Nik stood several feet away, behind a line of Servant-
Guard, their swords drawn and pointed at me. His mask had
been knocked away and a livid red mark marred his left
cheekbone. Blood trickled from his lip as a dreadful certainty
crept into his eyes.

Saints save me, what had I done? What had happened in
that split second I had lost my mind?

Courtiers surged away from us as if I was a madwoman
about to murder them all. Perhaps I was.

I looked at my bad arm. A smear of blood marred the end of my plaster cast.

"I've told you over and over again that she's sick, Your Highness," Melissa said. "I've never been able to control these murderous impulses of hers."

I tried to call out to him. I opened my mouth to plead with him. Help me, please. What's happening to me? But all that came out was a low moan, an animal sound that caused the courtiers around us to gasp.

Tears trailed down my heated cheeks, but I didn't even have enough control over myself to sob.

"The woman I love wouldn't hurt anyone," Nik said, voice rough.

"The woman you love kept plenty of secrets. This isn't even the worst one."

"No, she wouldn't lie. I trust her." He said the words, but he still stood behind a line of ServantGuard. He might as well have stood on the other side of the world.

"Did she tell you about this?" Melissa's inexorable logic damned me.

He jerked his gaze away from my face. I watched his expressive eyes change as he steeled himself, before he closed them entirely. "You should have told me," he whispered, but I could hear him across the hushed ballroom. "Why didn't you tell me?"

This isn't me, I tried to scream. No words, nothing of the truth made it through my lips. Just little gasps that made my chest heave.

Nik grimaced and turned away, as if he couldn't bear to look at me anymore.

"What's going on here?" King Julius's voice cut across the whispers of the courtiers until there was no more sound except my harsh breathing. Even the musicians had stopped playing.

I didn't care that the King was staring at me, his lips set in a grim line. All that mattered was Nik's broad back, retreating across the dance floor until he reached the rest of his family where they stood behind the King.

"There, there, Cindy," my stepmother said, wiping Nik's blood from my fingers with her handkerchief. Even now, she was gentle. The perfect nursemaid. "Now you will finally be useful," she whispered so only I could hear.

Panic raced through my veins, leaving ice in its wake. She had done this to me. She and whatever magic she held over my head. This was what she'd wanted all along. She was winning.

"Stop trying to fight it, cinder-mite. You'll only bring on a fit, and you already look terrible."

I hated the name so much. This whole time she'd been manipulating me, undermining me, and my nickname was just a way to remind me where I'd come from, how much power she held over my head.

"Lady Hargrove," the King's voice snapped out. "Explain this."

Melissa composed herself but not before I saw her small triumphant smile replaced with a remorseful pout. She was a born actress. She'd missed her calling on the stage. I struggled in my own mind as she turned to face the royal family, but my fingers didn't even twitch. For once my shaky legs betrayed me by not collapsing in terror.

"Your Majesty, I am so sorry," she said, voice ringing with false regret. "You can see my stepdaughter is not well."

While her back was turned, Ember crept across the marble floor, little half-hearted flames licking up only to flicker out. She reached my hem and hooked weak claws into the fabric.

The King looked me over. Behind him, Nik straightened his shoulders and turned, his face a polite mask, the bruise standing out stark on his cheek.

Melissa took my good hand in hers and stroked it. I tried to yank it from her grasp but failed. She could do anything while I stood here, a voiceless puppet.

"The excitement has been too much for her, I'm afraid. Before we traveled to court, I asked you for a decision, Your Majesty. Now I must ask that you make it, before anything worse happens."

The King's gaze flicked to Nik, whose stony countenance didn't budge. "I asked my son to look into the matter."

My rage battered ineffectually at the walls of my invisible prison. Just moments ago I was engaged to that very same son, I wanted to shout. Don't believe her lies!

I felt Ember haul herself up my skirt, but I couldn't even reach to help her.

Melissa bowed her head as if acquiescing, but her words were stern. "Yes, your majesty. But we are out of time. In his will, my lord left everything to his daughter. Title, lands, and the Blood Bond to you yourself," she said. "But you can clearly see she is not fit to manage any of those. In fact, I believe these responsibilities and the stress of life at court make her condition worse."

My eyes flickered shut, and I closed my lips on a groan that threatened to escape. Father had left the title to me specifically, in a way Melissa couldn't circumvent. The dresses, the presentation at court, the manipulation, it had all been a charade to steal my inheritance.

A sudden rush of grief and regret made me remember my father's face. If he'd really wanted to care for me, why had there been all those years of silence and exile?

"I'll admit the girl is suspect. This violence is criminal, especially against the Crown Prince, but one isolated incident does not revoke all her rights."

"Unfortunately, this is not the only time she's attacked someone, Your Majesty." She ducked her head as if embarrassed. "Two months ago she was taken in a fit that killed her own father."

Nik's face crumpled.

No, I shrieked inside my head. I did not, there's no proof!

"We found her sobbing over his dead body, obviously remorseful but just as obviously guilty. I was too lenient and now my husband is dead, killed by his own daughter who was too sick to know the difference."

The tears glittering in her eyes were real, but I knew the remorse was an act.

"You knew she had this tendency and yet you saw fit to expose my court, my family, to her?" King Julius's voice lashed through the room like a whip.

"You'll remember, Your Majesty, you requested her presence. So you could make your own judgment. I'd hoped court would socialize her," Melissa said. "I thought it might anchor her to reality. As soon as I realized my mistake, I tried to keep her away from anyone she might harm. But Prince Nikolas continued to visit her, pulling her further and further off balance."

The King turned his sad, judgmental gaze on me. "What have you to say for yourself, Cindy Hargrove?"

My name is not Cindy, I yelled, but it came out a menacing hiss that made the courtiers around us gasp and back away. I realized I was just proving her story and clamped my teeth shut on the noise.

"Your Majesty, she has become overwrought. I beg you forgive her for causing a scene and let me take her home."

"There is just the small matter of your husband's will," the King said.

Melissa paused as if she'd forgotten. "I ask only that I may keep her safe with us, closely guarded so she cannot harm herself or others."

"And the title and wealth that would have been hers would serve you well to keep her comfortable," the King said. Then he glanced at Nik. "My son is the one who knows the most about this case. Nikolas, what is your opinion? Is the girl incapable? Could she have a husband, a family, a life?"

At least the King was giving his son the chance to refute everything that had been said. He must know that I was Nik's intended bride.

I raised my head and looked at the man I loved with all my heart and willed him to know what was in my mind, not what was being staged before him. When my eyes met his, my heart caved in.

Nik's green gaze held love and remorse. And an implacable resolve that disregarded everything that his heart told him. He glanced at his father and shook his head. My entire world fell apart with just that one gesture.

"Very well. Cindy Hargrove is declared unfit. Her titles and property go to the Widow Hargrove, who is declared Viscountess of Yarrow in her own right and guardian of her stepdaughter. Her permanent status will be determined at her trial, which we'll set for a later date."

Even if I could have spoken at that moment I wouldn't have. I had nothing to say, and the man who had the most reason to come to my defense stood mute. In a single gesture he had crushed every moment we had spent together. The self-respect I had fought for, everything I had attempted to build with him, had ended in fiery disillusionment. He had proved that under all the interest, all the affection, I was just as unworthy of love and trust as I had been when I'd sat in the ashes of the fireplace.

Except, for a few brief days, I had felt what it was like to be someone worthwhile, and I knew I deserved better. I had been tricked into accepting less my whole life. Now, instead of acceptance, my face flushed in anger, a very different anger than what had overwhelmed me minutes ago.

This felt like it belonged to me.

My hand clenched and I realized I could control my limbs once again. My mouth was still out of reach but my fingers at least obeyed me.

"Thank you, Your Majesty," my stepmother said. "I will take Cindy home. She is not well."

No, I wasn't well, and when she gestured for Isol to help me out to the hall, I knew I couldn't leave here without fighting what had been done to me. For years, my pride had been buried under the contempt of others, the soot of the fire-place, and the neglect of the father who should have loved me most. But Nik had started to uncover it, and now my pride bled and demanded justice. Words had been taken from me so I mustered all the strength I could to fight whatever spell she had me under and planted my feet. Isol didn't expect the resistance, and when I followed it by flinging her hands off, she stumbled back.

With a savage cry I went for Melissa, fingers curled into claws. She'd wanted a violent stepdaughter and now she had one.

I bit and scratched and grabbed her fading golden hair. She shrieked, and it was extremely satisfying to note the terror in her voice. I had her. But then she kicked at my legs, and I collapsed.

The ServantGuard was slower now that it wasn't the Prince I was after, but finally hands pulled at us. I didn't care. I just wanted to go knowing I'd fought back.

Someone grabbed my feet, and I felt the laces on my shoe snap. Then Melissa's leg struck out and pain exploded in my half-healed arm. I cried out and hunched over in agony.

"Guards, control her," I heard the King say. "You can't overcome one crippled girl-child?"

Strong hands pulled me upright and held me fast.

Melissa staggered to her feet, breathless, with four scratches along her cheek and neck. A savage satisfaction raged through me at having left my mark.

"Take her to one of the cells. She's obviously dangerous in this state," the King said.

"No!" Panic laced my stepmother's voice. "No. She

should come home with us. A familiar place with familiar people will calm her down. She'll only remain in this state if you keep her here. Let me take her and nurse her back to health."

She had to know whatever she'd done to me was wearing off and she didn't want me anywhere near the King when it did. Because I was going to tell him everything.

The King had the guards carry me out to avoid any more scenes. I had one last glimpse towards the royal family while I was being carried out. Nik still stood there, his face averted in pain.

CHAPTER TWENTY-FIVE

The ServantGuard were nice enough to drop me on the townhouse doorstep into Melissa's loving care.

She helped me upstairs as the staff crowded the doorways to gawk. Word must have gotten back about my "breakdown" already. I blamed Anella.

Whatever foul spell Melissa had used to steal my voice and body had worn off on the way home, but I was still shaky and didn't trust myself at all. Once inside my room, Melissa dumped me at the dressing table, and I slumped, clutching my broken arm to my chest.

My display in the ballroom proved only one thing.

I was powerless. With Nik and the King against me and Grandmama out of the country, I had no one to protect me from Melissa anymore. And I had nothing left to fight back with.

Melissa made a show of smoothing my luminous skirt, now torn and smudged from our scuffle, before she smirked and patted my cheek.

"There you are now. Don't you feel better?" she crooned.

"What did you do to me?" I said. I couldn't even muster the energy to snap at her as exhaustion dragged at me.

She gave me a sweet sympathetic look. "I made you useful," she said. "Of course, I no longer need your cooperation. So things will be much simpler from now on."

She opened the satchel she always carried and drew out a slim knife, which winked in the light of the gas lamps.

I shrank back.

"Calm down," she said and grabbed my uninjured arm. "I'd give you something for the pain but that seems pointless at this juncture."

I tried to jerk away, but her fingers clenched and she held fast. She nicked the skin of my wrist and carefully held an empty vial to catch my blood as it dripped.

A few drops slid down the inside of the glass before she pulled it away and held it up to the light. "It was a mistake to not complete my control from the beginning. I need you. But I don't need your mind. Don't worry, the future queen's sick relative will always be taken care of."

Future queen? Was this all really just a bid to put Anella on the throne?

She handed me a handkerchief. "Keep pressure on the wound until it closes. I don't want you bleeding to death on me."

I had a mind to do that just to spite her, but I found myself obeying once again. And Melissa sailed out of my room knowing I would follow her instructions.

I couldn't stop shivering as the bright red stain crept slowly across the white linen I held to my wrist. I'd thought that if I'd stayed away from her, I'd be safe. But with my blood she could do whatever she wanted to me. She'd used it to control me.

She'd used it to ruin my reputation and steal my title and my future.

I covered my face with my good hand while shuddering breaths made my whole body shake.

Ember finally crept out from the folds of my dress and I scooped her up to cradle her against my chest. Her flames were still subdued but she had enough strength to grip my fingers with her small claws.

I didn't hear the door open but suddenly Renny was there, kneeling at my feet.

"Miss Cindy, what happened?" she asked quietly.

I sniffled and drew my hand away, taking some deep breaths.

"It's done," I said, my voice thin as a whisper. "Melissa's won."

"Miss Anella said you went mad. Started tearing apart the ballroom."

"Not mad," I said with hopeless conviction. "Spelled. She did something to me. Made me act that way. I couldn't control myself. But I could see everything. I could watch it all fall apart and do nothing to stop it."

Renny saw my seeping wrist and took it gently in her hands. With deft fingers she bandaged the cut to stop the bleeding.

I stared at the red staining the white cloth. "Now Melissa has what she wants, she'll keep me spelled for the rest of my life. That way I can watch as she takes everything else from me."

I choked on a sob and covered my mouth as tears escaped to leak down my cheeks. Maybe it wouldn't be so bad. Maybe Melissa would keep me locked up in the house so I wouldn't have to watch as Anella seduced the man I loved.

"It's all right, Miss Cindy," Renny was saying. "It's all right. We won't let any of that happen. We...we'll think of something."

She helped me to my feet and quietly and efficiently stripped off my ruined ball gown before dressing me in my nightgown and tucking me into bed. She put Ember in the fire so she could recover.

The whole time Renny murmured soothing words, things that sounded calm and purposeful.

When she left, a muffled command made its way through the door, and I recognized Melissa's voice ordering Renny to lock me in. The latch clicked.

I lay under the covers, still and silent. I wanted to cry, but I couldn't even though my throat was tight and aching. My future had looked so different this morning. But after all Nik's talk about changing the way the world saw me, he'd proved the same thing my father had when he'd written me out of his life. I wasn't worth loving. It was too hard and they didn't want to bother.

I sat up, restless, and climbed out of bed. My stool still sat beside the fire, and I sat by the banked coals, scrunching my toes in the ashes. I wrapped my unbroken arm around myself and leaned closer to the coals, looking for that sense of well-being I'd always felt here before. This was where I belonged.

Then why did it feel cold and uncomfortable?

I sat up. The fireplace didn't feel like my home anymore. And if I was honest with myself, it hadn't since the morning Father had called me to the roof. The morning he'd died and Melissa had taken over my life.

I frowned. What had really happened on the roof?

Ember had shown me what she'd seen that day but maybe I'd missed something there in the cellar. If I'd had some kind of fit, it had been manufactured like all the other fits I'd had since.

By Melissa.

"Ember," I said.

The fire sprite crept from the glowing coals.

"What happened the morning my father died?"

She chirped a question. Her voice was stronger now.

"I know I've seen it already. I want to see it again."

Ember murmured as she circled the hearthstones and finally sat. Her body faded, leaving only the wispy flames which stretched and danced before forming pictures, clear as sight even if they were transparent.

I seemed to be looking past a few wisps of hair and a giant ear at a figure standing at the edge of a roof. This was Ember's perspective. She'd hidden under my braid that morning.

Father spoke but the pictures were only pictures. Nothing but the shape of his words could tell me what he said. But I remembered this. He was saying something about how his thoughts were too thick. That he couldn't make sense of anything in the house.

Then I'd felt thick and hazy, too.

Father's face grew alarmed and he stepped forward. As he came the world began to sway and suddenly the ear was on the ground and my vision was covered with more hair.

That was the moment I'd fallen. Ember pushed herself out from under my braid to see Father kneeling beside me, holding my head. It gave me a moment of vertigo to see my face from someone else's perspective.

Father stroked my cheek, talking silently. Around us, sugared pastries lay on the roof.

The light caught on a gold pin on his lapel, a flower caught under glass.

I leaned forward, trying to read his lips. I couldn't hear his words, but now that I was paying attention, I recognized the shape of Ember's name.

I'd assumed he'd scared her away. I'd assumed she'd hidden herself. But now I concentrated on his words, desperate to make them out. They were the last things he'd ever said.

"Burn it out," it looked like he was saying. "Ember, burn it out, now."

Then the light flared before plunging into blackness.

Eventually the dark image faded back into the orange of the crackling fire and Ember coalesced out of the flames.

I sat silent for a long moment tallying up all the details I'd seen, trying to fit the pieces together. Ember climbed my leg and sat warming my hands, but she didn't make any of her usual noises.

My father had asked Ember to burn. And I remembered lying on the roof as fire warred with the darkness inside me.

"The pastries," I said. "They were poisoned." I'd

discounted the thought before because I hadn't died. But Melissa had insisted I eat one, and Father had taken one before he'd started talking to me. Melissa was an accomplished herbalist as well as whatever magic she practiced. Poisoning us wouldn't have been difficult.

"And you...you burned it out of me," I said. "He asked you to."

She laid her head against my thumb.

"Who paid the price?" It was a rhetorical question. A fire sprite burned out impurities, in body and mind. If I wasn't conscious to tell her who I was, there was only one other person who could have.

He'd been trying to protect me. And I'd bet all of my stolen lands and title that he had known who he was protecting me from. He'd been trying to tell me, he'd been warning me that his thoughts weren't his own.

Melissa had had her hooks in him from the beginning.

The day he'd married my stepmother was the day he'd sent me to the kitchen and told me he never wanted to see me again.

He'd been trying to protect me then, too. It wasn't until Melissa noticed me in the foyer of the manor that everything had gone downhill.

This whole time I'd thought he'd abandoned me. I'd thought he hated me. But what else could it be besides love? When he'd felt his thoughts sliding away, when he'd realized he was losing control over his life, he'd done what he could to save me from the same fate.

My cheeks were wet, and I scrubbed at the tears.

And I'd ruined everything he'd tried to do for me. I had trusted Melissa. I hadn't fought for myself or for him, and now I was feeling the same loss of control. I had no way to tell which thoughts were mine and which belonged to the compulsion magic.

I stood shakily and lifted Ember to my shoulder.

Then I stepped out of the ashes and limped to the window. Outside the palace glowed, but I wasn't looking at the intricate facade. Below my window the roof sloped out over the kitchen and creeper vines grew along the shingles and up the brick.

I'd been wrong about my father. He hadn't taught me I wasn't worth loving. He'd taught me I was worth protecting. He'd left me a viscountess, until Melissa stole the title.

And Grandmama had forced me to respect myself.

Even Nik had wanted to make me a princess until he'd thought I was a murderer.

But none of them could fight for me. They were either dead or out of reach. Which meant I had to fight for myself.

If Melissa needed my blood to control me, then I just had to take my blood out of her reach. Far enough that I could learn how to defend myself from her.

I dressed in the simplest gown I owned, packed some extra underwear and my books in a carpetbag, and tossed the bag and my crutch out the window. I happily left the jeweled canes behind, and I went barefoot since I'd lost one of my shoes when the lace broke. Then I climbed carefully onto the windowsill while Ember clung to my braid. At least Melissa hadn't ordered me to stay in my room, because I would have obeyed her like a dog. She probably never thought someone like me would even consider climbing down the roof.

As I ducked under the sash my necklace swung free and glinted in the firelight. I looked down at Melissa's gift. I'd been so gullible to believe she wanted me to remember my mother.

The pin on my father's lapel had glinted in the light, a flower preserved under glass. He'd been under her control, too.

I'd worn the necklace night and day since she'd given it to me. And since then I'd talked myself into obedience.

I turned the glass bauble over in my hand. On the back a rust red thumbprint marred the silver setting. My blood?

I yanked the chain over my head and tossed the necklace into the fireplace. Let it burn.

Then I slid down the shingles feeling lighter than a crippled murderess with a broken arm had any right to be. I went slowly trying to be quiet, and when I got to the edge I said a prayer. The ground was only one story down and I went over the side, prepared to land in a painful heap.

A pair of strong arms caught me and I squeaked.

I fought my way free and someone set me on my feet before I could fall. Ember flared up, weakly, sending a brief flickering light across a familiar face with light eyes and dark hair.

"Merrick," I gasped, clutching my chest. "What are you doing here?"

"I have been keeping watch over you since I was discharged," he said, his voice a low rumble in the alley.

"Keeping watch?" I frowned. "Why?"

"I told you, you saved my honor."

I winced. "Merrick, I'm disgraced. I don't think you want to be around me anymore. Do you even know what they've accused me of?"

"Is your honor undamaged, Miss Hargrove?"

I remembered how he'd described his honor while he'd stood outside the back gate. He'd told me the difference between what people thought and what you knew about yourself.

"My honor is undamaged," I said. I'd done nothing to break it.

"Then what they say does not matter to me. I told you, you own my service now. Wherever you go, I will follow."

I blinked. Then decided to take him at his word. There was no one else I could trust right now, and I was starting to understand Merrick as well as myself.

I nodded. "I have to get out of the city," I said.

Merrick straightened. "Yes, miss." He bent to retrieve the carpetbag and my crutch, which had fallen to the cobbles nearby.

I led the way out of the alley without a backward look while Ember clung to my braid and Merrick followed behind.

I knew what it was like to be valued, and I went to find a place to be valued again.

Nik stood against the frame of one of the massive windows

lining the ballroom. The musicians had gone home, the lights had all been doused, and the guests had long since departed disappointed.

He'd heard the whispers as they left.

The Prince had not made his announcement. But who could blame him after that scene with the Hargroves.

Nik closed his eyes and knocked his head against the stone behind him. He'd imagined the night so differently.

Slowly he straightened and walked out onto the gleaming dance floor to the exact spot where Cindy had stood crying. Incoherent with confusion and madness. The mind he loved so much gone in those moments, leaving nothing behind but violence.

He squeezed his eyes shut and took a deep calming breath. But the calm didn't come. He couldn't help imagining every little thing he could have done differently.

Except he was the Crown Prince. And his path had been set before he'd even met the woman who loved to read, and laugh, and cared so deeply for people.

In a moment of helpless anger, he reached up and tore the Valerian Dark Sun from its ribbon and tossed the silver emblem away, where it skittered into a corner.

If he'd been anyone else, he could have made a different choice. Anyone besides a prince could have married the woman he loved, madness or no madness, and promised to care for her forever.

But a prince couldn't marry a murderer. No matter what the circumstances.

And Nik was a prince before he was a man. Before he was anything.

A dark object lay on the gleaming marble, and alone in the empty ballroom, Nik knelt and picked it up.

It was a shoe. A shoe with wooden supports for the ankle. Its laces were torn, and its toe was scuffed. Nik held it to his chest and rocked.

CHAPTER TWENTY-SIX

Snow swirled in the gray twilight as Nik's horse trotted into the stable yard, and he directed it to the waiting hands. He kicked his foot free and jumped down into the manufactured warmth of the stables. Half a dozen mages worked just to keep the precious horses warm in the winter.

He brushed the snow off of his shoulders as his body-guard slid to the ground behind him. The new boy was doing much better now. At least he'd kept up for most of this trip.

Nik had fully intended to keep in touch with Merrick, but the stoic ex-bodyguard had disappeared four months ago, about the same time that—

Nik cut off the thought before it could form fully and stab him with memory.

That's why he'd been traveling for the last four months. So he wouldn't have to remember every time he turned around.

He gave his horse one last pat and started toward the

stairs that led up into the palace. He didn't even wait to get inside before he stripped off his gloves.

A figure stepped toward him from the last stall, a shawl wrapped around her thin shoulders.

"Eriana," Nik said. "What are you doing out here? It's snowing."

"Waiting for you." Her pale fingers shifted on the edge of her shawl. "We knew you were due sometime today."

He swept her into his arms. "I missed you, too, but you could have waited inside." He paused a moment, dreading the question that hadn't been answered before he left. But Nik had been brought up to do his duty whatever the cost, so he braced himself and asked, "Has Grandfather made his decision yet? Who am I to marry?"

Since he hadn't made his announcement at the ball, his grandfather's ultimatum had gone into effect and by now, Nik was ready to face the consequences. He wouldn't pretend to like it. But he would face it.

He leaned back and realized her face was twisted with its own kind of dread.

"What's wrong?" he said immediately, his heart sinking into his boots. "Is it Mother? Or Father?"

She shook her head. "They're fine. But Grandfather has taken a turn for the worse."

Nik pulled away with a sigh. "He's always saying that."

Her green eyes sparkled with unshed tears. "No, Nik. This isn't like usual. It's really bad this time."

His brow furrowed as his breath came quicker. The Disciple of Calahan was really sick? Saints defend him, if the old man died, Nik would be king. Now, today. Not in some nebulous future.

He swallowed. "You're serious."

"The caretakers don't know how much time he has."

Nik slapped his gloves against his thigh and then started for the stairs. "I'll go right now," he said.

Eriana rushed to follow him. "Nik, there are preparations to be made. Your coronation—"

"Can wait. Eriana, this could be my last chance to see him."

He sped up as she stopped walking.

"I know," she whispered behind him.

His bodyguard kept up as Nik raced up the stairs of the Guard's Tower to the spelled cupola on the roof.

The mage on duty must have correctly interpreted the look on his face because the man didn't make him wait for the ritual words before opening the portal and ushering Nik through.

Nik stepped across the threshold, felt the moving platform effect under his feet, and shook off the vertigo on the other side in order to stride down the window-lined bridge. The new bodyguard retched behind him, but Nik didn't pause.

Outside the windowed bridge, snow blew in curls and waves, obscuring the mountains that were less than a stone's throw away.

The big library at the end of the hall stood empty and silent, one lone caretaker standing at the wall as if to guard the place.

"Where is he?" Nik asked as the caretaker opened his mouth.

The man pursed his lips and pointed toward the Disciple's private chambers.

Nik pushed past the curtain to find the Disciple lying in his bed, his wan face turned toward the door as if he'd been expecting his grandson any moment.

"Grandfather," Nik said and knelt beside the bed. Three caretakers waited at a respectful distance. Nik would have kicked them all out but for once it looked like the old man needed all the help he could get.

The Disciple lifted a tremulous hand. Nik took it in his palm and waited, but the Disciple didn't say anything. For the first time since Nik could remember his grandfather couldn't muster the strength to comment.

"What is it?" Nik asked one of the caretakers. "What's wrong with him?"

The man shook his head. "A wasting sickness. It started a couple months ago, and has gotten steadily worse since. The best healers have been here to see him, but they all say they can't find anything to treat. In the end it looks like exhaustion is what will...what will..."

"Kill him," another voice said, and Nik looked up to see Colin enter the room.

Nik's brother stepped up to the other side of the bed and laid his hand on their grandfather's shoulder. The old man closed his eyes in as near to contentment as he could get and his breathing evened out in sleep.

"I know you wanted to say goodbye," Colin said. "But

you should get back now. There is too much to do. To prepare. I'll send word if...if anything happens."

Nik bowed his head under the weight of it all. This wasn't supposed to happen yet. He was supposed to have more time.

He was supposed to have someone by his side. Now he understood why the Disciple had been so adamant he marry soon. He'd never felt lonelier than right now.

He took a shuddering breath and drew his hand away from his grandfather's. He was a prince. And that meant he couldn't have what he wanted. He only got what was given to him.

Nik stood and squared his shoulders before he turned to face his responsibilities.

Nik stumbled back through the portal to the palace and didn't even wait to change out of his travel-stained clothes before seeking out one of his parents. He found his mother first in her room getting dressed for dinner.

"Nik," she said and drew him into a hug despite her elaborate state gown.

Nik took a moment to breathe in her perfume, rose and lavender, and let himself pretend for a moment that he was only six and the worst thing that had happened was he'd skinned his knee. Reality intruded all too soon.

Queen Terese pulled back and smiled, but despite her warm greeting, her eyes were serious. "You've heard?"

He dropped his gaze to the thick carpet under his boots. "I saw."

She drew in a deep breath and straightened her shoulders. "Then you know what we have to do. Your father is meeting with his councilors now to prepare them for a smooth transition. He expects you to join him as soon as you can, but I imagine you can change first. I've started planning your coronation, but I'm sure you will want some input. You can speak to my steward about the arrangements."

Nik swallowed, fighting back his growing panic, and clasped his hands behind his back. He could at least look like he was ready to be king even if he didn't feel like it.

"And there is one more thing."

Nik braced himself.

"Your wedding. Naturally it would be nice to get it out of the way before the coronation, but because of the timing I imagine you'll want something smaller, more subdued."

His jaw ached as his teeth clenched. "And who am I marrying? Since Grandfather can't pick and I..." *Mucked it up.*

Queen Terese kept her composure aside from the slight tightening around her mouth. "Your father and I will be choosing your bride," she said. "But we will gladly take any input you have. If you have strong feelings either way."

Nik did have strong feelings, but he doubted he'd be able to put them into words. The biggest one was regret.

"Very wise, Your Majesty," a familiar voice said.

Nik stiffened as Lady Melissa Hargrove stepped out of his mother's dressing room carrying an herbalist's satchel.

"Nik, you remember Lady Hargrove," his mother said. "She's my personal healer now."

The woman who'd smashed his fragile illusions four months ago gave him a benevolent nod and a deep curtsy.

Nik couldn't do anything besides stare.

Three faint scars traced down the Viscountess's face and neck, the only visible mark left by an angry young woman who'd lost all control over herself. Lady Hargrove's expression remained serene even as he nodded stiffly. She showed no reaction and didn't mention or reference his actions that day four months ago.

The worst part was that he couldn't blame her for any of it. Now that he knew the truth he could look back and see she'd done what any worried stepmother would have done. He couldn't even link her to Christoph's framing.

In the last four months Nik had spent all his time traveling to check on Rannard interests around the country, including Christoph and Lainey. They'd leaked information on their whereabouts just like they'd planned and no one had even made a half-hearted attempt on the King's Mage's life. For now, it looked like he'd been declared a blood mage for nothing. All on the false suspicions of one misunderstood young woman.

Yes, Lady Hargrove had lied and she'd kept secrets. But so had Cindy.

He swallowed.

Now that he'd thought her name he couldn't help but remember her face, her words, her actions in a cascade of memories, some beautiful and some ugly. And Nik realized this was how he would always have to remember her, with a mix of the good and the bad. He couldn't remember their time dancing under the phoenixes without remembering the way their dance at the ball had ended. He couldn't remember her face without remembering how it had contorted with rage and incoherence. He couldn't remember how much he loved her without remembering that he could never have her.

"Excuse me," Nik said, a little stiffly, but both women nodded in understanding, and he fled his mother's rooms.

When had his mother invited Lady Hargrove into such an intimate position in her household? With Cindy discredited, the Viscountess was free to take whatever honors were thrown her way, but Nik still couldn't look at her without a flood of embarrassment and grief.

He felt like he'd been gone years instead of months. Between Lady Hargrove's rise to his mother's side and the Disciple's imminent death and Nik's coronation, everything in his life had changed in the last few hours.

Saints, what was happening to him?

He raced down the stairs hoping to find some peace. At the bottom in the small alcove where the stairs ended and large glass-paned double doors led out into the gardens he heard a noise he hadn't expected. A sniffle and a hiccup.

He stopped, one foot still on the last step and turned to find the source.

Night had fallen and no one had come through this corner of the palace yet to light the lamps, making it even darker under the stairs.

When his eyes adjusted he finally found Anella, her hair the only point of brightness in the shadows. She hugged herself, arms crossing her chest, and she gasped like she was running a race.

Alarmed, Nik stepped off the last stair and into the shadows. He'd readily admit that he detested Anella, but she looked like she was in such pain. And whatever lies Cindy had fed him, she'd also taught him to stop and help when he could.

"Miss Anella?" he said.

At the sound of his voice her hands dropped, her shoulders straightened, and she stopped hiccupping. She swiped at her cheeks with a quick hand but from her posture he couldn't tell anything had been wrong. He'd always thought of Cindy as reserved, but in this moment Anella seemed just as accomplished at hiding her feelings.

He dug in his pocket and handed her his handkerchief.

She took the square of linen and dabbed her eyes, but she wouldn't look at him. Finally she handed it back. "Thank you," she said.

"Are you all right?" he said quietly.

She didn't answer for a minute and he almost turned to go, but then she looked up.

"Do you know what it's like living with an ambitious parent?"

He opened his mouth, but she laughed and went on. "Of course not. Your parents are already the highest they could possibly be."

He closed his mouth, thought, then said, "Your mother is certainly making herself invaluable to the crown."

"Sometimes I feel like she doesn't really see me. The real

me. I'm just a tool to whatever end she has in mind. It doesn't matter what I want, only what she wants."

Nik tugged at his collar. "I know what you mean." He'd never thought he'd say those words to Anella of all people, but there they were.

"My mother would like you to marry me," she said.

Nik stiffened as a wave of anger and regret coursed through him. He could tell himself he understood everything Melissa had done but the thought of the Viscountess arranging her way into his life made his skin crawl.

"But what do you want?" Nik said, trying to follow her line of thought.

She turned her head so she was staring out at the snow swirling through the gardens. "To be safe," she said.

A familiar stab of pain made him gasp. "That's all Cindy wanted, too."

She glanced at him and he winced. He hadn't meant to say it out loud but she'd caught him off guard.

Anella stared at her hands and Nik shuffled his feet.

"You still love her, don't you?" Anella said.

Nik didn't answer. What could he say? Yes, but I can't marry a murderer?

Anella drew something that glinted out of the reticule beside her and stared at it in the palm of her hand. "Cindy wanted you to have this, but you were away. And then just now, I was thinking you'd forgotten all about her already and maybe it would be better for her if you did."

She tilted her palm so he could see the pendant lying against her skin.

A sprig of yellow and green lady's mantle lying forever

332 | KENDRA MERRITT

blooming under a dome of glass backed with silver. He recognized the necklace immediately and his gut clenched again. Would he ever be able to think of her without wanting to hit something?

"But maybe it's as hard for you to forget her as it is for her to forget you," Anella said, her eyes on the necklace.

"How is she?" Nik said quietly, allowing himself this one thought, this one question before he knew he would have to shove all the emotion back inside himself and be a prince again.

"She's not doing well," she said. "I won't lie to you. The ball was a huge blow and she's been ill most of the time since. But I think she's turned a corner. She wanted to apologize. She...she wishes she'd told you the truth."

Nik swallowed and looked down. He couldn't look at another woman while his heart dwelt on the one he couldn't have.

In a rustle of skirts, Anella stood. She stepped close to him and reached to clasp the chain around his neck. He let her.

"You should have this," she said. "You don't have to forget about her, just because you can't have her. I know she doesn't forget you."

He could only nod.

Her fingers smoothed the chain where it rested against his collar. The gold and glass didn't glint the way he remembered, as if it had been dulled somehow.

It hung where the Dark Sun had always hung, before he'd tossed it away the night of the ball. He hadn't worn the symbol of his status since. Cindy's necklace seemed like a fitting replacement.

The traitorous part of his heart that never listened to his head leapt and thought maybe she forgave him for the part he'd played in her humiliation. It could be her way of saying she wouldn't mind seeing him again.

He tried to shake the thought. Meeting would be too painful for both of them after everything they'd shared together.

But it would give him the chance to explain. She hadn't been coherent enough at the ball for him to tell her his decision and there'd been too many onlookers to wait for a private moment. If he went to her now, he could apologize. He could tell her he still loved her. He could tell her it wasn't her fault.

And he could hear her forgive him.

CHAPTER TWENTY-SEVEN

With the preparations for the coronation and the transfer of his father's power to him, he didn't find another free moment for several days. By then Nik decided that if something was important he was just going to have to make time. So he slipped out of the palace between a meeting with the Monarch's Council and a meeting with the Council of Ruling Dukes and dragged his bodyguard into the city.

The new bodyguard held his horse while he climbed the steps to the Hargrove townhouse and knocked. It felt odd to walk up openly like this. He didn't have to sneak to the back door or worry about the neighbors reporting his visit.

Footsteps echoed inside and he took a deep breath. In just a few moments he would see her. In just a few moments he would know without a doubt how she felt about him after everything that had happened at the ball.

He wished he hadn't been so quick to knock.

The door opened and a butler ushered him inside with a correct bow.

"Your Highness, we weren't expecting you," Lady Hargrove said, sweeping into the hall, her wide skirts making her seem like she was floating.

Nik swallowed down the nervous panic. "It was a last minute opening," he said. "I was hoping to see Ci— Miss Hargrove. I wanted to speak with her. To say goodbye." For the final time. No matter how she felt about him, whether she hated him or understood his decision, he would not have the luxury of visiting a former fiancé once he was married.

His parents had not given him their decision on his future bride yet. But he knew it couldn't be far off if they wanted him to marry before the coronation. The Disciple still clung to life but he'd not been lucid for days. Nik was running out of time.

Lady Hargrove's eyes softened and she reached out to touch the back of his hand in sympathy. "Of course. I understand. Let me see if she will come down. She has kept to her room mostly since the incident."

Nik waited in the hall, slush melting off his boots, trembling with a strange mix of hope and helplessness. What was he doing here? The only thing he would accomplish was torturing himself and Cindy. After the ball he hadn't even wanted to think her name but now he was standing in her house.

Were they really calling it "the incident"?

A noise at the top of the steps made him straighten and his heart sped up. But it was Lady Hargrove returning, her eyes sad and her mouth pulled into an unhappy line.

"I'm sorry, Your Highness," she said as she reached the last step. "I can't convince her to come down. To tell you the truth, I think she's too embarrassed. She believes she humiliated herself irreparably in your eyes."

"I see," he said because he couldn't think of anything else to say.

She gave him an apologetic grimace. "She spends most of her time nowadays reading, which isn't a terrible hardship. Maybe some day she'll be ready to see you again."

He nodded, but if Cindy wasn't ready to see him after four months, he doubted she'd be ready to see him after six, eight, or even a year.

"I won't tell you to forget each other," Lady Hargrove said as she ushered him toward the door. "I know how hard it can be to shake a first love. But know that she is safe and taken care of here. Even if you can't be together, that should make you feel better."

Something in her words soothed the ache inside him and made a tiny spark of well-being light up. The first he'd felt since the ball. Unbidden, an image popped into his head of golden hair and dark exotic eyes. Copper skin against his fingers.

But then he found himself standing on the front step with the door closed behind him and he blinked in consternation. Cindy's eyes were brown, not black, and her skin was cream with hints of rose. The golden hair and exotic features belonged to Anella, but why would he be thinking of her?

Nik turned and frowned up at the facade at the house. Windows stared at him like judgmental eyes, and he thought he caught a hint of movement at one of the curtains and a delicate face pulled away too quickly.

He looked back down at his boots, a scowl pulling at his

features. None of this was his fault. If she'd only told him what was going on, they could have avoided the whole mess. But now she wouldn't even see him to let him explain.

He stomped down the steps, past his bodyguard. He didn't mount up but strode along the street, letting the physical exertion distract his body while his mind ran in unsatisfied circles. He hadn't realized how much he wanted closure. Last week he'd assumed he'd go on forever resolutely not thinking of her or what had happened.

But now his discontent had multiplied and he felt like he was living with a glass shard in his chest that stabbed him no matter which way he turned.

At the end of the row of townhouses Nik turned to head back toward the palace and nearly ran into a young woman carrying two laden baskets of laundry.

Without thinking he reached out to steady her. "Here, let me help," he said. And took one of the baskets. Behind him his bodyguard gasped in shock but Nik ignored him. He had two hands, why shouldn't he help?

The young woman looked up with a grateful smile but when she saw his face, she gasped and jerked back.

The band of unhappiness around his chest tightened.

This was Cindy's maid. Renny? He thought her name was Renny.

They stood awkwardly for a moment before he cleared his throat. "This way?" he said jerking his head at the alley that led to the back of the Hargrove townhouse.

She shook herself, then nodded and led the way through the narrow passage between back walls. The bodyguard made a noise of distress when he realized he couldn't follow and hold the horses at the same time. Nik ignored him while the young man dithered and finally decided to tie the horses at the mouth of the alley so he could follow his prince.

Nik followed Renny to the gate where he'd kissed Cindy and he fought down the memories while she unlocked it.

"Thank you, Your Highness," Renny said. "Someone is coming to help me get it downstairs so you can just—"

The gate scraped open with a screech, and Nik looked up to see Cindy's footman, Jason, standing in the opening. The young man's eyes narrowed when he saw the Prince and his mouth twisted in a snarl.

"You," he said, then launched himself at Nik.

The footman's fist connected with his jaw, snapping Nik's head back, and he stumbled into the wall.

His bodyguard yelled and threw himself between the footman and the Prince, but he needn't have bothered. Renny was already hauling Jason back, swearing like a wharf rat.

"What do you think you're doing?" she whispered furiously. "Hitting royalty. You're going to get yourself killed."

Nik levered himself off the wall and touched his lip. He'd bitten straight through it and bright blood colored his fingers.

Nik spat and glared at his bodyguard, who had started to draw his sword. "Stay out of this."

The footman should consider himself lucky. If Merrick had still been around, he'd have been dead before his blow landed. Nik could forgive the young man his slowness this once. He didn't really want to see Jason dead.

Maybe banged up a little, but not dead.

"What the hell was that for?" he said.

Jason glowered and tried to surge forward, but Renny

held him back. "I gave her up so you could have her," he said. "And you threw it all away. You destroyed her."

Nik winced and then rallied. "She didn't tell me she was a murderer. Even if it was an accident, I couldn't marry her after that."

Jason threw off Renny's clutching hands and crowded Nik against the wall. Nik stood straight against the assault. "There's no proof," Jason said. "There was no conviction. You just said she was unfit and that was that. You let Lady Hargrove win."

Nik pushed Jason out of the way and ran a hand through his already mussed hair. "There will be a trial once there's time. I thought it would be better if it was quiet. But the Disciple of Calahan is ill, so it will have to wait."

Jason stepped back a pace as Renny stared at him.

"You'll be king soon," Renny said.

Nik's teeth creaked as he ground them together. "Yes," he said shortly.

She and Jason exchanged a glance.

"Then you'll be the one Miss Cindy can appeal to," Jason said

Nik shifted his feet. "Technically," he said.

"As the King you'll be the final source of justice for any Valerian, noble or common," Renny said.

"I already made my decision," Nik replied, his chest hurting. "Don't ask me to do it again."

Jason's scowl twisted. "You made it wrong. So we damn well will ask you to do it again."

"You weren't there," Nik said, voice harsh with pain. "You didn't see her attack me and her family."

"What you saw was surely strange," Renny said. "But it wasn't Cindy. Jason's known her his entire life and he's never seen her attack anything."

"Then how do you explain her actions at the ball? She didn't just attack, she drew blood."

"Miss Cindy said she was spelled."

Nik hesitated. "She what?"

Renny clasped her hands before her. "She said Melissa did something to her. She could see and hear everything, but she couldn't control herself. She could only watch as everything fell apart."

He shook his head. "It sounds like something any murderer would say."

Jason poked him hard in the chest. "She's not a murderer."

"Then what happened to her father?"

They both went quiet.

"He fell off the roof," Jason finally said. "Cindy was the only one who saw it."

"Lady Hargrove said everyone would believe she killed him," Renny said. "So she had to pretend to be quiet and sick and incapable of murder."

"And then Lady Hargrove accused her anyway." Nik's brow furrowed and he started to chew his lip before wincing in pain.

Then he shook his head. He was self-aware enough to know he was grasping at straws because he wanted to believe what they told him.

"None of this is proof," he said. "You're asking me to trust someone who lied to me."

"Everyone lies," Jason said with another glower. "Your job is to decide who has a good reason and trust them anyway."

"If this is all true, why wouldn't Cindy tell me herself?" Nik threw his hand out to gesture up at the house. "I came to talk to her and she refused to see me. She had her stepmother throw me out like some sort of criminal."

Renny straightened and threw a startled look at Jason who looked just as alarmed.

"Miss Cindy isn't here," Renny said slowly.

Nik shook his head in confusion. "Did Lady Hargrove install her somewhere else? Somewhere more comfortable?"

"Miss Cindy ran away the night of the ball," Renny said. "In the morning I found the window open and she and Ember were gone."

"She's not in the city at all," Jason said. "Lady Hargrove isn't the only one who's looked."

Nik jerked, shock and worry and confusion all warring inside him. He looked up at the gently sloped roof, imagining a slight blonde figure navigating the shingles with a broken arm.

"Why...why would she run?" he asked, more to himself than anything. "If she was innocent, all she had to do was stay put until she had a chance to speak at her trial."

"Maybe she didn't believe you'd listen to her," Jason said.

Renny gave him a quelling look. "She was in a bad way after the ball," she said. "She was frightened. Not of what had happened to her, but of Lady Hargrove. She said now that the Viscountess had what she wanted she didn't need

Miss Cindy's cooperation anymore. I think Miss Cindy thought she might kill her. Or something worse."

It still sounded like a fairytale. But the pieces didn't quite fit together, and Nik was starting to realize there were gaps in the story that didn't make sense if Cindy really was a murderer.

Lady Hargrove seemed to loom over it all. She hadn't told him Cindy was gone. She'd pretended she was still upstairs in hiding. Why wouldn't Lady Hargrove ask the crown for assistance? If she really cared about Cindy, why wouldn't she get some help in tracking down her sick stepdaughter?

Unless she already had what she wanted. Like Cindy's title, lands, and wealth. Like her place in the court. And the trust of the King and Queen.

How long before she suggested to them that Nik should marry Anella?

And with the one witness to Lord Hargrove's murder out of the way, there was no one to fight for Cindy's innocence. Because the only other person who had a reason to fight for her had betrayed her.

A strange sort of calm swept over him. He'd not only betrayed the woman he loved, he'd utterly convinced her she had no other choice but to flee. Either from him or from her stepmother, it didn't matter. He'd wanted to come here to explain how much he still loved her, how conflicted he was. But he was too late. Four months too late. He hadn't trusted her, so she hadn't trusted him.

The damage was done.

Now all he could do was try to fix it.

Jason might have been right about her believing he

wouldn't listen. But the footman had been wrong about trust. Not everyone lied. Cindy had never lied to him. She'd hidden herself, she'd protected herself, she'd made him promise not to ask. But she hadn't lied.

You had to choose who to trust in life, and that trust had to go the whole way.

Nik paced to the gate and back.

"We have to find her," he said, and turned to face the two servants. "Will you help me?"

"Of course," Renny said without hesitation.

But Jason frowned. "How do you propose to find her?" he said. "Lady Hargrove has tried, you know. She's not in the city."

"We'll need help from a friend. I know someone who's very good at this sort of thing. He's in hiding himself right now, but he'll come if I ask."

"And what then?" Jason asked. He tapped his foot and held the Prince's gaze.

"We prove she's innocent," Nik said with vehemence.

CHAPTER TWENTY-EIGHT

I placed the last volume of Ballaslavian poetry on the shelf next to its fellows and caressed the spines of the books. Late afternoon light streamed through the window of the library and illuminated the dancing specks of dust I had raised with my movements. The smell of leather, paper, and ink seeped into me and melted the tension from my neck and shoulders. This felt more like home than any fireplace ever had.

Ember burbled from a nearby candle flame as she danced and twisted in the sunlight.

"Here you are, Miss Hargrove," Father Philip said, coming into view around a bookshelf. "I finally found that volume I was telling you about. It was misfiled in my office."

"I told you I could catalog those for you," I said with a grin. "Make sure everything you've squirreled away is accounted for so we can find it again."

Father Philip looked sheepish. "Well, I don't really like

anyone moving my piles, but you're so careful, I might as well let you keep track of everything for me."

I took the leather-bound volume he held and weighed it in my hand. "Do you want this one back anytime soon?"

He closed his palms over the backs of my hands where I held the book. "Your research right now is more important than mine. Keep it until you're done." His intent gaze held mine for a moment and I nodded solemnly.

"Thank you."

"Oh, and Merrick was looking for you." He stepped back, breaking the mood with a grin. "He said something about you being late for a lesson."

I glanced at the big grandfather clock at the end of the library. "Oh Saints, I forgot. I'll have to leave this for later."

Father Philip chuckled as I grabbed my crutch and hurried out of the Refuge library. Ember jumped from candle to candle to follow me.

I passed a couple of Disciples in the hall who all smiled at me and nodded, murmuring, "Miss Hargrove." The Refuge of Saint Wonderment, two days outside Namerre, served as a sanctuary of study and scholarship for those who wanted to worship the Almighty through research. People like Sister Claudia who studied the migratory patterns of Valerian song-birds. Or Brother Mathieu who was compiling the history of Namerre's sewers. None of them paid much attention to things outside their areas of expertise, making it the perfect place to hide.

Only Father Philip and Merrick knew where I'd come from and what I'd been accused of. To the others I was just the newest librarian, studying the compulsion magic that had leaked out of Torraca nearly twenty years ago.

The Refuge House formed two sides of a square opposite the stables with the stable yard occupying the center space. Patches of snow left slushy puddles on the gravel and dirt as they melted in the winter sun. Merrick stood, arms folded across his chest, a placid pony lipping the brown weeds beside his boots.

I limped across the open space, avoiding the puddles. Father Philip had commissioned the local cobbler to make me a new pair of shoes since I'd shown up on his doorstep barefoot, and I didn't want to get them wet and ruin the leather so soon.

"You're late," he said. "I hoped maybe you'd rethought this scheme of yours."

"Nope," I said with a grin. "I still want to learn to ride."

Merrick's scowl deepened and I suppressed a laugh. Now that I knew him so well, his scowls were as comforting as a smile from anyone else.

"Don't see why. I'll drive you anywhere you want."

I laid my hand on his arm. Someone who didn't know him would miss the way his gaze softened.

"I know," I said. "And I appreciate your devotion, but I really want to learn."

Because it only added to my independence. And because it had been important to someone I still loved. Even if I had to love him from a distance.

"It's a new challenge," I said. "Grandmama taught me I have to challenge myself in order to grow."

"Just so long as you know it's going to be hard at first. It requires a lot of leg control and yours might not be up to the task."

I tried not to grin. Trust Merrick to not pull his punches and to grumble through anything that I might find hard.

He needn't have worried. I wasn't looking for a miracle. But even if my legs didn't work very well, that didn't mean I had to hobble around and never try anything new. I could learn what worked for me. If I couldn't do something the normal way, I could find a way around it.

He helped me into the pony's saddle with a bunch of grumbling on his part and huffing on mine.

"We'll work on mounting later," he said, almost out of breath by the time I was settled.

He was gruff and terse, but he led me around the stable yard and the puddles with a gentle hand and he patiently reminded me every two minutes to keep my legs tight and my heels down in the stirrups. I knew I wasn't supposed to clutch the pony's mane, but I kept losing my balance and grabbing anything to keep myself upright.

Through the aches and the hard work, I kept telling myself that learning this would make it so I could go anywhere I wanted. I'd never be stuck relying on a carriage or some other rider's generosity again.

By the time Merrick declared a halt to the lesson, sweat stung my eyes and my legs trembled, but I knew that with some practice I would eventually be able to stay in the saddle. Who knew if I'd ever enjoy it as much as...well, as much as some people. But at least I'd have the chance to find out.

I hid how much my legs wobbled as I left Merrick in the stable yard. He'd agreed to another lesson tomorrow, and I didn't want him to rethink his decision, but I was glad the rest of my activities for the day could be done sitting down.

I must not have hidden it very well because Merrick stopped me at the door of the Refuge House.

"Here." He thrust a small bottle of thick ointment into my hands. "For your legs. Rub it into the muscles that hurt tonight. It'll help."

I opened my mouth to thank him but he cut me off with a small bow with his hand over his heart.

I shook my head at his formality and limped up the stairs.

I'd set up my own study in the far corner of the library. One of the large stained glass windows depicting Wonderment's canonization made an alcove sheltering a desk. Blue and orange and purple light spilled over the desktop where several books decorated with multiple bookmarks waited in a stack. When Ember leaped up to the nearby lamp, clear yellow light illuminated my space.

Out of sight of my bossy bodyguard, I plopped into my chair with a groan and massaged my calves through my gown.

Then I noticed a small misshapen package sitting on the volume I'd borrowed from Father Philip. I gasped when I recognized the handwriting and tore open the brown paper wrapping.

Along with my studies, I'd spent the winter trying to track down my grandmother. Any correspondence from her would have gone to the townhouse, and she didn't know what had happened at the ball.

I'd briefly thought about joining her in Torraca to study compulsion magic at its source, but I knew Melissa was still looking for me, and with the law on her side, the Viscountess would have had no trouble finding me if I'd tried to purchase passage on a ship legally.

But it seemed like one of my many letters had finally found its mark.

Out of the package I pulled two vials of murky liquid and a rumpled letter.

Granddaughter, the letter read. *I'm returning to Valeria for you. I never would have left if I'd thought Melissa would get the better of us yet again. I know you think you're safe where you are, but I won't be satisfied until we can plan your defense together.*

As for the compulsion magic, my search here has yielded the same results as yours.

In my original letter I'd laid out everything I'd learned so far, detailing the way Torraca used magic to squeeze as much power out of plants as possible, conserving the *vytl* energy that was so sparse in the desert.

The obvious use was in teas, tinctures, and lotions, spells that could be applied directly outside and inside the body. The less obvious technique preserved certain plants and the spells they powered under glass. The amulet or pendant stored a spell which worked over time.

Like the necklace Melissa had given me.

All of this was perfectly admirable and hardly any different than when we'd developed magecraft after all the enchanters had died out during the Time of Blood and Hope.

But once a person's blood was added to the mix, the spell became linked to them on a deeper, more insidious level. Teas became potent, personal poisons, and amulets reached deep into a person's thoughts. They would doubt their own convictions and accept someone else's.

And thus, compulsion magic had been born.

Every time I'd fought, every time I'd thought to myself "this time I'll refuse," the spell she'd tricked me into wearing would take hold of my thoughts and convince me I wanted to obey my stepmother.

Blood magic was brutish and primitive in comparison. It only removed a person's life, not their convictions.

I couldn't even be sure when it had started. Not when she'd given me the necklace. At least I didn't think it had been right away, otherwise I wouldn't have been able to even speak to Nik, or sneak out of the house.

But maybe after I'd broken my arm. When I'd openly defied her and she could no longer manipulate me into cooperating.

I went back to the letter.

Since this magic was developed here, I have found several ways to protect oneself. The one that I've included seems to be the most useful. This potion negates magic entirely. Drink it and no magic will be able to touch you. Inside or out. It is very effective, but it only works for a short time since it's made without magic. So timing is everything.

Only take it if you are in immediate danger. But do not fail to do so.

I don't know if you've come across this information as well, but my sources have warned me so I will warn you. There is a difference between a spell you wear and a spell you ingest. Something about magic in the bloodstream. The necklace she gave you was not a permanent spell. By removing it you removed her influence over you. However, if Melissa gives you a compulsion spell that you have to drink, that spell will take a permanent hold. You must take the antidote immediately or she will control you for the rest of your life.

Carry the antidote with you. Protect yourself. If you fall under her spell before I get there, I will never forgive myself.

Stay safe, Granddaughter. I will see you soon.

I clutched the vials of antidote, my knuckles going white. Melissa had a way to make her control permanent. She'd said it was a mistake not to complete her control before. Was this what she'd meant? She must have been learning how to make the spell permanent.

I remembered watching myself do things that weren't me, say things I hadn't meant, and I trembled.

But I'd escaped. She could never bespell me again as long as she couldn't find me.

I just had to stay here, away from the capital. And that wouldn't be hard. I had no intention of leaving the Refuge again. I had everything I wanted here. Friends and a purpose and even Grandmama once she got here. What did it matter if the man I loved still believed I was a violent murderer?

That was where I was content to leave it.

But none of my research or Grandmama's letter explained why Melissa had stolen my title along with my will.

If she just wanted to put Anella on the throne, she could have slipped Nik a compulsion spell anytime we were at court. She was crafty enough to get me to tie my own noose around my neck. I'm sure she could have managed with him.

That was why I'd asked Father Philip for the old book on Valerian nobility. What was it about my title that Melissa needed?

I turned to the table of contents and ran my finger down the text.

Land Division.
Inheritance.
Chain of Fealty.
Rannard Blood Bond.

My finger stopped, a cold suspicion making my stomach drop. Could that be what she was after?

Something had been destabilizing the Blood Bond. We'd assumed it was a blood mage. But what if it had been something else? A type of magic we hadn't seen before in Valeria?

I flipped to the chapter heading and scanned the pages, looking for...

There.

Every noble of Valeria is connected to the Rannards through the Blood Bond, forged when their blood was combined during Erestan the Gentle's rule. And therefore, every noble is responsible for responding when the monarch calls for aid in times of strife. Nobles can send the monarch their strength, their energy, and even sometimes their magic, if the noble is also a mage.

The power in this Bond can only be released by a spell, presented to the noble when they come of age or assume the full responsibility of their title.

I sat back, the edge of the desk cutting into my palms.

My blood was part of the Blood Bond, but I'd been declared unfit. No one had ever given me a spell to access the Bond and no one ever would now. But all my titles and responsibilities had passed to Melissa. And I had to assume that included the spell to access the Bond.

I didn't have to close my eyes to imagine Melissa leaning over me with the knife telling me, "I need you, but I don't need your mind."

She'd taken my blood the night I'd escaped. I'd assumed it was to renew the spell keeping me under control. But what if it had been for something else, some deeper purpose?

Who else could she affect through the Blood Bond?

Nik. His siblings. The King and Queen.

And one other.

I gasped as I realized where the Rannard family tree ended.

The Disciple of Calahan. The one who was supposed to choose Nik's bride. The one whose death determined when Nik would inherit. The one who was kept isolated because of his importance to the Valerian throne.

If he died before he could name Nik's wife, Nik would be made king. With Anella beside him as queen.

Could Melissa poison the Disciple through the Blood Bond? Was that possible? I flipped through the section again, looking for details.

Of course it didn't say anything about killing the royal family.

I tapped my teeth. Who else could I ask? Who else could I trust?

There was only one other person who even knew what I was researching, and I'd already trusted him with my safety.

I went to Father Philip. I stood in the door of his study, clutching the books that had led to my discovery. "What do you know about the Rannard Blood Bond?"

He blinked at me. "What on Térne..."

I explained.

He looked at my notes. He looked through my books. I waited while he double-checked my logic, my experience, and my proof.

Finally he sat back, his fingers steepled in front of his mouth. "It's not a lot to go on," he said.

"I know."

"I don't know enough about the Blood Bond to be able to say whether she can use it to affect the Disciple but…"

"But?" I said.

"Rumor is, the Disciple of Calahan is sick," Father Philip said. "And preparations for Prince Nikolas's coronation are underway."

My hands clenched on my skirt.

"Then Nik's as good as dead," I said the same moment the realization struck me.

"That's a little melodramatic."

I shook my head. "If she kills the Disciple, what's to stop her from killing Nik so Anella can rule alone?"

Father Philip remained silent for a long while, and I worried he didn't believe me. He didn't believe what Melissa was capable of.

"We have no proof," he said. "We won't get anyone to listen to our accusations without solid evidence."

"We don't need to get anyone to listen. All we have to do is stop her, right?"

His eyes met mine. "You're not serious? Miss Hargrove, you can't go back there. You know what might happen."

I took a deep breath. I knew better than he did. If Melissa caught me, forced me to drink a compulsion spell, I'd lose my free will forever. "I know. But you said it yourself. No one will listen. Not even to you. But I can get into the townhouse. I can destroy the blood she took from me. That way she can't touch Nik or the Disciple."

He held my gaze. "Are you sure?" he said, and I knew he

wasn't asking if I was sure I could do what I said. He was asking if I was sure I wanted to risk myself.

But this wasn't just my future I was deciding. It was Nik's future. Valeria's future. I might have been content to stay here, hidden away from Melissa's machinations, but Nik was the one in danger. I couldn't wait for Grandmama to help. If the Disciple was sick now, Melissa could kill him tomorrow.

I would have to go back to Namerre, where I was known as a murderous madwoman. To save a man who had betrayed me.

In the end, it was an easy decision.

Nik tapped the frame of the carriage with his fingers. He jiggled his leg against the seat. He crossed and uncrossed his arms. Nothing worked to relieve the irritating need to act that had settled under his skin. He wished he could have ridden his horse but one didn't show up at the Chapel of the Almighty on SanctDay sweaty and smelling like an animal.

His siblings eyed him suspiciously from the other side of the carriage, but he ignored them.

They could have just given their SanctDay Pledges at the palace chapel, but Nik had wanted to get away from the constant cloying presence of Melissa Hargrove. He couldn't trust himself to hold his tongue around her anymore and it wouldn't help Cindy to reveal everything he knew.

And he hoped the travel would help with the jitters.

It wasn't working.

"Have you heard from Christoph and Lainey yet?" Colin asked, eying him.

"No," Nik said, far too loud, and Colin and Eriana winced. As Colin hinted, that was the real problem with him. He couldn't go after Cindy until he had a mage to help and Christoph wasn't answering his letters. The blood magic charges were still active, so Nik didn't expect Christoph to risk his life to return. But Christoph would be able to tell him which mage to hire and trust with Cindy's story.

But the man had disappeared.

"The ServantGuard I sent to keep watch over them said they moved unexpectedly a couple weeks ago," he said.

"And he didn't have enough sense to follow them?" Eriana said.

Nik jerked his head in a negative. "He didn't know who exactly he was watching. I thought it safer that way." And now he had three people he had to worry about.

The carriage jolted to a stop and Nik burst through the door before his bodyguard could open it.

He strode down the street, avoiding the throngs of people who saw him and stopped to bow. He was fairly recognizable even without the Valerian Dark Sun. Cindy's necklace rested in its place and he reached up to touch it for the fifth time in the last hour.

He tried to recall her face, tried to remember the way loose tendrils of her honey blonde hair had fallen around her heart-shaped face. But the image in his mind kept fuzzing and shifting until he saw dark gold ringlets and black eyes in an angular face.

He shook his head, trying to get rid of the image of Anella and bring back Cindy, but he'd lost it already.

He growled to himself and pushed into the covered Pledge market where rows of stalls sold all the fresh greenery for the worshippers heading to the Chapel. He had to get Cindy back. Before he forgot her completely. Or worse his parents decided to wed him to Anella. His mother and the Viscountess of Yarrow already whispered together like long-time friends, and he wouldn't be surprised if they were planning the wedding.

And Saints help him, there was a piece of him that wouldn't protest. He didn't know what was wrong with him, but a corner of his mind was whispering how perfect Anella was, how beautiful, and poised, and stoic. It would be easy to choose her, and he was tired of everything being hard.

He stopped abruptly in front of a Pledge vendor's stall and gripped the rough edge of the countertop. Little bundles of herbs and flowers, ready to be bought and laid on the altar, marched across the table in perfect rows. He took a deep breath, concentrating on the sharp smell of rosemary, the subtle sweetness of vervain, and the spicy undercurrent of dittany.

"Your Highness?" the vendor said. "Your Highness, are you all right?"

"Nik?" Colin and Eriana had followed him, their own bodyguards spreading out to watch for threats.

"I'm all right," Nik said. "Just needed a moment." What was he doing here? Something had been driving him. Something with blonde hair and dark brown eyes.

"Did you want to choose a Pledge?" Eriana said hesitantly, as if speaking to a child.

The vendor's face brightened, and he reached under his counter. "I have just the thing, Your Highnesses. Calahan's Pledge, fresh and clean, free of parasites and blemishes, a perfect offering for the Almighty." He pulled several bundles of irises out, all tied with a ribbon as if he'd always expected royalty to stop by his stall one SanctDay. Maybe he'd been waiting for this moment his whole life, stocking irises based solely on that desperate hope.

His siblings stepped forward to politely check the beautiful purple blooms before they paid the man in silver Julians.

"Nik?" Colin said when he waited too long and the vendor held a bundle out to him.

"No," Nik said, his voice coming out hoarse.

"What?" Colin said.

"Not that one." He reached instead for a small bundle of simple daisies, their petals just as perfect as the irises if much humbler.

"Nik, that's Saint Needsmeet's Pledge," Eriana whispered.

He knew that. And he knew how odd it looked, a prince reaching for the Saint of Service's Pledge. But something about the simple white flowers made his head clearer, and as his fingers closed on the stems a voice came to him out of the fog in his mind. And with it a face. And with that a name.

"Are you sure you want that one?" Colin said.

"I'm sure," Nik said, straightening. In his head he saw Cindy defending her footman, he saw her standing between

Christoph and Merrick, he saw her tumbling into a river and laughing about it.

He paid the vendor and gathered the bundle of daisies in his hands. "I'm Pledging to Saint Needsmeet today. Because a monarch's greatest calling is to serve his people faithfully."

"Isn't that what Calahan does?" Eriana said.

"Yes, but only because Needsmeet first showed him how. Leading means meeting a person's needs. Seeing what hurts them and fixing it, however small or big that may be."

He turned toward the Chapel, leaving his siblings gaping behind him while he clutched the daisies and his memories of Cindy close.

CHAPTER TWENTY-NINE

As I stood in the snow across the street from my old home, a familiar terror crept up my throat. I'd escaped, I'd made a new life for myself away from the dangers of my stepfamily. But here I was, back in the city where I was considered a murderer, putting myself back in the line of fire.

I shook my head at my morbid thoughts. As long as everything went according to plan, Melissa would never know I was here. Nik would be safe from her machinations, and I could fade back into my new life.

I'd left word for Grandmama, in case she showed up at the Refuge before I returned. But I hoped I'd be back before she got there. I didn't want to see her face when she realized where I'd gone.

Merrick leaned against the wall, holding the horses. Their bodies shielded me from anyone looking into the alley from the street. A part of me was worried I was putting him in danger as well. But a larger part of me was glad he'd come.

His loyalty had never wavered, not even when I'd told him where we were going and what we were doing.

"There," he said.

I craned around him to see the family carriage pull up in front of the townhouse, Jason sitting on the box, handling the reins.

"One, two, three," I counted the figures who stepped into the carriage, wrapped in warm coats and scarves. "That's all of them."

The carriage pulled away from the townhouse, toward the palace, and I wished them a long arduous journey. Not that I wished ill for Jason, but I needed plenty of time to sneak into the house and rummage through my stepmother's things to find the blood she'd stolen from me. Hopefully with that, I would be able to prevent her from poisoning the Disciple anymore.

"Now, Merrick," I said. "Ask for—"

"Renny," Merrick said, pushing off the wall. "Yes, I remember. She'll be able to smuggle us into the house."

I flashed him an apologetic grin as he handed me the reins. Then he disappeared across the street to knock on the servant's entrance.

I chafed the leather of the reins between my hands while I waited and limped from one side of the alley to the other. It felt strange to lurk here in the shadows when technically I could walk up to the front door and waltz inside uncontested. Ember flowed around my neck, like a heated scarf, and chirped in my ear.

"I know. I hope this works, too."

Too soon Merrick returned to the alley. Alone.

"What's wrong?" I said, my heart speeding up in my chest. If we couldn't get into the house in the first place, I had no idea what to do next. My entire plan revolved around finding my blood.

"Renny's not there. They told me she went to the palace with the family. She's to help them dress since they'll be there for dinner with the court."

I blew out my breath. "Muck," I said.

"Language," Merrick admonished, but I could see his lip twitch in amusement.

Three women had gotten in the carriage. So who was left in the house? Melissa had to have gone to oversee everything. And Anella was the one seducing the Prince. That left Isol. Could I handle Isol?

"We'll have to come back later," Merrick said.

I scowled at the house. "But we're here now." My eyes traveled over the facade and rested on the second floor windows. I glanced at Ember, and up at the chimneys. Then I looked Merrick up and down.

"You're pretty tall," I said thoughtfully.

Merrick's eyes narrowed. "I don't like it when you look like that. The last time you got that expression you told me you wanted to learn to ride."

"And that turned out just fine. I didn't fall off the entire way here."

He sighed and I knew I'd won.

"What do you need me to do?"

I led him around to the alley behind the houses and pointed up to the edge of the roof where I'd dropped down the night after the ball. "Give me a boost?"

"Miss Hargrove—" he started, his tone telling me exactly what he thought.

"I made it down just fine four months ago. And my arm is almost completely healed. Look, I can grip with all my fingers now."

He crossed his arms.

I raised my chin. "If you don't help me, I'll have to try it by myself. I'll stack up a bunch of boxes and climb up, one by one, all wobbly and unstable—"

"All right, fine," he said. "I think I liked you better when you sat in the corner and didn't talk."

I grinned. "That's so sweet. Now shut up and give me a boost."

He didn't even grunt as he hoisted me over his head and I caught the edge of the roof under my arms. He shifted his grip to my knees, and I pushed against him with all the strength in my traitorous legs.

I slipped once, the rough shingles gouging into my elbows as I scrabbled for purchase. Then I gritted my teeth and with a graceless swing, I managed to get both legs up on the shingles. I rolled up the slope of the roof.

"Miss Hargrove," Merrick said from the alley.

I shifted onto my elbows and carefully leaned out over the edge so I could see his face turned up toward me.

"Be careful," he said.

"I will. Don't lose my crutch," I said as an afterthought.

In another moment he'd tossed my crutch up beside me. I grinned as I scootched myself farther up the roof, trying to keep my movements furtive. Hopefully no one looked out the windows of the houses on either side of us. They'd assume I was some kind of really inept cat burglar.

When I reached my window I tried to raise the sash.

Locked.

"Ember," I said. "Can you get in there? Through the chimney?"

She burbled in amusement, then uncurled from around my neck. She surged up the side of the house, using her claws to climb, and I lost sight of her as she tipped into the top of the chimney.

Less than a minute later a glowing shape tumbled out of the fireplace in my old room and scampered across the floor to the window. She clicked open the latch and I shoved the window up.

"Thanks," I said as I slid off the windowsill and steadied myself against the wall inside. "Just don't tell anyone you can open locked houses, all right?"

She chuckled and clambered up my skirt to circle my neck again.

I snatched my crutch from outside the window and hobbled across the room to poke my head out the door. My fingers dipped in the pocket of my skirt, and I pulled out the antidote Grandmama had sent.

I clutched the vial to my chest as I crept along the deserted hall. I knew Melissa couldn't be in the house, but I couldn't shake the feeling of danger. And if she managed to spell me even once, I would be gone forever. It made me nervous as hell.

I reached Melissa's room and listened against the door before turning the latch.

Under my ear Ember hissed, and I spun, catching myself against the doorframe. I raised the hand with the vial, ready to down it, but it wasn't Melissa that had made Ember react.

"Isol," I said, breath leaving my lungs in a whoosh.

My stepsister stood behind me in the hallway, dark hair swept back in a severe knot, her eyes steady on my face and her hands clasped in front of her.

She tipped her head, as she regarded me. Her eyes held the same intelligence as Melissa's but there was no malice there. Only confusion.

I tried to calm my racing heart, telling myself I'd known she was here. Isol had never hurt me. She'd stood by while her mother had manipulated and lied to me. But she hadn't hurt me. And she'd even tried to help me in her own way.

But in the end would any of that mean anything?

"You were gone," she said. "You escaped. But now you're back. Why?"

"You know what your mother is planning," I said. "You can guess."

She tipped her head the other way. "I really can't. I don't understand people."

"What do you mean?"

"The way they feel, the things they do and say. Sometimes I think I'm broken because I look at the world and I'm not like everyone else in it."

"You're not the only one," I said under my breath. Then I raised my voice slightly. "Being broken's not all that bad. It just means you're strong in different ways. You're smart. You watch and you understand things. You know your mother best of anyone. You can help me."

"Mother is easy," she said. "She'll climb to the top. If you get in her way, she'll destroy you. If you prove useful, she'll use you. You, I don't understand. You had the chance to tell the Prince I was involved in framing the King's Mage for blood magic. But you didn't. Why?"

"It would have hurt you," I said.

She raised an eyebrow and I tried harder to explain what I'd felt when Renny had told me what she was planning. "I knew it had to be Melissa's idea. And I didn't want you caught in the middle of your mother's scheme."

"You don't know me. How do you know I'm not like her?"

I shook my head. "I don't. But you've never done anything to prove to me you are. Everyone deserves a chance to be who they want to be. Not who others make them into."

She glanced down, a flush tinging her coppery skin.

"It's too late for me," she said, echoing her words from four months ago.

"I don't think it's ever too late," I said. A part of me was screaming about the delay, that Melissa could be coming back right now. But another part of me recognized how important this was. Isol stood on the edge of something big. Something deep. And I could reach out my hand to her. Or I could push her in.

"Who do you want to be?" I said.

She blinked. For a long moment she stood there, so long I worried she wouldn't ever answer me. Then her lips curved. It wasn't quite a smile. More like what someone who'd never tried it thought smiling should look like.

"I want to be someone like you," she said.

I couldn't help laughing. "No one's ever said that before. I hope you don't end up regretting it."

She eyed me sidelong. "You'll trust me?"

I held out my hand and with a wondering look she took my fingers between her own. "I'll trust you." I didn't know if I could keep that promise yet but it seemed really important to Isol that I make it.

"I came to destroy the blood Melissa took from me," I said. "Do you know where she keeps it?"

Her eyes narrowed and I could see a million thoughts crossing her mind at once. "Yes. But it won't help you. The damage is already done."

I sucked in a breath. "The Disciple?"

Isol nodded. "He'll be dead within a day unless you can somehow counteract her spell."

"You can't do it from here?"

She shook her head. "Not that I know of. She says she's teaching me, but I know she's holding things back."

I chewed my lip. I still had the anti-magic potion in my pocket. It was the only thing I had to fight against her.

I showed her the two vials I had brought and hurriedly told her about Grandmama's research. "It negates magic. Do you know if it will work on the Disciple?" I asked.

Her eyebrows bunched together. "I don't know. All of her poisons are bound with magic and blood. So I suppose it should."

"Then I have to get to the Refuge of Calahan." Hopefully Merrick knew a way.

"Still, that will only stop her until the Disciple dies naturally. She'll have Anella married to the Prince, no matter what."

It wasn't anything more than I'd already guessed but the confirmation still made me clench my hands until my nails bit into my palms.

"She destroyed my life just to put Anella on the throne."

Isol looked at the floor. "My father was a Torracan prince. Exiled after the revolution. She promised him she would use his compulsion magic to put one of his children on the Valerian throne. Because Valeria helped depose him."

"She must have loved him very much." To destroy her own monarchy.

"Their love might have been the only true thing in either of their lives. They were both used to manipulating everyone else around them. The compulsion magic only made them better at it." She cast me a penetrating glance. "It won't be long before Mother has Prince Nikolas thinking he's in love with Anella," she said.

I looked up sharply. "She has a compulsion spell on him now?"

"The same one she used on you."

I seethed. She used me against him even now when I wasn't even in the picture anymore. "I thought I destroyed it."

Isol shook her head. "In the fire? It was made in fire. To truly destroy it, you have to smash it. She had Anella give him the necklace, saying it was a gift from you."

"I'm sure Anella just loved that," I said.

She eyed me. "Anella might want to be queen. But she wanted to do it her own way. So Mother put her under a compulsion spell, too."

My eyes widened. "What?" Selfish, greedy Anella was a victim.

"I told you, if you get in her way, my mother will do everything to either use you or destroy you. I learned to do as she said after Anella tried to defy her and lost her own free will."

"I...I had no idea," I said.

She saw my look and shook her head. "Don't make the mistake of thinking Anella is a nice person just because she's a victim. She was just as nasty before, and she had her own agenda that would have hurt more people than it helped."

I squared my shoulders. "She still deserves to be free," I said. "All right, so we have to save the Disciple and then we have to have to get the spell away from Nik."

It seemed simple enough when I put it that way but I could barely imagine a way to start.

"I'd like to get my blood away from her anyway. She might have already damaged everything with it, but I can't let her keep it."

"I'll get it for you."

She started to turn, but a flash of movement caught my eye. I glanced toward the stairs and caught the blur of a pale face and dark hair around the corner.

"Bess," I said, loathing making my chest tight.

"Be careful," Isol said. "She tells my mother everything."

I had to stop her before she warned Melissa we were coming. I hobbled after the scullery maid and reached for her sleeve. "Bess, please don't."

She spun and slapped my hand away. "Why couldn't you have stayed gone? You were right where you were supposed to be in the kitchen, lower even than me. Then you went and played like you were one of them." She waved upward. "Now here you are, like you have something anyone wants."

"I have plenty," I snapped at her. "Just because people like you tried to make me believe otherwise doesn't make it true."

Her eyebrows went up. "Oh, look who grew a backbone. Much good it'll do you. My lady's clever and powerful. She'll put you right back where you belong."

She whipped away from me, faster than I could grab and dashed down the stairs. I started after her, hobbling down each step.

Muck, I couldn't keep up. And I couldn't let her get away.

I hefted the only weapon I had. I threw my crutch, tangling her legs just as she reached the bottom of the stairs. She fell with an angry scream. Then she was up. She flew up the stairs and lunged at me, her fingers curled into claws.

I fell under her. We slid down the steps as we grappled, each edge jouncing my spine. Ember leaped on her, claws aflame and Bess screamed, this time in pain.

Voices shouted and figures poured out of the kitchen below us.

A tremendous crash echoed around the front hall as the front door burst inward and hit the wall behind it. Merrick rushed through to drag Bess away from me.

I sat up, trembling, while Ruben and a couple others from the kitchen took charge of the screaming scullery maid.

"Miss Cindy. Glad you're all right," Ruben said as if I'd just strolled in the front door.

"Ruben, it's good to see you," I said, matching his tone and pretending I wasn't sprawled across the steps. I levered myself to my feet and winced. Merrick surged forward and lent me his arm.

Isol came down the stairs behind me. "What should we do with her?" she said, gesturing at Bess.

"Can't say anyone will be sorry to see the last of her," Ruben said. "Except maybe the lady of the house. But she doesn't need to know the details." Ruben grinned up at me. "Leave her to us, mite," he said. "We'll keep her locked up tight. After today, she won't be able to find a decent post within five miles of Namerre."

Just before heading back to the kitchen, Ruben leaned over and squeezed my hand. "Welcome home," he said.

I couldn't meet his eyes. How did I tell him I was only here to save the Disciple? Then I'd leave again and never come back.

Isol looked at me. "We should head to the palace."

I nodded and turned to Merrick. "Can you get me to the Disciple of Calahan?" I said, meeting and holding his eyes.

His grimaced. "Why—?" Then he sighed. "Is it the only way to save him?"

"Yes. Can you get us to the Refuge?"

"Maybe," he said. "We'll have to get into the palace."

"Good enough." I turned back to Isol. "You'll have to find Nik and get that compulsion spell away from him."

She angled her chin. "I would have thought you'd want to do that."

I flushed and shook my head. "I don't...I don't think he should see me." He still believed I'd murdered my father.

She stared at me steadily, but I didn't change my mind. "Very well," she said. "I'll meet you at the palace once it's done. You'll be careful? She put that compulsion spell in one of her potions. If she makes you take it, it'll be permanent."

I swallowed. Melissa had been planning my demise even when I wasn't in her clutches.

"I still have the antidote," I said. "That will protect me." I hoped.

"Just be sure to take it early. It would be better not to let her dose you at all."

I snorted. "That's a given."

She smiled again and started back up the stairs.

"Isol," I said, catching her hand. "Thank you. For Nik."

"I'm not doing it for him," she said. "I'm doing it for you."

CHAPTER THIRTY

"Nik!" a voice called from the other end of the hall and Nik turned to see Eriana rushing toward him. "You have to come right now."

"What is it? What's wrong?"

She took hold of his hand and hauled him toward the other end of the palace, both their bodyguards following. "We've called a special meeting in the green parlor."

The green parlor was an awkward room tucked between the water closets on the first floor and the servants' staircase. When Nik pushed through the door, he found the space occupied by the group of people he'd privately started to consider his "conspirators," the ones who knew the truth and were willing to help him prove it.

Eriana joined Colin beside the fireplace while Jason and Renny stood in the corner looking awkward and out of place.

And opposite them all sat Christoph and Adelaine.

"You came." Nik strode across the carpet to clasp Christoph's hand. "You got my letters."

Christoph's brows drew down. "What letters?"

"The ones I sent..." Nik trailed off realizing that wasn't particularly helpful. "If you didn't get my letters, then why are you here? You're supposed to be in hiding."

Christoph's lips thinned. "This was more important."

"More important than your life? If you're caught here, you could be killed on sight."

Adelaine went pale but she raised her chin and squeezed Christoph's hand.

The former King's Mage nodded gravely. "I know. But more people will die if I didn't come back. Someone is tampering with the Blood Bond."

"We knew that—" Nik started but Christoph waved a hand to cut him off.

"I think I know how it's being done now. I've been monitoring the Bond since we learned the Disciple had fallen ill. And now I think I can distill enough to know that someone is using Miss Hargrove's blood to gain access to the Bond."

Nik staggered and caught himself against the table. Colin straightened as if to help, but Nik's sharp gesture kept him back.

"It can't have been a willing contribution," Christoph said, eyes traveling from Nik to Colin and back again. "She saved my life once. So we came back to help her break free from whoever is using her."

"Lady Hargrove," Jason said as Renny nodded vigorously. "Who else would have Cindy's blood?"

Christoph sat up. "Then something really is going on in the Hargrove house? I can help her. I can—"

"You'll have to find her first," Nik said. "She's been missing since the ball."

His vision swam as Anella's face tried to superimpose itself in front of him. He dug his fingers into the tabletop with one hand and grasped Cindy's necklace with the other. He knew now that it wasn't a gift from his former fiancé. She hadn't even been in the city for the last four months. But he couldn't help holding onto it as his last link to someone he was having a hard time remembering.

The edges cut into his fingers as he repeated the details of Cindy's appearance to himself.

Slowly the room steadied and he found the conspirators looking at him.

"Are you all right?" Christoph asked, eyes narrow. "You look...you don't look like yourself."

"I'm fine." He shook his head and concentrated. He couldn't afford to let Christoph get distracted now that he was here. Especially when all that was wrong with Nik was lack of sleep and a pushy Viscountess.

"Are you sure?" Christoph's face set. "I have a couple spells that might help."

Nik cut him off with a gesture. "Not now. After...you can do whatever you like after we find Cindy." He made an effort to focus on Christoph and Lainey. "Can you track a person? Like a bloodhound or like the police sometimes do?"

"You mean magically?" Christoph frowned. "It's possible. There are plenty of association spells I should be able to use. But I will need something she owned. Not just something she touched once, either. It needs to be something she handled a lot."

Christoph looked at the footman and the maid in the corner, obviously assuming they would have access to Cindy's old things. But before either of them could react, Nik held out his hand to his bodyguard, who produced something from one of his many pockets.

It was a shoe with wooden supports for the ankle, its laces broken and its leather old and worn.

"Something like this?" Nik said.

"That's Cindy's," Jason said. "She wore it every day since she was thirteen."

Christoph glanced between Nik and the shoe. "That'll work."

"How long will it take?" Nik asked as Christoph took the shoe from him.

"Only a few minutes to set the spell," he said. "After that it will tell you direction and proximity. How long it takes you to find her will depend on how far she is and how fast you ride." Christoph cast him a grin and set to work, turning the shoe around and around in his hands as he muttered words Nik didn't recognize.

"As soon as we know how far she is, we can make our plans," Nik said. "We'll have to stop Lady Hargrove from... poisoning the Disciple. However she's doing that."

Nik turned to Jason and Renny. "Have you found anything in the house? Anything that indicates she's a mage?"

Renny shook her head. "I'd hardly know what to look for, but everything seems normal."

"Does she suspect we know the truth about Cindy?"

The two servants looked at each other before Jason answered. "We don't think so, Your Highness."

"She's very preoccupied with court right now," Renny said. "She's acting like you're already engaged to Anella."

Nik ground his teeth. His own preoccupation hadn't left much time to convince his parents he did not want to marry Anella. And given that she was all he could think of recently, he wasn't sure what he was going to do when they made the decision for him.

"That can't be right," Christoph said behind him.

Nik spun to the mage. "What? What is it?"

"She's here. In the city."

Nik glared at him. "She can't be."

"We would have found her by now," Jason said. "We've been looking for ages."

"I'm just telling you what this is saying. Here, see for yourself. She's somewhere close."

He held up the shoe and Nik snatched it. The moment his hands touched the leather he felt a sharp tug in his gut, one that made him whirl around and nearly stumble to the door. She was here, it told him. She was close.

Nik had fully intended to go about this the right way, equipping himself for an expedition. It would have given him time to prepare himself to see her again, figure out what he wanted to say, how he would approach her.

But with the shoe in his hands and the throbbing in his gut, he found he couldn't wait. He wouldn't have to wait. He could find her today, in the next hour, even.

He glanced over his shoulder at the others. They had all stood and now they waited, watching him intently.

"Well," he said. "Are you coming?"

✳

"How much trouble will you be in if we're caught?" I asked as Merrick tied the horses outside the bustling palace stables.

He glanced at his old uniform, which would hopefully get us into the palace and past all the guards. "A lot."

"Are you sure you want to risk it?"

He turned from the horses and looked me in the eyes. "This is the only way to get to the Disciple. Our honor dictates no other course. The risk to us is negligible compared to the consequences of inaction."

He said that but I still felt like the only reason he was doing this was because I'd asked him to.

Ember raised her head from my shoulder and chirped a question.

"He means you have to stay quiet and out of sight," I said. "You can't draw attention to us."

She hummed serious assent and settled against my collarbone, morphing to look like a simple orange and black beaded necklace.

Merrick led me past the dormitory for the kitchen workers, workshops for the carpenter and blacksmith, and more laundry rooms than I would have imagined being part of one household, however big.

We used the narrow servant's stair to climb to the extensive attics not far from where I'd come to save Christoph.

"This is the Guard's Tower," Merrick said as he stopped in a large square room. He pointed up. "Up there is the portal to the Refuge of Calahan."

I gazed at the steps stretching up and around the cupola and clutched my crutch. "How many more stairs?" I said, trying not to gasp with the effort I'd already expended to get here.

Merrick glanced at me, then around at the staircase winding up the walls. "Here," he said and led me to the first step.

I climbed up as he turned his back to me.

"Climb on."

"It's a good thing I have no dignity," I said as I wrapped my arms around his neck and he straightened until I dangled behind him like a cape.

He didn't reply as he took my crutch and started climbing, far faster than we would have gone if I'd insisted on walking.

I tried to make sure my arms crossed his collarbones and my hands clasped his chest so I didn't strangle him. Three steps from the top, where the light from the windows above us lit the stairs, he stopped and lowered me to the ground.

"This is it," he said. "If we're caught now, I'll be declared a traitor to the Realm and shot. And you'll be hung as a murderer."

I gaped at him as he started up the last couple stairs.

"That's what you consider a negligible risk?" I hissed to his back.

He didn't respond and I had no choice but to hobble after him.

In the square windowed room high above the palace, colored tiles made a geometric pattern on the floor and a young man in a rumpled suit sat tilting his chair back on two legs while he read a worn paperback.

His chair thumped to the floor when he saw us and he sprang to his feet. A wide grin split his face. "Merrick," he said. "I haven't seen you in a while. Did the Prince get a new bodyguard?"

Merrick came to a stop and clasped his hands behind his back as if he was still entitled to wear the uniform he'd tossed on over his civilian clothes. "Yes," he said shortly. "Will you open the portal? His highness is sending his personal healer to the Disciple."

The young man's face twitched in a confusion of hope and sadness. "Oh yes." He threw back his shoulders. "The Byway Portal attendant awaits your command."

Merrick nodded sagely. "I am ready to cross the Byways," he said. "Open the portals."

The young man knelt and touched the tiles under our feet. Lines of blue fire raced between them and in a moment of clarity I realized the spell was already woven into the pattern. The mage was only here to power it and guard the portal.

Merrick glanced at me, growled something that sounded like "Brace yourself," and took one step forward.

Afraid I was about to be left behind I hurried to follow him and found myself stepping onto something that felt like a moving platform. The air raced along underneath me as colors swirled and streamed alongside.

Another step and the world stopped moving with a jolt I felt in my stomach.

I gasped in surprise and wonder. The room around us looked very similar to the one we'd just left but there were subtle differences. The mage that stood before us was much older with a steady gaze and stoic expression. And the view from the windows convinced me we'd reached our destination. The day had been gray and threatening snow when we'd stepped onto the glowing spell lines. Now bright sunlight glinted off crisp white peaks through the windows. How far had we come with that one single step? You couldn't even see mountains from Namerre.

Merrick looked at me curiously. "Do you feel all right?" he said.

"Fine," I said, blinking. "Why?"

Merrick shrugged. "The Prince never likes that journey. It's made him sick on more than one occasion."

I had a hard time imagining Nik bent over the colorful tiles heaving up his breakfast, but Merrick was moving on and I hobbled to catch up.

"I can't believe it was that easy," I whispered, glancing back at the mage who hadn't moved from his post. "Shouldn't there be more trouble? Someone checking your status or something?"

"It's my uniform. I'm recognized and trusted here."

"But why didn't they know about your demotion?"

"The records for that day are sealed and certain circumstances were kept secret for Christoph's safety. The Prince decided no one needed to know the truth about my discharge except my commander. I think he was trying to spare my feelings."

His lip twitched and I realized that this was Merrick at his most amused.

"The Disciple is protected by his isolation and the mages that guard the portal," Merrick continued. "The caretakers are only here to see to his comfort. Now that we're in, we should be fine."

The long, windowed hallway opened onto a cozy library lit by half a dozen mage globes and large windows that faced the valley. A man in a crisp black suit and white gloves hurried up to us, his eyebrows drawn in confusion and alarm.

"What are you doing here?" he said. "We are expecting no visitors. The Disciple hasn't woken in weeks and is too ill to be disturbed."

Merrick gave me a little shove toward a doorway covered with thick velvet curtains before he moved to intercept the man I assumed was a caretaker of the old Disciple.

I hurried toward the opening and didn't stop to listen as Merrick told his lie a second time, about how I was a healer sent specifically by the Prince. This part was my responsibility, and I couldn't afford to be delayed now when we were so close.

I pushed through the curtains and stopped suddenly. The dim room was lit by one mage globe, but I could make out a large bed and a figure lying unmoving under the covers.

Another caretaker dozed in a chair in the corner, the lines around his eyes and mouth depicting many sleepless nights.

I hurried as quietly as I could across the room and leaned over the bed.

The old man lying among the pillows still breathed, but

his breathing was shallow and his skin looked gray. He could be minutes from death.

Ember raised her head from my collarbone. Her glow cast a yellow light across the Disciple's face and I winced. He looked even worse than in the dark, but it gave me an idea.

I pulled her from my neck, brow furrowed. "Ember," I whispered. "You can see impurities, right?" She had to be able to see them if she was also able to burn them out.

She chirped assent. Then she climbed down the front of my dress and onto the bedcovers. She looked the Disciple up and down and then trilled a high warbling note.

Suddenly the Disciple's skin lit with color, red and yellow and a sick grayish green snaked across his face and neck and arms as if following his veins. I could even see the dull glow through his sheets.

"Almighty save us." I sucked in a breath. "It's everywhere."

Isol had said it was a spell. Some magic poison Melissa had sent using my blood as the link.

I rubbed my face, feeling the time—and his life—ticking away.

Ember burbled a determined sound and I knew what she was saying.

"No," I said, shaking my head. "You can't burn it out of him. He's not awake to hold onto who he is and we don't know him well enough to do it."

I set my jaw. I only had one defense against magic. Would it even work? Grandmama had said it was time sensitive, but did that matter if the poison was delivered through a blood link?

I dug in my pocket, pulled out one of my vials, and pulled the cork.

"What are you doing?" the caretaker asked sharply from the doorway, Merrick behind him. "Get away from there." The other caretaker woke with a snort.

He lunged forward but Merrick blocked him. I thrust the vial between the Disciple's teeth and held his nose.

As soon as I'd poured it down his throat, I stumbled back. The first caretaker took hold of my arms while Merrick was occupied by the other.

I ground my teeth. We were mucked now. If the antidote didn't work, nothing would save us from our executions.

Someone groaned and everyone in the room froze.

The Disciple raised a trembling hand, his skin reflecting much subtler colors in Ember's warm light.

I was still closest and I took his hand, which was waving about, and leaned over the bed. "How do you feel?" I said.

"Awful, thanks for asking," he said, voice grating with disuse.

I smiled. That sounded very promising. And it sounded like the Disciple was still himself. Nik had mentioned how crotchety his grandfather was. "I'm glad it's only awful," I said. "Dead was the other option."

He blinked up at me. "Who are you?" he said.

Before I could answer, both caretakers had pushed forward. "Ambrose!" they said, before babbling a million questions at once. From their reactions it was obvious they considered the old man more than the king they served. He was their friend, too.

I gathered Ember and backed away toward Merrick. He gripped my shoulder and leaned toward my ear.

"If you want to get out, we have to do it now. They won't expect you to leave after saving him."

I nodded. We were done here.

No one noticed as we pushed our way out of the room, except the Disciple who asked, voice growing stronger, "Who was that young woman? The one who glowed."

CHAPTER THIRTY-ONE

Merrick carried me down the stairs the same way he'd carried me up, then we slipped quietly along the halls of the main floor. We had to find Isol without being spotted ourselves. I was counting on the fact that the court would be at dinner, and no one would be in this part of the palace. We didn't see anyone as we made our way into the Grand Foyer with its soaring ceilings and marble columns. The big windows let in little light as the sun went down, and the servants hadn't been through to light the lamps yet.

When footsteps hurried towards us we flattened ourselves against a column until I recognized the figure running past.

"Isol!"

She turned swiftly at the sound of my voice. "Oh, good. There are a couple of guards following me. I think they know I'm not supposed to be here since I didn't go in to dinner with the others."

"I'll take care of them," Merrick said.

"Did you find Nik?" I asked Isol as he strode away. "Is he free?"

My heart sank when she shook her head. "He wasn't at dinner with the court, and his bodyguard says he's been unavailable all day. Something about some sort of meeting. I would have just kept looking, but I didn't want Mother to see me."

"Isol, you have to find him. We can't let Melissa have control over him. She could make him do anything."

"You're turning out to be far too clever for your own good, cinder-mite."

The voice made me stiffen as a chill swept through my blood, leaving ice in its wake. I spun to see Melissa Hargrove smirking in the twilit hall. Anella stepped behind her, a sullen pout on her face.

My heart sank. After four months away, Melissa didn't look surprised to see me standing in the palace. Bess must have sent a message ahead before I'd even seen her spying on us.

Isol stepped between us, her chin raised in defiance. "Stop this, Mother," she said, her voice quavering. "We know what you're planning. Just—just let us go."

Melissa glanced at Isol, her smile stretching into a rictus of pain and determination.

I shuddered while I fumbled at my pocket. I needed to take the antidote before she touched me. Before she could bespell or drug me. Folds of fabric muddled my fingers, keeping them from the cool glass of my last vial.

Melissa chuckled at Isol. "I raised you to be smarter than that."

She stepped forward, closing the distance between us, and grabbed Isol's wrist. She leaned in until her lips were level with her daughter's ear.

"You know I can't let you go with all you know," she said. Before I realized what was happening she had laid a thin, gleaming blade against the copper skin of Isol's arm and sliced down.

Isol cried out and staggered back. I tried to catch her. I put my arms around her, but her legs crumpled, and I couldn't keep us both upright. We landed hard against the marble floor.

"Isol?"

The cut wasn't that bad, but she looked up at me eyes wide and disoriented. "S-spell..."

I looked at the knife in Melissa's hand. Of course it would be poisoned with her magic.

"You are much more trouble than I first imagined, cinder-mite," Melissa said with a sigh, as if I had a habit of trampling her flowers. "I will have to be more careful this time around."

"Just kill me and get it over with," I said, hoping to distract her. This time my hand dipped smoothly into the pocket of my skirt, and I drew out the last vial.

"You know better than that. You're too valuable alive. It was so hard convincing the Prince you really weren't going to go back to your normal self. But from now on you'll be here to prove it."

I pressed the cool glass shape into Isol's palm, meeting

her startled eyes, and I gave her the tiniest nod. It was the last one but it would save her life.

"So, you'll just have to stay and be my good little invalid." That was when I noticed she carried her own vial of liquid, colored with just a trace of blood. My blood.

My own personal mind poison.

I tried to stand, but Melissa reached across and grabbed my throat. Ember leapt from my neck and sank fiery fangs into her hand. Melissa's lips peeled back from her teeth, and she flung Ember across the room where the fire sprite hit the wall and slid to the floor.

I screamed, and Melissa used the opportunity to pour the dark liquid in my open mouth. I thrashed and choked and gagged and tried to get away, but her grip tightened on my neck, and I had to swallow in order to breathe.

"Stop!" The voice I loved so much rang across the hall, and Melissa stepped away.

I fell back coughing and trying to spit out what was left in my mouth, but it was too late. Melissa's eyes gleamed with triumph and a small smile lurked in the corners of her mouth.

A cold, heavy weight pressed into my hand. I looked down.

I clutched the knife she had used to cut Isol. In our scuffle she had passed it to me. I knelt on the floor of the Grand Foyer with Isol bleeding beside me, the offending weapon in my palm.

Saints protect me, she'd done it again.

"Prince Nikolas," Melissa said. "She escaped from the house. I was giving her something to calm her down."

I trembled on the floor, ignoring Melissa's voice and waiting for the feeling of disorientation and disconnection to wash over me.

Ember crawled toward me, her flames flickering against the gleaming marble floor.

I could imagine the magic coursing through my blood, bringing permanent disconnection with it. Ember cuddled against my hands and looked up at me, her tiny flaming body pulsing. She chirped one solemn question.

I closed my eyes. Then I pulled her toward me and pressed her against my heart.

She dissolved into me, heat and light spreading across my skin, into my veins, along my entire body. I could feel her singing in the back of my mind, burning away every dark corner of Melissa's magic. Not just the recent dose but everything she'd ever done to me, the poison lurking beneath my surface waiting to take hold again. The pain swept through me in waves, agony and wonder combined.

The ends of my hair crackled and lifted in the heat.

And through it all I kept hold of myself. I was me. I wasn't a victim, I wasn't less than everyone else, I wasn't a murderer, and I wasn't Cindy. I held tight to those truths as Ember burned away everything else.

Brilliant white-blue light flared behind my eyelids and the warmth and pain faded.

I opened my eyes and took a deep breath. And then another. After three breaths I realized I felt normal. Ember had done it. She'd protected me from Melissa's magic.

"She stabbed my daughter, Your Highness," Melissa was

saying. "There's no other explanation. She must be in the grip of another fit."

"No, I'm not," I said. I flung the knife from me so it skittered across the floor.

Melissa turned, her face stunned and her eyes wide. "What?"

I used the column to climb unsteadily to my feet. A tall, princely figure led a group of people farther down the hall, but I ignored them. Instead, I met my stepmother's eyes.

"I didn't stab Isol, I am not an invalid, and I didn't murder my father. You did."

"Cindy, you're obviously not well. Let me take you home—"

"That is not my name."

The confusion and shock on her face was gratifying. "I-I don't understand."

"Then let me explain. I got rid of your poison. Your magic won't work on me anymore."

Her eyebrows came together, and the corners of her mouth dipped in a frown. She reached towards me, but heat flared in my chest as Ember flowed from my center, materializing in front of me and spreading fiery wings to block her. The fire sprite hissed and flapped and Melissa stumbled back.

"Don't. Touch. Me," I said.

"Miss Hargrove!" Merrick called and raced toward me. He took my arm and I sagged into his support. "Did she hurt you?"

Ember circled us, shaped like a falcon, keeping my stepmother at bay.

I shook my head. "I'm all right." I could feel eyes watching me. Green eyes, I knew, but I didn't want to look. I didn't want to meet them and acknowledge everything between us. Anella clung to his arm, holding him back. I would have run if I could, but there was still work to be done here.

I met my stepmother's eyes. "I won't let you have him," I said.

Her eyes narrowed and her fingers curled.

Merrick drew his sword and Ember screamed.

"What is going on here?" Nik's voice had rung, but King Julius's voice boomed around the hall.

I grabbed Merrick's arm, but he'd already dropped his sword. No amount of loyalty to me would keep him from old habits, and it was a capital offense to draw a weapon in the presence of the King unless you were actually a ServantGuard.

"Whoever is responsible for this flaming bird," the King said, glaring at Ember. "Please contain it."

I held out my hand and Ember flashed around us once more before lighting on my fist. Her talons shifted and molded around me without breaking my skin, and she kept her wings half unfurled as if waiting for an excuse to take flight.

"Lady Hargrove," the King said. "What is your step-daughter doing in my palace? She is supposed to be in your custody. At home."

"Father." Nik stepped forward, flinging Anella's hand from his arm. "I have reason to believe that Lady Hargrove has been lying to us since she joined the court."

"Be careful, Prince Nikolas," King Julius said. "Your personal feelings cannot blind you to the fact that you're accusing a member of the Queen's household of treason."

The Queen's household? Melissa must have been busy while I was gone.

"It's true, Father. You should at least consider the possibility."

I bent to pick up my crutch and then straightened when I realized the King was looking at me.

"Can you answer a few questions, Cindy?" He spoke slowly, the way Melissa had when she wanted everyone to think I was sick and weak.

"Please don't call me that, Your Majesty," I said, startling King Julius. "Cindy is short for cinder-mite, a hurtful nickname. My name is Aschen."

Someone made a noise from the group of people, but I ignored them and focused on the King. If I didn't look at him, I wouldn't have to feel anything for him. Merrick put his hand on my shoulder and squeezed, bolstering me. I was grateful for the support, but Isol still lay against the column, blood leaking sluggishly from her arm. The empty vial lay on the floor beside her.

I touched Merrick's fingers. "Help Isol," I said.

He nodded and knelt beside my stepsister.

"Aschen then," the King said, recalling me. "All this was put behind us months ago, do you really want to dredge it all up again?"

I drew myself up. He was going to ignore everything that had been done to me just to save face?

"Your Majesty, you are the final source of justice for

Valerians, and I have the right to ask you to hear me out on this matter." I hadn't come here to defend myself, but here I was in front of the one person who could declare my innocence.

"Cin—" He stopped himself. "Aschen, you can't really request a hearing. You were declared unfit to retain your holdings and rights."

"You mean while I was spelled?"

The King fell still and looked at me. "Spelled?"

"Do I appear unfit in my current condition?"

His gaze swept me up and down, and I realized what I must look like with my hair coming loose and Isol's blood on my dress.

The King sighed. "Perhaps you would like to discuss this privately?"

"No." I raised my chin. "I have been maligned and mistreated, and I will not be hidden away or ignored again."

A chorus of whispers swept around the foyer and I realized how many courtiers had followed the King from the state dining room. For a moment I faltered and found myself staring at Nik. Between the lapels of his jacket a bit of silver and glass gleamed at me like a baleful eye.

I limped toward him, my gaze fixed on that tiny point of light. Out of the corner of my eye I saw several guards step forward, but Nik's gesture told them to stand down. My fingers tangled in the chain and Nik's hands went to my arms.

Before he could touch me, I ripped the pendant from his neck and spun away.

"Isol?" I called.

She clutched Merrick's supporting arm and scowled pointedly at her mother. "Smash it."

Melissa screamed and dove for me as I flung the pendant against the wall. The glass shattered and the gold glittered in the fading light as pieces of the necklace fell to the marble.

CHAPTER THIRTY-TWO

"Viscountess, control yourself," the King's voice whipped out. "Miss Hargrove, what the hell is going on?"

Nik had caught hold of Melissa's wrists, keeping her clawing fingers from me, and I backed away from them.

"Your Majesty," Isol said. "Aschen just saved your son's life."

The courtiers fell silent, and in the hush, I could practically hear Melissa glare at her daughter. The air crackled with it.

"Please explain," the King said, and I could see him struggling to be reasonable.

"That pendant held a very powerful compulsion spell, one that bound Aschen for months and your son for weeks," Isol said. "It's a wonder he wasn't my mother's puppet already. She was making him think he loved Anella. The only protection from that is if he was in love with someone else."

I felt nauseous.

Julius sorted through all the questions he obviously wanted to ask and came up with just one. "What?"

"Where would you like me to start, Your Majesty?" Isol said calmly. The antidote I'd given her was clearly working now.

She looked quizzical and then said, "Oh, the end. I'll start at the end, then it will all make sense."

King Julius opened his mouth to laugh or protest, but Isol continued without waiting.

"My father was a Torracan prince deposed during the revolution Valeria helped foment. My mother planned to put his blood on the Valerian throne in revenge for his exile."

Julius looked at Anella, who raised her chin and met his gaze. I remembered what Isol had said about Anella being under compulsion spells as well and I stepped toward her.

"How was the Prince's life in danger then?" King Julius said.

Isol blinked. "She would have killed him the same way she killed my stepfather, then Anella would have ruled alone."

Anella grimaced and then jumped when I touched her hand. I raised my eyebrows and nodded at the bracelet she wore, a gold chain with a bubble of glass laying flat against her skin. She met my eyes, hesitated, and then held her wrist up for me. I undid the gold clasp and let the bracelet slip from her wrist to crack against the marble floor. I crushed it under the heel of my new shoe for good measure.

Anella shuddered.

King Julius rubbed his forehead. "Let's be very clear here.

You're accusing your mother of killing your stepfather and framing Aschen for it."

"Yes," Isol said.

"Why?"

Isol just looked at him. "If you'd let me go in order, your majesty, this would make much more sense."

King Julius opened his mouth, thought better of what he was about to say, and waved Isol on.

"My mother needed the Rannard Blood Bond, but she didn't have noble blood. When my stepfather wouldn't let her use his, she killed him. Aschen was supposed to die as well, but she survived somehow." Isol gave Ember a sidelong look. "So my mother framed her and decided to use her Bond instead. It was the only way she could get to the Disciple to ensure Nik assumed the throne before the Disciple chose some other bride."

Melissa's eyes narrowed. "At least you're too late to save the old man," she said through her teeth, glaring at me.

"Oh, I'm still alive and kicking," another voice said.

The courtiers turned with a gasp and as each one recognized the new figure standing in the hall they fell into bows and curtsies.

The Disciple looked much more hale than he had just an hour before, though two caretakers flanked him just in case. And his bright green eyes found my face in the crowd.

"Thanks to this young lady, here."

"Grandfather," Nik said.

"Father, you're well," Julius said, striding to the Disciple.

The Disciple waved a hand. "Yes, yes. But continue,

please. I wish to see the end of this story. Now, before I die of old age."

Nik rolled his eyes but King Julius spun to Isol.

"If all this is true," he said. "Why didn't you come forward before?"

Isol met his gaze, raised her chin, and said, "Because I was the one who helped my mother murder my stepfather."

Gasps spread across the hall as her words registered.

Isol stood firm. "I didn't know what we were doing at the time, but afterward she told me I'd be tried as a murderer."

That sounded familiar.

"But now I've realized that blackmail only works if the person being blackmailed doesn't want to face the consequences of their actions. I'm willing to face the consequences if it means confronting the real murderer."

King Julius's face settled into hard lines and he turned to my stepmother. "Do you have anything to say for yourself, Lady Hargrove?"

Melissa raised her chin, her smirk still firmly in place. "You have no proof."

I looked guiltily at the glittering pieces of the necklace I'd smashed and Anella's broken bracelet.

Isol didn't seem fazed. She took a couple vials from a pouch at her side. "Here is Aschen's blood, which my mother was using to kill the Disciple. And here is a sample of the poison she used."

I fought not to laugh. Isol had thought of everything.

The Disciple himself stepped forward to take the vial of red liquid in his white hands and turn it over and over.

"The law is clear," King Julius said taking the other vial. "I need a mage to confirm the spells before I can convict."

"I'm here, Your Majesty." Master Christoph stepped from the group of people standing with the Prince.

King Julius scowled as the ServantGuard around us drew their weapons with a menacing susurrus of steel. "You have been charged with blood magic." The King gestured to the ServantGuard. "Arrest him. Unless he runs. Then kill him."

"Wait," I said. I was too far to fling myself in front of him like last time. "It wasn't him. He was framed."

King Julius barely cast me a glance. "Then prove it."

"Oh, I can do that," Isol said. "I kept receipts."

From the same pouch, Isol pulled the note I'd seen the day I'd stopped Merrick from killing Christoph, plus several other papers.

Isol should consider becoming a solicitor. She certainly had the mind and the poise for it.

King Julius looked like he'd be struck in the back of the head, then he raised his gaze to the ceiling as if asking for patience from the Almighty. "You're saying your mother framed him, too?"

"Of course," Isol said. "If he'd been around during the ball, he would have known something was off about Aschen's actions."

I flushed. And by interfering I'd assured that Melissa's plan went off without a hitch.

Julius looked at Christoph, who'd stepped forward to examine the vials of liquid. "Well?" he said.

Finally, Christoph grimaced. "I can tell Aschen's blood has been tampered with. And it was used as a conduit to access the Blood Bond. But I am not familiar enough with Torracan magic to know what this one does." He touched the poison. "It contains some sort of spell, but that's all. As far as I know, it could be a tonic to cure a sore throat."

The King looked truly upset. "Then I cannot convict her."

Nik stepped forward. "Father, wait—"

"It is the law," the King snapped. "All I can do is reinstate Aschen's title and responsibilities. She is now Lady Hargrove, Viscountess of Yarrow. But without a mage who can confirm these spells, Melissa Hargrove cannot be convicted."

"Then it appears I am just in time."

The court turned as one to the wide doors where three figures stood. My heart leaped when I recognized Grandmama, looking tired and careworn but triumphant. Beside her stood the Torracan ambassador and another man with the darkest skin I had ever seen. He wore a wraparound coat of a deep, lustrous red, and his loose trousers were an eye-smarting shade of orange.

"Your Majesty," Grandmama said. "My friend here from the Torracan College of Magery specializes in the magic of Torraca, and he's made a study of the compulsion spells from the revolution."

"You can make sense of this?" The King held up the vial Isol had produced.

The Torracan mage smiled, teeth flashing white in his dark face, and he stepped forward gracefully. The ambassador exchanged a relieved look with my grandmother.

While the Torracan mage laid a hand over each vial, I

turned to Merrick, who had returned to my side. "Will you fetch the horses?"

He frowned. "Miss Hargrove, we're not leaving now, are we?"

"Please, Merrick?"

He glanced from me to the Prince and back again before his lips tightened and he nodded and headed outside.

I waited just long enough to hear the mage begin his assessment. As soon as I was sure Melissa wouldn't be escaping from judgment, I slipped toward the door.

I called myself a coward a dozen times in my head, but I couldn't stand in the palace one more moment. And I didn't have to. I could leave just as quietly as I'd come.

I should have at least said something to Grandmama, but she knew where to find me now. And Isol didn't appear to need me. She was handling everything far better than I was. As soon as I reached the doors, Ember launched herself into the air and circled me as I struggled down the steps.

Merrick waited outside the main entrance with the horses. I could tell from the set of his mouth that he wanted to say something but wasn't sure if he should.

"Miss Hargrove," he finally said as he helped me into the saddle. "I don't think we should be leaving."

"Why? We did our duty. The Prince is safe, and I'm no longer a murderer." I twisted to strap my crutch behind my saddle.

"No, you're a viscountess. Do you really want to go back to being a Refuge librarian?"

I hadn't really thought that far. All I'd wanted was to get

away, but I raised my chin and glared at him. "I liked being a librarian, thank you very much."

"But you could be a princess."

I sucked in a breath and my hands clenched on the reins. It was the thought I'd been avoiding, but now I couldn't help following it to its conclusion. If I wasn't a murderer, Nik was free to choose me as his wife.

But did I still want him to?

He'd turned away from me once. He hadn't defended me when his words could have changed everything. I couldn't pretend that it hadn't hurt me deeply.

I didn't want to face that again. And nothing said I had to put myself in a situation where I would have to.

I urged my horse forward, away from the palace and down the drive. "The Prince is free to choose whatever bride he wants. That has nothing to do with me anymore."

"He didn't take his eyes off you," Merrick said, drawing even with me, his horse puffing a plume of breath in the cold air. "And he had that look that said he was afraid he'd done something stupid he'd regret for the rest of his life."

I snorted. "That must be some look."

"You had it, too. When you came out that door."

My jaw clenched. Why wouldn't this horse go any faster?

"You still love him, otherwise you wouldn't be running so hard."

Of course I still loved him, even after everything that had happened. But love without trust sounded like a recipe for pain and disappointment.

I had already given him up. I didn't have to do anything else except ride away knowing he was free.

"Miss Cindy, wait!"

I sighed and turned to see Jason pounding down the palace drive, Renny not far behind him.

"Please don't call me that."

He shook his head. "Sorry. It's what I've called you since we were six. Miss Aschen, then. You can't leave, yet."

"Why not?"

"He needs you."

I jerked in the saddle and had to clutch the horse's mane to stay on. I shook my head. "He doesn't."

Jason planted himself in front of me and took the horse's bridle.

I glared. "Let me go."

"No."

"Jason, I'm not afraid to run you over."

"Wait." Nik's quiet voice went down my spine, making me stiffen.

My shoulders tensed and I thought about kicking my horse into a run whether Jason held its head or not, but Merrick maneuvered ahead of me and used his horse to herd mine in a circle. I met his eyes with a scowl.

"Your honor is your own," he said. "No one else can break it but you."

No one could break my honor. But they could definitely break my heart.

I steeled myself and turned to face Nik. For the first time in four months I met his gaze, and had to catch my breath at the look of naked fear and longing I saw there.

He cleared his throat before he spoke, but even then his

voice was hoarse. "I was afraid you would be gone before I could catch you."

"You can thank Merrick and Jason for that."

Nik grinned at the footman, who moved to stand behind him with Renny.

"I'm beginning to appreciate outspoken servants."

Jason rolled his eyes and the Prince flashed him another grin. Clearly there was more understanding there than there'd been when I'd left.

Nik turned back to me and his smile fell. "Aschen."

The sound of my name on his lips made my skin flush against the frosty air. I'd wanted him to be the first one to use it. But we can't always have what we want.

He shook his head. "Why didn't you tell me your name wasn't Cindy?"

"Because it was Cindy. For a long time. I was never brave enough to claim my real one when everyone else was content to think of me as Cinder-mite."

"I suppose that makes sense." He fell silent, and I wondered if everything between us was going to be this awkward from now on.

Still, I sat there, silent. I wasn't the one who had things to say.

He cast about for a topic like he was avoiding what he really wanted to get out. "I see you learned to ride."

"Yes."

"Do you like it?"

"Well enough." I didn't have to make this easy for him.

He reached under his arm. "I should probably return this."

It took me a moment to recognize my old shoe. He handed it up to me. "Christoph spelled it so I could find you. But you were already here."

I fondled the broken laces with a frown. "Why did you want to find me?" I said quietly.

Nik rubbed the back of his neck. "Renny and Jason told me the truth, and I realized I'd made a huge mistake. I had to find you so I could fix it. So I could apologize."

I held my breath as he stepped forward and put his hand on my knee.

"I have several apologies, Aschen. It doesn't matter what I thought I saw that night at the ball. It doesn't matter how sick you were or weren't. Whatever was happening inside your head or body, I should have loved you enough to stand by you. In the end it doesn't even matter if your stepmother was controlling you. I betrayed you the moment I abandoned you. By loving you, I made a promise, and I should have kept that promise through any illness, any lies, any truth."

I shook my head. "Nik, I understand what you did that night. You're a prince, you couldn't—"

His free hand slashed through the air. "No. Who I am is defined by my actions, not by my title. You know that better than anyone."

I remained quiet for a moment. "Fine," I said at last. "You mucked up. Badly. But I forgive you."

I wrenched my horse's head around, but Nik skipped ahead and stood in front of me again. "Then why are you running?"

"I'm not running. I'm leaving. There's a difference."

"Why? Give me a good reason to let you go, and I'll never follow you again."

"Nik," I said, throat thick. "You're free. You don't need me anymore. You can marry anyone you want."

His face went white with hurt, and I hid how much I regretted my words.

"Aschen, it was the thought of you that kept me from succumbing to your stepmother's spell. You heard Isol. What more proof do you need that I still love you?" His voice grew soft. "It is not me who has changed."

I flushed and raised my chin. "What's that supposed to mean?"

"Look at you." He gestured to how I sat straight and strong in the saddle. "You rode in here to save my grandfather's life and my freedom. You're calling yourself by a new name. You lived for four months without being caught. Can someone as competent and confident as you still love a man who has failed her?"

I clenched the reins in one fist and placed the other on my hip, staring down at him indignantly. "I saved you because I could, and because it was the right thing to do," I said. "Aschen is my real name. And I don't care how much I've changed, I will always love you, Nikolas Alyxander Humphrey Rannard."

The brilliant sunset behind the palace was nothing compared to the triumph that spread across Nik's face. "Then you'll marry me, Aschen Hargrove?"

"I'd like to see you try and stop me."

We stared at each other in the deepening gloom as the words we'd said echoed between us. I willed my heart to slow its rapid beat. Had he really just proposed again? Had I really said yes?

Merrick cleared his throat. "I guess I'll tell Father Philip he's not getting his librarian back."

Nik glared at the bodyguard. "I wondered where you'd disappeared to. I should have known you'd hide Aschen from me."

I snorted and leaned over to dismount. I slid down and paused to get my legs under me. When I had my balance, I turned and found Nik just inches away. That suited my purposes just fine.

Above us Ember shrieked and circled, sending sparks showering down around us.

I put my arms around his neck. I could feel his warmth even through the thick coat that protected me from the harsh cold. "Leave Merrick alone. He didn't do anything I didn't ask him to. Now, stop talking and kiss me."

His smile was lopsided. "But I have more apologies to make."

"You should save them for later. You may need them. I hear husbands occasionally mess up."

He opened his mouth to protest, but I pulled his head down and kissed him. With the touch of his lips, my world finally came back together.

CHAPTER THIRTY-THREE

I warmed my hands by the gigantic fireplace and tried to ignore the fuss around me. The anteroom was supposed to be a sanctuary for a select few but it felt like everyone and their aunt had joined us to say hello before I presented Eriana to the court.

"Remind me what I'm doing again," I asked Nik who stood beside me, smiling and nodding to everyone coming and going.

"Trying to relax," he said.

I made a face. "No, really. Your mother made it sound very complicated."

"You will present Eriana, then all you have to do is stand next to me and look like a happy bride."

I grinned up at him. "That part should be easy enough." It was my natural state these days.

Nik and I had been married less than a month ago, in the royal chapel. Grandmama had given me away and Father

Philip had officiated the ceremony. I'd been more worried about falling on my face in the aisle than saying my vows but everything had gone off without a hitch. Isol had served as one of my bridesmaids before she'd left for Torraca to study their magic. She and Anella had earned their pardons from the King, although I had no idea what Anella was doing now. She'd disappeared without a thank you or a goodbye. I tried to wish her well, at least in my own mind.

Melissa languished in prison somewhere, due to the Torracan expert's testimony. And now no one would be able to practice compulsion magic in Valeria. Once their prince had been threatened—and with the Duke of Chatham out of the way—the Bicouncil had been perfectly happy to include the new legislation in the laws against blood magic.

A tug on my indigo skirt made me look down at Renny, who murmured an apology and adjusted my hem. She headed up the battalion of maids my new in-laws had assigned to me, while Jason served as my personal footman. Nik hadn't been too happy about Jason's proximity until I'd explained to him that the footman was making eyes at Renny. And he was being much more deliberate about this courtship than he'd ever been with me.

The door of the anteroom opened again, and Merrick stiffened beside me. The bodyguard had been reinstated with full honors and now served as my official shadow. So, not much difference there except he had his uniform back.

He relaxed again when he recognized the figure of the Disciple. Nik's grandfather was technically supposed to stay in the Refuge for his protection, but the old man hadn't gone home after our wedding and no one was brave enough to make him.

"Why are they keeping you standing here like this?" he said, striding up to us. "Come here, my dear. Sit. Sit." Ambrose pulled up an armchair and took my arm to lead me to the seat. Then he settled himself beside me.

"What about me, Grandfather?" Nik said with an affronted look.

"Find your own damn seat," he said.

I couldn't help laughing out loud as Nik made a face and passed Lainey and Christoph on his way to check the throne room. "That wasn't very nice," I said.

"He'll live," Ambrose said. "Learn this now, before it's too late. You can't coddle husbands. It turns them soft."

I nodded solemnly and beckoned to the King's Mage. "I'll remember that."

"I suppose you have to get used to this circus at some point, my dear," the Disciple said, glaring at Adelaine and Christoph as they curtsied and bowed respectively.

"I kind of like the circus," I said. "Christoph, I've been meaning to ask you a fa—Lainey, what on Térne are you carrying?"

Lainey swung a jeweled cane from one hand. "It's the newest fashion. To emulate the Prince's bride."

"You have got to be joking," I said with a laugh. I'd struggled to fit in at court with my strange gait and the canes and now carrying one was considered fashionable?

"I know, it's absolutely ridiculous what some people will think is in good taste. But I thought it might make you laugh."

"She's promised to get rid of it after she showed you," Christoph said.

"He's sour because I've threatened to use it to hit the next person who says what a pity it is I threw away my family for my husband."

I gave them a sympathetic look. The royal family didn't want anyone knowing the real reasons for the Duke of Chatham's arrest and death, which meant that Lainey's family was still angry with her choice. Although Lainey herself didn't seem fazed by the ostracism.

"What was it you needed, Your Highness?" Christoph said, recalling me to my own problem.

"I've been meaning to ask you a favor."

He gave me a little bow. "I'm at your service."

"You have to take that spell off my shoe," I said desperately.

Lainey burst out with a laugh too loud to be lady-like, and Christoph hid his mirth behind his hand.

"Oh dear," she said. "Is he still using it then?" Her voice was suspiciously unsympathetic.

"He keeps showing up at the most inopportune times," I said, my eyes narrowing with annoyance. "I love the man, but sometimes a girl just doesn't want to be found."

They kept laughing.

"I'm sorry, Your Highness," Christoph said. "I did try to remove the spell soon after your acquittal, but Prince Nikolas wouldn't let me. I believe his response was the royal equivalent of 'shove off.'"

"Give him time," Lainey said. "He's still worried you'll

disappear again. I'm sure the impulse will wear off eventually," she said when she saw my sour face.

Nik stepped up beside them, and Lainey and Christoph smothered their amusement.

"Ready?" Nik said to me.

I smiled and gave him my hand as the others excused themselves. Ember raised her head from the flames in the fireplace and she leapt up onto my shoulder, her fiery talons gently gripping my collarbone. She hadn't abandoned her falcon shape since the day I'd saved Nik. I think she secretly liked being mistaken for a phoenix.

"Waiting is boring," Eriana said as we joined her and Colin before the big double doors that opened onto the throne room. Given the formality of the occasion, we all wore the royal indigo. Even me.

"At least they didn't let you bring a sword," Colin said. "We'd all be dead by now."

Eriana stuck her tongue out at him.

"Just pretend you're Althaea the Wolf stalking Erestan's enemies," I told her.

"Don't give her any ideas," Nik said. "She'll leap into the throne room with a war cry."

I gave her a conspiratorial wink behind Nik's back.

He knocked on the inside of the door, letting the footmen on the other side know that it was time. There was a blast of trumpets before the doors were flung open.

I looked at Nik in surprise as he took my arm. "Do they always do that?"

He grinned. "Only for princesses." He bent down and kissed me on the forehead. "Or when I ask them to."

I squeezed his arm as I walked away from the fireplace and into the throne room.

This time there was a fanfare. This time the silence spread as everyone turned to watch me come in the room. I took a deep breath and stepped into my new life, my partner on my arm.

Psalm 139:14

ACKNOWLEDGMENTS

If it takes a village to raise a child, it at least takes a mob to finish a book. Thanks go to all these people and more:

Mom and Dad, for laughing at all the appropriate moments that one time I read the first draft in the car somewhere in England.

Arielle, Miranda, Lacey, Betsy, and Alison, for grounding me when I thought I was seriously crazy.

Darby, Todd, and Chris and so many others in the Pikes Peak Writers, for thinking that I actually know what I'm doing.

Wendy, Janet, Ralph, Don, Bruce, Apryl, Paul, and Audrey for telling Aschen to get off her ass and do something.

Kim Killion, always for an amazing cover design. And for unlimited patience and going back to the drawing board over and over.

Fiona McLaren, for copy edits. And for pointing out

every single time someone smiled. There were a lot. I'm sure you got tired of them.

Sasha Grossman, for double checking everything. And for knowing more about how my series is formatted than I do.

And Josh, for taking Abby for donuts every Saturday, no matter how the week went. She and I both count on that time for different reasons but we both appreciate it more than words can tell.

ABOUT THE AUTHOR

 Books have been Kendra's escape for as long as she can remember. She used to hide fantasy novels behind her government textbook in high school, and she wrote most of her first novel during a semester of college algebra.

Kendra writes familiar stories from unfamiliar points of view, highlighting heroes with disabilities. Her own experience with partial paraplegia has shown her you don't have to be able to swing a sword to save the day.

When she's not writing she's reading, and when she's not reading she's playing video games.

She lives in Denver with her very tall husband, their book loving progeny, and a lazy black monster masquerading as a service dog.

Never miss a new release!

Visit Kendra at:
www.kendramerritt.com
to sign up for exclusive excerpts, updates, and book recommendations.

facebook.com/kendramerrittauthor

twitter.com/Kendra_Merritt

instagram.com/kendramerrittauthor

goodreads.com/kendramerritt